OF SWORDS & ROSES

SHORT STORIES

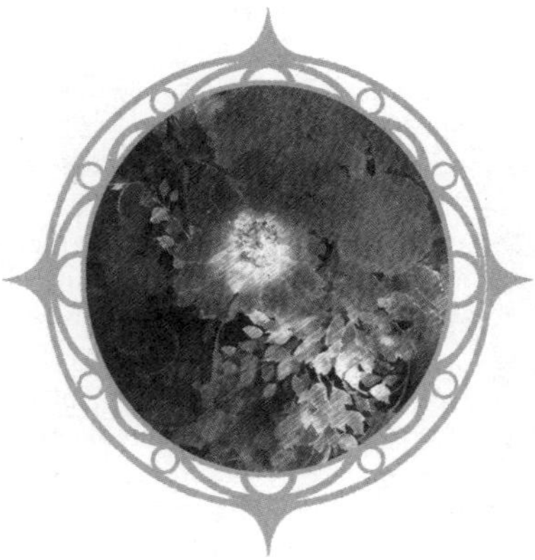

This is a FLAME TREE Book

Publisher & Creative Director: Nick Wells
Editorial Director: Catherine Taylor
Editorial Board: Catherine Taylor, Gillian Whitaker, Josie Karani,
Jemma North, Jocelyn Pontes and Simran Aulakh.
Special thanks to Tim Leng.

FLAME TREE PUBLISHING
6 Melbray Mews, Fulham,
London SW6 3NS, United Kingdom
www.flametreepublishing.com

First published 2026

26 28 30 29 27
1 3 5 7 9 10 8 6 4 2

ISBN: 978-1-83562-796-9
Special ISBN: 978-1-80694-252-7
Ebook ISBN: 978-1-83562-798-3

The cover image is created by Flame Tree Studio from sketches and layered files, new photos and stock images from Shutterstock combined and crafted in Photoshop. No AI, AGI or LLM was used in this process. The cover features specially commissioned artwork © 2025 Xinyue Chen. Shutterstock elements are courtesy of Innoria, Oniks Astarit and Apostrophe. The internal illustrations are © the respective creators – see the back of the book for further information on the artists.

A copy of the CIP data for this book is available from the British Library.

Printed and bound in China

Represented in the EU for product safety and compliance by Authorised Rep Compliance Ltd, Ground Floor, 71 Lower Baggot Street, Dublin, D02 P593, Ireland. Contact at www.arccompliance.com

FSC www.fsc.org MIX Paper | Supporting responsible forestry FSC™ C005748

Of Swords & Roses

Short Stories

Romantic Fantasy

Foreword by Kristen Cipriano

FLAME TREE
PUBLISHING

Contents

Foreword

Kristen Cipriano 8

The Pixie's Ploy

Erica Barnes 14

The Queen's Eye

Keyan Bowes 27

Red Like Blood

Kim Chance 48

A Silken Bridge to Bind the Stars

Deborah L. Davitt 65

Monster Masquerade

Sarina Dorie 96

When Frost Loved Flame

Umenyi Evelyn 114

By Any Other Name

Jonathan Ficke 133

Stolen Shadows

Jess L. Freed 140

The Rose and the Blade
M.A. Gardner ... 157

Fragments of Us
Georgina Kamsika ... 173

What Honor Dictates
A.L. Keane ... 187

Half Made of Shadows
Sasha Kielman ... 204

Shadows of Silvermorn
AJ Lancaster ... 229

Ring of Wax, Armor of Bone
Jessica Lévai ... 248

The Hedge Knight Drinks
M. McNamara ... 268

The Gentle Art of Necromancy
S.C. Mills ... 291

The Duelist and Dreamweaver
Charity Ogechi ... 305

Always for Her Favor
Jennifer R. Povey....319

It Befits Her
Ziggy Schutz....331

The Thornblade's Promise
Laura Shenton....339

Libeunfeyer
S.S.N. Smith....349

Oberon's Rose
Gemma Sterling....365

Sometimes a Sword Is Like a Lover
Celia Winter....381

Light Tangled in Shadow
Aubrey Wroth....392

Biographies....406

Foreword

Kristen Cipriano

A Love Your World Depends Upon

Is there anything more fascinating than falling in love? It's a phenomenon nearly all of us will experience in our lives at one point, or sometimes many. It will steal our breath in moments, make our hearts ache in others, and bring us a sort of inexplicable joy that no other human experience can replicate. Love in the real world comes with its own sense of extraordinary highs, devastating lows, tangled emotional experiences and a yearning that oftentimes, to our logical minds, makes no sense.

The love in the fantasy worlds you will read about in this book take this experience we all instinctively know and cherish (and in darker times, sometimes despise), and raise the stakes to a level we rarely encounter in our real world. Whether it's thousands of lives hanging in a delicate balance dependent upon the success of an arranged marriage, or the heart-wrenching process of watching your lover step out onto the battlefield, the love in these romantic fantasy stories gives you everything you appreciate about the real thing – but in emotionally heightened, often desperate situations where it's not just about whether or not our two lovers end up together; it's about whether they – or the kingdom or world as they know it – will survive along with their love.

Falling for the Enemy

Perhaps the most relatable aspect of these stories to our real-world love sagas is the mere fact that we cannot choose whom we fall in love with, and nor can we control what family or those around us think of our beloved. The characters in these stories know these situations intimately, as they find themselves falling for their mortal enemy, or perhaps ruining a plot to take down an opposing kingdom from the inside, as they realize it's too late: their loyalties have shifted due to the uncontrollable whims of their hearts.

And isn't that the most exquisite and maddening facet of love? That we cannot help ourselves, that old prejudices or assumptions fall away far too easily the moment someone's mere presence speaks to our heart? These stories demonstrate that almost nothing can get in the way of true love – not an enemy uniform, family tradition, societal expectations or even a sword.

This is my favourite aspect of the romantic fantasy genre and is exactly what drew me to write *The Queen Rises* series. Set in an elven kingdom where females are treated as second-class citizens and are not allowed to have magic, how could the female protagonist possibly fall in love with the King's top guard? What barriers need to be broken for her to see anything redeemable in the male responsible for upholding the very subjugation she suffers?

As you will see in these stories, love cuts through everything logical and expected and exposes the truth some of us are still afraid to accept: that deep down, we are all worthy and capable of love. We are not our identities or labels. We are not all that different. And possibly most surprisingly, even when it comes to our supposed enemies, there is often more to love than there is to hate.

The Inevitability of Love

How radical it is, in these often hate- and violence-filled fantasy worlds, to dare to fall in love. How radical it is to shed what your lineage or general or king expects of you, to shirk your responsibilities and oath-bound duties, and even endanger your own life for a stolen kiss or a moonlit garden stroll. How radical, and yet, how deeply satisfying it is to honour what the heart truly wants.

For these characters as for us, they simply cannot resist the longings of their hearts. These stories remind us how inevitable love is. How once it's taken hold, we cannot help but act on it or risk making ourselves miserable for the rest of our lives. No court strategy, war games or revenge plot can compare to the destruction of our souls that occurs should we try to fight the yearnings of our hearts.

We can try for a time, and many of our characters make this futile attempt. When I was writing Fiana, the protagonist in *The Queen Rises*, I was struck by how often this character wanted to deny her feelings, and yet how ineffective the self-denial ultimately was. She so steadfastly maintained her story in her own mind that she was not in danger of loving Evander, until it was ultimately too late and so obvious what had taken root within her, that the moment she was given information that he was a safe person for her to love, her internal excuses entirely fell apart.

Her journey, and the journey many characters in these stories undergo, reminds us that the mind is utterly powerless when it comes to love. It can delay, make excuses, put up obstacles and attempt to justify why we cannot love that person; meanwhile, the heart simply waits patiently for the smallest sliver of an opening in the carefully constructed web of logic that keeps us apart from our beloved. All it takes is a microscopic crack in that mental façade for our internal defences to collapse fully and for our hearts to win out.

Truly, love is a dangerous and wonderful thing.

Beyond This Book

If you find yourself enraptured by the stories in this book and are left with this feeling of wanting more, the romantic fantasy genre is filled with reads that will consume you in similar ways as love itself. Of course, I would be delighted if you explored *The Queen Rises* series, but the genre as a whole is full of mystical worlds, high-stakes battles and war games, and love stories that will leave you feeling breathless.

I find the genre is often misunderstood by those who do not read it frequently. The truth is, in order to craft a romantic fantasy, what you are really crafting is a fantasy novel with romance as the main plot driver. As an author, I spent far more time building the world of *The Queen Rises* than I did writing the romance scenes, even though they are my favourite. I have spreadsheets, timelines, pages of notes, definitions and magic rules occupying as much space on my hard drive as the manuscripts themselves. A strength of the genre is that these books often become viral page-turners that fans of romantic fantasy cannot stop raving about. A weakness is that outsiders can take this fact to mean that the genre is more about writing what sells versus crafting intelligent plots, captivating characters and fully immersive worlds.

If this book is your first entry to the genre, I hope you will realize that the latter simply is not the case. Romantic fantasy may be wildly entertaining and a welcome escape from our real world, and yet it also carries themes deeply relevant to our lives and the world at large, just like the most highly respected literature in print today.

Let these stories show you how much beauty and depth this genre has to offer. I genuinely hope you enjoy these stories as much as I did, and that they remind you of the all-consuming power something as simple as love can have in our lives.

The Pixie's Ploy

Erica Barnes

"Watch your tongue!" Aderyn's giggles betrayed her warning. "If any of your teasing got back to the king…"

"Oh, don't be so worrisome." Honeycomb smiled as she finished the last braid on Aderyn's golden hair. The pixie's elegant work was completed with a flourish of her fingertips, vines and colorful flowers entwining themselves into Aderyn's hair. "Your dearest husband will never be any the wiser."

Dearest. It wasn't the proper word, but Aderyn couldn't find the right one. Was he not supposed to be her beloved? He whom she most treasured? "I'm not sure he is ever any wiser."

Honeycomb moved to sit in front of Aderyn, adjusting her emerald and amethyst dress as she sat. "If I may, Your Majesty—"

"You may always," Aderyn interrupted, her blue eyes staring into Honeycomb's bright green ones. Behind the pixie, the setting sun provided the second most stunning view from Aderyn's balcony. It made the gold flecks of glitter on Honeycomb's ebony cheeks sparkle.

Honeycomb watched Aderyn for a moment before continuing. "Your husband is a fool. To choose anything other than being with someone as wonderful as you...I do not understand it."

"He is the king. He has matters to attend to." Aderyn sighed, plucking a berry from their basket of food. She popped it into her mouth and remembered asking him to join her for dinner that evening. She also remembered the subsequent groan of frustration and irritated tone as he explained all he had to do that day, from meetings to creating a treaty so they did not go to war with the merfolk. He told her to go bother her favorite lady-in-waiting instead.

"You are the queen. You are the most important matter he can attend to." Honeycomb shook her head and looked out at the kingdom. "Before we met all those months ago, I had only heard rumors about what a jewel you are. Your intelligence, your charm, your heart. How you cared for all the people, from the poorest villager to the wealthiest noble. From the tallest elf to the smallest pixie. I never believed someone so virtuous existed, but...here you are."

"Oh, please. You praise me too much."

"I do not praise you enough," Honeycomb insisted. Her soft hands took Aderyn's, and for some reason, Aderyn felt her heart begin to flutter like Honeycomb's wings. "Please hear me when I say your husband is not worthy of you."

"So what if he is not?" she asked, dejected. Her thumb traced small circles on Honeycomb's hand. Wyn was not perfect. Perhaps she was not even in love with him like she used to be, enamored by his ambition and strength. But that did not change her circumstances, either. "We are married. Through thick and thin, 'til death do us part. It is our duty to stand side by side and rule our kingdom together. I would not show weakness to our enemies now, especially when we are on the brink of war."

"If you are not a united front behind closed doors, soon enough, it will come to light." Honeycomb paused a moment, looking for words she seemed to have trouble finding. "You could be with someone who adores you."

"And...who would that be?" Aderyn asked softly, looking at Honeycomb through long lashes. Her heart thundered in her chest now, afraid to believe that her daydreams may not be so far from reality. The stolen glances, the late-night talks, the passing touches and caresses. Maybe she wasn't the only one who thought about them long after they had happened. "There are no suitors knocking at my door."

"Perhaps they are already in your room."

Aderyn's breath hitched. Was this a pixie's prank? Or was it something more? "Do not toy with me."

"I would not hurt you like that. You are the only person that..." Honeycomb trailed off, seemingly at war with what she was going to say next.

Then her lips were on Aderyn's, and it didn't matter what she was about to say.

Her lips, unsurprisingly, tasted of sweet honey. It was a kiss so impossibly gentle and passionate that she wondered if Wyn had ever really kissed her before. Aderyn's hand came up to cradle Honeycomb's cheek, and it was all the invitation the pixie needed to deepen the embrace. They were a tangle of limbs, and Aderyn would have been pleased to take it further if it would not have been reckless to do so on her bedroom balcony.

Honeycomb pulled away with such fierceness, the same thought must have occurred to her.

"I can't do this…not to you," Honeycomb murmured, almost to herself.

"It is my choice as well," Aderyn tried to reassure her. "I…I care for you, Honeycomb. You are more than a lady-in-waiting. You have been my best friend and confidante in a world that has become increasingly lonely. You've done nothing wrong."

"Don't say that. I do not deserve such kindness." Honeycomb stood abruptly, bringing a hand to her forehead as she paced the balcony.

Aderyn stood as well, suddenly feeling vulnerable. "What are you not telling me?"

Honeycomb turned to Aderyn, a pained expression on her face that did not match the sparkle on her cheeks. "I…I have been keeping a terrible secret from you. I have not wanted to tell you for fear of losing you, but I cannot keep you without you knowing."

The knot that formed in Aderyn's stomach felt too large, too twisted. She wanted to be sick. What could possibly be so bad that even the flawed pixie would deem it too horrible to speak? "Alright. Then what is this terrible secret you have kept?"

Honeycomb made her way to the balcony's ledge, her back to Aderyn as she looked out at the kingdom. The seconds stretched on and on, the silence deafening. Then Honeycomb's voice was so quiet, Aderyn was afraid she might have misheard her.

"I am a member of the Banished."

Impossible.

Aderyn took a step back. It did not feel like a reveal out of guilt over morality. Like Honeycomb was afraid the queen would judge her. No…this was much deeper, much darker.

An assassin had been sent to kill Aderyn. And she'd fallen into the trap.

"I see," Aderyn said, slowly, quietly. Her regal mask slipped back into place. So everything she had felt over the past few months…it was all planned. Orchestrated so that Honeycomb could get close enough to stick the knife into her heart. "Do I get the courtesy of knowing who has hired a Banisher to end me?"

Honeycomb winced. *Good.* The pixie moved to retrieve a piece of parchment from her satchel. Aderyn looked over the contract that was handed to her, and she couldn't say she was surprised to see whose signature was at the bottom.

Wyn Samson was scrawled just above Honeycomb's own name.

"When I say that your husband is not worthy of you," Honeycomb said, voice low and steady, "I really and truly mean it."

"And you are?" Aderyn asked, voice monotone. "You signed just like he did."

"I want to be," Honeycomb said. "I took the job when I didn't know you. When it wasn't personal. It was a lucrative hit that would ensure I didn't starve. Then I got to know you, and every day that passed began to feel like there was a weight that pressed harder and harder against my chest. Thinking of a world without you in it…I couldn't fathom it."

Aderyn's lips pressed together. "What, exactly, did he say was the reason for wanting me gone? What is his plan?"

Honeycomb hesitated before continuing. "He has a deal with the merfolk. There is a princess waiting to be married off, but Wyn is obviously not eligible to take a wife. The merfolk agreed that if…you were out of the way…they would agree to the arrangement to join both land and sea together. There would be no war."

"I guess a separation would have been too civil," Aderyn muttered. This was more than a simple political move. Wyn held a hatred for her that was far deeper than she had even realized. She turned to Honeycomb with cold eyes. "And what was *your* plan? How were you going to do it?"

Honeycomb cringed. "Aderyn, please…"

"Your Majesty," Aderyn corrected.

Honeycomb's eyes widened in hurt momentarily, before she gave a single nod in understanding. "Your Majesty…I intended for it to be painless. Wyn said it must be discreet for obvious reasons. It was to look like you died of natural causes or an unfortunate accident. I had considered…while you slept, or perhaps when we shared a meal."

Aderyn looked around at the long-forgotten picnic. "Like this?"

"No, no, no…not like this," Honeycomb said with a sigh. "It has been some months now since I realized I couldn't go through with…"

Aderyn nodded. She didn't need to finish that sentence. "What changed your mind?"

"You changed my mind," Honeycomb said in confusion. "Just you."

"I mean at what moment did you decide I would get to keep my life?" There it was. There was the anger. Aderyn strode toward Honeycomb, fire in her eyes, and her words sharp as ice. "Which of the moments when my husband *encouraged* our interactions did you decide to void the contract?"

"When I fell in love with you," Honeycomb said, words just as sharp, but far more desperate.

The two women stood there, staring at each other truly for the first time. Aderyn didn't know what to believe. For all she knew, this was still a part of the pixie's ploy. A way to get Aderyn to let down her defenses so she might shove the poison down her throat, or stick a dagger in her back.

Then again…it would have been an impractical strategy. Why tell her all of this if she were only going to follow through with the assassination? Could it be possible that she really did want to lay all the cards on the table? That she were being honest when…well…

"How do I know?" Aderyn asked, the bite leaving her voice. "How do I know if any of this is real anymore? My husband wants me dead, and I have feelings for the pixie he sent to kill me. How do I know that I'm more than a mark to you?"

"You return my feelings?" Honeycomb asked. She had the audacity to sound hopeful.

Aderyn's expression was enough to let the pixie know that now was *not the time*.

"Please...please hear me," Honeycomb said, wings fluttering as she moved closer to Aderyn. When she took the queen's hands, Aderyn didn't move away. "I did not mean to get these feelings, but I have them now, and I have never been happier than I have been these past few months. I would do anything to ensure your trust and your safety. It's why I told you all this in the first place. Your Majesty, I would run away with you. I would renounce my place in the Banished."

"Would you kill my husband?"

Honeycomb looked taken aback for only a second. Then she shook her head forlornly. "While I would, in fact, kill for you, that is the one thing I legitimately *cannot* do."

"Does this go against some code of yours?" Aderyn asked.

"It goes against the contract," Honeycomb said with a sigh. "As a safety precaution, the writing states that Wyn is safe from my hand. It is a magically bound contract that I cannot go back on. If I were to, say...kill him just for the bounty, then I would die as well."

"Is that commonplace, or did my lovely husband think of that?"

Honeycomb gave a small smile. "Your husband is quite… paranoid. As he should be, I suppose."

Aderyn took a deep breath, breaking contact with Honeycomb. So many thoughts and emotions ran through her at once, she didn't know which to land on first. As she placed her hands on the stone ledge and looked out at the kingdom…her kingdom…Aderyn finally landed on which gut reaction she wanted to cling to.

Revenge.

"Would you die for me?" Aderyn asked, voice even as she turned to face Honeycomb.

Honeycomb seemed to be putting the pieces together, brows furrowed. "It would be hard for us to be together if I were dead, but…yes. I would."

Aderyn's expression softened for the first time since the news of her almost-fate was revealed. It was time for her to stop playing by rules no one else played by. It was time she reminded everyone – including herself – that she was more than Wyn's accessory.

"I know how you're going to make this up to me."

* * *

Honeycomb adjusted her dress, fixed her dark curls, and straightened her back as she walked down the grandiose hallway of the castle. The only image running through her mind was Aderyn's betrayed expression when she first told her why Honeycomb had even come into her life. It was the image that moved Honeycomb's feet to the dining hall, even when all she wanted to do was turn the other way.

She pushed the large double doors open and found only one other person in the high-ceilinged room. At the end of the long dining table was King Wyn, poised, distant, and ever the smug-looking bastard. Honeycomb walked to the seat beside him, and then gave her best curtsy. The king raised a full glass of wine in toast.

"There she is, my favorite pixie in all the land." He gestured toward the chair, officially granting her permission to take a seat. "I assumed when you called with good news, it was to announce that the deed was done?"

"Yes, Your Majesty," Honeycomb said politely. She plastered on her best fake smile, and gazed at the feast the king had put together. Anger bubbled up inside Honeycomb at the happiness he felt thinking the most wonderful human was dead. What a toad. "The deed is done. Your path is clear to marry the sea princess."

"Marvelous," he breathed, taking a long sip of wine.

When he offered her a drink, Honeycomb shook her head. "Thank you, but I don't need any. A Banisher must always keep a clear head."

"I respect that," he said approvingly, giving her a nod before moving on to his roasted boar. "Tell me...was it difficult? Did she fall for it? She was always rather...

pig-headed. I was honestly afraid she'd catch on and never let any suspicions go."

Honeycomb bit back a million retorts. "No, she never saw it coming."

"Well, go on, then, details, details," he urged, shoveling food into his mouth, clearing his throat between large bites. "How will I tell the people she perished?"

"I made it as quiet as possible," Honeycomb lied. "I felt like a convenient fall would sound too dramatic and unbelievable."

"Agreed, agreed," he said, coughing on the food he continued to celebrate with. "So what method did you go with?"

Honeycomb sat for a minute, letting him eat as much as he could. Then she said, "I poisoned her at one of our picnics."

"Excell—"

Wyn was cut off abruptly, as if the wind had been taken right out of him. Honeycomb smiled at him as he struggled to get a word out, smacking his throat, opening and closing his mouth. Like an illness had overtaken him within seconds, he looked to Honeycomb with panic in his eyes. He pointed an accusatory finger at Honeycomb, but couldn't quite get the words out.

"Are you feeling alright, Your Majesty? You don't look well," she said with faux concern.

Wyn's face reddened, though it had nothing to do with suffocating. He slammed his fists down on the table, shaking the dishes with a clatter. He pointed at Honeycomb again, and then mimed writing a signature.

Honeycomb smiled. "Oh, yes, that. You see…I didn't break our deal."

Wyn's eyes widened. At that moment, the doors opened again, and Aderyn strutted through with a confidence that made Honeycomb tingle. She was hot when she was cunning.

"You forget I know all the same guards and chefs that you do," Aderyn announced. "You also forget they like me better."

Wyn's face was so much more satisfying than Honeycomb thought it would be. He looked to Honeycomb in confusion, but Aderyn clicked her tongue. "She didn't put anything in your food. I did."

The king's face turned from a shade of red to a shade of blue as the poison worked its way through his system. Honeycomb smiled and stood, walking over to Aderyn. Just for fun, she threw an arm around Aderyn's waist. "How did your talks with the merfolk go, my love?"

Aderyn grinned slyly, hands clasped together in front of her. "I was able to make a deal of my own with them, one that didn't involve a marriage. Something the princess was relieved about once I told her of your plans for me."

Wyn fell to the floor, and Aderyn knelt down beside him. Honeycomb watched with a certain pride over the woman she'd come to love. She thought running away with the queen would have been better, but this had a satisfaction to it as well.

"You always bit off more than you could chew, didn't you?"

Wyn managed one last, cold glare at his wife before his body stilled, never to move again.

Aderyn stood, more regal-looking than ever before. She turned to Honeycomb, and with a smile the pixie had once been afraid she wouldn't see again, the queen walked briskly over to Honeycomb and placed a passionate kiss on her lips.

"I was afraid you might actually want me to die, you know," Honeycomb said with a smile through multiple kisses.

"Life is far more interesting with you in it," Aderyn said, hands tangled in Honeycomb's hair.

The two laughed, then separated long enough to look at Wyn's lifeless body. "What now, Your Majesty?"

"Aderyn," the queen corrected, looking to Honeycomb with a soft expression. "Call me Aderyn."

"Addie…" Honeycomb said with a smile. "What do you wish to do now?

Aderyn grinned. "I am going to get a guard to clean this up…and then we are going up to my quarters to think of a wonderful reason for Wyn's demise."

"Is that all we're going to do?" Honeycomb asked with a playful pout.

Aderyn grinned in a way that Honeycomb found all too promising. And it only made her love the queen more. "No, that is not all we're going to do."

The Queen's Eye

Keyan Bowes

I love the sound of elephants at dawn.

From the fort's battlements, I watch our troops greet the rising sun. Its rays sparkle off the dew, illuminate the royal dais where Rani Vijya stands. The horses line up on the riverbank facing east and bow. The elephants raise their trunks, trumpeting. My sword-sisters hold up their polished blades in salute. Then I break into song, the song of the growing light, the song of Sonagur our beloved homeland. My clear voice carries across the field to the listening troops. This is our daily moment of peace and calm and hope.

But not today, not for me. A dark anxiety clutches my chest.

* * *

Afterward, I take my brazier to the inner courtyard and light the morning seeing-fire. But as I drop pieces of sandalwood into the flame and sing the invocation, I shudder involuntarily. My apprentice Githa looks at me, concerned, but I say nothing.

The vision will not be a good one.

I stand in a field of battle, my breathing rapid as my Queen lowers her curved sword. It drips blood. Around me elephants stampede and scream and trample the foe. Everything is red, and the dying and maimed limp away from the field of horror. In the distance, fires burn. Bodies of the slain lie disregarded on the ground. She falls, and only I am standing.

War is coming, and our Queen will be drawn into it.

* * *

The parade over, the troops head to the meal-hall: gray-braided veterans with the gold of martial honors in their hair; seasoned warriors who run the force; wide-eyed youngsters of the newest cohort.

"Aren't you coming down to join us, Nyna?" my friends call up to me.

I can't. These people are the some of the bodies I saw lying on the vision-field. I shiver, their names whispering through my mind. Jythi. Veera. Abheya. Pravira… With an effort, I stop this silent recitation.

I must tell my Rani. Now. I'm the Queen's Eye, and it's my duty to inform her of visions that affect our State.

* * *

Rani Vijya's just returned from the parade, still formally dressed in royal red, her silken black hair adorned in gold. As always, she sees me alone, for she must be the first to hear about my visions. Her eyes darken with concern as she senses my distress.

"Nyna, what's wrong?" she asks. "What did you See?"

"War," I whisper. "War and loss and death." I do not say that in my vision, her standard lay fallen across her lifeless body, her bloodied sword gripped in her still hand. My beloved Queen.

"What? How? We have the strongest standing army among the Six States. And good diplomatic relations with them all."

She rises from her throne, comes over to me and grasps my hand. "Did it reveal the enemy?" she asks. "Your vision?"

"The dead wore many colors. I couldn't say who was an ally and who a foe."

There's so little I can tell her. "I do not understand what I have seen, do not understand what the war is about."

"All wars are the same," she says with the weariness of experience. "Someone seeking more power, more land, more wealth. Or an outside distraction to unify their people." Our Queen has balanced the powers of the Six States for thirty years in a precarious and hard-won peace.

But I sense this foretold war is different.

After I've left my Queen, a vision opens in my mind, even without fire or song. "I think," I whisper to myself in dismay, "I think it's because of the Cascade of Stars."

The legendary and fabulous jewel, the Cascade of Stars. The Jewel we surrendered to the Lalgur invaders at the end of the last war. The Jewel that was lost to Sonagur before my generation was even born.

* * *

That night in the camp gathering, I sing the song of the absent gem striving to return to its rightful home, of the war that must follow if it doesn't. The music is stirring, and soon everyone's clapping along, tears in their eyes. But later, the Queen's Shield, the Leader of the Troops, confronts me. Anvi and I have been dear friends since childhood, but today she's furious.

"Nyna! What did you mean by singing that? Now the soldiers are talking only of how the Cascade was taken, how it must be returned to us. Are you trying to incite this war you've visioned?"

I stand firm. "The song sings through me. I must voice it."

"You *must*, Nyna? Are you a pawn of destiny or something? Whose throat is it that sings?" I can't tell if her reaction is fear or disbelief or anger because she stalks away.

Drawing my blade, I practice my sword drills before lighting my brazier once more and singing the song of the dark. Perhaps tomorrow will bring more clarity. Sometimes, my visions change with the winds of chance. I hope to leave this one behind, and tell my Rani of the change.

But this time, my visions only grow darker, and the imperative to sing to the troops more urgent. When Githa comes for her usual session, I dismiss my apprentice for her own protection. Let this dire vision be only mine.

Will I sing our army to its destruction?

* * *

On the third day, I know what I must tell my Rani: we need to bring home the Cascade of Stars. The Jewel must return.

The Queen lounges on the couch-throne, looking deceptively relaxed. But her stern gaze locks on me from the moment I enter. Though I adore this woman, I'm nervous.

"Nyna." Her voice is too quiet, too incisive. "Your songs are stirring up unrest in the ranks, provoking them to a war that no one wants. Our neighbor-state Lalgur is unsettled enough with the old King's failing health and the death of their Eye. I have no patience for this."

Haltingly, I explain about the Jewel, and the war that the visions prophesy.

"The Cascade of Stars was lost forty years ago, when my father gave it to the conquering Prince from Lalgur," says the Queen. "Why is it important? For thirty years we've been at peace with Lalgur, after we won back our land. The Jewel they may keep."

"The Cascade…wishes to come home," I say.

"The Cascade wishes?" says the Queen, "Can a stone have wishes? I will not send my troops into battle, sacrifice lives, and bring the hardship and cost of war on our people for a colored pebble."

She's right. The bloodied battlefield reappears in my mind's eye. War will be devastating, and the cost to us all, terrifying. And yet…

"It's more than a pebble," I say, being careful as I contradict my Monarch to respectfully use all her titles, Mother of the Land, Grain-Giver, Defender of Sonagur. "It's a symbol of our nation. Without it, all the peace and prosperity of Sonagur will end." This much my visions reveal.

"It may have been such a symbol once. It is no longer. Nyna, you will stop."

"The battlefield vision was a warning that we must bring the Jewel home," I say. "I cannot help but sing its songs. I must not stop."

The Queen looks at me, her beautiful eyes hard enough to hurt my soul. "Your songs are against the interests of the State. You say you cannot stop. I say it cannot go on. I will have to imprison you."

Immediately, guards remove me from the Audience Hall.

* * *

My prison is luxurious, a small palace that's been used in the past to incarcerate inconvenient royals. The ruling family is strict with its own, and wayward sons and daughters are suppressed. This Queen has not had much use for it. Her daughter Princess Ajitha has a fine sense of duty, suitable in our Heir, and young Prince Moehan has only just left childhood behind. His sister's opposite, he's a charming and lighthearted young scamp. But that's all right; his eventual role will be to marry strategically, not to reign.

I do not have a brazier or sandalwood or any of my herbs with which to See.

Only, my songs haven't faded to silence though they have no audience. I sing the dark each night, and it tends toward the Jewel. In the morning, facing the sun, I sing of light – and it echoes of the Jewel. I cannot tell if my songs prevent the war or incite it, but I know they must be sung. They are not creating the truth, they are telling the truth.

There's news that the Lalgur king to whom the Queen's father gave the Cascade of Stars has died of doddering old age. This information flows into my songs.

Our guards bear these songs back to the camp, repeating them to all the troops. Aanvi the Leader comes to chide me again about my singing, reproaching me for its effects on the troops, on the strategic situation, and on me, the Queen's blinded Eye.

The Rani visits me. "Nyna, I am trying to get the Jewel returned," she says, "But we cannot honorably demand back my father's gift. We can only hint that it would be an acceptable token of friendship." She takes my hands in hers and draws them to her heart. "So far, Lalgur has ignored the hint."

The talks continue, couched in maddeningly oblique diplomatic language. Meanwhile, the Queen wants me to stop my inflammatory music.

But I can't. Sonagur must bring home the Cascade of Stars, or face destruction. Our people have to know this. The Jewel insists.

The Queen engages new guards who haven't heard the songs. Then she has me gagged. Kindly, comfortably, but thoroughly. I'm ordered to be silent at the times my gag is removed for me to eat or drink, and can only communicate with notes.

* * *

On pieces of paper I write the words of my songs in dark ink. Some talk of homesickness, the staple of prisoners and exiles. The poems refract the voice of the shining colored rock that dreams of home.

My silence does not block my message. The papers fly from my window in the tower room where I now spend my time composing poetry, to swoop and flutter on the breeze. Some land in the camp, as I learn from the Queen herself when she comes again to visit.

"Why, Nyna, why?" she asks, her lovely eyes soft and reproachful. She holds me close in her arms and whispers, "Why must you keep doing this?"

I must stop writing this poetry, she says. She does not want to have to chain me. She would like me to return to being her Eye. She wants me back. My heart is breaking.

"It's the Cascade of Stars that speaks," I say softly. This is my duty, to speak true. "We must bring back the Jewel."

"Let's say it is the Cascade speaking," she says. "It wants a bloody war with Lalgur, one that could involve all the Six States as both sides call in alliances. Does it care if we win or lose or how many die and what it costs us?"

"It's a jewel," I say. "I don't think it understands a lot of political economics. It just wants to come home."

"Why now?" she asks. "It's been gone nearly a lifetime!"

"The death of Lalgur's old King, perhaps?" I suggest. "Your father gifted the Cascade of Stars to him personally. Maybe it was bound to him but not to his successor. Or maybe it sees that Lalgur is weak now."

"Nyna, the Cascade is an idiot," says the Queen, exasperated. "If we declared war, at least three of the other five nations would unite against us."

The vision of the devastated battlefield returns to me, with the bodies of our dead, with our fallen standard and fallen Queen. It was a field of destruction, not a field of victory.

"The Jewel is an idiot," I agree. "It's trying to force a war. Nevertheless, we must bring it home."

"Has this idiot jewel never heard of diplomacy?" asks the Queen bitterly. "That's how it went into exile."

"But it's not working, is it, this diplomacy?" I whisper.

* * *

The poems don't stop, I don't stop, and the Jewel's voice is increasingly eloquent.

It talks wistfully of the quiet nights, when only the camp sentries wake. The owls calling, the nightjars tut-tut-tutting with a sound like a bouncing pebble, the jackals yipping outside the camp. It sings of the dawn breaking with the cat-screams of the waking peacocks, the glint of the blades of my sword-sisters as they drill, the clang of the river-ferry's gong.

It talks about the rigid life imprisoned in a foreign crown in an arid land.

It talks of an opportune time to destroy the kingdom that holds it hostage, with the old King dead, and the throne unstable and Eyeless.

* * *

The Rani Vijya orders my hands bound. The restraints, originally made for obstreperous royals, are shaped like gloves of solid gold and linked at the wrist. Once I slip my hands into them and they're locked, I cannot write. I cannot eat and my attendants must feed me. The gloves are only removed for a short time each day to allow me to bathe and dress.

So I dance. The dance of the warrior, fighting for home. My eyes seek the window, my twinned arms reach for the horizon, for my beloved land. My arms swing an imaginary sword in a double-handed grip. My golden hands touch my ears, evoking the clash of blades, the whinny of horses and shrieks of the dying. My feet stomp out the sounds of battle, the elephants destroying armies beneath their weight.

The guards watch, enthralled, saying that the Queen's Eye must have understood the future aright. We should fight, they whisper, knowing they shouldn't say it aloud. We should bring back the Cascade of Stars.

And afterward, with the litheness of sword-sisters whose bodies are trained to obey their minds, they dance in the camp. They reproduce all the steps exactly, the yearning arms, the listening ears, the stamping feet.

* * *

The guards bring me to the Queen. They remove the rigid gloves of gold, they remove the gag.

"What shall I do with you, Nyna?" Rani Vijya asks. "You have been my dearest, most trusted advisor. You've always been loyal, always devoted. Now you're stirring up trouble."

I'm silent. What can I say?

"I'm considering an alliance with Lalgur," the Rani Vijya says. "Offering my son as consort to their Princess. We'll ask only the Jewel as bride-gift."

"Prince Moehan?" I'm astounded. "But…he's barely of age." Born late in the Queen's life, he should remain with her at home in Sonagur for another ten years before he follows his future to another state.

"My son's life belongs to Sonagur," the Queen says, "as does mine, as does that of everyone born royal."

She believes it. She lives by it. Would that Monarchs of all the Six States were so honorable! The extravagance and debauchery of some other palaces proves they are not. Thus this Queen commands not just our loyalty but our devotion. And my love, a voice whispers in my mind. It's there between us, unspoken.

"Besides," she continues, "it's his destiny to go abroad. What will he do here in the shadow of his sister?"

A royal alliance usually involves months or years of negotiations and complex treaties involving land and water rights and tithes. This offer of marriage would be a huge gesture to Lalgur. The Queen's sacrifice may yet avert this awful war.

I look down at my freed hands, elated that we might avoid the war, hoping the young Prince will be happy in his new home.

* * *

Late in the evening I have a visitor to my comfortable prison, and it's not the Queen. It's Prince Moehan. "Aunt Nyna, have you heard I am to be married into Lalgur?" he says. His unhappy voice makes him seem even younger than he is, recalling the child who chased around the fort, watched our parades, and fed peanuts to the elephants.

"The Queen your mother mentioned it," I say cautiously. "It would be a good alliance."

He looks down, then away out of the window. "Have you seen the Neelgur princess?" he asks.

"Which one?" There are three.

"Noora…she has my heart."

A hundred questions flood my mind, but I ask only one. "How did this happen?"

He turns back to me, looking shy. "Do you remember the Neelgur state visit, two years ago? For discussions of my sister's alliance?"

I recall it. Our Princess Ajitha had married the Neelgur prince.

"Noora's older sisters were attending the meetings, but Noora and I – we were children, and no one needed our presence. So we walked by the river, and into the woods, and we promised ourselves to each other."

I listen to him with my heart sinking.

"A child's promises are not binding between States," I tell him.

"I know it, Aunt Nyna," he says miserably. "We meant to ask formally when we came of age. But now… I'm being sent to Lalgur."

"Does Neelgur know?" I ask. There's a diplomatic fiasco in the making if Noora's people were planning to ask for Moehan.

He shrugs. "I think so. Noora said they would ask as soon as she was old enough."

"You've been meeting Noora?" I'm aghast.

"Yes, down by the river where their border touches ours, in the arrowshot."

"Young prince, the arrowshot is the neutral zone between our two territories, and not where you should be. Does your tutor know?"

"But the herders go there all day with their animals," he protests.

"You are no herder," I say gently. He's a royal pawn, and we can't have him captured. "How often have you met the Princess Noora?"

"Maybe once a moon? For nearly two years?"

I stare at him. "Have you told your mother all this?"

This boy cannot be sent to Lalgur.

He looks shy. "Aunt Nyna, I thought you might find a way to tell her."

* * *

The Queen is not pleased. "The wishes of the Jewel. The wishes of my son, who is hardly more than a child." She glares at me and my heart sinks though I reveal nothing. "Tell me, my beloved Eye, is this any way to manage a State? On the whims of a pebble and an infant? Thirty years of diplomacy, now collapsing into this?"

"If you send him to Lalgur..." I say softly. "Neelgur's Princess Noora will be embarrassed, and she'll talk. The Lalgur princess will be insulted when she hears, because her new husband bears loyalty to another. And both States will blame Sonagur."

"Hmph. And if he goes to Neelgur?"

"That, too, is a worthwhile strategic alliance. The equal of Lalgur. Except for the Cascade."

"Except for the Cascade," the Queen agrees, looking at me directly. "I have no other sons to offer Lalgur."

* * *

The Queen does not release me from my prison, but she does visit and keep me appraised of the situation. Neelgur has opened negotiations for Prince Moehan. I suspect the lad has been meeting Noora in the arrowshot despite being forbidden.

"This is going to be embarrassing," Rani Vijya says. "Do you have any *helpful* visions?"

* * *

"Lalgur understands that Moehan's affections are elsewhere," the Rani tells me one day. "They are no longer interested."

I'm relieved, even though it brings us right back to the beginning and the Jewel remains with Lalgur.

"But Nyna, they've asked for you instead."

"What does that mean?" I ask. "I'm a mature woman, no substitute for a young Prince."

The Queen gives one of her rare smiles at my comment. Then she's serious again. "The King's Eye of Lalgur died a few weeks before him. After the King's death, his apprentice, bereft both of the King and the master who was like a father to him, fell into despair. He took his own life. So they have no Eye."

They have no Eye, and they want me.

"I have told them we cannot," she says, looking at me fondly. "Where would I get another Nyna? Where would I get another Eye?"

As she sends me back to my palace-prison, I refrain from pointing out that she effectively doesn't have one now. Blocking my visions won't prevent them from happening. I remember the dead on the battlefield of my vision, the fallen standard, the fallen Queen.

Sonagur, land of my birth and my heart. I can hardly bear even to think of leaving my dearest homeland, my beloved Queen. There would be no return. Even short visits would depend on the grace of the new Monarch to whom I would bear responsibility.

* * *

I send word to my apprentice Githa to come to me, to bring her brazier and herbs. What I know and the Rani doesn't is that she's on the verge of coming into her powers. She sings the song of Dawn, she lights the brazier, she sees and understands my vision. I prepare to install her as the Queen's Eye.

"We're sword-sisters," I tell her. We've taken the oath to die for our State if we must. I know this in my gut. My life belongs to Sonagur even as much as the Royals' lives do, as much as the Queen's does, and I know my duty.

I will ransom the Cascade of Stars with myself.

The Rani Vijya is distraught when I tell her. So am I. She forbids me but there is no better option. For the sake of Sonagur. Also for her sake, though she does not know. I still have not told her of the fallen standard in the first vision, and now I cannot think of doing so.

Eventually, she acquiesces.

Now I have three weeks, three weeks to make my farewells to all my people, all my places. All the songs of home that I sang for the Jewel, they're also my songs. The battlement where I sing the Dawn. The riverside where the moon ripples on the water, where the sun rises, where the peacocks cry in the trees. The soldiers' dining hall where I bid farewell to the sword-sisters, the women I love as friends, as family.

The Rani Vijya, Queen of my nation, Queen of my heart.

Time floats by like a leaf on the river and stops at last on the new moon.

* * *

The Cascade of Stars is huge, for a jewel. A dome the size of a dove's egg, it shifts between shades of green and blue and almost black. Within it is the starry shower of dancing silver and gold sparkles.

In its presence, my songs change. It's the gladness of homecoming, the bliss of return, the call of the place. I wonder if the Queen's grandmother had bespelled it into loyalty to our nation. Anyway, it's overflowing with joy.

The scent of the herbs from the brazier float in on the breeze. The visions of bloody battlefields recede into improbability, and there are no dead. The elephants call to the parade, not war. The Queen's standard flutters above the dais.

I sing and I dance, the dance of home. It's the Jewel's song I sing today, the end of all its yearning. Then I bow to Rani Vijya for the last time. There are tears in her eyes as she enfolds me in her arms. "You are the true jewel," she whispers. "And I lose you for a stone."

* * *

Outside, my friends waiting to bid me farewell line my path out of the palace. Jythi. Abheya. Pravira. Veera. My apprentice, Githa, who will replace me as the Queen's Eye. My dear old friend Aanvi, the Queen's Shield. So many others, all my sword-sisters. The Rani watches from the palace balcony, above the crowd, her tears unshed.

I am not Royal and I can let my tears fall as I take up my pack to leave my Queen, my homeland, and all I love forever.

The Sage of Lalgur is waiting for me with the riders who will escort me to the border. He watches me come out of the palace and turn and look upward to my Rani standing on the royal balcony. He sees the tears streaming down my cheeks, the tears I cannot quell.

"Have you agreed to this?" he asks gently when I make my way over to where he stands. "We were informed you volunteered to come to Lalgur."

"I have." My voice is clear, if a little unsteady. "My duty is to go with you."

"On behalf of Lalgur, I thank you and refuse," he replies. He looks from me to the Queen in the high balcony above. "Your heart is bound to the Queen of Sonagur. How will you make space for our new King?"

Refusal! We'd never considered the possibility. Terror runs through me. It's a diplomatic disaster. We have the Jewel. It's not going back. But if I don't go, if they won't accept me…is this where that darkly foretold war starts?

Rani Vijya comes running down. "Sage of Lalgur, we cannot return the Jewel, nor can Sonagur break its word." She looks at me, and though I can see what it costs her, she says, "Nyna, you must go."

"Queen of Sonagur, how can you send her to us? All her loyalty is to you."

"O Sage, I will go to Lalgur," I say firmly. "I will do my duty to your new King, have no fear."

He looks at me dubiously. "Will your visions even come in a foreign land for a stranger?"

Suddenly, my apprentice Githa comes forward and touches my arm. "Let me go instead," she says. "I'm not yet installed as the Queen's Eye." That was to happen after my departure.

The Sage of Lalgur looks confused. "Who is this?" he asks.

"This is Githa, who has been my apprentice for ten years. She is to replace me after I leave."

"Accept me, O Sage, as the Eye of your new young King," Githa says. "Since childhood, I have trained with the Queen's Eye. That training is complete and I have come into my power. Tonight, I was to have been installed as the new Eye. But today my heart and my fealty is my own, unbound. I am ready to bond to the young King."

He looks thoughtful. "Do you have your elders' permission, young Eye? And do they vouch for you?"

Githa looks at me, then falls at the Rani's feet. "Give me leave to go, honored ones," she says formally. "I am grown now. My destiny, like Prince Moehan's, may also lie in another land."

Rani Vijya looks at me.

"She's ready," I say in answer to her unspoken question. "Githa will be a powerful Eye."

So it's decided.

Githa mounts the horse that was to have carried me, and joins the Sage and the group of escorts. They gallop away from the palace to the farewell cries of her friends.

The Rani takes my hand. "Come, my beloved Eye," she says, and joyfully I follow her back into the Palace.

Red Like Blood

Kim Chance

Shriveled brown leaves blanket the forest floor and crunch beneath my boots as I tread farther into the deepest part of the wood.

The winter wind, a haunting, soprano trill, rattles the air. Skeletal trees sway in the howling gusts, their branches twisting towards me like gnarled, knobbed fingers, eager to yank me into the darkness.

Those in my kingdom say this is a place of nightmares, a cursed land where the vilest of creatures roam.

But this forest has been my haven since childhood. I have nothing to fear here.

Besides, monsters do not always inhabit fearsome places.

Sometimes they dwell in castles.

I pick up my pace. Each exhale is a silver ribbon that swirls above my head, and the frigid temperature nips at my cheeks, making me pull the thick, woolen cloak tighter around my shoulders.

For once, I am grateful for it, the heavy fabric that marks me for who I am. I may be required by the king's law to wear it, but out here in the wild, the scarlet hue means nothing. Out here, the cloak is simply that, a cloak.

Up ahead, the path begins to widen, revealing a small glen where slivers of moonlight illuminate the darkness. There's a flash of movement and a moment later, a low growl shatters the quiet of the wood, echoing across the glen.

I come to an abrupt halt, my pulse quickening as an enormous silver wolf emerges from the shadows.

Hackles raised and upper lip curled back to reveal a row of sharp, gleaming teeth, it takes one step towards me, then two.

I hold up both my hands and step solidly into a pool of moonlight. "Svea, it's me."

The wolf's demeanor changes in an instant and then it charges, running towards me at full speed. There's a flash of golden light as the wolf barrels into me, knocking me to the forest floor. "I've missed you too," I chuckle, as a face appears above my own.

"Evander," Svea breathes, her voice raspy from being in wolf form for so long. "I was so worried you wouldn't come."

"I always come," I remind her, reaching to cup her smooth cheek.

She leans into my touch, her golden-brown eyes softening. "I know, but your brother—"

"My brother may be the heir to the throne, but he is *not* my master." I pull her gently towards me, my nose skimming the tip of hers. Svea's shoulders relax, the tension there draining as my lips brush against hers, gently, teasingly. "I will always come for you."

I kiss her fully this time, and she tunnels her fingers into my hair as we come alive together. Fire ignites in my chest as her lips part, and I taste the sweetness of her mouth, her tongue swirling around mine.

I could live for a thousand years and still never get enough of her, never tire of the feel of her body pressed against me, her soft lips moving against mine.

A groan rumbles in my chest as she pulls away gently, tendrils of her long silver hair, the same color as her fur, falling into my face. "More," I grumble, tugging her back down against my chest. She smells of the wood, of pine, and of snow and sunshine. It's intoxicating.

Svea laughs as she untangles herself from my arms. "We can't just lie here in the middle of the forest."

"Can't we?" I nuzzle the sensitive skin on her neck. "I am perfectly content right here."

"What a wicked little princeling," she coos, swatting at my hands. "Come." She stands up, extending a hand to help pull me to my feet.

Now that we're upright, my eyes drink her in. She is nearly a foot shorter than me, but her lean frame is carved from hardened muscle. Waist-length hair, rosy cheeks, and full lips, slightly swollen. There's a wildness in her eyes and in her movements that might frighten some, but never me. Not from the moment I first saw her back when I was twelve years old.

Face throbbing and bleeding, I'd run into the cursed forest that day without even thinking about my actions. I didn't care that it was forbidden, that the wolven of the wood would likely roast me over an open flame if they caught me. All I knew was that I had to get away from the castle, from my brother, and from the marrow-deep ache in my chest. I'd run until my legs gave out, stumbling into this very glen.

Lying there, bleeding and raw, Svea had nearly given me a heart attack when she'd shown up in her wolf form. I braced myself, waiting for this wicked, cursed creature to tear my flesh into ribbons just like all the stories claimed. But then she'd transformed before my eyes.

"Why do you bleed?" the most beautiful girl I'd ever seen asked me.

I was so shocked, I'd answered with the first thing that came to mind: the truth.

"My brother acted out in lessons today. He was foolish, his behavior not fitting for the heir to the throne. It was deemed he be punished for his actions."

The girl's brows dipped. "You bleed for your brother?"

"I do. It is against the law to strike the future king."

"So…they struck you." It was not a question, and the sympathy that filled her features made my throat burn.

I pointed to my red cloak. "It is what I was born to do. I bleed for my brother so that he may rule. My blood for his."

She stepped closer, reaching up to swipe a finger across my brow. "And who bleeds for you?" She sniffed the blood on her fingertip.

"No one. I am just the spare." Despite only being born eight minutes before me, my brother's life was of far more value than mine.

She had stared at me for a moment, her head tilting thoughtfully as she studied me. Then she surprised me by rising onto her tiptoes and placing a delicate kiss on my bruised and bloodied cheek. "Not *just*."

It was then that I realized the stories weren't true. And it was the first time someone had ever looked at me as something more. Not just the spare, but *more*.

Ten years had passed since our initial meeting, and I'd been sneaking across the boundary line to meet her ever since. Our mutual interest in one another had turned into a friendship, and it didn't take long before I handed over my heart. Thank the stars above she'd exchanged it for her own.

"I can't stay long. He's increased the number of patrols on the border, and lately, I feel his eyes on me more often than not. I fear he suspects something." I tuck a tendril of hair behind her ear. "I shouldn't have risked it; I don't want him to find me here, but I had to see you."

"More patrols?" Svea lets out a huff. "The kingdom has nothing to fear from these woods. My people do not make a habit of leaving the sanctuary of the trees, nor do we snatch up villagers for supper. We have no real quarrel with the people of Galiea…but we will protect our home if necessary." She sweeps out her arms to indicate the forest around us. "History proves that."

Shame creeps up my spine like a spider. "I hate all the pain my family has caused yours." I grip the hilt of the sheathed sword at my waist, squeezing tightly as if it might blot out the past.

Were it not for my great, great, great-grandfather, King Raelin, and his greedy ambition of expanding Galiea's territory, there never would have been a conflict. He'd been determined to build the grandest kingdom in all the lands, and to do so would require razing the forest entirely. Svea's pack had fought to save the forest, and many violent and brutal altercations occurred leading to unfathomable death on both sides.

King Raelin had underestimated the wolven of the wood. Once he knew that he could not defeat them, he'd spun stories of their land being cursed, of massive, horrible creatures that feasted on the flesh of humans. Wolves that would tear your heart out with a single swipe of a claw.

He'd used fear to keep the people from questioning his failure, and that fear remained to this day.

Svea's face softens. "You already take the brunt for your brother's awful deeds, do not add anything else." She reaches up, smoothing the crease between my brows. "Besides, you're here with me now. That's all that matters."

"Are you sure you're not just planning to split me open, feast on my entrails, and gnaw on my bones?"

"I'm afraid not." Svea shakes her head, playing along. "You're made of far too much gristle." She winks at me, and a laugh rumbles in my chest.

"You're certain?" I hold up my hands to mimic claws. "The villagers still speak of the big, bad wolves in the wood."

Svea lets out a playful growl and pounces, jumping up to wrap her arms around my neck, peppering my cheeks with kisses. More laughter spills from me.

"How long do we have?" she asks once she's released me, the joy of this stolen moment already ebbing.

"Not much longer. My brother will wonder where I am." The words come out resigned, and they sour my stomach.

All of Svea's features harden, her eyes flashing. "Your people fear these woods when the real monster lives behind their stone walls."

She's not wrong. Though my brother and I were born on the same day and are alike in looks – same dark hair, same slate-colored eyes, same tall, broad-shouldered build – we are *not* the same.

There's an old wives' tale that speaks of babies born at the same time. It's said that two infants result from the splitting of a single soul into two.

But perhaps the splitting of a soul is more complicated than we can possibly know.

Perhaps it can go horribly wrong.

I can't know for certain what it is that made my brother so very unlike me, but the jagged, uneven scars carved into my back are undeniable proof of Eris's cruelty and spite.

Svea's eyes turn predatory. "He pretends to be a man of honor when behind closed doors, he is more vile and wicked than any can imagine. He torments people for pleasure, and he is particularly cruel to you, my love. He would kill you if it didn't mean taking away his favorite form of entertainment."

I don't deny this. My brother has long since made a sport of watching me bleed. Once he learned that his childhood punishments would be dispensed on me, he would purposefully act up to ensure I received a lashing. Into adolescence, he would force our trainers and the guards to beat me within an inch of my life in the name of learning proper fighting techniques. Now that we're men, he still looks for ways to torture me, to break me.

But I am not easily broken. My bones may shatter, but I will not.

"Why don't you leave?" Svea's voice takes on the same pleading tone it always does when she asks me this question. "You could come live here, in the forest with me. My pack will hide you. We will keep you safe."

I put my hands on the tops of Svea's shoulders and squeeze gently. "You know that I would love nothing more than to spend every minute of my life with you. But my father grows weaker by the day. Before long, Eris will sit on the throne and his power will be unmatched. The only thing that keeps him from unleashing the entirety of his cruelty on the people of Galiea is me. If I am there to torment, he has no need to find other targets."

Svea's lower lip trembles. "You are so brave, my love. And you are kind and good and honorable. You are everything your brother is not, and he despises you for it. He *will* kill you. One day, things will go too far and he will delight in it. He will dance over your bones." Her voice cracks. "Then what will I do? You are *mine*. Do you understand? Body and soul, mine."

I lean down and press my forehead against her. "It won't happen, Svea. I'm strong enough to survive him."

"But what if—"

"No," I'm quick to silence the thought. "There is no what if, only what is." I press my lips to her skin for a quick moment. "I will not let him take this from us. Meeting you in the forest that day was the best thing that ever happened to me. I will survive him and I will love you. Those two things are as true and as real as the stars in the heavens." I pull her closer. "I will survive him and I will love you. Always."

A tear trails down Svea's cheeks as she closes the distance between us, her lips finding mine. Her arms wrap around my neck so tightly, I can feel the fear and worry coursing through her. And the love. It's stronger than any weapon my brother has ever wielded against me.

Heat rushes through me as our kiss deepens, my heart fluttering wildly in my chest. A groan escapes me as Svea trails her fingers down my back. I cradle her head, carefully leaning her back as I deepen our kiss. Every single inch of my skin feels like it's on fire, but the burn isn't painful, it's incandescent.

Crack!

Behind us, a stick snaps in two.

"What do we have here?" A cold voice drawls, dousing the flames.

Svea yanks away from me, a snarl ripping from her throat as her eyes land on the intruder. My own reaction is quieter, but just as fierce. I step in front of Svea, my hand resting on the hilt of my sword.

"What are you doing here?" I spit the words.

Eris steps farther into the glen, the folds of his indigo cloak appearing almost onyx in the dim light of the forest. "I could ask you the same thing, little brother." His eyes swivel away from my face, landing on Svea. "But I think the answer is more than clear."

Behind me, Svea lets out another snarl, which only makes the gleam in Eris's eyes shine brighter.

"Tell me, brother. Was this your plan all along? To form some kind of alliance with the wolven of the wood? To take one of them as your own?" He cocks his head. "If it is female flesh you crave, you needn't resort to bedding wild animals. There are plenty of pickings in the castle."

Rage explodes inside me and I surge forward. Svea's strong hands reach out, yanking me back to her side. "Don't," she warns, her voice low. "That's exactly what he wants."

"Ah, she speaks!" Eris claps his hands together delightedly. "How wonderful. That will make this whole thing much easier."

I do not like the smug twist of his features, an expression I've come to associate with punishment and pain. "What thing?"

"The expansion, of course."

I stare at my brother, trying to make sense of the words. Svea catches on before I do, her fingers digging into the skin of my arms. Energy crackles through the air and I can feel her getting ready to shift back into her wolf form, to fight.

Eris holds out his arms, continuing. "You see, once I figured out that you were sneaking across the border, I had to know what it was that you found so alluring in these woods. So, I followed you. And now, everything is clear." He takes another step closer, his eyes narrowing as any traces of amusement vanish from his features. "You seek my crown. And you plan to use the wolven as weapons against me."

The idea is so absurd, I laugh, the sound echoing across the trees. "You're mad. I want nothing of yours."

"Yet, here you are," Eris sneers.

"You're a fool," Svea calls out, her body vibrating. "You know nothing about us."

Eris cocks a brow at Svea, his eyes traveling from her face to mine, to the way we're pressed against one another. "Wait…are you *in love* with her?" He looks so shocked, it is almost comical.

I glance down at Svea, her face lined with predatory protectiveness, but also fear and worry and so much love. More than I've ever known from another soul. I don't owe him an answer. Not about this.

Eris's laughter rings out and he claps his hands together again. "By God, you are. How odd." His smile morphs into a smirk. "But I'm afraid I can't allow such things to continue.

It wouldn't be befitting to have my queen lusting after my own brother."

"Your queen?" The full weight of Eris's words land, nearly squeezing all of the air from my lungs. "She will never be *your* queen." Svea echoes my words with an animalistic growl.

Eris's eyes seem to dance with glee. "Oh, but she will. You see, you're both going to return with me to the castle. You," he points to me, "will be taken to the lower level where you will receive your rightful punishment for crossing the forbidden boundary, and you," he indicates Svea, "will accompany me to the throne room where I will announce our engagement to the king."

"You really are mad," Svea's voice is low and deep, "if you think I would even consider marrying the likes of you. You are not my king. Why would I ever agree to something like that?"

"Because if you don't, I will make sure that Evander suffers more than any human ever has," Eris answers nonchalantly, as if he were asking the maids for a pot of tea instead of threatening to mercilessly torture his own twin. "I will make sure that every day, every waking moment, is full of unfathomable pain and torment. Every second filled with agony and blood. When I am through with him, you'll both wish he were dead."

The threat hangs heavy in the air, and neither Svea nor I find words.

"So you *will* marry me and you will ally your people with our kingdom. We will finally raze this forest and build a road to the sea. We will build an empire together. And if you refuse…" Eris's eyes land on me. "Well, I guess we'll see how long it takes your bones to shatter, brother."

Svea's form slumps and emits a pitiful sound from her throat. It's the one an animal in a snare might make when it realizes it will never be free again.

It's that sound that unravels something inside me. Whatever tiny thread of duty or obligation I had that connected me to my brother, that allowed me to endure his abuse and his torment for so long, snaps in two.

In a fluid motion, I shove Svea away from me, towards the safety of the tree line, and rip the sword from the sheath at my waist.

"No!" I'm screaming and charging at the same time. Eris's eyes register a flicker of shock before he spins out of the way, yanking his own weapon free.

Our blades collide in the center of the glen, the sound of clashing steel like a booming peal of thunder. Rage fuels each of my steps, every attack and parry, every strike and dodge. My brother's face has lost its smug satisfaction and he grits his teeth, snarling as he lunges, a move that would easily pierce my heart were it not for my quick feet.

I step sideways, twisting out of Eris's reach, and send my own blade slicing through the air. Eris is quick too, his own blade smacking against mine with such force I feel it in my knees.

I shove against his blade, yanking my sword back and throwing myself to the side as Eris strikes again. I spin away as Svea's voice cries out, the tip of the blade snagging in the fabric of my scarlet cloak. It rips down the center.

I yank the clasp around my neck, freeing myself of it just as Eris takes another swipe – this time narrowly missing my throat.

"If you're smart, you'll surrender now," Eris calls out.

Energy ignites the air as Svea shifts into her wolf form, leaping to my side with hackles raised. "No, Svea," I tell her, holding out a hand. "This is between my brother and me."

I strike again, throwing everything I have at Eris, my rage spilling from my throat in a feral yell that sends crows fleeing from the trees.

We move around each other like wraiths, our motions mirroring each other in strength and speed. Sweat drips down my face and neck as I swing my blade, slicing it through the air. The years of pain and punishment swirl around me, every single lash, every drop of my blood spilled for my brother, every broken bone, every tear I cried as I child – all of it whips me into a frenzy until I am unstoppable.

My brother realizes it too, his eyes going wide as I knock the sword from his hand, cornering him against the twisted trunk of an old oak tree.

Panting, we stare at one another, the tip of my sword poised just below his chin. "Let us get one thing perfectly straight, *brother*," I growl. "I bleed for you no longer."

Eris winces as if he's been struck and then squeezes his eyes shut, awaiting the death blow. But I pull my sword back. "I'm not going to kill you."

One of his eyes pops open and then another. "You're not?"

"No," I take another step backward. "Because I am not you. I am *better* than you."

I lower my sword.

Then time itself slows down as several things happen at once. My brother lets out a wild cry and rushes towards me, pulling a dagger from a hidden sheath. He raises the dagger, preparing to plunge it into my chest.

But there's a flash of silver as Svea leaps at Eris, her sharp claws glinting as they pierce him.

Eris screams in pain, wild and full of rage, but the sound is quickly cut off when Svea snarls, her white fangs gleaming as she rips out his throat.

The forest falls silent. It is as if every creature, every bird, every spirit in the trees is holding its breath, waiting to see what will happen next.

I toss my sword and drop to my knees in front of Svea, her snout crimson with blood. She lets out a whimper, refusing to meet my gaze.

"It's okay," I whisper, reaching out to touch her. I run my hand down her back and feel her trembling. "He's gone, and he can't hurt me or anyone else anymore."

There's another burst of golden light as Svea transforms once more, her blood-covered face appearing before mine. Her eyes swim with tears. "I wasn't going to let him take you from me."

"I am yours," I soothe, gathering her up in my arms. I wipe the blood from her face with my tunic and hold her close until she stops trembling.

"So what now?" she asks, her eyes drifting to Eris's lifeless form.

"The king will demand blood for the death of his heir. If they find his body and if the truth of what happened here tonight was known..."

Svea swallows. "He would come for me...and my people."

I nod. "Yes. He would not rest until this forest was destroyed.

"So your brother wins after all?"

I don't answer right away, my thoughts spinning wildly in my head. I walk over to Eris, studying him for a moment. It's like looking at my own face – even in death, we still mirror one another.

And it gives me an idea.

Rolling his body to the side, I make quick work of removing the cloak from his shoulders. I dust it off and fasten it around my shoulders. "Well?" I ask, modeling it for Svea. "How do I look?"

Her brows are bunched together, but she responds. "You look...like your brother."

A smile lifts my cheeks. "Exactly."

It takes a moment for my words to click, but Svea's smile matches my own once she understands. "Evander, you're going to take his place." Awe makes her eyes widen.

"The kingdom deserves better than the heir they got." I straighten my shoulders, stealing one last look at the crumpled scarlet cloak lying discarded on the frozen ground. "For my entire life, I've bled for my brother. Now, I will bleed for them. I will serve the people of my kingdom with kindness and mercy. Two things Eris knew nothing about."

I give Eris one last look. "I wish my brother could have known love, could have been different, but perhaps it's better this way. Maybe now he can find some peace. Maybe we all can."

"The people will be lucky to have you," Svea breathes out, beaming with pride.

"And you?" I tug her towards me. "I cannot do this without you by my side." I dip my head and steal a quick kiss. "Say you'll rule with me, Svea. Promise me that you'll stay with me."

Svea presses up on her tiptoes, bringing her face level with mine. "Always."

She seals her promise with a long, lingering kiss.

A light snow begins to fall, the flakes catching in our hair and eyelashes. "I should return to the castle. I'll need to alert my father that the spare has 'disappeared'." The right side of my mouth twists up in a smirk. "Terrible shame, that is."

"Oh yes," Svea replies, playing along. "I wonder whatever happened to him." She pretends to be thinking seriously.

"Only the stars know," I say with a straight face.

Svea's tinkling laughter fills the glen until I silence her mouth with mine, the heavy fabric of my indigo cloak shielding us from the snow.

A Silken Bridge to Bind the Stars

Deborah L. Davitt

Chapter I: The Invaders

When Lyra was young, she'd loved the royal nursemaids' tales of how the ancients had built an empire that spanned the stars, and had sent colonists to worlds through Gates – Gates that only those of royal blood could control. Troublemakers and convicts had been exiled, leaving nothing but peace and prosperity for those who remained behind. She pictured diamond dust whirling in the obsidian walls of the Gate temples, sparkling with the stars' own light, though all had stood in ruins for some two thousand years.

The royal tutors had little time for myth and legend. They focused instead on the collapse of the global empire after the Gates failed. With no raw materials arriving from the colonies to sustain the burgeoning population of Home, the empire shattered into petty, warring kingdoms. Of those kingdoms, those held by her grandparents, Rostiv and Castain, had been the largest, with the best claim to old imperial blood and legitimacy. And with her parents' marriage, the two kingdoms became Rosstain.

But when Lyra was nine, her tutors stopped talking about history, and started discussing current events. More with her older sister, Tahti, than with her. But Lyra got crumbs of the conversations that made her stomach sink with fear and dread.

"The Invaders are coming," Tahti told her one evening, staring out the window of the room they shared.

Their parents doted on dark-haired Tahti and their youngest child, Bhaitan. Lyra and her other sisters fell into a gray area between the cherished heir and the adored first-born. It didn't bother her, most days. Their nursemaids showered all the children with love, and their tutors often complimented Lyra for being able to read, write, and figure better than Tahti, despite the five years between them.

"I thought they were fighting in Ardain?"

A tightly whispered reply: "Ardain fell. So did Fryncia."

Her stomach lurched as she pictured the map. "That just leaves Esalia to our west?" The smaller kingdom jostled at Rosstain's borders, trying to carve off pieces.

Tahti wrapped her arms around her knees. "Father's calling up the levies. He's going to ride to their defense in the morning."

"But I thought Esalia was our enemy?"

Tahti raised her head. "The Invaders are *everyone's* enemy."

"Who *are* they? Where do they even come from?"

Tahti waved her hands impatiently. "They aren't even *human*! They're immortal, or nearly. They came through a Gate almost fifty years ago, and have been churning through country after country ever since—"

"But the Gates don't work anymore—"

"*They found a way*! They're monsters, Lyra!"

Dark shadows loomed in Lyra's mind. Human-shaped, with fangs and claws. "But what do they want?"

"It doesn't matter what they want. It only matters what it'll take to stop them from killing everyone here!" Tahti flipped a hand at her. "Go away."

Lyra stood, obedient. "Father will be all right," she assured Tahti. "He's brave. He'll win."

Tahti looked away, tears running down her face.

In the morning, the royal children bade their father farewell in the courtyard as he and his men mounted up. Swords and pistols at their sides, shining cuirasses, and long red cloaks. "We'll be back before the harvest," King Mitistav promised his wife, who stood holding their son, Bhatain, in her arms. "Don't let the Council run you around over taxes."

Queen Alania smiled, cool and reserved. "I have never yet allowed them do so, your Majesty."

"There's always a first time, *your Majesty*." He accorded her a formal embrace. Gave Bhatain a kiss – a kindness that Tahti received as well. Lyra and her remaining sisters received light tousles to their hair, and a reminder: "Behave while I'm away."

And then he was gone.

He didn't return in autumn. Nor by the following spring.

When Lyra was ten, Esalia fell. Rosstain stood alone with its back to the eastern sea. Without trade to the fallen kingdoms around them, they had to rely solely on their own harvests. And while the royal children didn't starve, the queen insisted on austerity measures to show solidarity with the rest of the kingdom.

Five years later, the Invaders besieged the capital. Queen Alania had stockpiled food and reinforced the ancient walls, forty feet thick in places. Defensive cannons roared while Lyra and Tahti watched from the highest tower in the castle. They could see the Invader lines moving in, even as a storm rolled in with them, blackening the sky. Lightning crashed, answering every salvo of the cannons with direct strikes on the walls, leaving purple after-images in Lyra's eyes. The thunder was so loud, so continuous, that when Tahti screamed and covered her ears, Lyra couldn't hear her voice. The storm consumed it, ate it whole.

The storm stirred something in Lyra. She walked to the window, blinded by each white flash. She could smell something behind the rain that pounded on the rooftiles. Something...*alive. Magic. They used magic to awaken the storm.*

She watched as the clouds rolled away, and great beasts with bat-wings and leonine haunches appeared in the sky.

They soared over the battlefield, the riders on their backs shooting at targets below, their weapons throwing crackling arcs of blue lightning. Beside them swooped birds seemingly made of fire, their riders pouring down arcs of white flame.

"Beautiful," Lyra whispered, but the thunder ate her words. *Beautiful and terrible at once.*

"Come away from the window, Lyra!" Tahti shrieked. "Come away!"

* * *

That night, their mother came to their rooms. As she entered, Lyra leaped up to curtsy. "Your Majesty!"

Tahti rose as well, asking, "Mother, what's wrong?"

"The king has fallen," Queen Alania whispered, her voice barely audible under the continuous growl of the storm that shook the walls of the ancient castle.

Tahti's voice became keen. "No...*Father*..."

Lyra wished she could feel something beyond the shame that she didn't feel more. She darted a glance at Tahti, but her sister had never accepted or required comfort from her before.

And it didn't seem that this had changed.

"A guard post inside the walls was set on by those... flying beasts. He'd just arrived there with his guards." The queen slumped into a chair, her eyes blank. "The horses spooked. Mitistav was thrown." She put her hands over her face, a wracking sound coming from behind that frail shield.

"No...heroic last stand. No fighting hand-to-hand with our enemies. Just trampled to death by his own men in a plaza half-drowned in flood water from the storm."

"What will we do now, your Majesty?" Lyra asked softly.

Alania raised her face from her hands. "We'll fight long enough to push them to the bargaining table. The Invaders have accepted peace terms before." Her mother's shoulders, always held proudly straight, slumped. "My only goal is to preserve the lives of our people."

"No!" Tahti exclaimed, her expression contorted. "Father wouldn't want—"

"Your father's death leaves us without a commander that our combined forces respect. Our people are demoralized and have been fighting nonstop for five years. How many more lives would you have me sacrifice, Tahti?" Alania lifted her head, proud and fierce once more. "How many more young men and women would you have join your father in the earth?"

Lyra lowered her head. "As your Majesty thinks best," she murmured, hoping Tahti would follow her lead.

Alania nodded acknowledgement to Lyra, and patted Tahti on the shoulder before leaving.

Tahti sobbed into her pillow for the rest of the night, screaming, "It's not right!" and "It's not fair!" and "Why did the Invaders have to come?!"

Lyra sat beside her, patting her shoulders gently whenever Tahti didn't snap at her for doing so. Bhaitan, still only nine – far too young to be a king – slept through the whole thing.

In the morning, Lyra went to the window and looked out at the walls of the city. The storm had abated overnight, so she had an excellent view as the western wall *rippled.* Shuddered. Collapsed. A great rent appeared in the earth, cracking wide through the city streets, and she felt a tremor in the stones under her feet.

We don't have a week in which to surrender, Lyra thought numbly. *Mother had best do it today.*

Chapter II: Surrender

One of the benefits of being the invisible middle child was that Lyra could vanish for hours, unlooked for. So she'd stolen time in the armory to learn the basics of swordplay from the guards. Snuck into the library to read tomes that her tutors hadn't thought suitable for her age. Now she found herself in the courtyard outside the Great Hall where her mother and her Council met with the Invaders. The Invaders' great beasts perched on the roofs above, and her breath caught as she studied them. The bat-winged ones proved to be scaly up close, in vivid shades of scarlet and vermillion, and their amber eyes followed her as she approached the guards at the door.

Those same guards merely glanced at her as she pressed an ear to the cracked door. "Lady Lyra," one of them whispered. "Don't get caught, y'hear?"

She smiled. But the expression felt odd. The *silence* in the castle in the wake of the great storm was unnerving.

The servants, red-eyed, barely spoke above whispers. And to smile in the face of death and defeat felt…wrong.

And yet here was Gorensi, one of her swordplay instructors of long standing, smiling at her with more affection in his eyes than her father had ever displayed for her. Trying, Lyra felt, to comfort her. "I won't get caught," she whispered, and peered into the hall.

Her mother sat at the head of the long rectangular table, her Council to her right. To her left? The Invaders, their faces concealed by elaborate masks. The ones in brown cloaks wore masks of horn or ivory, carved like owls and deer. The ones in blue cloaks wore armor like none she'd seen before, the metal clinging to their bodies like oil, seamless and fine. Their faces, too, were hidden by masks. Bears. Boars. Dragons.

Behind their masks, the Invaders' eyes glittered. Some lid-to-lid black. Others all the colors of an opal, changing in the light as they moved their heads. A voice at the back of her mind whispered, *Beautiful…*

Her mother's voice rose now. "It is our custom to offer treaty-marriages. To ally both sides and to allow… continuance. I myself married my husband after his father's armies had largely conquered Rostiv…."

Lyra stifled a gasp. The alliance of Rostiv and Castain had always been presented by her tutors as a treaty between nations and equals. *Mother and Father didn't marry by choice?*

She suddenly felt small and naive.

"We have no such tradition." The words were flat and only lightly accented. They seemed to emanate from one of the owl-masked Invaders. He stood, his arms crossed, hands tucked into his sleeves. Indifferent. Implacable. "We've opened the way into your city. Your fall is inevitable. You do not dictate the terms here."

"Spakr, hear them." A younger voice, also speaking lightly accented Rosstaini. "It doesn't serve the Lith to slaughter until none remain. If there's a way to ensure peace without having to scorch the land, I'd hear more." The speaker leaned back, his gleaming steel dragon-mask appearing predatory. Behind it, his eyes gleamed green and blue.

Lyra shot a glance at her mother. Read faint satisfaction in the queen's expression. "You are the king, then?" Alania asked, turning towards the one in the dragon-mask.

"We have no kings. I am the Vinr, friend to all and first among Rekkren." A shrug. "You may call me thus."

Alania's lips parted, and her councilors buzzed in consternation. "Ah. Vinr, then. You at least *lead* your people, yes?"

"In war I lead. With the advice of Spakren, Fragnen, and Rekkren. As you do." A gauntleted hand waved at the Council.

Alania licked her lips. "Let me be blunt. I viewed my own treaty-marriage as a chance to build bridges between my people and my husband's." She paused. "If you wed one of my daughters, I'd be willing to sign an agreement that her children would inherit the rule of Rosstain, in place of my son." Alaina's dark eyes gleamed cannily.

"That assumes that our people are fertile with yours," Spakr noted distantly.

Fascinated, Lyra pressed closer to the door. *She's buying time? So we can fight the Invaders off from within? Or... something else?* She blinked, a new thought dawning. *Tahti will* rage *to be married to an Invader. She's had her eye on that duke from Esalia. The one who took refuge with us and fought beside Fa...ther.* Lyra swallowed, suddenly realizing that the young duke might also be dead.

A sudden, rapid exchange of foreign syllables almost crackled in the air. Then Vinr's head swung back towards Alaina. "You can trace your blood back to the ancient emperors. The ones who ruled when the Gates opened freely."

It wasn't a question.

"Yes. I have documentation. You seek...legitimacy, then?" Lyra recognized the calculation in Alaina's gaze. *She thinks she's caught them. That they seek unquestioned claim to the lands they've conquered.*

Spakr and Vinr didn't answer. Just exchanged a measuring gaze. "Marriage, among our people, is not to be entered into lightly," Spakr warned now. "In the event that either partner betrays the other, both suffer. Both may die."

Wait, what?

Alaina snorted, a distinctly ungenteel sound. "So if a man lies with another woman outside of marriage, *both* he and his blameless wife can be put to death? How *just* your laws must be."

"It is not a law," Spakr replied, his voice indifferent. "It is the will of our gods. If one partner has carnal relations outside of the marriage, a wasting will come upon them. It has been known to consume both halves of the union, though not always. And if one partner kills the other…the gods' justice is swift. The same blow that slew one slays the other, within seconds of the first heart ceasing to beat."

Cold slithered down Lyra's spine at the expression on her mother's face. The fear. The uncertainty.

"Of course," Spakr went on, his tone still neutral, "if you did not plan to give your daughter a knife with which to kill her new husband on their wedding night…you would not be sentencing your child to death." A pause. "Consider very carefully what you intend when you bargain with us."

Alaina's chin lifted. "I seek to build a bridge, as I said. One forged of understanding."

As Lyra swallowed, she caught the dragon-masked Invader turn to regard the door she stood behind. It was as if he could see her through the heavy wood, and she lurched backwards, suddenly aware of her own trespass.

"Heard enough?" Gorensi asked.

"Far too much," Lyra countered tightly.

She slipped away as silently as she could, back up to the royal apartments, where Tahti slept, exhausted from a night of weeping. Where little Bhaitan was tracing the letters outlined by one of their nervous nursemaids, who greeted her with an anxious look. "Lyra, what news?"

"Nothing yet," she lied.

* * *

At nightfall, Lyra and Tahti found themselves both summoned to the great hall, bidden to wear their finest. Tahti wore gold brocade that skimmed over her curves, emeralds glinting in the heavy folds of her skirt. Lyra wore pale silver silk, unadorned. She'd been promised that for her next birthday, when she'd be presented to the court as an adult, she'd be given her mother's sapphires to wear at feasts and dances.

She doubted that this would now come to pass.

She wouldn't miss the long, stultifying evenings that Tahti had relished. She hadn't looked forward to dancing and idle gossip in the great hall or the gardens. But anxiety over what the future would now hold clutched at her stomach like bloody claws, twisting.

And as she looked down at the silk wrapped tightly over her arms, she compared it to the near-liquid armor that the Invaders wore, and sighed.

"Come on," Tahti snapped. "We must present ourselves before our conquerors." Her lips twisted. "We'll offer them dainties on trays like *servants*."

But before they could enter the great hall, their mother appeared, her expression stern. "Leave us," she ordered her attendants, who scattered with deferential bows. "There are hard truths that need to be spoken." She spared Lyra a glance before focusing on Tahti. "You were the heir-presumptive of Rosstain for nearly twelve years, my dear. You were trained to rule until Bhaitan's birth. Now you have a chance to take back that future. If you want it."

Lyra admired how carefully their mother had chosen her tactics, leading with an appeal to Tahti's pride. Tahti had wept when Bhaitan had been born. She'd sobbed for almost a week that it wasn't *fair* that the baby would be king someday. It had taken a direct order from their father to get Tahti out of bed for the naming ceremony.

But Lyra wished she could be anywhere other than *here*. The queen had made her decision. Tahti would be offered as a peace-bride to the Invaders; she would object but eventually obey, and that would be the end of it.

"What do you mean?" Tahti asked uncertainly.

Alania explained. And as she did so, Tahti shouted, "No! We haven't even *buried* Father yet, and you're already trying to sell me off to the monsters that killed him?"

Alania's expression tautened. "Silence."

She didn't even raise her voice, but Tahti's wails cut off abruptly. Alania went on softly, relentlessly, "One of my daughters must do this, to save the lives of thousands of people who will die if this war continues. Why should it not be you? You would rule—"

"I don't *care*. I won't do it! They're murderers. Monsters—"

"I thought the same of your father when I married him, and we had five children to attest to our *tolerable happiness*." Alania's voice harshened. "Stop being selfish and see where your duty lies—"

"I'll do it," Lyra said.

Her voice fell into the cracks between their words, and silence rippled out from the syllables.

The queen's head snapped towards her. "You're young. But…." Calculation in her mother's sharp gaze. "A year's betrothal would give us *time*."

"You don't care about Father," Tahti accused Lyra, her voice riding over their mother's. "You haven't even cried. You just want *attention*."

The words cut under Lyra's breastbone. Their father had been an absent presence for her even before the war. She remembered him holding Bhaitan at the naming ceremony. Taking Tahti out a-horse for hunting. Little more. But *Tahti* – her whims, her moods – had been the constant presence, the whirlwind that had consumed Lyra's life.

Because of it – or in spite of it – part of her craved her sister's approval.

"It's not that," Lyra replied. She knew that she couldn't confess her fascination for the Invaders. That they inspired terror and yearning in her, and seemed as far beyond humans as any mountain or storm. How could you hate a storm for its mere existence? "I've always known that I'd be married for political advantage," she continued, glancing at her mother. "Why not this one?"

And then the door behind them opened.

Alania turned, glaring, ready to upbraid whatever servant had just intruded…and then smoothed her features as several Invaders appeared in the doorway. "You've kept us waiting," ivory-masked Spakr said. "But it appears your time hasn't been ill-spent. You've ascertained which of your daughters is willing to participate in your treaty."

"Either of them will obey me," Alaina returned tautly.

"Obedience isn't required," steel-masked Vinr replied calmly. "Consent is. In marriage, I would place my life in the hands of my wife. She would become Vina to my people. Trust must be earned in both directions." He stepped forward, taller than any man Lyra had ever seen before, and taking up more space than seemed possible in the small anteroom.

But all he did was take her hands in his cold, armored grip and weigh them in his own, studying her palms. "You've used a sword."

It wasn't a question. "I-I've some training, yes. M'lord."

"Is that a problem?" Her mother's voice, from behind him, sounded oddly frail.

"No. If she's to be Vina, she'll learn both blade and pistol. To ride a wyvern or a firebird." That, from Spakr, who sounded pleased. "We'll teach her what she needs to learn." He turned, the owl-like beak of his mask appearing like a hooked blade. "The question is, will you accept being taught?"

Lyra swallowed. "Whatever I must."

"Well enough. We'll complete this *treaty* of yours." A hint of mockery in Spakr's voice as he addressed Alaina. "And we will use this castle as our base of operations until all of its conditions are met, including access to your temple ruins."

Past Vinr's elbow, Lyra saw her mother blanch. "You're staying *here*?"

"As the family of our future Vina, you will, of course, remain honored guests," another voice replied, this one lighter, more feminine, speaking from beneath a white mask that looked like a deer's head. "It would be inappropriate to break your kinship bond."

"If consent and willingness between partners is so important," Alaina replied rapidly, her eyes darting from Vinr to Lyra, "then...take the time afforded by my daughter Lyra's youth to...get to know her. A year's betrothal, before final vows are spoken, is all I entreat." Her expression shifted. "I would be a poor mother if my daughter's happiness were of no concern."

Lyra stared. Judging by Alaina's shuttered eyes, Lyra's happiness was her mother's least concern.

"There is no rush," Spakr agreed, shrugging. "We've spent fifty years in search of what we required of this world. Now that we've attained it, what's one more?" A pause. "To the betrothal, then."

"Oh, that will take at least a month to arrange—"

"Nonsense. I would speak the words of the wedding this moment, but for your touching concern for your daughter's *happiness*." Spakr's voice held knife-edges.

Vinr removed his gauntlets, revealing wide, strong hands. His skin shone as blue-green as his eyes, rippling into oranges and red as the lamplight flickered. He took Lyra's hands in his once more, and leaned down to whisper a single word in her ear: "Courage!" as Spakr intoned in the Invader tongue, tying their hands together with a cord.

A question in their tongue to Vinr, who gave some hearty affirmative. A sharp look at Lyra, and a question in her own language: "Do you consent to be bound to this man, and no other, for the term of one year, in preparation for spending your lives together?"

Lyra blinked, overwhelmed. "I—Yes. I do."

The cord *glowed*. Dissolved, melting into Lyra's flesh and Vinr's alike. She felt it spread through her like cold fire, and her heart stopped beating for an instant, before pounding triple-time.

Spakr gestured, and the deer-masked female came forward, another mask in her hand – a steel dragon's head, like Vinr's own. "You will carry this for your intended. Against the day she may call herself Vina."

It was nothing less than an order. And to Lyra's astonishment, the war-leader simply bowed his head to Spakr. "For the good of all, I will."

In spite of these whirlwind events, Lyra felt oddly safe among all these armored forms and masked faces. But before they could draw her away, her mother caught her arm in insistent hands, her fingers digging into her flesh like talons. Leaned down and whispered in her ear, urgently, "Discover what they *want*. Why they're here. We can use that information."

And then Vinr pulled her gently away, out of the room, while behind her she could hear her mother snapping to Tahti, "Go with her! The queen-to-be needs an attendant!"

Oh, gods, Lyra thought. *What have I done?*

Chapter III: Among the Lith

Lyra began by learning the Invaders' language. Their name for themselves, *the Lith*, apparently meant *the exiled*.

The first day she took instruction with Tahti on her left, she realized that they were the only unmasked people in the room. Before their long table, Spakr paced, speaking in rapid, lyrical Lith, and Lyra felt too uncertain to ask him to translate. But the students beside her weren't shy. They asked questions and seemed to argue.

And when that first lesson ended, she'd asked the students what their names were.

"I am Fragna," a hawk-masked male with gleaming golden eyes replied.

"And I am Fragnr," replied the deer-masked female Lyra recognized from the betrothal.

"You can't *both* be Fragna," Tahti retorted, perhaps mishearing the word.

"But we are," they chorused, laughing.

"And Fragna you are, too, or could be. You're old enough to put aside your childhood." The female Fragna gestured at the white mask over her face. "To become what you must, for the good of all."

"I am *twenty*. I'm an adult and should be married by now," Tahti seethed.

"But you still carry the name of childhood." The deer-masked female shrugged.

Lyra interposed quickly, "If Fragna isn't your name, then what does it mean?"

The pair exchanged glances. "Scholar. Student. Or questioner."

The male chimed in. "Inquirer, in criminal matters."

Lyra exhaled. "So, am I Fragna right now?"

More laughter. "You're learning. But you haven't yet given up your childhood. Your name. Your face. That will come in time."

They moved off, and Tahti glared after them. "I'll never give up my name." She stared at Lyra. "They just want to efface us. Turn us into *them*. They'll probably set up re-education camps all through the kingdom. Just like this one." She caught her sister by the arm. "Don't you start believing them, you understand me? That's the real reason Mother insisted that I *attend* you." Her lips worked. "To keep you Rosstaini."

But there is *no Rosstain*, Lyra wanted to reply. *Rosstain is a myth. There's just Rostiv and Castain, jammed together by conquest and marriage. I wonder if the people outside these walls still hate each other, even if our parents were...*tolerably happy. *If they've even noticed a difference between the rule of our parents and the rule of the Lith.*

But she couldn't say that to Tahti. Not while her sister squeezed her arm cruelly tight. "I remember who I am," Lyra finally replied. *But I also know who I'm not.*

* * *

Her language lessons were supplemented, however, when her original palace tutors joined Spakr in teaching. They appeared uneasy before the Lith, but the Fragnen took diligent notes on the history of Rosstain, asking demanding questions. Lyra learned to do the same, pushing her teachers as hard as they'd ever pushed her.

Her afternoons, by contrast, were spent in sword-play and pistols. Sometimes Vinr was her instructor, though she would've cheerfully faced the rack before admitting to Tahti how much she enjoyed his instruction. And she certainly didn't mention the cool tingle that suffused her fingers any time she came in contact with him – even through his armor.

Tahti refused to participate in those lessons. She simply sat in the courtyard, her face carved into a mask of disapproval and anger.

A year into her training, Lyra managed to get in two hits on Vinr before being thrown to the ground like a ragdoll. They rolled across the courtyard, Lyra half-laughing, half grunting with effort as she set her feet against his hips and shoved, forcing his weight away before slamming an elbow into his masked face.

"Good!" Vinr said, sitting back.

Lyra sat up, accepting the hand he offered to haul her back to her feet, the usual cool tingle rushing through her. "You *let* me get those hits in."

"I provided openings for you to see, as I would with any trainee. What you did with it was all your own work." He nodded. "Much progress today. Soon you'll earn your armor."

"Armor like yours?" she asked. Part of her delighted in the notion – she'd been found *worthy*, and by a demanding tutor. But part of her also felt discomfited. She couldn't imagine how the people of the city might see her, dressed like…one of the *Invaders*.

Her eyes fell to the dragon-mask riding at Vinr's hip. The one she'd agreed to wear when they were wed. Though a year had passed, and she was of age, no one had yet spoken of completing the ceremony. She wondered if it would feel like a cage to her.

If his felt like a prison to him.

"Yes, like mine," he replied as her mind raced. "Every Vina must prove herself worthy of leading, which means proving herself worthy of being followed. This is part of it." He gestured at the courtyard. "You're worthy enough to call yourself Rekkra, this day, if you wished it. But only you can tell me if you're ready to call yourself Vina." His eyes were serious behind the mask. Intent.

She hesitated. "If I prove myself worthy of leading your people," Lyra noted softly, "I could be proving myself unworthy to lead my own." She glanced at Tahti, who sat embroidering on a wall. Watching them.

He inclined his chin. "Possible," he replied as they moved towards the pump in the courtyard. He worked the handle, so that she could dunk her head under the rushing water. When she came up, short-cropped hair dripping down her neck, he added, "Your mother spoke during the treaty negotiations of building bridges between our people. Were those just pretty words and stalling tactics?"

Lyra winced. "From her, perhaps." She looked down at the flagstones. Every time she saw her mother lately, the urgency that blazed in Alaina's eyes was almost too much to bear. *What have you learned? What do they want? Why is it taking you so long to win your betrothed's confidence?*

She couldn't tell her mother that she had no intention of betraying Vinr's trust. Even if it meant betraying Alaina's.

"And from you?"

Lyra looked up. "Bridges can be swept away when rivers flood."

"Then we should ensure that the dams don't burst," he countered. Under his mask, his eyelids crinkled. "I'll see you here again tomorrow. When you prove that today's good work was not happenstance."

She felt a smile stretch her face as he left, which faded as Tahti closed on her. "You look happy," her sister accused.

Lyra composed her face. "There's pleasure in doing well," she replied. *What does she see when she looks at the wyverns? Monstrous beasts that killed our father, I'm sure – but can she see their beauty? Or does their very beauty offend her?*

Tahti leaned closer. "Have you even seen any of their *faces*?" she whispered. "Do you know what they look like?"

Lyra felt exhaustion wash over her. Not the good kind that came from exertion on the sparring grounds, but from emotional exhaustion. She wore one mask for Tahti and their mother. Another mask for Spakr and the Fragnen. Only around Vinr did she feel as if she wore no mask at all. "You know I haven't." Frank, open speech. None of the deference that Tahti still demanded in front of their mother and the human court. *As if any of our former lives matter now.*

Tahti's face tightened. "I saw Vinr without his mask yesterday," she whispered.

Lyra's eyebrows rose skeptically. "Their faces are for intimates only." *Not even with his* betrothed *has Vinr removed that damned mask.* She put her head to the side. *What's the play here? Is this Mother at work, trying to manipulate me?*

Her mother was the best player of court games in living memory. This felt too unsubtle to be Alaina's work. She could envision her mother going so far as to poison *her,* on her wedding night, to ensure that Vinr would die with her, but only if pushed towards such unsubtlety by forces outside her control.

Tahti's anger is behind this, then. The thought startled her with its cool lack of emotion. "Did you try to kiss him, sister?" A thrust like the point of a sword, testing for reactions. "Did your desire to be queen overcome your loathing? Or did you just want to ascertain whether or not he and I would both fall over dead if you seduced him?"

Tahti's hand leaped to slap, and Lyra caught her wrist before it could connect. She blinked, surprised at her own reflexes. "Don't."

Her sister's lips worked. "He was alone in the courtyard and took off his helmet to drink from this same pump." She gestured. "I was in the long gallery, passing by. His face is nothing but *putrescence*. A writhing mass of worms and rot."

Lyra stared at her, knowing from her own experience that there was no way in which the pump was visible from the window. *A lie. But why? Is it just that she wants me to feel as she does towards them? So that she feels…less alone, having me as her ally in hate?* "Thank you," she finally replied. "It's good to know where everyone stands."

Chapter IV: Bridges

Weeks later, Vinr brought his wyvern into the courtyard. Lyra stared up at the great beast, studying the bat-like sweep of its wings, the clawed hindlegs, the restless, serpentine tail. "Let me adjust the saddle for you," Vinr said, and moments later had her positioned atop the great beast. Then he slipped up behind, asking, "Ready?" and she nodded.

The wyvern leaped, its wings clawing at the air, and Lyra half-laughed, half-shrieked with delight, feeling Vinr's arms tighten around her.

After several minutes, the great wings spread out, catching the wind, and they soared over the castle and the city, giving her a clear view of the battle scars that pocked the fields outside. The crumbled outer wall.

The mass graves.

The exhilaration of the flight left her. "Did you bring me up here to show me the damage?" she called over the roar of the wind. *To remind me of your power?*

"No. I brought you here to give you a taste of what it means to be Vina," he shouted back, the wind tearing at his voice. "Both the good and the terrible."

"I know that you don't give your names to strangers," she commented carefully as he brought the wyvern in for a landing on a mountainous outcropping, miles away. "but I'd...like to know what your title really means."

She could hear the smile in his voice. "Good question. You would be an excellent Fragna. Perhaps even a Spakr someday."

"Could *you* be a Spakr someday?"

"My father was Vinr once. And is Spakr now – the one you know." He helped her slide down from the wyvern's back. "So, yes. Once I'm too old for sword and pistol, and once someone else may call himself Vinr...it would be an honor to be considered wise enough to become Spakr." A faint shrug. "Of course, many who called themselves Vinr have died in battle, too."

She considered it. "Spakr means *speaker.*" She was fairly sure of that. "Someone who gives the laws. Speaks for the gods. Teaches others."

"Excellent!" He pulled a leather bag of wine from the saddle, and a single cup. "Vinr means *beloved companion.* Which is what I am to all the Rekkren. Their leader, as well as friend to all the other castes."

"The Rekkren are the warriors. So you lead only them? Not the rest of your people?"

"A warrior might not know when to plant grain or how to build a house. It would be stupid for me to tell the Stadren or the Smitjen how to do their jobs. No, it is the Council that governs. We all have voices on it. The Vinr and Vida are friends to all, however. The loudest voices on the Council, too."

He gestured for her to join him on a patch of soft moss under a gnarled oak. She'd never been so alone with any man before, but the Lith had a way of cutting through Rosstaini propriety, so she sat beside him and picked through the food he'd brought with them. Simple fare. An uncut wheel of cheese, an unbroken loaf of bread, and cured meats. He even handed her a knife so that she could cut the food to her liking – a gesture of trust she instantly recognized.

"Will you eat with me today?" She'd never seen him eat or drink.

"Perhaps," he replied slowly. "It's…an intimacy."

"My birthday has passed. So has the year of our betrothal," Lyra replied, looking away. "Are we not to wed soon?"

His shoulders shifted. "Only if you're ready to become Vida. I can wait longer. The other Lith grow impatient, however."

"Why?" Lyra blinked. She hadn't thought the Lith had any opinion of her at all.

His eyes shifted color, from blue-green to yellow-amber. *Caution*, she thought, *wariness*. "You may be the key to all we Lith have sought here," Vinr admitted, and filled the single cup with wine.

She keyed on the word, as he'd surely meant her to. "Lith. Exiles." She nibbled on her cheese. "Were you exiled from your home? Is that why you're here, on this world?"

"We were exiled *to* where we came from," he replied, his eyes turning violet. *Is that regret? Sorrow?* "The gods of that world changed us. Made us what we are now, over generations. We no longer die of natural causes, but on the world of our exile, it's a curse to watch someone starve, unable to die of the hunger. Do you understand?"

And after a moment, it all came together. "The Gates," she whispered. "Your ancestors? They came from *here*. They were exiled from *this* world. Sent as colonists, or prisoners."

He nodded. "You're quick. Your mother and her advisors refused to believe this."

Lyra sat upright under the oak, mind racing. "So you're… human."

"More or less. The gods of our new world changed us in many ways." His voice sounded weary.

She turned towards him, not having realized until this moment, as relief coursed through her, how much her sister's poison had coiled through her heart. "Under that mask…"

"No worms or rot, if that's what you're asking."

"You heard Tahti." Shame colored her cheeks.

"A Fragna did. Your lack of belief was also noted. I was grateful to hear of it." A wry note. "I wasn't looking forward to a future in which my wife might recoil from me."

Lyra swallowed. "Show me your face. Please." She paused. "Perhaps…you might even tell me your name?"

He reached up and unlatched the steel dragon's head. As he did so, his armor unfurled. Pulled back from his skin, retreating into the mask, into other hidden reservoirs on his body, leaving him wearing little but trews and his weapon-belt. The shimmering blue-green of his skin glistened in the dappled light under the tree, catching glimmers of gold and red as the leaves above swayed.

Then he let his hands fall, revealing eyes that appeared exactly as they had under the mask, though he averted his gaze from her in evident discomfort. And for the rest? Achingly human, with dark tousled hair, rough beard stubble, and a strong jawline.

Hesitantly, Lyra reached out, sliding her fingers along the line of his jaw. "You…feel real." The cold-fire surged in her fingertips. As if the power inside her yearned towards the matching energies in him.

His lips curled. "So do you." An exhalation. "The name my parents gave me at birth was Rikr." Vinr's eyes rose fractionally to meet hers. "No one's called me that since I put on my first mask as a Rekkr." He studied her face. "I wouldn't object to hearing it from your lips in private. As I would call you Lyra, once you've become Vina."

A quick, bright surge of panic, mixed with anticipation. "Why do your people…bury yourselves under these masks? Why do you *efface* yourselves so?" She cast about for an explanation. "Did your gods demand it?"

He shook his head. "Our new world was harsh. Names, identities, wealth, all the dross with which you distinguish yourselves from each other…it all seemed selfish. So our ancestors gave them up. As we all must. For the good of all." He turned his face, and she felt his lips brush the palm of her hand. "That doesn't mean that we don't take joy in our lives, that we don't care for our spouses or families. It just means that we're all obliged to care about *all* of our people." A pause. "And once we're wed, your people will be my people. I will be obliged to care for them as for my own."

Her eyes fell to the dragon mask still tied to his belt. But she needed to know more. To understand all the things that had been unspoken.

"So…you returned to the world that exiled you. To…punish us?" That didn't sound right. "You said that the Lith were impatient. That I might be the key to something." *Mother has wanted this information for a year. Wouldn't she be delighted to know what I'm about to learn? Though…I surely can't tell her.*

Vinr nodded, leaned back against the tree, letting her hand fall with his to his lap. Light. Undemanding. "I was born on the Lith world."

"Wait. How old *are* you? The Lith arrived fifty years ago!" Lyra blurted.

"Aye. I was your age when we arrived. But I'm nearly a stripling by my people's standards, mind. Spakr is past three hundred." He raised her fingers to his lips. "Can you accept my *antiquity*?"

"You don't look or sound antique!" Lyra felt her cheeks flush and looked away hastily. "But I've interrupted enough."

His chuckles faded. "We opened a Gate from our side," Vinr went on. "Suddenly, we thought we could go *home*. Though for most of us, it was a home of myth and legend. But it closed behind us, and we couldn't open it again from this side. Ten thousand warriors, crafters, and scholars, all cut off from home." His fingers tightened on hers. "Everywhere we went, we were attacked. Spakr – who was Vinr then – responded in kind. His only goal was opening a Gate and either getting us back to our people or bringing our people through."

Her mind whirled through the possibilities. "You think I can open a *Gate*?" Lyra asked, stunned. "No one can – no one *has*. Not in centuries."

"They were tied to the blood of the ancient rulers. Your mother claims lineage going back to them. It's worth a try." He shrugged. "And if it doesn't work, we'll be no worse off than we were already."

"That seems a terrible gamble."

He nodded, closing his eyes. A gesture of trust, she realized. "Is your world so terrible, then?" Lyra asked, hesitantly settling her head on his shoulder. He felt warm, she noted distantly. "Would all your people come through at once? I don't think we could feed them all."

"My people number in the millions. They can't all come through. But simply opening trade routes would help. Your grain for our metals, and the like." One of his hands moved up, running lightly along the nape of her neck, tangling into her hair. "Will you go with me to the temple near here? Will you try to craft a bridge across the void, between the stars with me?"

"Between the stars. Between people." She nodded against his shoulder. "Yes. I will. I'll be your Vina."

His eyes opened, looked down into her own, before he brushed a light kiss across her lips. "Between us, no masks," he whispered. "Never. But for all others—"

He reached down, unhooking the mask from his belt. Offered it to her with gentle hands.

And she took it and covered her own face, feeling the liquid steel mold itself to her features. Felt the armor sleeking down from the mask to slick along her skin, under her clothing. But she raised the faceplate once more, long enough for him to lean in and kiss her, his hands tight against the supple armor she now wore. "I'm ready," she whispered. "Let's go."

Monster Masquerade

Sarina Dorie

"Each princess comes with a monster," the fairy godmother told the crowd of princes who stood against the wall of the eighteenth century style grand ballroom of the palace. "There are no exceptions. That is how things are done in our kingdom."

Edwin stared at devastatingly beautiful princesses dancing with their devastating monsters to waltzes played by a quartet. Candlelight glittered from gilded filigree arches and gold leaf in pastel murals depicting scenes of cherubs in classical art. Everything was decadent and excessive, even the princes in their expensive armor around him.

Prince Edwin raised his hand, waiting for a nod from the fairy godmother before asking his question. "But surely there are some exceptions," he said. "Because I heard about this one princess who got rid of her monster without—"

"Do not believe rumors." The fairy godmother stared down her long nose at him, as if daring him to contradict her.

Edwin's friend Antoine gave him a sidelong glance, but his other two friends didn't seem perturbed by the question.

Edwin hoped he hadn't raised suspicion from the other princes by asking a question that would make them think he didn't belong here.

He feared he hadn't prepared enough for tonight's festivities – or the massacre that would follow. As much as he yearned to prove himself worthy as a prince so he would be permitted to keep his current identity, he should have realized it wouldn't come without a price.

That price might be his life.

All young ladies present wore pastel gowns, many reminiscent of medieval nobility. A Persian princess in flowing robes of gold looked like she had stepped out of *A Thousand and One Nights*. Another in twelve kimonos, each layered on top of another, didn't even break a sweat as she waltzed.

Each princess waltzed in time to the music with a hulking creature at least three times her size.

The monsters came in a variety of colors and shapes, no two the same. Some of them were covered in fur with claws that could fell a man in one swoop. Other beasts were serpentine and covered in scales that glittered like rubies or sapphires. Nearby was a creature resembling a dragon with wings and teeth that could crush a prince. The ghostly phantoms were the scariest, appearing and disappearing like mist, cloaked in shadows and mystery.

All princesses and beasts wore masks. This was a monster masquerade after all.

The fairy godmother pointed at the princes in turn. "Remember the rules of the party and the rules of the curse. Only the brave and wise will be able to break it." She turned her gaze on a bored-looking young man slurping a green gelatin salad loudly.

It was obvious from his smile that the young man was trying to annoy the fairy godmother. He slurped even louder.

Edwin didn't like this rude young man who had been born with privilege and a life of ease. He suspected his rival took his rank and position for granted.

The fairy godmother continued with the grace of someone used to handling churlish clods. She could have been a princess herself with her voluminous pastel dress and the endless panels of lace and ruffles. The only detail that marked her as different was her grandmotherly age.

Occasionally Edwin thought he caught sight of a shimmer along the fairy godmother's back, the wings that mere mortals weren't supposed to be able to see, but he was no ordinary mortal. He hadn't been born a prince.

That had been a gift of his own fairy godmother, to give him the dream he had always yearned for. Now that he was here on the princess quest, he felt less certain about this part of his adventure.

He had known the road to becoming a prince would be full of peril and danger, but he hadn't considered he would need to participate in the monster masquerade.

"No prince will be able to compete for a princess's affections while she is held in the thrall of her monster," the fairy godmother said. "And that is your goal, to find the princess you wish to court, marry, and take home."

Edwin had listened attentively during the prince orientation before the ball. The curse was a revelation for some princes who had been raised in ignorance about the reasons a supposedly evil fairy had "cursed" the princess population, but Edwin had been taught early on why princesses needed their monsters to protect them.

Surely some of these princes had learned the same lessons he had, even if hormones had made them forget.

The music ceased. Beasts bowed to their princesses, and princesses in turn bowed to her beasts.

"Seize your chance before the next song starts!" the fairy godmother said. "And remember, you'll need brains more than brawn."

The crowd of princes surged forward.

"I'm ready to seize my princess!" a rowdy prince in a purple cape shouted.

The fairy godmother had definitely not said to "seize a princess". Edwin turned to find the prince in question being mowed down by a shaggy beast with horns. He wasn't surprised.

A prince up ahead elbowed his peers out of his path. "I claim the most beautiful princess!"

"I will prove how brave I am and slay multiple monsters so that I can have many wives," another prince said.

Edwin thought they both were idiots. There was more to a partnership than beauty. And it was folly to want more than one wife when establishing a relationship with one princess – and her monster – would be more than enough.

Edwin did not run. He took his time. He strolled through the sea of princesses, studying the monsters that represented each beauty's personality. The lovely redhead wearing silver stared blankly at the room around her, while the cunning eyes of her chimera twitched restlessly. The icicles growing in the creature's fur hinted that she was cold in temperament. Steam fumed from another monster's nose, signaling that the princess had a fiery temper.

A prince in a green cape roared from Edwin's left as he charged toward a twisting wyrm that looked like it was made of vapor. The man's sword sliced through the wyrm, but the creature remained unscathed. The prince screamed as the wyrm opened its maws and swallowed him whole. As the monster was transparent, the prince could be seen upside down, wiggling inside the wyrm's belly.

Edwin supposed he should have felt bad for the man, but that prince had been rude to the fairy godmother during orientation, constantly interrupting and talking over her, inferring he knew more than the expert in the room.

As Edwin approached a giant lounging lizard, a prince in armor shoved Edwin out of the way. "You can't have her. I saw her first."

Edwin assumed the other prince must have been referring to the beautiful young lady dressed in a gown that glittered with a thousand diamonds that had been sewn into the fabric. Her monster was just as resplendent, the scales of the beast each inlaid with precious stones and gems. Edwin suspected he understood the prince's motivation in selecting this princess.

Seconds later, Edwin heard the prince scream from overhead. Edwin watched in shock as the prince was catapulted over the crowd and out the window. He hadn't liked the prince, but he hoped he landed in some bushes outside without thorns.

Edwin perused the monsters, his gaze settling on a blocky beast pale as parchment, black squiggles decorating the hide. As the beast shifted its tail to the side to swat a pretentious prince away, Edwin noticed the way those squiggles moved. He stepped closer, his curiosity piqued when he saw those were words written across the beast's limbs and belly. They shifted and danced as his gaze swept over it.

"May I have this dance?" Edwin looked from the princess to her dragon.

The princess stared at him blankly. She was pretty, with brown hair and tawny skin that was striking against the lavender gown she wore. Her expression was full of vapid emptiness compared to her larger-than-life dragon.

It was the dragon who spoke, her voice as sweet as honey. "I will consent to one dance, but only because you asked so politely and didn't try to slay me with a sword."

The dragon held out a claw to Edwin. He reluctantly took it. The scent of vanilla and dusty pages wafted from her.

"Is this your first time at the monster masquerade?" Edwin asked.

"No, it's my third year. Each time I've managed to leave unscathed." The dragon's lips curled back in a smile.

Words drifted across the dragon's chest: *In vain have I struggled. It will not do. My feelings will not be repressed. You must allow me to tell you how ardently I admire and love you.*

"Ahem, my eyes are up here," the dragon said.

"I beg your pardon," Edwin said. "I didn't mean to offend. I couldn't help noticing you're a fan of Jane Austen. I'm guessing *Pride and Prejudice* must be one of your favorites." Now that he was a prince, he could more easily acquire novels that promoted free thinking from outside their kingdom.

The dragon giggled in girlish delight. "Why yes! I love the classics."

"As do I," Edwin said.

A prince screamed from elsewhere in the room. He hoped it wasn't one of his friends. Edwin tried to ignore the sound.

"What other literature do you enjoy?" he asked.

"Excuse me," the book dragon said, deftly stepping aside.

A prince in armor flung the princess in lavender over his shoulder and attempted to carry her off. The book dragon plucked the doll-like figure from the man's back and set her aside. The armored prince whirled, crossbow in hand.

Edwin considered stepping forward to stop the dragon or the prince but decided against it. This was not his battle.

"Dear me. I was afraid it would come to this." The book dragon opened her mouth and black ink vomited out, a landslide of poetic phrases typed in Garamond, Times New Roman, and Courier gushing onto the rival prince.

"*Once upon a midnight dreary, while I pondered weak and weary...*" became jumbled under a pile of: "*Do you think I am an automaton? – a machine without feelings? and can bear to have my morsel of bread snatched from my lips, and my drop of living water dashed from my cup?*"

The mountain of words from Edgar Allen Poe and Jane Eyre became buried under *Orlando*, Virginia Woolf's sentiments surely mirroring the monster's own: "*A woman knows very well that, though a wit sends her his poems, praises her judgment, solicits her criticism, and drinks her tea, this by no means signifies that he respects her opinions, admires her understanding, or will refuse, though the rapier is denied him, to run through the body with his pen.*"

Edwin feasted his eyes on the dragon's rant that was the equivalent of fire. He, in fact, liked this so much more, appreciating someone who could express herself with words.

The book dragon turned back to Edwin. "Have you had enough? You can flee now without incurring shame. I have no desire to be carried off and forced to go with you to your kingdom."

"Nor did I say I intend to carry you off or force you anywhere," Edwin said with a bow. "I simply asked for the honor of a dance. Nothing more."

The dragon tentatively took his offered hand. "I'm not ready to marry."

"Nor am I," Edwin said.

"Then why are you here, if not to slay a monster and carry off a princess?" the dragon asked.

"There is more to life and relationships than marriage," Edwin said. "Friendship and companionship." That, and this was one of the items he had to accomplish on his quest to be a real prince. He couldn't tell if he was passing that test or failing.

The dragon leaned in and sniffed. "You are no ordinary prince."

Edwin held still, lest the dragon give him a papercut or accidentally maul him with razor sharp wit.

"No, I'm not." Edwin didn't care to elaborate.

"Who are you?" the dragon asked with suspicion.

Edwin smiled. That was his secret.

* * *

During orientation, the fairy godmother had explained the purpose of monsters to the princes as though they were dimwitted. In all fairness, most of them were.

Princes sat in rows of cushioned chairs before the fairy godmother lecturing at the head of the lavish room. Edwin thought it had been a mistake to serve wine and hors d'oeuvres as several princes were now reclining across the seats.

"That monster might have been a princess's protector in her early years, but there is a point in life where they are no longer needed," the fairy godmother said. "Now that these eligible young ladies are ready for marriage, you must disarm the monster she manifests to keep her safe. Only then will you be able to take a princess for her hand in marriage."

"But what if she isn't ready for marriage?" Edwin asked, thinking it had been a perfectly reasonable question.

The other princes laughed and mocked him.

"Why don't you just ask her monster if he's ready to get married?" one of the haughty princes had demanded.

Edwin crossed his arms, as vexed by the loutish prince's jeering as he was by the assumption that all monsters were male.

A gawky prince next to Edwin crossed his arms, shaking his head. He muttered under his breath. "They're a bunch of fools. Ignore them."

Edwin noticed the shrewd appraisal in the fairy godmother's eyes. "If the princess is not ready, her monster will fight to the death for her."

"Death to the monsters. Death to the monsters!" a group of enthusiastic princes chanted.

Edwin raised his hand, not waiting to be called on. "And if a prince kills her monster, won't part of the princess die as well?"

"Indeed," the fairy godmother said.

"Don't worry." A hunky prince in a green cape, and with so much muscle it appeared he was lacking a neck, thwacked Edwin on the back. "Only the monster side of the princess will be destroyed. She'll be helpless and complacent. She'll be a doll."

A doll. Edwin found it all disgusting. This was why it was so much better to be a prince than a princess.

Boys didn't have to manifest avatars to keep themselves safe.

"If that is what you most desire in a mate, then yes. If you slay her monster, she will be complicit and docile," the fairy godmother said, eyeing the prince who had spoken out of turn. "But if you wish to acquire a princess who will rule as your equal—"

The arrogant prince talked over the fairy godmother. "Too many cooks spoil the broth. And too many rulers create anarchy for the kingdom."

This was the fifth time the young man had interrupted. Edwin wondered if every orientation was like this for the fairy godmother and this was what she had to put up with.

"I see you've got this all figured out." The fairy godmother crossed her arms. "Why don't you finish teaching the lesson?"

The prince did so.

The gawky young man who felt as much contempt for his peers as Edwin whispered, "Don't pay them any mind. You've got the right idea about it. I have eight sisters, and they've all got monsters. I survived long enough to make it this far in life."

The young man introduced himself as Antoine. He leaned in closer. "Do you want to get out of this stuffy room and read the manual for the ball without these dudes prince-splaining the rules?"

Edwin was relieved at the idea of escaping, even if it was only for a moment. Antoine gestured to a prince in armor and a young man dressed in colorful robes that contrasted with his dark skin. The four of them met in the hallway.

"This is Abidemi," Antoine said, pointing to the man in vibrant robes.

Abidemi wasn't wearing a sword.

The prince wearing armor lifted his helm so that his face was visible. He introduced himself as Xavier. He had to be the handsomest prince Edwin had ever met, with his thick black lashes and dusky complexion. He was also surprisingly studious.

"Let's read the manual to ourselves and take notes," Xavier said. "If there's anything we're uncertain about, let's mark those sections to see if anyone else has gleaned the answers from the text." He grinned with the kind of smile that was certain to break a few princesses' hearts.

And maybe some of the princes. Abidemi couldn't take his eyes off Xavier.

"Did everyone bring highlighters?" Xavier asked. "If not, I have some you can borrow."

Abidemi let out a wistful sigh. "I would love to borrow your highlighter."

Edwin studied the booklet, took notes, and compared information with the other princes.

"Was there anything unclear about the 'persuade the monster' part?" Xavier asked with the seriousness of a schoolmaster. "Or do we all have the basics down?"

"My only question is, why do those other princes all think 'persuade' means 'destroy'?" Edwin asked. "This task is about collaboration and mutual respect, not violence."

It was true Edwin hadn't been raised in a wealthy household where they felt that violence was the answer to every problem, but surely there had to be more than the four of them in three dozen princes who felt otherwise.

Abidemi shook his head. "Some of those boys must not have had a momma who raised them with manners."

"Or had eight sisters to show them the error of their ways," Antoine said. He rolled up a sleeve, showing off a puckered pink line on the back of his wrist. "But I do have scars from my mistakes with my sisters. Tread carefully, not heedlessly like these fools."

Edwin had been an only child. He had no scars. His fairy godmother had used magic to transform him, gifting him with a whole and perfect new body.

Now he could go on quests and save the kingdom from dark magic, fight the tyranny of wicked rulers, read books from the neighboring kingdom without incurring the wrath of elders, and not have to bow down to anyone. He was allowed to make decisions for himself.

But he still had to prove himself as a prince with this final test.

The Princess Quest Test at the Monster Masquerade awaited.

* * *

Candlelight from chandeliers glittered off gold leaf decorating the pastel ballroom where princesses waltzed with monsters to melodic music – and some princes attempted to slay them.

"You're holding up noticeably well," said the book dragon to Edwin as they danced. "Are you certain you've never been to one of these balls?"

"I'm quite certain."

A crimson stain from a nearby prince splattered against the pale parchment of the book dragon's neck. Edwin feared what he might see if he looked.

When green spotted the book dragon's hide, followed by a violet streak, a prince behind Edwin moaned. "Please no! Anything but that!'

The book dragon turned away from Edwin, toward the other masked monster, "Excuse me, could you take that activity elsewhere?"

Edwin glanced over at the prince, cowering on the ground in fear. His gleaming armor was splattered with color. The monster torturing him was holding a paintball gun, a vicious grin on her face as her princess stared on.

Edwin and the dragon resumed dancing.

"I noticed you haven't once gazed at my princess this entire time we've been dancing," the dragon said.

"Well, that would be rude, wouldn't it? You're the one I'm dancing with." Edwin stared up into the dragon's brown eyes. "Or was I supposed to ogle your decoy?"

"My decoy?" The dragon's lips curled upward with mirth. A line from Edgar Allen Poe scrolled across her neck like a necklace inlaid with words. "Yes, I suppose that is one way to think about my princess."

Edwin felt wholly inadequate for this masquerade. He feared the princess and her monster saw through him and questioned whether he truly was a prince if he didn't behave enough like the others.

Edwin supposed he should at least try to blend in with the others. He turned to gaze at the princess's dark hair pulled up so that curls cascaded down her back. She was beautiful, smiling at him, though her eyes were vacant.

"What made you ask me to dance if you're not interested in marriage?" the dragon asked.

"I liked your personality. Or what I gathered was your personality from the quotes dancing across your arms. I thought we might share common interests." Edwin shrugged. "I just thought, maybe we could be friends and get to know each other and see if our feelings are mutual. It seems more civilized than throwing your avatar over my shoulder and running off."

The book dragon drew back. "You aren't a prince! You're an imposter!"

Edwin's face turned red. Now he'd done it. He was about to be caught and thrown out.

The dragon laughed. "Forgive me. I jest."

Edwin conceded that his life before becoming a prince probably gave him a perspective most of the other men in the room lacked, aside from those who had enough sisters or a mother who had influenced them with their female gaze.

"Do you know how my curse will be broken?" the book dragon asked.

"Yes," Edwin said. He knew this as much from the manual as his own experience before his wish had been granted and he'd been given the body he'd yearned for. "When you find someone who truly loves you as you are, your personality and avatar will be united as one."

When his fairy godmother had united his own monster with his body, she had explained princes did not have the same problem. They didn't have to exist as two separate people, developing a monster to protect themselves from princes. As much as Edwin tried to forget his other life, and to believe he had always been a prince, his past experiences shaped the person he was today.

He wouldn't understand the plight of princesses without that past.

Out of the corner of his eye, Edwin noticed Antoine was riding on the back of a dragon with a princess in a kimono seated beside him. Somehow they both managed to hold on as the creature undulated in time to the music. Abidemi had given up all pretenses of being interested in princesses and was dancing with Xavier. They looked like they were enjoying themselves.

Edwin only felt tense and awkward. He wished he could be as authentically himself with this dragon as his friends were with their dance partners.

There was only one way to do that. He was going to have to admit the truth and hope the dragon didn't slay him.

"I need to be honest with you," Edwin said. "I'm only here at the masquerade because it's on my list of tasks that I need to perform as a prince. If I prove myself, I will get to keep on being…me." Sweat prickled the back of his neck. "But I haven't always been a prince…at least not in body."

The dragon tilted her head with curiosity.

When his fairy godmother had transformed him from a princess to a prince, his avatar of that doll-like body had been dissolved. Now that his monster was hidden within the flesh of a human form, he didn't need a decoy to distract would-be suitors from noticing his personality.

Edwin drew in a deep breath to fortify himself with courage. "I'm now the prince I've always known I was deep inside, but I didn't always have this body. I once was a princess, and my fairy godmother made my wish come true. She dissolved my avatar when she gave me my body."

"What?" the dragon roared. Words flung off her scales and peppered the crowd, causing other monsters to give her dirty looks.

Edwin flinched back. He had feared an angry reaction like this.

"How do I get a fairy godmother like that?" the dragon asked.

That wasn't the question Edwin had been expecting. "I – um – I don't know. I could try contacting my fairy godmother for you. Do you want to be turned into a prince too?"

The dragon bit her lip, giving it serious consideration. "No. I think I would wish to be a shapeshifter, so I could be a dragon or a human woman, but not have to worry about two bodies."

The music ended. Edwin glanced around at the great hall. Servants were carrying off bodies of moaning princes as well as a few unfortunate monsters that had been slain. A rush of more princes from the sidelines surged forward to seek a princess during the next song.

The dragon shifted from foot to foot awkwardly. "Do you want to dance again?"

"I would love that, but could I ask your name first?" Edwin asked.

"Where are my manners? I should have introduced myself! But I guess I assumed I was going to bury you under a mountain of inky words, and there wouldn't be much point. I'm Princess Magdalena, but you can call me Mags." The dragon grinned. "All my friends do."

Edwin took that as a compliment.

He introduced himself.

The fairy godmother gave him a thumbs up. Apparently he had aced Princess Quest Test.

When Frost Loved Flame

Umenyi Chisomaga Evelyn

Chapter I: Velmora's First Masque

The banners over Velmora's Keep sagged under their own weight, stiff with frost, their silk roses stained crimson against pale stone. The courtyard below seethed with horses, torches, and voices – nobles in sable cloaks, merchants hawking sugared almonds, jugglers tossing knives as though to mock the evening's true purpose. For all the colour, the air smelled of iron, pine smoke, and fear.

Lady Serenya Veyrath stood at the edge of a marble colonnade, her hands gloved in pearl-threaded velvet, her cloak fastened with a clasp shaped like a rose entwined with thorns. Snow caught in her dark braid, silver ribbons glimmering faintly where they tangled with strands of black. Her eyes – frost-sharp blue, steady and unreadable – scanned the crowd without ever seeming to.

Behind her, a low voice murmured. "You should not stand so near the wind, my lady. The court already says you keep company with cold things."

Serenya glanced over her shoulder at Maelric, her sworn sword. A man broad of shoulder and grave of face, he wore his blade openly even within the keep, his loyalty sharper still. "Let them say what they like," she said. "Words cannot cut flesh."

"They can cut deeper," he replied, not without gentleness.

Serenya almost smiled. "Then I had best be all ice and armour." She drew her cloak closer, though her heart was warmer than her face betrayed. Tonight was not a simple feast. Tonight was custom – the masque held before the Crown paraded a betrothal, so that whispers might do their cruel work before vows sealed their fate.

The masque before her marriage.

Not to the man she once loved.

A voice intruded on her thoughts. "Cousin."

Lord Eryndor Veyrath approached, every inch the courtier: green velvet doublet, gold mask, a smile that could disarm or gut depending on his whim. He bowed, mock formal, before offering his arm. "You haunt the edges like a ghost. Shall I lead you back into the light?"

"Not all games are played in the centre of the board," Serenya said coolly, though she accepted.

Eryndor chuckled.

"Ah, but all eyes are there. Careful, cousin. The Queen watches everything."

"I know."

Together they entered the Hall of Frostlight. Crystal chandeliers blazed above, casting a thousand fragments of light on rose-carved pillars. Masks glittered, silks swirled, and the air pulsed with music – flutes, viols, the soft thrum of a harp. Yet the crowd parted when Serenya entered, not from deference but hunger.

Whispers followed her like smoke.

"The Veyrath girl returns from exile."

They say the Queen will bind her to the Prince "before spring thaws".

Serenya ignored them, though her jaw ached with restraint. Her silver mask hid her eyes, but nothing could hide the weight she bore.

At the dais, Queen Ysmera reclined, pale hair strung with pearls, gown black as frozen rivers. Her gaze was a blade that measured and weighed, and beside her stood Prince Caledric – broad-shouldered, sun-dark, a scar along his jaw that looked earned, not ornamental. His eyes found Serenya, and lingered.

He descended from the dais with the ease of a man accustomed to power. "Lady Serenya," he said, bowing slightly. "Three winters, and yet the court feels colder without you."

"Your Highness." She curtsied, precise. "I fear the winters are colder everywhere."

Eryndor excused himself, melting into the throng, his smirk lingering like smoke.

Caledric extended his hand. "Dance with me."

To refuse would shame her house. To accept would feed the Queen's purpose. Serenya placed her hand in his.

They moved into the waltz, circling the hall as courtiers murmured. His grip was steady, his gaze direct, and his words measured carefully for her ears alone. "You know why you were summoned back. My mother desires stability. The realm requires it. Our union will secure the marches and silence the border lords."

Serenya tilted her chin. "And what do you desire, my prince?"

His lips curved faintly. "A partner. A queen who is not afraid to wield steel with silk. And perhaps..." His eyes searched hers. "A woman who does not flinch from me."

It was well said. Too well. Serenya answered with a smile so practised it felt carved into her bones. "Then I hope I prove worthy of such a place."

But her heart betrayed her. For in the music, in the light, she saw another face – dark hair unbound, eyes glinting like storm light, a scar cut across his cheek like lightning striking earth. Kaleen. The Thorn King. Her Kaleen, once. His laughter had been fire in the snow. His kiss, defiance.

They had called it love. The Queen had called it treason.

The music ended in polite applause. Serenya withdrew her hand, curtsied again, her pulse unsteady.

Before she could retreat, the eastern doors thundered open.

A knight strode in, snow crusting his mail, helm under his arm. He knelt, voice carrying over the hush. "Your Grace – the Thorn King's banners have been sighted at the northern pass."

The masque shattered. Whispers broke like glass.

"He lives? Impossible."

"They swore he was broken, scattered, slain."

Serenya could not breathe. Her blood turned to ice and fire both. She saw him as though conjured – the scar, the half-smile, the way his hand had once held hers as if the world itself might break first.

The Thorn King. Kaleen.

Queen Ysmera's voice was steel.

"Summon the war council."

The hall dissolved into panic. Dancers fled, courtiers calculated, alliances shifted with the wind. Caledric's hand went to his sword. Eryndor's smile curved darker, as though he had been waiting for this.

Serenya stood motionless. Only Maelric's quiet presence at her back kept her rooted.

In the cedar-scented hush of her chambers later, she pressed her palm to the frost-kissed window. Snow fell beyond, veiling the hills. Somewhere past that veil, he was coming.

Not a ghost. Not a tale.

A king remade of thorns and winter.

Though the court named it war, Serenya knew better.

He was coming for her.

And though fear should have filled her, her pulse quickened with a forbidden truth.

Her heart, long buried in frost, remembered how to burn.

Chapter II: The Thorn King's Promise

Velmora's War Room

The council chamber of Velmora's queen reeked of candle wax and fear. Maps lay sprawled across the oak table, inked with lines that told of mountains, rivers, and the frozen frontier where Kaleen's banner had risen again.

"He should have stayed dead," Lord Meris spat, his jewelled fingers trembling as he jabbed at the parchment. "We struck him down, we buried him beneath the black earth. Yet now his shadow stirs again. How many times must we kill the Thorn King?"

A ripple of unease stirred the council. The queen, silver-veiled and sharp-eyed, lifted her goblet with regal calm. "Kaleen thrives because his people love him," she said, her tone smooth as polished ice. "And love, my lords, is more dangerous than swords."

"Love?" sneered Baron Etrion. "What loyalty can come from farmers and beast-kin? His 'allies' are half-creatures, mongrels—"

"—who tore through your riders last winter," cut in Lady Sira, a bitter smile on her lips. "Perhaps mongrels fight better than pampered knights."

The queen's knuckles whitened around her goblet, but her voice did not waver. "Enough. Velmora has Serenya, the jewel he covets. And so long as she remains in our court, Kaleen will come. That is when we strike. But hear me – underestimate him, and he will unmake us all."

A silence fell, thick as smoke. Somewhere beyond the walls, a bell tolled, and each noble shivered as though it rang their doom.

The Thorn King's Hall

Snow whispered outside the stronghold, but inside, fire and brotherhood ruled. Kaleen's hall blazed with warmth: torches hissed, spits turned with venison, and long tables groaned with bread and mead. Soldiers shared bowls with smiths, and laughter rumbled like a hearth. The king's court was not marble and silk but oak, steel, and loyalty.

Kaleen sat at the head, cloak of black fur thrown about his shoulders. His hair, dark as frost-bitten earth, brushed his jaw, and his eyes – grey like storm clouds – watched his people with a quiet pride. He was no tyrant. He ruled as if each soul here were kin.

By his side stood Daren, his commander and brother-in-arms, broad-shouldered, scar down his cheek, grin sharp as a whetted blade.

"You know, brother," Daren said as he sloshed mead into Kaleen's cup, "if the nobles of Velmora saw this hall, they'd choke on their golden forks. Look at us – farmers drinking with bowmen, blacksmiths calling wolves to heel. What chaos."

"A chaos that keeps us alive," Kaleen replied, the corner of his mouth curving.

At that, a heavy thud echoed as a half-horse warrior strode in – hooves clanging on stone, quiver rattling with black-fletched arrows. His mane glistened with frost, his amber eyes fierce. He bowed low.

"My king," rumbled Tharos, the centaur archer. "The scouts return. Velmora moves soldiers along the northern ridge. Too disciplined for a simple patrol."

A wolf padded in beside him, massive and pale as moonlight, its fur dusted with snow. It curled at Kaleen's feet, golden eyes watchful.

Daren leaned on the table. "They're tightening their grip because they fear you. And they should." His grin was wicked. "I say we break their lines before the snows deepen. Let Velmora choke on their own blood."

A murmur of agreement rippled through the hall, fists thudding on the table. But Kaleen raised his hand, and silence fell.

"No," he said, his voice calm yet iron-bound. "We do not waste lives in fury. Velmora took Serenya. This is not about pride, nor vengeance – it is about a promise."

He rose then, and all eyes lifted. Firelight caught the faint scar across his chest, the mark where steel had pierced him the night he fell. He remembered it – the darkness, the cold grave – and the voice that pulled him back. Serenya's voice.

"She bound me to this world," he said, softer now. "I swore to her, before the gods and before death itself, that I would find her again. That promise is not mine alone – it is ours. Serenya will be queen, and we will see her returned."

The hall erupted in cries, steel striking shields.

"You speak as if she already wears the crown," Daren chuckled, though his eyes gleamed.

"She will," Kaleen said simply.

A raven swooped through the smoke-filled rafters then, black wings whispering omens. It landed upon Kaleen's chair, cawing once, as if sealing the vow.

Tharos stamped a hoof. "Name the day, and my arrows will darken their skies."

"And my claws their throats," growled the frost-wolf, its voice deep and guttural in the hush.

Kaleen placed his hand on the beast's fur, steady and warm despite the cold of his power. "We will march when the snows guide us. Not before. Velmora sharpens their blades on fear – let them. We sharpen ours on loyalty."

Daren clapped his king's shoulder, laughing. "And when we take her back, brother, I expect she'll scold you for making her wait."

"She will," Kaleen said, smiling faintly. "And I will be glad for it."

The hall roared with laughter, steel and hoof and claw striking the stone in unity. Outside, the snow fell thicker, as though the world itself bent towards the Thorn King's vow.

Chapter III: The Night He Came

The Queen's council chamber reeked of smoke and sweat. Tension hung so thick it felt like another body at the table.

Lord Varros slammed his fist onto the map. "Strike his camps in the night. Burn his tents. Burn his food. Let his men starve."

"Starving wolves bite harder," muttered Baron Etrion, voice sharp as glass. "Better to strike the head. Kill him. Send a blade into his tent. Without their king, the beast-pack scatters."

A younger lord scoffed, "An assassin? You think the Thorn King sleeps like a lamb? He wears shadow like armor."

The room erupted. Voices clashed, threats layered over curses. Serenya sat at the far end, wine swirling slow in her cup. She barely listened, her thoughts elsewhere.

"Serenya."

The Queen leaned forward, crown catching the firelight. Her eyes were hard, watchful. "I need more than silence. This alliance binds more than crowns – it binds our families, our children's children. Stand with me now, and we secure a future beyond war. Refuse…" She let the word hang, thin as a blade. "…and you know what refusal means."

Every gaze swung to Serenya. Her throat burned. She wanted to scream, *I cannot.* But the weight of the room pressed her down.

"I stand with you," she said softly, each word pulled like a tooth. "I know refusal would be treason."

The Queen-to-be studied her, long and hard, before nodding. "Good. Then let us end this war together."

The meeting dragged on, then ended. Serenya slipped away down the corridors, her crown heavy, her secret heavier.

By the time she reached her chamber, night had swallowed the keep. She dismissed her maid, pulled the pins from her hair, let her gown slide from her shoulders. She stood in only her shift before the fire, stretching, breathing.

The shutters rattled with the wind. And then—

Silence.

The air thickened. Frost crept across the stone floor, glimmering pale in firelight. Her breath curled white in the air.

Her heart thudded.

"Kaleen," she whispered.

He stepped from the dark. Handsome and dangerous. Snow dripped from his hair, his cloak steaming with cold. The fire hissed, bowing to his chill. His eyes – storm-grey, hungry, alive – locked on hers.

"You bring winter with you," she said, half-breathless, half-amused.

"Better than the hot air of your council," he shot back.

Her lips twitched. She wanted to laugh, to cry. Instead, she whispered, "You're alive."

In three strides, he was on her. His hands caught her face, his mouth claimed hers – fierce, unrelenting, a kiss that shattered years apart.

She gasped against him, shoving him lightly though her fingers curled in his chest. "Do you know what they'd do if they found you here?"

"Freeze them solid," he murmured, voice sharp as ice.

"You've always been reckless," she breathed, though her hands were sliding up his chest of their own will.

"And you've always loved it." His grin was danger and mischief.

She tried to glare, but his lips brushed her ear, and her knees nearly gave out. His hands roamed – waist, thigh, the curve of her back – claiming her as if he'd never let go.

"You shouldn't be here," she whispered.

"And yet here I am." He pressed his forehead to hers, breath cool, almost teasing.

Her laugh came shaky. "Do you ever listen?"

"Never," he said, kissing her again.

This time slower, playful, a war of heat and frost. His cloak smelled of snow and wild journeys, but beneath it was him – warm, familiar, hers.

Her fingers tugged his hair. "You're dripping on my floor."

He growled softly into her mouth. "I'll melt it later."

She snorted against his lips, and he kissed the sound away, lifting her easily. Her back hit the wall, his body pinning hers. Desire surged sharp as hunger, terrifying as battle.

Her words broke against his kiss. "If anyone hears—"

"They'll learn something," he cut in, smirking, mouth trailing her jaw.

"You're insufferable," she gasped, clutching his shoulders.

"And you're addicted," he fired back, hands sliding where only he had ever dared.

She should have stopped him. Instead, she melted, fingers trembling as they clung to him. For a moment, there was no war, no council. Only him, his storm against her fire.

At last, she pushed him back, panting, trembling. "You didn't come only for me."

His eyes burned. "I came for what's mine. You. Always you."

Her throat closed. She wanted to say yes, to beg him to take her away, to forget crowns and kingdoms. But his steps were already retreating, his shadow folding around him.

"Wait—" she whispered, reaching.

But he was gone.

Her chamber door rattled with a sudden pounding.

"My Queen," came her handmaiden's muffled voice. "The council has reconvened. You're needed."

Serenya forced her breath steady, pulled her gown over shaking shoulders, and walked.

* * *

The lords were quieter now, faces grim. The Queen-to-be stood at the head of the table, crown gleaming like cold fire.

"There is another way," she said, voice slicing through the chamber. "No assassin. No raids. A weapon older than his cursed bloodline."

Lord Varros leaned forward. "Nightbane?"

The Queen-to-be nodded. "It will coat a sword. One cut, and his magic fails. The Thorn King bleeds, he dies."

A murmur rippled. Some smiled. Others shifted uneasily.

Serenya sat very still. Nightbane. She had heard of it in whispers – an ancient poison that burned through magic like fire through parchment.

Her heart pounded so loudly she thought they'd hear. But her face stayed calm, eyes lowered.

The meeting ended. The lords dispersed, already scheming. Serenya rose slowly, legs weak.

Back in her chamber, she shut the door and leaned hard against it.

"Kaleen," she whispered, pressing her forehead to the wood.

He had come for her. He was out there, fierce as the storm, alive in her arms.

And now, they had sharpened a poisoned blade for him.

Her chest ached with terror. With longing. With resolve.

If the council thought they could kill him, they had underestimated the one thing stronger than their poison.

Her love.

Chapter IV: Frost, War and Love

The war came one month later.

Drums tore through the castles at dawn. The Queen's decree had been swift: Serenya would ride at the very front. Not at the back with the healers, not beside the generals – but in the very first line, where swords tasted blood first. It was punishment dressed as honour.

The plains stretched wide, the earth trembling under the stomping hooves of Kaleen's war beasts and the sharp cries of his soldiers. His creatures – scaled, furred, winged – lined up beside men with spears, bows, and burning eyes. They were a strange brotherhood, bound by him, their Ice Prince.

And yet, wherever Serenya moved, the line curved away. Kaleen's men and beasts parted subtly, letting her stand clear. It wasn't fear – it was a mark of respect, as if she carried an unseen crown. She noticed, her lips twisting into a bitter smile.

The enemy banners rose like fire against the pale sky. The Thorn King's army – dark steel, snarling beasts, faces painted for death.

Kaleen rode past his lines, his ice armour glowing faint blue, frost hissing off his sword. He stopped where Serenya stood.

"You should be behind the walls," he said, voice sharp.

"You should be beside your brothers," she shot back, tone laced with sarcasm.

His jaw tightened, but his eyes – his eyes lingered on her like he might never look again. "Stay close to me."

"Close enough to get frozen?" she teased, though her chest ached. "Your power tends to leave frostbite."

He gave a crooked smile, even here. "And yet you always come back for more."

Around them, the battle began.

Steel clashed. Arrows sang. Fire met ice, screams split the air. Serenya's blade danced, silver streaks cutting down enemies who came too close. Beside her, Kaleen fought like a storm in human form – every strike laced with shards of ice, every enemy he struck falling stiff and frozen.

"Your tricks never get old," she called over the roar, panting as she kicked back a soldier.

"And yours?" He blocked two spears at once, then smirked at her. "Still reckless. Still beautiful."

"Still distracted," she snapped, slicing down the man behind him.

He chuckled, breath clouding in the cold mist his power left behind. "That's why you're here".

Their banter came like breath between clashes. Sarcastic, heated, alive.

She fought at his side, blades of enemies glancing off her armour, her laughter fierce even as death brushed past.

"You're enjoying this," Kaleen growled, freezing three men in one sweep.

"Better than court dinners," she shot back, ducking under a spear. "At least here no one stares at how I chew."

He snorted, shaking his head as he cut down another. "You're impossible."

"And you love it."

"Yes," he whispered, almost too soft for the battlefield. "Gods help me, I do."

Then she saw it – the glint of poisoned steel in an enemy's hand, aimed straight for Kaleen's side.

Her heart lurched. "Kaleen! The sword—"

But her cry was drowned in the roar of war. The soldier lunged. Without thought, Serenya moved.

The blade sank into her instead.

Her gasp broke Kaleen's world apart. He caught her as she fell, her blood hot against his freezing hands.

"No. No, Serenya, no." His voice cracked, raw, a sound torn from the deepest part of him.

She tried to speak, but blood touched her lips. "I – told you – to let me protect you," she whispered, a weak smile trembling.

Then Kaleen roared. It was no human sound, but the cry of a storm. His power surged, frost exploding from his body in a wave that swept across the battlefield.

Men froze where they stood. Screams cut short, bodies turned to ice statues, faces locked in horror. Half the enemy shattered in the storm of his fury, the rest fled, stumbling over one another to escape the wrath of the Ice Prince.

When silence fell, only the crackle of frozen flesh breaking under the weight of the wind remained. Kaleen knelt in the snow and cradled Serenya, his tears freezing as they fell on her pale cheek.

His men approached slowly, heads bowed. One of the frost wolves whimpered, pressing its muzzle to Serenya's still hand. The bond of brotherhood was unspoken, but heavy in the air – they grieved for her too, for the one who had fought beside them without fear.

"Get me a healer," Kaleen's voice was steel. "Now."

They carried her back, her body wrapped in furs, Kaleen never leaving her side. His icy fingers brushed her face again and again, as if his touch alone could keep her tethered.

The healer came, an old woman with hands steady as stone. She studied Serenya, then Kaleen. "The poison is deep. But there is a potion. She will sleep for days…five, maybe more. But she may wake."

"May?" Kaleen snarled. His eyes burned, the ice in him raging to be unleashed again.

The healer did not flinch. "Her will must meet the potion's strength. That is not mine to command."

Kaleen lowered his head, pressing his forehead to Serenya's.

They gave her the potion, bitter and thick, poured carefully past her lips. Kaleen kept vigil by her bed, never sleeping, never leaving. His men and creatures guarded the halls outside, silent, their loyalty fierce as his grief.

Five days passed like years. Kaleen whispered to her every hour, his words broken, sarcastic, loving – just as she loved.

"You'd mock me for sitting here like this," he murmured one night, brushing hair from her face. "You'd call me dramatic. Maybe I am. Maybe I always was – for you."

On the dawn of the fifth day, her hand twitched. Kaleen froze, heart hammering. Slowly, her eyes opened, weak but alive.

She looked at him, lips curving in the faintest smile. "Kaleen," she whispered, voice hoarse.

He choked on a laugh, on a sob. "Serenya." He kissed her forehead, his icy power soft around her like a shield. "You came back to me."

Her eyes fluttered, still heavy with sleep, but her hand found his. "Always."

And for the first time since the war began, Kaleen believed in tomorrow.

By Any Other Name

Jonathan Ficke

Radiant spring sunbeams dappled my leaves and shone bright upon the curl of my crimson petals. The occasional bee danced among my stigma and stamen, taking and leaving pollen before flitting off to continue her dance among the other flowers of the garden, but my purpose was not in going to seed.

All the garden's blooms – both those with which I shared root and stem and those I knew only by pollen – existed to serve our mistress. I existed to pursue her love, that she may one day embrace my scent, my beauty.

Juliet's voice – that golden chime I'd come to love from the songs that drifted from her window overlooking the gardens – rang through the air. The still garden air shifted with the vibration of her skirts as she drew near to the cool bed of earth at my roots.

"Ahh, such sweet smell." Her voice, half sigh and half word, drew ever closer.

She grazed one of my petals, a touch so soft it barely rose above a passing breeze. Joy ran through me from corolla to root, and from there to all the others. Juliet. Smelling my scent. Touching my petals.

The others echoed my excitement, envy palpable as their emotions mingled with my own.

Oh, what a touch. Juliet's fingertips gently, oh so gently, alighted upon my delicate petals, coaxing me open, baring my corolla to the air. She moved with grace, leaving no trace of her passing save my ravenous desire as she moved to my stem. I feared my thorns may draw her blood, but my fear was misplaced. She felt her way around my thorns as though she knew where each one lay.

"Juliet," a deep voice echoed through the garden. "Are you ready?"

One moment, I basked in her rapturous attentions, and the next, as though waking from a dream, I lamented her absence.

"Just a moment, Adamo," she answered.

A burst of joy ran up along the roots. One of the other blooms was experiencing the thrill of Juliet's touch that had been mine not moments before. The joy rose in an ecstatic crescendo until a snap of the stem severed that joyful song from our chorus of envy.

Juliet had chosen another, and I was left to drink the damp earth, bask in the warm sun, and to ponder what could have been while listening always for the vibrations that marked sweet Juliet's coming.

* * *

Not every day did I have the privilege of a visit from Juliet, but most days did involve the attention of Piero, the gardener. My leaves tasted the bitter stale tobacco that trailed him. He hummed while he worked, a rough, atonal vibration that sounded only the worse for the memory of Juliet's songs.

Piero carried bags of peat and mulch to moisten and cool the earth around my roots. When the skies failed to co-operate with rain, he was my source of life-giving water. I was, in all likelihood, planted by Piero, nurtured by Piero, given life by Piero. But Piero carried the shears.

"Yes, yes," he said, his voice a merciful interruption to his atrocious humming, but the cold rasp of steel on steel, the blades of his shears cutting and recoiling, was far more terrifying than any terrible song.

Scream. Cut. Silence. A bloom fell to the earth.

He moved through the stems, his touch rough, impersonal, cold.

The clear snap of blades silenced a voice. Again, and again, and again, voices fell from our chorus, never to be heard again.

When his rough hand pushed my stem to the side, exposing me to his fatal attentions, I strove with desperate futility to drive a thorn into his unfeeling hands. Though the sharpened sting drove into his hands, he did not flinch or falter.

The steel, cool when filtered through the sensation of another, radiated painful, uncaring frigidity when it settled round my stem. I screamed in incoherent panic, but I knew I was powerless against Piero's deathly ministrations, so I thought of Juliet's touch. The memory calmed me. I quieted and awaited my fate.

"Piero," Adamo said. "I have need of you."

The steel left my stem and the rough hand left my side. But a softer hand gripped me – not Piero, the acrid stench of tobacco had faded – and I panicked, driving a thorn into the interloper's flesh. The smallest drop of hot blood ran down the thorn to my stem, tracing the path to the earth.

"Dammit." Adamo withdrew his hand. "Dangerous and beautiful. No wonder Juliet loves you."

As the tension faded I heard nothing but cries of relief and triumphant celebration from the other blooms. I shared one of those cries, relief that I had survived Piero's cull. As the drop of lifeblood neared the ground, I felt no triumph. I had harmed the man who'd saved me.

Adamo's touch had not been unfeeling like Piero's. It hadn't been like Juliet's, either. It was singular, unique. As the sun drifted towards the horizon, I found myself longing for the stranger's touch again, and I hoped my desires were not too evident to the others.

* * *

While the sun slept, I drew my petals closed. The cool evening hung in peaceful quiet beneath bright moonlight. Amidst the darkness, water condensed upon my petals. The dewdrops accumulated, and eventually slid down my length following the same pathway as Adamo's blood.

The air of the garden, normally peaceful in the nighttime, broke. Someone moved with rough purpose, disturbing the silence with footfalls.

"Juliet," Adamo shout-whispered into the night. "Come down to the gardens, come down to me, I love you and cannot wait a moment more."

Adamo spoke of my Juliet, and he continued, sounding her praises, expressing his unfulfilled desires, desiring to be even as little as a glove that might touch her cheek. The others muttered their agreement. He gave human voice to the desire of every flower in the orchard, though envy tinged the flowers' voices.

"And if I come down?" Juliet spoke from her window. "Will you take me away from this place?"

Away? She would leave us?

"Come to me and I will take you anywhere you wish to go," Adamo said.

Juliet paused, her silence stretched into the night. "Wait for me," she finally said.

"Always," Adamo said.

While he waited for Juliet, he touched one of the others and a wave of revulsion followed. The others joined in cries of alarm. Then Adamo's fingers touched my own petals, knocking the silvery droplets of dew free, shaking my stem, and I was silent amid the storm of blossoms screaming. I had mind only for the firm, insistent fingertips on my stem, but like Juliet before, Adamo released me.

The other blooms voiced their confusion. But I had no answer. I felt what I had felt when Juliet had doted upon me earlier. This was a person who could fulfill my purpose, but how? Was I not made for Juliet?

"I would be with you," Juliet whispered as she hurried into the garden. "But the only thing I love in this place are these blooms, and to go with you means to leave them behind."

His fingers returned to my stem, and so too did the certainty that I never wanted him to release his grip. I made no effort to cut him with my thorns, but it was not necessary. He deftly avoided them as if he knew precisely where to touch.

"Juliet, my love, I swear by the light of the moon that I will always love you and will take you to a place where all the gardens of your imagination are at your feet."

"Swear not by the moon," Juliet said. "It's light waxes and wanes. I must have a love that is as unchanging, as limitless as the sea."

Love. A love as variable as the shifting moonlight. Love that *could* be as variable as the waxing and waning of the moon.

Incredulity radiated from my roots. They demanded an explanation for my feelings, accused me of betraying Juliet. But this love in my stem was not transitory. It did not abandon Juliet. I loved her no less than I had the moment

Adamo's touch awoke me to this revelation, but to love him as well? Could such a thing be possible?

Juliet's fingers joined Adamo's on my stem. The heat of her hand joined his. Why not burn bright, each equal?

The others screamed objections in a raging cacophony.

Crack.

Fire.

Silence.

Adamo and Juliet's hands moved together, lifting me free from the tangle of stems and leaves to fly through the night in both of their grips.

"Let's go, my love," Juliet said.

"Together," Adamo said.

Free.

Stolen Shadows

Jess L. Freed

Smoke curved and slithered along castle walls, brushing up against stone and snuffing out lighted sconces. A shiver of triumph writhed through Klisha's spine as darkness descended. At last, she would save her beloved.

A soldier stepped forward, sword in hand. "You should have stayed dead," she snarled.

"I never wanted this." Klisha's skin heated as she commanded the shadows to swallow the soldier whole. The soldier's eyes widened as darkness stretched outward. Her weapon clanged on stone as the shadows engulfed her, armor and all.

A terrible death for a terrible person.

Klisha sighed as shadows retreated to her fingertips. This was never going to be easy, but still, it gnawed at her insides.

She once was a milk maid in love, and now she was a killer.

Wisps of light filtered into the castle, allowing a glimpse out the frosted window. Soldiers clashed against her shadow creatures in a snowy landscape, blood spraying onto white flurries.

She brushed her fingertips across the window, ignoring the way her reflection detailed her yellow hair blending with shadows. Instead, she focused on her precious mountain, the place she and Malson had run away together. It towered in the distance, snow-capped and looming over all. Her blood boiled as the memory of her death flashed through her thoughts. The glass shattered, shadows pouring through the window, and wrapping around every enemy soldier.

They killed her and took Malson. She shoved the sickness of guilt to the side. Now was the time for action, not mercy.

"You cannot run from me," a voice rasped, the voice of Death.

Klisha covered her ears as the hair on the back of her neck rose. Death's voice was like boots across gravel, echoing and scraping across her mind. "You will not take me back, not yet." She dropped to her knees, her pulse straining as she tried to force the voice from her thoughts.

Death cackled. "My shadows cannot protect you from what is coming."

"It's a good thing I stole more than just shadows then." Klisha clawed at her neck, until at last her fingers clutched the small silver hourglass bobbing on a chain.

"My shadows will destroy you from the inside out before the sun sets."

Klisha ripped the hourglass from the chain, holding it outward. "I have all the time I need." A half-smile tugged at her lips. If only Death had a face so she could have seen the shock.

"You've been warned," Death growled, retreating from her mind.

Not only had she stolen Death's shadows, she had also swiped an hourglass from Father Time. "I'll save him first."

She twisted the hourglass in her fingers, unwilling to admit out loud that she didn't understand how to use the device. The power of the shadows pulsed through her veins, seeping into her bones, obeying her every thought. On trembling hands she pushed herself upward, thinking of her Malson, her beloved.

The reason she escaped from the land of the dead.

The silence of death tinged the air, a stillness stretching through the castle and into the frozen landscape. A shiver raced down Klisha's spine as she slipped the hourglass back onto the chain around her neck. The sun sparkled across the snow. There was enough time before sundown, it would be okay.

Hopefully.

Klisha raised her arms in the air, allowing the shadows to caress her skin, protecting her from any harm. With her chin held high, she raced through the castle. "Malson!"

There was nothing she wouldn't do for him.

He was her everything.

Tears blurred her vision as the aching memories rushed back. The way they'd dragged him away in chains while a sword swung over her neck. It was a torturous end. But she could rest in peace once Malson was free.

Power seeped from every pore as she commanded Death's shadows to lift her, streaming her through the castle. "Malson!" she screamed again, searching for his curly red hair.

The shadows stretched through the first set of cells, extinguishing the glowing fires dotted across the stone walls. Darkness was her friend, but Malson would be the light. He would be here in the dungeons... Somewhere.

Her heart slowed and her blood went cold.

Death was coming for her once more.

With a trembling hand, Klisha flipped the hourglass. Grains of sand fell from one end to the other, sparkling a bright light in the darkness. "Please, I need more time," she whispered.

A cloaked figure emerged and the shadows bent to their owner as if wishing to return. "Only Father Time can control the hourglass." Death's voice was kinder now, almost like satin and silk, as if attempting to soften the blow.

Klisha covered her mouth, trying to hide her own shock. It had been a quick decision to steal the hourglass. Apparently a useless one too. "But I need," Klisha hiccupped, "to find him."

Death hovered above the stone floor, floating closer to Klisha and tsked. "You need to think about yourself." He stretched out a cloaked arm and the shadows drifted toward him, but never touched him.

Klisha urged the stolen shadows back to her command and the darkness snapped toward her. "They like me."

Death snorted. "It's a mystery why, but yes, it seems they do."

The tiniest smile tugged at Klisha's lips. "Did you just snort?"

"Perhaps."

Klisha twisted her hands and the shadows danced around her and Death, pulsing to the rhythm of her heart. "I tried to escape. The shadows were an accident though."

"I know." Death's cloak billowed in anger. "When they are returned, there will be a long conversation between me and my shadows."

"If," Klisha emphasized, "if they are returned."

Death growled.

"Tell me where I can find him and I'll return your shadows."

"You have no bargaining power here," Death sneered. "You will get sicker and sicker until my shadows burn you from the inside out. Your soul will disintegrate and there will be no place for you in the afterlife."

Death's cloak rippled in the darkness and Klisha had the sudden desire to toss back his hood. What lived under there? In her head, she imagined a skeleton, but no one had ever seen Death. She bit her lip. "I don't care about my soul. I care about Malson."

"Do you know why they killed you?"

Klisha swallowed against the lump forming in her throat. "His mother didn't want us to be together. So we ran to the mountains." She sniffed. "But still, they followed."

Death cackled. "You are the first to successfully steal my shadows, so I grant you this one gift. He is not here in the dungeon, but in the Seaside tower." The shadows retreated back to Klisha as Death evaporated.

Klisha stumbled backwards, clutching the useless hour glass. The Seaside tower? He hated the ocean. He hated the place where he was raised. Maybe that would be the place his mother would have imprisoned him for running away with a milk maid.

Klisha's eyes darted from one end of the dungeon to the other.

Death was at least right about the first part… Malson was not here. Klisha blinked and shook her head. If he was in the Seaside tower, that must be where she would go next.

With a snap of her fingers Death's shadows wrapped Klisha in a blanket of darkness and thrust her into the sky. The snowy landscape turned to a speck as Klisha flew through clouds.

Heat rippled through Klisha's body as the shadows raced her through the skies. Her vision spotted at the edges as her sickness deepened, her heart pounding erratically as her body warmed. She was dead and no longer belonged in the world of the living, and Death was right: it was burning her alive from the inside out. Death should have been colder, not scorching. She sighed. She needed rest.

"Keep me safe," Klisha whispered, hoping the shadows could manage flying her while she slept.

The shadows cradled her head as her sight darkened.

* * *

When ocean waves crashed against a rocky shore Klisha snapped awake. She licked the salty sweat from her lips. Her eyes widened as the Seaside tower came into view and she commanded her stolen shadows to fly into the window at the peak.

Adrenaline blasted through her veins. "Please be here," she pleaded. Her body quivered as searing pain overtook her senses. A single tear dripped down her cheek. There wouldn't be time to travel anywhere else.

If her soul disintegrated as Death claimed, there wouldn't be a chance to steal his shadows again. The shadows crashed through the window and shattered glass scattered throughout the sky, reflecting orange sun rays setting over ocean waves.

Shadows swirled around her as she landed in the window. Shrill screams echoed as half-naked women shielded themselves from broken shards.

Klisha's heart dropped.

There in the center of the four-poster bed lay Malson, shirtless with his curly copper hair wearing a light layer of sweat.

"Malson?" Klisha croaked his name as her knees buckled beneath her weight. Thankfully, the shadows caught her before she could fall. Her knuckles whitened as she gripped onto the swirling darkness – her one and only lifeline. "You were taken… I saw…"

Malson tilted his head. "And your head was removed from your body."

"That's the first thing you have to say to me?" Klisha scanned the room, settling her gaze on the women huddled in the corner. Dread drenched her stomach as pieces started to connect. "Leave now," she growled to them.

Whatever was going on, they weren't at fault.

Malson's lips thinned as he watched the shadows escort the half-naked women through the doors. He turned back to Klisha. "Death is not known for his mercy, how did you come back?"

"I came back for you." She raised her chin. "I stole Death's shadows to save you."

Malson's brows furrowed for a split-second before his features softened. "My love."

Klisha's shoulders eased, despite the sickness boiling her blood. "I was worried you were imprisoned."

Malson flashed a charming smile and strode from the bed. "Mother was displeased, but I'm safe." He cleared his throat. "I'm sorry you had to witness me trying to move on." He gestured to the door where the women had left.

Streaming sun rays deepened to dark orange and hues of pink. Klisha looked from the broken window and back to Malson. The sickness would take her soon, but at least Malson was safe. "You should move on," she murmured, despite the lie burning her throat. She choked down bile that threatened to pour over. "But I thought it would've taken longer than the day I've been dead." Teary eyes blurred her vision as she looked at her beloved. This didn't make sense.

A flash of darkness flared, and Death appeared, still shrouded in his cloak. He snapped his fingers, and his shadows wrapped around Malson's neck. "Tell her the truth."

Klisha ran toward Death. "Stop this!"

"No," he snarled. "Tell her now." The shadows tightened around Malson.

Klisha tried to command the shadows to stop, but they ignored her, continuing to constrict around the man she loved. "Just tell him what he wants." She sniffed. "I don't have long left." She tore the hourglass from her neck and tossed it out the window.

There was never enough time.

Malson coughed, eyes wide with fear. "I…don't…know."

Death's cloak merged with the shadows as the room darkened, leaving only splashes of sunset painting the blackness. "Tell her who had her killed." He pointed outside. "And quickly."

Klisha kicked Death's leg. "It was his mother!" Without the power of Death's shadows it did nothing, but at least it felt good. She continued her assault, kicking and hitting whatever was hidden underneath his cloak. But the question lingered in her heart… Why was Death so insistent? And there was something off with Malson.

"The truth and I won't kill you," Death said, unbothered by Klisha's attack.

She paused and shuffled closer to Malson. "There's nothing that could take away my love," she said, uncertain about her own words.

Malson scratched at his neck, and the shadows loosened their hold on him. He gasped. "I had her killed."

Klisha's blood turned to ice as she paused her onslaught. "But we were in love."'

The shadows released Malson and he ran a hand through his curls. "You were in love." He shrugged. "I enjoyed your company for a time."

Klisha's vision turned red as anger rooted deep inside. A small part of her wanted to whisper it wasn't true, but she had seen and heard enough. "I was a fool." Death's shadows softly caressed her cheek.

Malson rolled his eyes. "The exact reason you needed to die. You couldn't take a hint."

"I've done so much for you! I came back from the dead. For you!" Klisha screamed. "And you couldn't have the decency to break off our relationship with words?" Her voice grew louder with each syllable. "How much of a coward could you be?"

Malson held his hands up in surrender. "Are we done here?"

"You are." Klisha's hands tightened into fists, knowing exactly what she wanted to do in her final moments.

Death nodded. "Go ahead," he said to his shadows.

The shadows whirled with purpose around Klisha and power once again surged through her body, fully submitting to her command. She straightened her spine. "I came to save you, but instead, I'll end you."

Malson pointed to Death. "He said I'd live with the truth."

Death chuckled. "I said I wouldn't kill you. There were no promises made for what she would do."

Klisha tossed her hands in the air and the shadows writhed like snakes ready to strike. Darkness descended as the sunset disappeared behind the ocean and Klisha gave herself over to the shadows willingly. "Kill him," she commanded.

In that moment, her soul merged with the darkness. It was as if her hands were the ones wrapped around Malson's neck.

It was only when his body lay lifeless that the shadows retreated and Klisha blinked open her eyes. The heat of the sickness had evaporated, leaving her feeling stronger than ever. She stared at her hands and the shadows encircling. "How am I still alive?"

"You're not," Death said.

Klisha gasped. Death stood, not cloaked, but dressed in a black suit. Dark hair, a chiseled jawline, and a gleaming smile. "You're handsome?" She would have expected a pile of bones or an elderly man, but not this…

"I am many things, but no one has ever called me that before." He winked.

Klisha blushed and looked away. The sun had set over the ocean…apparently she did have more time. "What's happening to me?"

"It seems my shadows grew to like you a bit too much." Death stroked his chin. "I never thought we would have a Lady Death."

Klisha's eyes widened and she patted down her body. She was also wearing a black suit, this one fitted to her every curve. "But how?"

"The correct question is, *but why*?" He reached out a hand. "There's only one way to find the answer."

Klisha accepted his hand and a jolt of excitement zapped through her as her skin brushed against his. "Thank you," she whispered, "for revealing the truth to me."

Death intertwined his fingers with hers. "Don't thank me yet."

* * *

A meadow of wildflowers dazzled below as Klisha flew hand in hand with Death over the Land of the Dead. She had been here before, but this was different. The first time she had ached for Malson and was unable to see the beauty of the afterlife. Now, she flew with wide eyes. She squeezed Death's hand. "Where are you taking me?"

"To Father Time," he said, eyes intent on the horizon.

Klisha pressed her lips together. "Great, another being I stole from."

Death snickered. "Have you not figured it out yet?"

"Can we just skip to the part where you tell me what's going on?" Klisha glared.

He raised a brow. "You never stole anything. When you snuck into my chambers with the intent of robbing, I allowed it to happen. Father Time just happens to leave his trinkets around."

Klisha's jaw dropped. "Apparently Malson was not the only liar in my life."

Death scowled. "Do not compare me to that sad little man. I never lied to you."

"Why did you do it?" Her thoughts spun on one another, tangling into knots. None of this made any sense.

Flowers in the meadow below grew thicker as they flew deeper into the afterlife. Death slowed their speed as thrones woven from trees came into view. When their feet softly landed, Death released Klisha's hand. "You'll understand soon what it is to feel the death of others." He looked up to the clear blue sky. "The level of heartache I felt when your head was removed was the deepest pain I had felt in over a thousand years."

A thousand years. Klisha shook her head. "Who would have thought Death had so much empathy?"

Death smiled. "We feel all that they feel. Empathy isn't just a theory to us. The one guarantee in life is that all will meet us. Hopefully we can help on the journey to the Land of the Dead."

Klisha clung to a single word. "We?"

Death rolled up his sleeves and tapped the edge of a throne constructed of moss and tiny yellow flower buds. Swirls of silver mist spun and a small man in a tall yellow hat emerged. He wore three hourglasses around his neck.

"Ah," the man said, looking up at Klisha.

Death gestured to the man. "Father Time is the oldest of the Council. Time was needed first for the world to form. Then came Life and eventually Death."

Klisha swallowed and glanced around. "But there are dozens of thrones."

Father Time cleared his throat. "Most of us were human once." He pointed to two thrones, made of dead twigs, all intertwined with one another. One sprouted mushrooms and the other was barren. "The empty one materialized at your sunset." He cleared his throat once more. "It seems the world's magic has chosen you. Sit and take your place as Lady Death."

Klisha took a step backwards. "This can't be right."

Father Time yawned. "You can prove us wrong by sitting on the throne. If nothing blooms, then we are wrong."

They would be wrong.

They had to be wrong.

Because a life as Lady Death was too difficult to fathom. Life as a milk maid was all she had known. And of course, Malson. Her blood boiled at the thought and she stormed over to the throne, flopping down in pure anger.

Nothing happened and she wiggled to make her point. "See? There's been a mistake."

Dark shadows streamed from beneath the throne, drifting upward. On instinct, Klisha flexed her fingertips and siphoned the shadows into her body. As power coursed through her veins, black roses bloomed across the dead twigs of the throne. Klisha's eyes widened in shock. Not because they had been right, but because the surge of magic felt so right. She raised her chin, embracing her new role.

Death nodded in approval. "You look ravishing."

Klisha's cheeks heated as her eyes met Death's brown swirls. "I still don't understand why you allowed me to borrow your shadows." She gripped the edge of the throne. "None of this would have been possible without my plan to rescue Malson."

"You needed the truth." He looked up at the blue sky. "We all did, once upon a time."

Her shadows intertwined with his of their own accord, skimming and merging, showing off the ability together and separate all at once. Klisha leaned back on her throne, watching in awe as the shadows whirled in delight.

Death brushed a hand through the display and the shadows scattered. "As much as I enjoy watching our shadows blend, it was ruining my view of you."

She tucked a stray hair behind her ear, never taking her eyes off of Death. Malson had been a facade, what she had believed love looked like, but Death? He wasn't just striking, he was honest and empathetic. But could he love? Was it possible for her to love in this role? She sucked in a tight breath. "What comes next?"

Death closed the gap between them and kneeled at her feet. "What do you want to come next?"

Father Time tapped his wrist. "Time waits for no one. The Council will meet in a fortnight." Silver mist stretched and with a snap, the little man was gone.

Klisha's breath stilled in her chest. No one had ever asked her what she wanted. As a simple milk maid, her life had so little meaning until Malson had come along.

And that was the mistake, never once putting herself first.

She looked to Death. Part of her wanted him, but she wasn't ready to admit that. Instead she turned to what her heart ached for more than love. "I want to see the mountain again."

Death raised a brow as he stood to his full height. "Then it will be so."

"You must think I'm insane though?" She rose from her throne.

"Insanity looks good on you."

Klisha chuckled. "I need closure." She inhaled his musty scent, and the warmth radiated off his chest. She sighed at the comfort she felt leaning closer to him.

Death brushed a finger under her chin and raised her gaze to meet his. "I'll give you anything you need or want." He snapped his fingers, and there they were, standing at the top of the mountain.

But this time, it was with someone worthy of her heart.

It fluttered now as she looked at Death. "What if I want to kiss you?"

Time stood still as he wrapped his arms around her, lifted her into the air, and pressed his lips against hers. Snow fell softly as she sank into his warmth, thankful for the moment she had decided to steal his shadows. Thankful that Malson had betrayed her, because no kiss had ever felt like this. Nothing in her life had felt like this.

The kiss consumed her very being, keeping her warm from the ice and snow. And now she had reclaimed the place of her death with an even stronger memory.

Klisha pulled away, a gleaming smile splaying across her face. "Isn't Death supposed to be cold?"

He traced her lips with his fingers. "It can be. It can also be warm." He pecked her cheek. "In time, you will come to know this life as well as I do."

"I look forward to every second, as long as I get to keep kissing you."

Death spun himself into a nearby snowy boulder, with Klisha in his lap. "We have all the time we could ever desire."

Klisha bit the inside of her cheek. "For you, everything can wait." She once again fell into his embrace as shadows swirled around in delight. Tomorrow, she would learn about her role as Lady Death. For now, this moment was all that mattered.

The Rose and the Blade

M.A. Gardner

The Hall of Judgement was colder than Calien remembered.

Once, he stood here under a gleaming breastplate with banners unfurled above. The king's voice rang praise for victories achieved. Now, the same banners hung heavy in the stale air. Courtiers whispered behind bejeweled hands as he walked the length of the chamber. Each step echoed with the clang of his armored feet like a strike of a blacksmith's anvil.

He bowed low before the dais. His hair, unkempt and uncut for weeks, covered his eyes, yet he did not dare to raise his head.

"Syr Calien," said the king, his sharp announcement echoing. "'Twas once my most loyal knight. Now the most disappointing."

The simple words were a dagger to his heart. Calien learned to suffer worse. "Milord," he answered, his voice hoarse, but steady. "Your command, sire?"

Laughter rippled through the gathered nobility. They savored his humiliation like a great feast. The scandal of one of their own falling from grace was an exquisite aperitif. The king allowed the silence to linger before he leaned forward on his throne. "Your disgrace is unforgiven. Unforgotten. My orders cast aside, as were your oaths. Blood was spilled, and deep alliances threatened. And yet…" His fingers drummed on the carved dragon armrest. "…a task is upon us better suited to a *man* who formally held a place in honor." It didn't take a linguist to detect the scorn the king heaped upon a single word. "A man with nothing left to lose."

Calien forced his tightened jaw loose. He dared not speak, for that would only betray the bitter serpent coiled within.

The king snapped his fingers, and attendants opened a side door. A woman swept into the grand hall. Her gown flowed around her, the violet silk caught the overhead light. Her eyes flashed with fire hotter than the torches along the stone walls.

"Lady Mirenya," the king announced. "My ward. She is to wed the Duke of Avelmûr, to procure a peace this realm so dearly needs. You, Syr Calien, will deliver her safely to her betrothed."

Murmurs turned to gasps of astonishment. A noble lady's life entrusted to a disgraced knight? Scandalous.

Calien allowed his gaze to rise from the floor to meet the lady's gaze. Her beauty was undeniable, but so too was the fury etched upon her face. She didn't curtsy, nor nod. She stood as though she were the matriarch and he but a lowly servant to fetch her dinner.

Lady Mirenya turned to the king. "My lord king," she said, her voice cool, "am I but a parcel to be carried by any hand you see fit?"

"You are a rose of the realm," the king replied. The impatience that flickered beneath his mask of calm was not lost on the courtiers. "Even the most beautiful rose must sometimes be transplanted to where it will flourish. Syr Calien will be your guard until you stand in Avelmûr joined to the duke."

Her gaze rested on Calien. Her eyes were like a storm – beautiful and dangerous. "Then the transplant will be twice cursed," she murmured for all to hear. "A prisoner escorted by a traitor."

* * *

The corridors beyond the hall were hushed. The thick carpet runner swallowed Calien's footsteps as he trailed Lady Mirenya. Staff bowed as she passed. Her chin remained high as though she bore a crown instead of the king's will.

At last, she stopped in an antechamber where light from tall windows painted her in gold. She whirled upon Calien with the precision and suddenness of an assassin's dagger. "*So*," she said, the single word laced with disdain, "you're to drag me to my gilded cage?"

Calien stood at the threshold of the great room. His broad shoulders shadowed the archway. He removed his gauntlets with slow, deliberate precision. "I am charged with your safety, milady. Nothing more."

A sudden laugh – sharp and without mirth. "Safety? That is laughable. I've heard the stories. Stories of a knight who abandoned his post. Stories of a knight who betrayed his king. What safety does such a *storied* knight possibly offer?"

"You need not trust me," Calien declared, his tone even. "Only walk the path, and I'll see you safely to its end."

Mirenya stepped closer. He could see clearly the defiance alight in her storm-gray eyes. "What then, Syr Calien? After I'm delivered like a broodmare to a man twice my age?" She scoffed. "Will you kneel before the altar and offer congratulations?"

Her words were a hammer blow to his chest. They mirrored truths he dared not voice. He allowed the silence to stretch between them. Finally, he answered in a low, steady voice. "What I think of your betrothal is of no consequence. I was not summoned to question the desire or will of my king."

"No," she said bitterly. "You were summoned because no one else would have you."

It cut deeper than the most skilled sawyer. For just a moment, his stoic mask cracked. His eyes, dark and wounded, met hers with a flash of heat. Something in his gaze made her falter, and her chin rose a fraction to hide it. "You may despise me, Lady Mirenya," Calien whispered, his voice hardened by restraint. "Know this: whatever the stories may be, I'll not let you come to harm. Even if it costs me my life."

Her gaze wavered. She searched his face – perhaps looking for mockery. Perhaps for weakness. What she found was granite. She drew back, a flicker of unease masked with a scoff. "We shall see, *knight*."

With that, she swept by him. The scent of violets lingered in her wake. It was as sharp and cloying as her words.

Calien exhaled. The slow breath helped to calm his shuddering heart as he fastened his gauntlets. She was spoiled. Proud. *Impossible*. However, beneath her scorn, beneath her contempt, he glimpsed something fragile: a fear she buried beneath barbs.

He struck down the thought like an enemy on the field. She was his charge and nothing more. *A rose of the realm*, as the king had declared. And he was merely the blade sent to transplant her.

* * *

The moon hung low over the Great Forest, and pale light spilled across a dark canvas. The company traveled all day, their retinue only a few guards. Calien thought it too few, but the king insisted that secrecy was safer than banners and trumpets.

Calien rode at the head of the short column, his eyes scanning the woods along the trail. He rested his hand on the pommel of his sword. It wasn't out of fear, but habit. Mirenya, cloaked in gray, rode directly behind him with her back straight and her chin lifted in defiance of the shadows that gathered at the tree line.

The forest grew quiet. No crickets. No rustle of leaves. No fluttering of bats. Calien's grip tightened. He raised a gauntleted hand to signal a halt.

Mirenya sighed. "Why do we stop?"

He looked over his shoulder. "The forest is listening."

She prepared to retort, but an arrow hissed from the treeline. One of the guards fell from his saddle with a cry of alarm, the shaft buried in his neck.

Chaos erupted.

Figures slipped through shadows. They were tall, gaunt, and their faces hidden by masks of bark and bone. Their movements were too swift. Too fluid. Inhuman.

Fae.

"Ambush!" Calien bellowed and drew his blade.

The guards moved to protect Mirenya, but their attackers moved with unnatural grace, their blades glinting in the moonlight. Calien urged his horse into a trot and intercepted the first attacker with a punishing swing that sundered wood mask and fae skull alike. Blood as black as sealing wax spilled across the leaves.

"Stay behind me!" he shouted at his charge.

Mirenya was no passive observer. Another fae leaped towards her, and she wrenched a dagger from the fallen guard's belt and slashed. The dagger caught flesh, and the fae hissed. It recoiled, its eyes wide like pools of molten silver.

Calien allowed a grin of surprise and grudging respect, but there was no time to dwell on her. A fae spear impacted his side and found a gap in his armor. Pain lanced through him, hot and sharp. He staggered but forced his sword up to cut down the enemy even as his vision darkened.

"You're bleeding," Mirenya gasped.

Calien wrenched the spear free. "Better me than you," he hissed.

The guards fell one after another, outmatched by the ferocity of their foes.

We will not hold, he thought. He seized Mirenya's reins with a blood-slicked hand and dragged her horse to the tree line. "We must go!" he roared.

A fae dropped from the canopy above, its claws outstretched. Training fueled his actions, and he threw himself between her and the fae, his sword flashing. The collision sent pain radiating from his wound, but the fae toppled, cleaved from neck to hip.

Mirenya stared at him, her face pale. Her scorn faltered. "You're mad."

"Perhaps," he replied, his armor stained with fae blood. "You're alive."

They vanished into the trees, the sound of battle fading. When the silence returned to the woods, Mirenya spoke. "You saved me."

Calien's lips formed a smile, showing his blood-stained teeth. "I was commanded so."

* * *

The woods swallowed them completely.

Branches clawed their cloaks. Hooves stumbled on roots. The night closed like a fist. Calien pulled them into a hollow where an old elm leaned over a ramshackle hunting cabin.

Calien dropped from his saddle, his boots thudding into the earth. He grasped the edge of the cabin to steady himself. His breath was harsh, and blood darkened his side, weeping through chain and studded leather.

"You're hurt," Mirenya announced and dismounted with her gown catching for just a moment.

"Tis nothing," Calien insisted, but his pallor announced otherwise.

She clenched her jaw. "Sit. Before you fall."

He started to protest. His pride demanded it. But the ground shifted beneath him, and his legs buckled. With a grimace, he obeyed.

Mirenya kneeled beside him. Her hands trembled slightly as she tore strips from the hem of her gown. "Hold still," she ordered.

He allowed a raspy chuckle. "You'll deface fine silk for a traitor?"

Her eyes gleamed. "Better ruined silk than a corpse as an escort."

She bunched the cloth into his wound. He hissed, his teeth clenched, but he didn't flinch. Her steady hands surprised him. Her touch was firm but not cruel. Moonlight filtered through the canopy and set her hair ablaze.

"You fight as a demon possessed," she said at last. "You throw yourself onto blades as though you care not for your life."

"Perhaps I don't," he replied. Then he caught the sharp look she gave him. "I care for yours," he added. "That is my charge."

Her fingers stilled. For a heartbeat, she seemed about to reply, then she shook her head and shoved another length of cloth into his wound. "You're a fool," she muttered.

Calien wheezed what might have been laughter. "I've been called worse."

Their eyes met. The air in the hollow was taut, filled with words they dared not speak. Mirenya looked away first and bound the silk with a final tug.

"It will hold," she declared, "until we find a healer."

Calien studied her face. The proud tilt of her chin warred with fear beneath her calm. He thought her nothing more than arrogance wrapped in silk, but he witnessed her face a fae with a dagger in her hand and fire in her eyes. She was not just a rose to be transplanted.

"Thank you," he whispered.

Her lips parted to answer, but instead, she rose and spun on her heel. "Rest, Syr Calien. We ride as day breaks." She stepped into the cabin and closed the door.

Perhaps there was more to Lady Mirenya than silk and fury. Perhaps there was more to the journey than duty. Calien wondered for the first time if his heart was in greater danger than his body.

* * *

The ruins of Aeltar Keep were like the broken maw of a long-forgotten monster. Walls, once proud, lay shattered and reclaimed by a forest primeval. Calien guided his horse through a rubble-strewn courtyard, his eyes glancing to and fro for new threats. Behind him, Mirenya rode with her back straight. Her gown was marked by dirt and blood.

"Surely this place is haunted," she declared.

Calien dismounted with a wince and scanned the shadows and overgrowth. "Aeltar fell at the peak of the fae conflict. No one's lived here in over a century. It'll be safe for us."

Mirenya slid from her saddle and landed less gracefully than she intended. Her ankle wobbled, and Calien's hand shot out to steady her elbow. For a heartbeat, neither spoke. His grip was firm and warm, even through the leather of his glove. She drew back in haste and covered her unease with a glare.

"I am not porcelain," she growled. "You needn't touch me as though I am. I'm perfectly able to walk on my own."

"I'm aware," he replied. "But strength spent foolishly will abandon you when you need it most."

She scoffed away a retort. She didn't examine the truth in his words.

He turned towards the ruins, and Mirenya followed.

The great hall still bore fragments of grandeur. Faded banners hung limp. A hearth blackened by ash still had a tarnished andiron that once gleamed. Cracked and split columns remained upright, their marble resisting nature. Light shone through gaps in the roof and illuminated motes of dust that swirled like courtesans at a dance. For all its ruin, Aeltar still possessed beauty.

Mirenya's hand traced the stitched crest on one of the banners. "My grandmother told me stories of Aeltar. She claimed knights here swore their oaths with roses twined to their swords to remind them of beauty and blood."

Calien's gaze softened. "*The Rose Oath*. I was but a boy when I first heard it. That honor is long forgotten."

The silence was heavy with things left unspoken. Finally, Mirenya whispered, "Why did you betray your order?"

Calien stiffened. "I did what I thought was right. I protected lives, *not titles*."

"That answer explains nothing," she insisted.

Their eyes met. The fire in his eyes matched the fury in hers. "I refuse to kill innocents. Honor without mercy is not thus."

Her breath caught. Her sharp tongue failed her. She now saw not a traitor, but a man who carried grief like armor. She looked away, and to her horror, she felt her resolve falter.

Before either could speak, wind howled through the broken hall, and upon it the sound of distant horses.

"They've found us," Calien muttered and spun toward the courtyard, his sword already in hand.

Mirenya's fingers brushed the banner once again, as if she gathered strength from the stories of roses and blades.

She stepped next to Calien. "Let's see if *The Rose Oath* still has power."

* * *

Calien's sword arced in the moonlight, and he cleaved the last of the first wave of fae. From the rubble, another group emerged. They were smaller, nimbler. Mirenya's dagger flashed as she met them. Her eyes were alight with defiance. For the first time, Calien saw her not as a charge to protect, but as a warrior to partner with against the tide.

A fae dropped from a ruined balcony. Calien raised his sword, but a misstep on rubble sent him staggering. Pain radiated from his side. Mirenya reacted and shoved him aside. Her dagger sank into the fae, and she met Calien's eyes for a heartbeat. Shock, worry, and something unspoken passed between them.

"You!" Calien gasped and clenched his teeth. "Foolish girl!"

"And you!" she retorted, her breath heavy. "Reckless knight!"

Neither could laugh at their exchange. There was no time. Together, they fought their way across shattered stone and to the edge of the forest. Calien worked through the pain with the strength of desperation. Mirenya stayed close, her shoulder brushing his time and again, their movements in sync.

When they crossed the tree line, it was as if the boundary of a great wizard's spell was broken. The fae stopped as one and turned to the north. The frustrated shrieks echoed as they disappeared into the darkness. The night grew still once more. Calien sank to one knee with a hand pressed to his reopened wound.

Mirenya kneeled beside him. Fear and awe mingled in her storm-gray eyes. "You cannot keep doing this to yourself," she whispered. Her hands moved to press against his wound.

"I'm alive," he said, his voice ragged. "And you..." He caught her wrist and gently turned her hand over so she could see the blood staining it. "...are alive."

Her chest rose and fell rapidly. "We are," she whispered. She didn't move but simply let her hand remain in his. The air between them felt charged.

Calien's eyes softened. "I didn't expect...gratitude," he admitted, his lips close to her knuckles. "I think... I think it is the first thing I've desired in a long time."

Mirenya's head tilted. Slowly, she leaned closer. "Perhaps," she whispered, "you deserve it." The words were a whisper, but they carried the weight of something else.

He straightened and met her gaze for the first time since they'd left the hall, "I protect those I care for, Lady Mirenya. Whether you like it...or not."

A silence lingered. Neither wanted to break the fragile intimacy, and both were drawn toward it. At last, Mirenya exhaled and shook her head with a mix of exasperation and something warmer. Fonder. "You're insufferable!" she hissed, but there wasn't any venom in her tone.

"Indeed," he replied with a small bloody smile on his lips. "But you'll find insufferable is preferable to dead."

She allowed a small laugh. Calien drank from it. It was raw and real. No courtesans to impress or judge. "A fair point, Syr Calien."

* * *

They rode the last of their journey in silence, side by side. The brisk dawn caressed their faces. Exhaustion clung to them, and the adrenaline from the previous night's ambush sapped their strength. They decided to risk travelling through the night to reach their destination early. Their shared experience wove a tenuous bond that neither acknowledged. The forest began to thin, and the towers of Avelmûr rose against the painter's palette of a rising sun. The nascent light caught on the ivory spires and they gleamed. Calien scanned the battlements and noted the rhythm of the guards. He glanced at the positions of the sentries. Somewhere inside the castle, the duke awaited.

They paused on a rise just before the splendor of Avelmûr Castle unfolded. Mirenya's hand brushed his arm. It was light. Hesitant. He felt a jolt at her touch.

"I..." she began. Her storm-gray eyes clouded with words unspoken.

"You need not speak it," Calien murmured. "I hear it in every glance. Every movement. I value your trust."

Her gaze lingered on him, conflicted. Fire and sunlight mingled in her storm. She leaned closer, enough for him to feel the warmth she radiated.

His breath caught. "Mirenya…" he whispered, for a moment forgetting his position.

The moment stretched. Then, as if drawn by the same unspoken need, she tipped forward, their lips meeting in a brief, daring kiss. It was soft at first. Hesitant and questioning. Then firm. A promise shared between them. Calien's hand rose to caress her cheek, tilting her head as the kiss deepened. The world narrowed to the press of their lips. The steady beat of hearts. The mingling of fear and relief. Danger and desire.

When their lips parted, their foreheads rested together. Their breath mingled. Their hearts stuttered in unison. Mirenya's eyes searched his. Vulnerability? Contentment? Pride? "I'm not meant for soft words," she murmured.

"You're meant for more than you know," he replied. His fingers brushed a stray strand of hair from her face. "And I…" He swallowed. His emotions threatened to betray him. "I would survive any peril for you."

Her hand lingered on his. The brush of his thumb against her knuckles spoke volumes. "Then perhaps, Syr Calien," she finally said, "this is only a beginning."

They rode the remainder to the gates; the castle loomed above. The duke waited, flanked by guards. His smile was tight, but polite as Mirenya dismounted. Calien followed suit and remained formal, though the ache in his side reminded him of the trials they had endured together.

"Milady," the duke intoned, "you arrive safely."

"Thanks to Syr Calien," she said, her voice carrying across the courtyard. "A man who proved that not all knights are as they appear."

The duke inclined his head in acknowledgement. "Then I owe him my gratitude as well."

Calien bowed and kept his hand near his sword. When he straightened, his eyes found Mirenya's. In that glance lingered the memory of their kiss and the promise that it held. The duke's guards led the retinue inside. Mirenya paused at the gate and turned back to Calien. Her lips curved into a dangerous, delicate smile as if to say, *Syr Calien, don't think this ends here.*

He returned her smile. A slow, rueful grin. He felt warmth in his chest that he hadn't known for years. *I wouldn't have it any other way,* he thought, and watched her vanish into the castle, the memory of their kiss burning brighter than the rising sun.

Fragments of Us

Georgina Kamsika

"Their very existence is an affront to the Lady." My first words to the new advocate are not my most diplomatic. They are a blade, unsheathed and gleaming between us.

She lounges beside our Commander's war table, her body sweet and plump and brown as a syrup-drenched gulab jamun. The mirrored chamber splinters the light, multiplying her reflection until she seems an infinite goddess arrayed in fractured gold.

The advocate dips her head, a smile playing at the corners of her lips like a secret half-told. "Yes, I had heard the more…unenlightened believe our goddess would spurn her own children for the crime of magic. How strange that anyone touched by her grace might think her capable of such cruelty."

My fingers tighten around my sword hilt, knuckles bleaching to bone-white. This is why I despise advocates, venom wrapped in velvet, masquerading as diplomacy. She moves through court like a jewelled knife, effortless, lethal, slipping between the ribs of our empire's elite.

But she has misjudged her audience. The Commander shares my wariness of unchecked power. Mages will never roam free beyond the walls of the jēla.

"I take no issue with their existence," our Commander chides, shifting in his ceremonial armour, the plates groaning like a restless beast. His colourless eyes narrow. "My concern is that they are fed. Sheltered. Loved. This you must ensure. We cannot afford more husks."

Behind him, the hollow ones stand in silent rows. Mages who rebelled. Mages who were severed. Their eyes are voids, their souls excised from the cycle of rebirth.

The advocate's smile remains treacle sweet, but her gaze is honed steel. "Sometimes love becomes control. Sometimes shelter becomes a cage."

The Commander slaps my leather-clad arm. "And for that, I rely on my general. The Empire runs by my will, but she is my hand that guides our Believers."

The advocate steps closer, her pomegranate silks whispering against the tiles. "Then I look forward to working closely with you, General." Her fingers brush my forearm, feather-light. "I have many ideas to share."

The way she says my rank ignites something treacherous. The way her gaze lingers on the breadth of my shoulders, the strength in my frame. I cannot drown in her eyes, dark as monsoon-drenched earth. I cannot trust her.

Yet she becomes my shadow. In the sunlit courtyard where I train my Believers, she settles primly on a patch of grass, plump fingers cradling a book. Not that she reads it.

Not that I look.

* * *

Slowly, inevitably, I surrender to her friendship. We share steaming puri at dawn. We stroll the perfume gardens at twilight, jasmine clinging to our skin. We steal kulfi in the temple's shadow, daring the midday sun like fools.

She sprawls on her curved stomach, one shapely leg kicking playfully in the air, a mirrored slipper dangling from her toes. Sunlight fractures around her, scattering diamonds across the tiles.

Our secrets divide us. I never speak of my youth policing the jēla, of the horrors I'd dispatched, or of the atrocities committed in the Lady's name by my fellow Believers. She, in turn, offers only fragments – a childhood spent fleeing patrols, a rogue mage for a mother, a life steeped in fear.

Perhaps I feel guilt. Maybe I fear what her truth would cost me.

We speak of our commander's endless conquests, of how he swept through our homeland before our parents drew breath. How he continues to expand into neighbouring countries. We smile over the Empire's celebrations and mourn her lost soldiers. In the hush of midnight, when no one can overhear, we mock his excessive demands.

We never speak of the jēla.

"I grew up on tales of warriors," I confess. "Swords and honour. Loyalty bound in blood. That's why the Believer's oath is sacred to me."

Her teeth gleam. "You're so noble, it aches. I always preferred the stories where the hero makes a noble sacrifice at the end." She twirls a lock of hair around her finger. "How *romantic*."

I promise myself to not fall in love with her.

* * *

The lie shatters when I watch her eat a mango. Juice glides from her lips, along her fingers, staining the silk of her saree like liquid gold. I ache to catch those droplets with my mouth, to press her palm to my lips and never let go. My stomach twists, alive with butterflies.

That's when she asks the question.

"Do you support mage rights? Or do you trust in your commander's more brutal methods?"

The butterflies settle.

"I don't dwell on it, but he keeps us safe."

"Safe. Huh." She hurls the gnawed seed to the waiting monkeys, then licks her fingers with deliberate slowness. "Are mages safe? What happens if they're severed? Where do the husks go?"

"Safe from what?" I snap. "Mages smile and weave spells until they've drained your blood and broken open the planes of existence."

"Has that ever happened?"

"I've heard stories—"

She scoffs. "Stories spun to justify chains. No calamity stains our history. Almost as if the threat is fabricated."

I see the danger now, coiled behind her beautiful smile and flashing eyes. She never cared for me. She wanted to unravel me, thread by thread, until my faith lay in tatters at her feet.

I should walk away. There is no point in listening as she twists my devotion into doubt. She might be called an advocate; I think of her as a powder keg.

But of course, I waste more time on her smiles. And of course, she explodes.

* * *

I do not fall in love with her. There is no plunge, no headlong rush into the abyss. The fast crash, the intense feelings, the meteoric pain at the inevitable exit wounds.

Instead I stumble a little, and she is there to catch my elbow. I miss a step, and she is beside me so I don't trip. I don't recognise this feeling. It's slow and sure, with no space at all between our heartbeats, no space at all between our lips until there is no me, no her, only us. I don't recognise this feeling, but it has a familiar face and a familiar name, and soon it's the only thing in my heart.

I don't fall in love with her. But oh, I find myself in love.

* * *

She is the one who uncovers the rot. My own Believers smuggling mages from the jēla in the dead of night, their stolen charges draped in funeral white. Had she not followed, their screams would have died unheard as their souls were flayed away.

The Believers pin them to the earth, blades poised to sever. They are unrepentant, righteous in their fury. "Mages have no rights. Their existence is an affront to the Lady."

My own words, thrown back like a curse. They taste foul now. She has changed me. "We are their guardians. We do them no harm."

Her gaze meets mine, warmer than the midday sun. However much she burns to change the world, she loves me for who I am.

"They're demons!" the Believers roar.

I execute my own. My sword feels heavier than ever.

"Do you see?" she asks. "Your Believers hold life and death in their hands. There can be no peace like this."

"The Commander rules over us as we rule over magic users." I reject the comparison. "These people are the exception, the rest of us are good."

Her lips tremble. "No one is good if they ignore the injustice surrounding them."

The blow wounds me. I stand there, my blade wet with the blood of my own people. And she stands before the husks of hers. There is enough pain for both of us.

"I don't ignore it. I fight it."

"Then fight with me." She holds out her hand. "Leave the palace. Leave him."

I want to bellow my agreement, seize her hand, and let the world burn if it means keeping her. But the blood dripping from my fingers gives me pause. Will I ever wash clean?

Loyalty is etched into my bones. The Believers are my cradle and my chains. "What would that achieve? Who would remain to protect them?"

A crooked smile. "What indeed, my love?"

* * *

The city throbs in the heat. Fetid and anxious.

The Commander is irritable, his ceremonial robes loose at his throat, his feet bare and cooled by scurrying servants. His sharp teeth flash in the unrelenting sun. His armies slow their inexorable advance.

I'm barely at the palace. The rising temperature leads to a rise in tensions. The jēla grow restless. The Believers are stretched thin.

There's a rumour that across the sacred river a jēla has fallen. For three days, the wealthy report demons in every shadow. The Believers chase phantoms.

This leaves the main jēla understaffed. I try to ease the mages' suffering. Cooling walks and an additional hour in their bathing pool. Nothing works.

"You could treat them like people," she says.

I'm exhausted. All I want is to rest with her, not be lectured to. "They're not like us. They could tear open the skies."

"And yet they haven't."

"Because they're contained!"

Her laughter blends with the fountain's song, the water spray the only thing cool between us. "Any one of them could destroy the jēla at any time. They choose not to because they're good. Because they fear reprisals."

I pat my sword. "Then the system is working."

She rolls onto her side, closing her eyes. I want to stay and comfort her, but a bell rings across the courtyard. Harsh, strident. Another problem for me to tackle.

* * *

The jēla grow worse. The mages are angry at their mistreatment, but I cannot get my Believers in line. The Commander has given them extra powers. Lockdown. Solitary. Brutal torture.

Some of the mages are dangerous. They are threatening to summon demons. But we are driving them to it. I cannot stand by and watch as my people destroy their chance at reincarnation. I want no more blood on my hands.

I bypass the security barricade, my own Believers stepping aside. It's dark inside the Commander's chamber. Incense curls up to the roof. An array of candles lines the floor. It takes me a moment to see what is happening.

Husks. Rows of them. Empty and lifeless, their only movement is in their chests as they breathe. A shackled mage stands to one side, lash marks striping his back. He raises his hands, magic writhing from his fingers like black smoke. A husk judders, its eyes flashing white, and then lurches forward.

"Control it!" the Commander barks. "You're worthless if you can't!"

The mage cries out in anguish. The cycle repeats.

The truth coils in my gut. The Commander's undefeated army is not human.

The Commander is defensive. "Soldiers need food. They get wounded. They die. Husks are more efficient."

I hear his words, but I remember the oath he taught me.

Protect them. Care for them. Control them. Sever them as a last resort.

How many souls has he stolen? How many countries have fallen because of this atrocity?

He mistakes my silence for loyalty. Let him. I have buried my dreams for this man, and he does not even care.

* * *

She is both elated that the scales have fallen from my eyes and devastated that it cost me my faith. Despite our love, she refuses to tell me her schemes.

"You'll never be free again. We'll be persecuted. Despised. Every one of your Believers will try to kill us."

Nothing I say will change her mind. She is adamant that I cannot, will not, help her.

The days pass. She leaves to meet with others from cities across the Empire. I try to find other Believers who feel as conflicted as I do.

I watch, and I wait.

She slips into the jēla, a shadow amongst shadows. I follow, though she begs me not to.

"You'll die."

"Then I'll die by your side."

"And I want *you* to survive our inevitable defeat." Her gaze is fierce.

"Inevitable defeat?"

"It's not a great story unless the hero dies, remember?"

"This isn't a story! This is your life!" I reach out and take her hand.

"This is the path I've chosen." There is a faint smile on her lips before she turns away, fingers trailing off. The gate clangs behind her.

Am I that foolish to think we could incite a rebellion and survive it? Is it an impossible dream?

No. I refuse to let her do this. She saved me from my blind loyalty, and now I must save her from her martyrdom. We could never do this by ourselves, so it's good that her people have magic and that I have trained an army.

Some of the Believers might be broken and ruined and corrupt. But others are like me. They want to protect and care for our charges. They have seen how bad things are. I must reach them, but I don't know how to rouse them. I'm no orator. I'm not her.

But I *know* her. I know how she crafts her words to hook a heart.

"We are here because we believe. Because we protect. Because we care."

I pause. My words are not honey. They do not drip with sweetness, nor do I win every heart the way she would. Still, there is a fragment of her essence in them. Most are listening. There are some nods and a few smiles. Only one or two have their arms crossed, their bodies defensive and cold. That's when I tell them what I've witnessed. Our Commander breaking his own oath. Summoning demons. Destroying lives.

"Mage lives! Who cares!" one yells. There's a murmur of agreement.

"People's lives. For do we not all think and breathe, live, and love? It's time to end this betrayal of all we hold dear!"

At first there are cheers. Then a small scuffle. Then a larger scuffle. Then swords are drawn. I am heartened to find my friends outnumber those against us. More Believers hear us. Some join the others; most join me.

We fight towards her. She has freed the mages. Hundreds stand ready, sparks at their fingers.

"The Lady loves all of her children!" I shout across the room.

The crowd parts. She takes my hand, her smile as sharp as my blade. "Enlightened at last."

I have been foolish, but I'm not wrong this time. We can both survive this. My dream of honour and loyalty, her dream of a heroic victory.

"Other jēla have also risen." She leads us out.

The city does not burn. No demons tear the sky. The lies unravel like old rope.

* * *

I hear the Commander before I see him, angry barks of rage over the sound of a lashing whip. But this time, I'm not alone. My Believers follow to my left, while the mages stand to my right.

"He's a demon, you know," the shackled mage gasps.

I didn't know, but perhaps I'd suspected. His empire-building was long before my parents were born. His invincibility in battle. Still, I must face him anyway.

The immortal's sword carves the air, centuries of slaughter humming in its edge. I block, but the force near shatters my bones. A backhand sends me sprawling. My sword clatters away. The taste of iron fills my mouth. He raises his blade for the final cut. "A shame. You almost—"

My Believers strike. Not at him, but at the tether binding the demon inhabiting him. The Commander falters for the first time in centuries.

My dagger finds his colourless eye. Black blood wells. He screams in fury and fear. I press the advantage, my blade biting a vulnerable joint in his armour. He crashes down, the earth shaking. My dagger finds flesh that has never known pain. A twist. A gasp. Silence.

I stand over the corpse of a god, bloodied but unbowed. I spit on his corpse and turn towards the dawn.

* * *

The rebellion does not end with the Commander's death.

It takes weeks to quell the chaos. Believers lost without their god-king, mages trembling at their newfound freedom, the Empire fracturing like a pane of stained glass. But we endure.

We stand together on the palace's highest balcony, watching the sun bleed into the horizon. The air smells of rain and jasmine, the first monsoon storm gathering in the distance.

Her fingers lace through mine, sticky with mango juice. She had insisted on eating one, laughing when I scolded her for ruining another saree. "What's the point of freedom if I can't be messy?"

She leans into me, her warmth a familiar anchor. "What now, General?" she asks, her voice steeped in the warmth of slow-burning incense.

I turn her palm up, tracing the lines of it with my thumb. "No more generals. No more advocates. Just us."

She hums, thoughtful. "Just us sounds like a story with no ending."

"Good," I say. "I hate stories where the hero dies."

Her laughter is bright and unburdened. She rises onto her toes, her lips brushing mine, sweet with mango, sharp with the promise of tomorrow. "Then let's make our own."

And we do.

What Honor Dictates

A.L. Keane

You appeared to me as a hazy apparition, a vision dark and immutable, a sword with no wielder. From the fog of rain and smoke came your assault. I knew you were there only for the shrill clash of your blade against mine. Battle and heavy rain became to us a bubble, a bleak backdrop to our encounter.

It was a bloody skirmish of a dozen men just outside the northern border. Our lords were at odds – broken oaths, land rights, trade disputes – I remain hard pressed to recall what honor this particular conflict concerned.

It hardly mattered, all the same. When there was you, there was very little else, even then.

Mud nearly sucked the boot from my leg as I deflected your blow with a brisk step back. In the same moment, lightning rent the leaden sky above us, and revealed to me the smallest glimpse, yet only a breath's worth of time to discern the visage of my combatant. Pallid skin, frenzied sneer, and a serpentine gaze. Bloodied rain plastered your pitch-dark hair into wiry fronds against your cheeks and throat, where it disappeared beneath the shadow of your ash-stained gorget.

You swung again, cleaving the rain-fog in a second strike of lightning. There was something oddly rehearsed about our duel, a rhythmic strike and retort, riposte and renounce. You moved through my guard with ease – brutal, wild, instinctual with your strikes. At the time, it did not seem to me that you conducted your attacks with the chivalry born of an honorable charge. You were fury and passion, and I was naive.

I know now that you would have bested me eventually, had the extraneous not interrupted our sacred foreground. In a heartbeat there was you, in another there was a shouting mass of wounded soldiers shoving me through an opaque sheet of downpour, wresting you from my vision.

A pitiful retreat, made only more disgraceful by the short cut of our duel.

You appeared to me as a sword with no wielder, and left as such – only the glint of a ruby fractal upon the hilt, and you were gone.

* * *

Months later, I served as honor guard for the funeral of my lord's distant relation. A hundred-full procession poured into the cobbled streets, clergy and royal blood alike. The late lord's golden coffin waded the thoroughfare below billowing violet heraldry. It was a sluggish crawl to the church, up winding steps to the finer parts of the city where the highest-ranking of the procession broke off and carried on the rest of the way.

The church itself was grand – pearly columns and marble arches, a red carpet laid down the aisle like a bloody gash through an otherwise spotless sight. The coffin was settled before the altar as the remaining mourners entered in through the massive tiled entrance behind me, filling the pews.

The proceedings muddle after that, a slew of formalities and speeches. Positioned beside the coffin, I grew well accustomed to the backs of many a noble's head, as one after another spoke fond words of their lord before the congregation. I, for my part, recall passing the time with nary a yawn, honor-bound as I am.

And then, there was you, an inky specter approaching via a sanguinary aisle between pews of formless faces: blackest of knights, bane of my glory. I was tempted to draw right there, to finish what had begun weeks before. Alas, duty forbade it in such a setting. Your glare betrayed a similar realization.

Yes, you recognized me. Of course you would.

Your presence startled me at first, followed by the sharp sting of my own oversight. Then I considered your being there, and found it impudent that a knight of your brutishness was invited to this noble gathering. Was the presence of such an animal not a disrespect to the man being honored? How could the entire room not balk at your very shadow?

It incensed me to no end, having your eyes burn relentlessly into mine, like you knew the mockery you made of everything around you and reveled in it. Your attention narrowed the church itself, folding it inward, entreating me to hold it. You held my gaze as you walked the length of the aisle, coming to a halt before the massive ornate coffin beside me.

It was the first time I'd seen you mud-less and unbloodied. Your armor was finer than I'd remembered.

"Honor dictates we relinquish our heart's desires in this lifetime, so that we might be worthy of them in the next," you said softly. "Whatever it was that stole your heart, my lord, I pray it is with you now – only to express my deepest honor, for I know you are a man worthy of it."

Your hand flexed against the ruby hilt of your blade before you unsheathed it, the sound reverberating through the hushed, marbled hall. I tried not to gawk when you took a knee, sword point down, and bowed your head in prayer.

That you paid allegiance to anything at all was astounding to me. That you showed respect to a man as noble as the one being honored, that you might have known him well enough to relay such sentiments...

I shifted uncomfortably, feeling suddenly exposed before the sea of burdened pews.

When I was a boy, there was an odd rat snake I witnessed in the eastern wood while hunting. It confused me deeply, at the time, how it tolerated certain rodents near its habitat. Perhaps it was in exchange for their pest-removing appetites, or perhaps not, but either way I learned even deadly serpents were prone to civility, when it suited them.

The thought failed to render the sight of you on your knee any less uncanny. I didn't know why it disturbed me so, and that only served to madden me further. The church walls poured in on me, suffocating.

I couldn't risk the scrutiny of your attention anymore, and for that, our duel did not conclude before nightfall. Nor would it for years to come.

* * *

I'd never known ecstasy like the weight of your sword bearing down on mine. The battlefield was where we did our best work after all. You were gloriously mad – irises blown wide in a frenzy, sweat and gore gleaming upon your brow. Each ragged gasp, each grunt of our long-awaited duel was its own relief.

A hundred other battles waged in our periphery. Bone-weary soldiers fought in an ever-roiling maelstrom around us, stretching across a ravaged valley as fire and ash bloodied the heavens. I'd imagined our final stand innumerable times in the months preceding this, the reality more grand and obscene than anything my fledgling imagination could have conjured.

You peered through the crossing of our swords, steel grating on steel.

"*You* again," you panted.

I roared, bombarding you with a sudden rush of aggression. Your eyes were shocked before you stumbled back, anchoring your blade into the ruined earth. What was once an immaculate length of smeltwork was now laden with blood and grime; the rubies upon the hilt, polished no longer, were mired in grisly muck – as tarnished as the rest of you after fighting for the better part of a day. Such carnage was becoming of you, however much I mourned for the majesty of your trappings.

"Do not tire now, beast!" I leveled my sword with your gaze. "For months I've awaited casting your soul from this world. I will be denied no longer."

I took advantage with a charge, golden blade held aloft, smoke burning my eyes. You didn't even flinch.

You *smirked*.

That was my sole forewarning before a series of rapid maneuvers left me helmet-first in the dirt, disarmed and bewildered. The quietus of my folly smothered me. I trembled, awaiting the felling strike, tears welling.

Alas, the reaper did not call. When I rose I saw naught but the war-torn valley under a ruddied, darkening sky.

You were gone. Again.

And you took my sword.

When I found your own – lying discarded only a pace away from where you'd bested me – I repaid the sentiment. Begrudgingly. (Traversing a battlefield without proper defense was simply poor judgement.)

I weighed the weapon, pictured your hand gripping the gory hilt just as I was, rubies glimmering in spite of their begrimed state. Discerning whether you'd left it behind as a token of mockery or respect was beyond me – I knew only that it was a promise, and that itself satisfied me.

* * *

Years later, in the heart of winter, instead of enemies we found ourselves unlikely allies. Our lords were engaged in a plot against a mutual rival, forcing our companies into a reluctant truce.

The cold was more frigid than years past and by no means curtailed by the ice storm that bore down from the frozen mountain peaks. My comrades were starving, freezing, frostbitten – and there you were, a shadowy beacon on the fringe of a hoary tempest.

You offered refuge for my men in spite of our mutual strife, a stalwart stone fortress built into the southern face of the mountain. It was dutifully manned and well stocked – how that was possible, I didn't know, considering the base's isolation. I chose not to question it for fear I might offend you.

"There is room in the eastern wing," you said. The forward gate shuddered closed behind us. "Your men are welcome to it for the remainder of the storm."

"You have my gratitude." I nodded. "It is a kindness I did not expect to find out here in the volatile wilderness. Let alone from the black knight himse—"

"Mark me well, *boy*."

My smile fell.

Your eyes narrowed, cold and portentous. "My generosity ends with the storm."

We did not talk again for the rest of the evening.

I thought myself the first to rise in the morning, hours before any of my fellows – but as I made my way to the training yard, clad in a warm set of armor, I found I was not alone. When I saw the spray of your black hair pluming under the torchlight with every practiced swing of your – *my* – blade, my heart stilled just as my feet.

I should leave, I thought. *Right now.*

You snarled, hacking a series of brisk attacks through the thick morning fog, fending off an encompassment of invisible combatants. It was odd seeing you fight without a barrels-worth of blood coating every inch of you. Like a painting without the varnish.

I wanted so badly to feel your blade against mine. We needn't even finish our long, drawn-out duel, the truce being what it was – just a respectful crossing of swords between two knights of great skill, if only for a short while.

"I know you are there, knightling." You spoke into the air, looking nowhere in particular.

I swallowed, face simmering for all the bitter cold. With a glance, I perceived myself as the sole intended recipient. *Damn it all.* My hand enclosed the hilt of my secondhand weapon, slowly rounding one of the main pillars and entering the training yard proper. The bulk of the snow had been shoveled in the night, piled into a mound against the northernmost wall. You were still swinging, wild yet seasoned, into the mist.

"I have a request, if you will indulge me," I offered.

You paused, swiveling to regard me at a decidedly glacial pace. Then, you laughed.

"Has your lord always had a penchant for more impertinent knights?" you said. "Or does he make an exception for you, I wonder?"

"You question the discernment of my charge and you dare speak of impertinence?"

"I suggest you entreat me," you said. "Quickly now."

I scoffed against my better judgment. I would not flatter you with undue respect. "'Tis of no account. Forgive me."

Nothing was worth such debasement, surely. Except turning from you was more dreadful than a half-stone mace clobbering the underside of my ribcage (a sensation I'd been unfortunate enough to experience once before). Almost as soon as I did, however, I heard the unmistakable sound of footsteps in snow behind me. In the next moment I was countering your attack, stumbling backward for the force of your charge.

I held my ground despite the thick layer of snow muddling my footwork, managing to nick your cheek in a fortuitous assault that took us both by surprise. Your restraint was broken the moment blood came away from the wound, a piddling smear of crimson upon your fingers.

I didn't fare well after that.

The next three mornings, still snowed in along with the rest of my men, were of similar routine. I would get a few sporadic hits in, only to get undercut by your fury and knocked into the snow. At the time, I would have seethed with the knowledge that you might be going easy on me, an affront to my pride.

That didn't mean injury wasn't a likelihood, however, and on the fourth morning, you carved a harrowing gash into the meat of my shoulder blade, deft handiwork slipping right between the plates of my armor. Boiling pain aside, I maintained the sort of composure befitting my rank as you wrangled me into (what I assumed to be) your chambers.

The extent of the damage was beyond my sight. Only the fire of a deep wound and an alarmingly *wet* sensation trailing down my back alerted me to its probable severity.

"Sit," you snapped, jutting a finger towards the bed.

The hearth blazed nearby, a blessed relief from the rattling chill. I sat down, tentatively peeling away what armor I could reach, though not without several winces and murmurs of pain. You returned bearing what I took for leech's gear, though with you I could never be certain. Perhaps you judged me too great a burden and came instead to put me out of my misery. Perhaps I'd even let you, tenacious as you were.

I'd managed to remove the sum of my upper plate, exposing the wound and my clammy skin to the bite of the morning air, fire notwithstanding. You walked, silent, to my side and motioned me to turn.

"I've the ability to tend to my own injuries," I said, pointedly.

You shrugged, handed me the folded up chest of healer's supplies, and waited.

In the end, the wound lay in too troublesome a place to manage on my own, and I acquiesced to your kind insistence to tend it yourself. Or, rather, I *would* have, had you not forcibly turned my back to you and begun cleaning the gash once your patience had worn thin.

The manhandling was really, *truly* unnecessary.

Your naked touch, however, was enough to make up for it. Even where the rag brushed me, it burned with the proximity of your skin through the damp fibers. You tended just as you fought – quick, efficient, no room for prudence. It was the worst care in ministrations I'd ever received, but I admired the severity you applied to everything you did.

I wondered just how far your intensity extended.

I wondered if you'd let me find out.

The morning chill was no longer a concern by the end. You snipped the loose thread dangling from my shoulder blade, humming approvingly as you regarded your needlework. I, on the other hand, felt much like a piece of furniture being scrutinized for imperfections.

When at last I regarded you, your attention was taken with situating the medical gear in its proper place – an array of torn cloths, salves, and iron instruments. I gingerly pulled my linen tunic over my head, hissing whenever I tugged the stitches in my back.

"Thank you," I said.

You paused. Then, "You've improved."

"There was little margin for improvement," I huffed, fastening the ties at my neck.

You chuckled with a slight, sideways grin, clasping the small chest closed.

"I am not the one at fault for my injury," I pressed. "We were only sparring and you – reckless as you are – mauled me as an animal!"

You held my gaze, blinking steadily.

I continued, "Had I known you'd attack me regardless of chivalric code, there would be little concern for injury in my r—"

"*Quiet*," you shushed, the faintest grin still plucking at your mouth.

I stared at you, wary. The more you insisted, the more compelled I felt to outface you, but I managed to hold my tongue for the moment.

"Be still," you said, dark gaze flicking over me inquisitively, long enough that I began to squirm. I realized you were moving closer and froze, rigid as stone.

"Move not an inch," you whispered.

The shock of your kiss cast me from this realm. Your mouth was warm. The scent of you hung heavy in the air – sweat and oiled leather. My senses had never felt so susceptible. When you groaned against my lips, I winced – *whimpered* – and felt all at once like bared sinew.

I jolted back, met your stupefied gaze, and promptly left your chambers. Not once did I turn to look at you, even as my heart thundered and ached.

The storm ebbed in the night.

* * *

The damp clung to my skin in a thick film. Torch aloft, I followed the filth-ridden corridor between rows of steel-enforced cells, the first few of which housed individual prisoners. Soon there was only the clink of my steps, two swords jostling against my armor, and a persistent trickling noise echoing across the stone walls.

They'd thrown you into one of the far-flung cells, where they intended to forget you, just as they had the ones prior. Such treatment was usually reserved for the lowliest of prisoners – treasonous wretches and rapists – not *knights* invited under pretense of an armistice.

I was a loyal servant of my lord. Implicitly, I'd thought. He was a man of honor, of great charity and strong moral character. I recalled the famine a handful of winters prior, the graciousness he'd displayed in opening the castle's granaries. I gave our kitchen's bread to starving peasants with my very own hands, by my lord's direct order.

But there you were – inky hair covering your face, veiling your shoulders and flickering with orange torchlight as I shone it into your cell. The bars cast a long shadow over your already dark form, and you regarded me with a weary, disgruntled expression.

"*You.*"

"Last summer, the old stone wall caved in just over there," I said, pointing to a dark corner at the end of the hallway of cells. I continued, musingly, "It's bothered me ever since. I've told the chamberlain to attend to it many times."

Your eyes narrowed. "Turn around, knightling."

"He's not a very good chamberlain."

I pulled back my cloak, revealing the length of two familiar blades, one of which had mysteriously vanished from the armory shortly after you were placed behind bars.

"Fool," you said, so quietly I wasn't certain you meant for me to hear it.

I unfastened one of the sheathed blades from my side, slipping it awkwardly through the bars. It clattered to the stone floor of your cell. You didn't move.

"Are you suggesting I saw my way through metal?" you asked.

I reached under my cloak again, digging into the inside pockets until I grasped an old key.

You stood abruptly and walked to the bars, torchlight revealing the entirety of your face at last. There had always been a jaded edge to your countenance, but you appeared even more worn than usual. Beaten and tired – a string of day-old bruises smattering the side of your face – but alive.

"And when your liege lord catches wind of your treachery?" you asked.

"He won't."

"He could."

"He *won't*," I insisted. You stared at me, unconvinced. I shook my head. "For years now, we have done this. I am not the fool you've always taken me for."

"Not any longer, you mean?" you said. "You are not helping your case, knightling."

"There is no case!" I snapped. "You will take this key, you will take that blade, you will leave this dank hole and you will live!"

My outburst shocked us both into silence. We looked at one another for a long time; you were considering, I was admiring. There was the odd chance you were stubborn enough to let yourself die just to pain me. I prayed that your will to live would prevail, but I burned every plane of your face indelibly into my mind, just in case.

Then I dropped the key through the bars, rested my hand upon the ruby-studded blade at my hip, and left.

* * *

There were only the two of us this time. Our previous duels had always been in the midst of some other conflict, fueled by the orders of higher-ranking men, never of our own making. Any lord we might've sworn ourselves to had died in the years since you'd escaped from my late lord's dungeon, and any lord that might come later would never get the opportunity to beckon our fealty.

I appreciated the change of pace, alone as we were, surrounded only by a light rain that was growing heavier by the moment. Fog encompassed us, steam licked off your shoulder plates in whorls, and I gripped the blade that had once been yours, readying my stance in the mud-muck underfoot.

You attacked me first – roaring, before the shock of clattering steel shuddered up my arms, down my back. You didn't waver, pressing your blade and pushing me continuously through the slick mire. I mustered the strength to wind my sword around the length of yours, bolting sidewards and coming up from behind. I kicked you forward, purposely needling.

You didn't like that.

I chuckled. You were so inflamed by such paltry bait.

A vein I'd never noticed before flared in your temple. Then – an onslaught of thundering attacks, each parry more wearying than the one before it, your dark eyes furious.

Rain came down in a heavy sheet – so clamorous I could barely make out the snarl before your every attack, or the din of our blades crossing again, again, again. We were in no war-infested valley; this was no skirmish in a northern border village; nor was it a cordial spar between mutually regarded knights. Neither of us were planning to walk away this time. And when we charged at one another, both of us coated in rainwater and mud and sweat, I knew neither of us would.

Your sword was in my gut, and mine in yours, a sharp ache blooming where the steel skewered my belly. You looked down, disbelieving, and saw a gush of blood coat the length of my blade as it disappeared between the gaps in your breastplate. When you looked back at me your eyes dilated with fear, and I reached for you, weakly, as we slumped together in the gory mire, swords still buried.

The movement dislodged something wrong in my gut. I coughed a spray of blood onto your cheek. You didn't seem to notice. We bled out together, eyes meeting in a frightful and wordless exchange as we simultaneously made peace with entropy. It wasn't so hard, in the end. You'd never looked more beautiful than when you were impaled on my blade, and I on yours – bleeding from the mouth, a dimming recognition in your eyes.

I listened to the memory of your voice, and understood the truth of it at last: *Honor dictates we relinquish our heart's desires in this lifetime, so that we might be worthy of them in the next.*

It is there, on the edge of the reaper's scythe, and only there, that you could ever be mine.

Half Made of Shadows

Sasha Kielman

Many traveled, near and far.
Many wandered, here and there.
Many sought magic without a thought.
But never I, the Lady of Shalott.

* * *

Never to steal a kiss in a bower,
Never to leave my tower.
Ever to weave,
Ever to grieve.

* * *

Weaving my spells into my creations wasn't the hard part. The waiting was.

Waiting for someone to approach my tower. Waiting for the project to be complete.

Waiting to replenish my strength before I could cast the next spell.

Being the powerful witch who lived in a tower weaving magic garments was a lonely life. But it gave me comfort to know my magic was being worn each day, that the more my spells and shawls embraced those brave enough to seek me out, the more my power would grow.

And yet.

I wanted to feel the sunlight on my skin. I wanted conversations more than correspondence, to pick my own fruits and vegetables at the town market rather than paying someone to bring baskets to my door.

I wanted to go to Camelot, see the knights in their armor and the nobles in their finery.

I wanted, and I waited. Still I longed for a visitor who wanted more than a magical garment. More than my magic.

I wanted to be wanted.

* * *

Hours passed by while I sat at my loom, weaving. My hands flew over threads as I whispered spells, enchantments, magic into the weave. I could hear children laughing by the river, women singing and chasing after them. The sounds of a happy life, echoing up into my tower. I smiled, thinking of the young woman who would wear the shawl I was weaving. My hands and eyes never strayed from my loom. Not until the sun was setting, my hands shaking, did I allow myself to rise from my stool, stretch, and pour a glass of wine. I drank deeply to refresh my body while I stood at the window to look out at the sunset. It was beautiful: red and orange and yellow. Someday, I would weave a blanket in those colors, to keep a couple warm at night, from sunset until sunset. I committed the colors to memory, then made notes in my journal.

I slept deeply, my magic depleted from a day's worth of weaving. But it had been a good day, a good spell. A warm, comforting shawl for a young woman about to start a new path on life's journey.

Much different were the nights after I wove dark enchantments into a cloak or a net.

Those who came from Camelot asking for enchanted nets for their knights never wanted to tell me much about the monsters they planned to ensnare and slay, but they haunted my dreams nonetheless. They always spoke in whispers when they asked for more private spells, such as an enchanted shawl to ease the pains of monthly bleeding. But when they spoke of monsters, they did not whisper, but left much unsaid.

The spaces between their words haunted my dreams.

I fought my way through cobwebs and thorns, monsters growling and trying to tear my hair with their claws. My enchanted nets could not help me; they disintegrated to ash in my hands. I tried to slash through with my knitting needles, but the more I struggled, the more I had to fight through.

I woke up gasping for breath, a creature clawing at my skirts.

But it was only my blanket wrapped around my legs.

* * *

My strength lasted most of the day on a good day of weaving, as it had thus. But there were days where I could do no weaving or knitting or embroidering at all. Days in which I felt as though there were lightning bolts within my own head, where I could not keep anything in my stomach save some bites of plain bread. Or days where I could not sit at the loom due to cramps and back pain from my monthly cycle. Between both, I lost at least a week per month to fighting my own body and trying to replenish both my magic and my physical health.

It made the good days all the more precious. While I could not feel the sunlight on my own face, I could appreciate it from my window on the days when it did not hurt my eyes and head.

I was but a shadow watching the river flow by.

* * *

The scent of roses was in the air when the contingent of knights galloped by. Another battle in a distant land, another war to be won? I would hear the outcome eventually. I had no loved ones to worry over in the corps, unlike my neighbors in Shalott and Camelot. Once again, I was distant, removed from the realities of daily life.

I continued my gardening, pulling weeds and savoring the feeling of the earth in my hands, until sweat dripped from my brow and I knew my skin would be pink and freckled from the sun.

It did not occur to me that perhaps the knights passing by took note of me, that they would consider my visible presence an omen. I hardly considered myself that important, but as I would learn later, the legend of the Lady of Shalott had spread through Camelot.

If only they knew how badly I wanted to see the castle and its town for myself.

But though I hardly took note of the knights, intent upon my work in the garden and in the kitchen – I brewed most of my own teas and remedies for headaches and cramps – my unconscious mind brought my yearning loneliness to the fore that night. I dreamed of a knight in shining armor, returning to me after a battle. I dreamt of helping him with his armor, healing him with my poultices and care.

I dreamt of our bodies entwined, tangled in the sheets.

I never saw my lover's face in my dreams. But somehow, I knew him, as if our minds and souls were entwined even though our bodies had not in the physical realm.

I wept when I woke, for who would ever want to sacrifice their freedom to join me in my tower? I had no loyal knight and true.

* * *

I wove, and I yearned, and I dreamed.

These were my days. Seeing as Shalott was not so far from Camelot, it seemed that adventure should have come my way sooner than it did.

I was working on a new blanket, commissioned as a gift for a woman who was expecting a baby in the spring. Ethel, a kindly grandmother and unofficial village matriarch, came to the tower alongside Abigail, the younger woman who filled and delivered my baskets of produce, fresh bread, and cheese.

"My lady," Ethel began. "Have you ever considered..." She paused for a moment, looking around at my loom, the many skeins of yarn and knitting and sewing implements, and books strewn around my room. "Have you ever thought about trying to use your magic outside of enchanted garments?"

I swallowed. I wanted to trust the village women, to be part of their lives, while knowing I was of Camelot, but not from it. Near the village, but not within it. A woman, but a witch.

And we all knew it.

I wanted to trust. To have friends. To be included.

"I have thought about it, yes," I answered. "But I'm not sure how well it would work, or what the consequences might be."

Ethel nodded.

"Why do you ask?" I asked. *After all these years* went unspoken.

Ethel met my eyes. "I know you are forbidden to leave this tower. And your works are a blessing, truly. But there is so much more that needs to be done besides fighting monsters and keeping to the chivalric code, and there aren't enough knights and nobles in Camelot to do all that needs doing."

I was aware. We all were aware. And the village women, while integral to the castle, were not the priority for the knights and lords who sought fame and glory through their valiant deeds. Nor was I, for that matter, for all I tried to lace my creations with care – and power.

"How do you think I can help?"

"Do you think it would be possible to cast a spell of protection on a person? Weave the magic the way you weave on your loom?"

"Would anyone be willing to come to my tower for me to practice upon them?"

Ethel turned to look at Abigail, who smiled and met my gaze. "Aye, my lady. You're a fair and kind lady, always treating those of us who come to you with respect, and never sharing our secrets. Mother Ethel and I will accompany those who are willing, to make everyone comfortable, if need be."

I found myself smiling. Perhaps I was wanted, needed, not just for my works, but for myself, too.

My smile remained as I returned to my weaving after Ethel and Abigail left. I would weave for a few more hours, then turn to my books. It had been some time since I'd had to research a particular spell; most of my woven enchantments came from heart and memory. But perhaps one of my older grimoires, passed down from sorcerers and witches before me, would contain some wisdom from the ancestors that might help the village women where Camelot could not.

I was up most of the night reading, all of my candles lit. I would ask Abigail to bring more – if I were able to use my magic for more than crafting, I could earn more money to make up for the expense.

I was excited when I awoke. I stretched my hands and wrists, and prepared tea for a day of research ahead. I made notes on spells and techniques that seemed promising or suited to my magic.

After lunch, I worked on my weaving for a few hours, then returned to my books. My mind turned over and over with possibilities. I slept fitfully once more, my dreams full of knights and monsters.

* * *

A few days later, it was time to put what I had learned and considered into practice. Ethel and Abigail brought a young would-be knight named Llewelyn to my tower. He would serve as a squire when the next contingent set forth from Camelot.

"Are you ready?" I asked him.

"Is one ever truly ready for their first battle?" he replied, meeting my eyes.

I nodded. Had I been ready when I first started using my magic, when I was enclosed in my tower? I had never had another choice. This young man had his whole future ahead of him.

"I will do what I can to help protect you," I promised.

I took a deep breath, and began. I wasn't moving threads through my fingers, but my mental imagery was the same. I was weaving a spell, though only through my magic, not capturing it in any material. I imagined wrapping the young knight in a blanket of protection, pouring magic over him from a pitcher. I let my magic flow through me and around him instead of channeling it into my weaving as usual.

I worked as if I were weaving, for a few hours. My guests remained silent while I cast my spell. I hoped that it would keep him safe and well.

* * *

A few weeks passed. The summer became ever hotter, and I wished I had more ventilation than just my window overlooking the garden and the river, Camelot in the distance. I could hear people splashing about more often, and their complaints regarding the heat. It felt tortuous to weave blankets and shawls and knit scarves, but they would be needed come winter. Socks and other undergarments were needed all year round, but I used different weights of yarn and fabrics.

I piled my hair up into a bun, as far off my neck as I could get it, and decided to let the blankets wait until September. I worked on tunics for the knights until I heard them returning, the clatter of armor and whinnying of horses rising from the southern road along with clouds of dust and cries from those in the village.

It was a few hours later that Ethel came to the tower, bearing a basket of enchanted items I had made that needed to be mended.

"What news?" I asked, taking the basket from her. "How fare the knights?"

"Well, for the most part," she said. "It was a difficult battle, and many were injured. But the battle was won, in the end. They return home to recover, before heading out again in a few weeks."

"That is good news. Perhaps I can try brewing some teas to aid in their recovery."

"I think that would be appreciated, my lady. I will see about getting you more jars or jugs."

"Thank you, Ethel." I paused for a moment before asking my next question. I was so curious to know if my magic had worked. "How did Llewellyn and his knight fare?"

Ethel closed her eyes for a moment. My heart sank.

"They were both injured by a monster, I'm sorry to tell you, my lady. But both are home and recovering well."

I felt as though I might faint and fall to the floor. My heart raced, and my ears were ringing. If Ethel continued speaking to me, I could not hear her. My eyes filled with tears.

I struggled to control my breathing. I felt separated from my body, as though what was happening forced my mind away elsewhere.

After Ethel left, I collapsed into bed and did not move for hours.

That night, I wept. I was a failure. Never had one of my enchanted garments failed before. Certainly, both the fabric and magic decayed over time – that was to be expected from a well-loved blanket or shawl – but they always protected the bearer.

I was protected in my tower. But those in Shalott, in Camelot? They fought the outside world in ways I never had to consider beyond that what they told me. My battles, against my own mind and body, were of a far different nature. And I was losing that battle that night, as I felt sick to my stomach with despair and anguish. What good was I if I could not use my magic for its intended purpose?

What good was I at all?

My mind raced as I considered what I could do to apologize to the young man. When I finally slept, I was once again assailed by nightmares.

The next morning, Ethel returned to check on me. It was a kindness I did not anticipate, and to which I was unaccustomed.

"Llewelyn fares better this morning. I hope you do as well," she said, eyeing me carefully.

I knew the dark circles under my eyes were even more prominent than usual. "Thank you, Ethel. I would make amends to him and the knight whom he serves, as well as his family. Rather than weaving this week, I will make poultices and salves in addition to teas. My garden should be able to provide many herbs, and I may ask you and Abigail for more ingredients."

"But my lady," Ethel said. "We all know you cannot leave your tower."

"I can," I replied. "I am forbidden to leave. I may not leave. But I physically can. At least, I think so. The consequence may very well be my death. But what is a life worth living? My enchantment failed. Someone might have lost their life because of me, because Llewelyn was injured. I owe it to their loved ones to try to help heal them."

I swallowed. I felt the truth of my words in my heart. I would regret it if I died at an old age, alone, having never even tried to leave my tower. And I would never be able to forgive myself if I didn't try to help the trusting squire who was grievously injured due to my failed enchantment.

"Will you help me?" I asked, meeting Ethel's eyes. "I will bring whatever I can to help his recovery."

She nodded, and took my hands in her own. No one had touched me like that since I was a child. My body was unused to it, and I startled, then blinked quite a bit.

Ethel noticed, but squeezed my hands nonetheless. "Thank you, my lady. Thank you for trying. We will come up with another solution to help those left behind in Camelot and Shalott. Until then, I will convey your well wishes to the injured and their loved ones. I'll return in a few days' time."

I blinked back tears as she left. I had ruminated on my own loneliness and despair often, too often, over the years of my confinement. I dreamt of having a lover in my bed. But simple touches, I did not realize how much I needed. My hands never brushed hers or Abigail's when we exchanged baskets and parcels each week.

And if I died upon leaving my tower, at least I would have known a caring touch from a friend for the first time. And I could be content knowing that I had faced my curse without fear.

* * *

My normally pale hands were red from overuse and hot water by the time Ethel returned. I had brewed teas, wrapped poultices, used up all my remaining beeswax to make healing salves.

I met her at the door, my basket upon my arm. There was not much to be said.

I swallowed, and took her left hand in my right. My other hand held my basket.

It was time.

I took my first tentative step outside my tower. I was holding on to Ethel's hand like it was tethering me to life.

I took a step, then another, looking back and forth between my feet and Ethel as if I were a child learning to walk again.

Once we reached the gate, I dared look up at the sky. The sun was bright and I blinked, then held my hand over my eyes to shade them for the first time. It was a simple gesture, but I had never thought about it before. People probably did it every day without thinking about it. I would never be one of those people. Every gesture, every interaction, would be something I treasured and would consider over and over again until the end of my days. It was fortunate for my magic that I had such a good memory – but not so fortunate for my nightmares and my loneliness. It wasn't the shadows in my tower that haunted me, but my own mind.

We walked slowly to Shalott. I took a breath with each step, fearing it might be my last.

When we reached the town's threshold, Ethel turned to me.

"Are you ready, my lady?"

I smiled at her. Llewelyn's words returned to my mind. "Is one ever truly ready for their first battle?" I replied.

Ethel squeezed my hand in response. "I felt that way when I had my first child. We all have our own battles to fight. I pray you'll survive yours."

I blinked back tears as we walked arm in arm into Shalott.

Dogs barked, neighbors waved and called out to each other in the streets and from windows, children ran to and fro, laughing. It was a small village, a happy one. It wasn't illustrious like Camelot, but it was charming.

Ethel led me to Llewelyn's home, where we were greeted by his mother and sister. They were kind, curtseying to me and pressing kisses to Ethel's cheeks.

I tried not to be overwhelmed with tears as I spoke to Llewelyn, but his soft smile put me at ease just as it made me feel guiltier for having failed him. I wrapped a new blanket around him despite the summer warmth, and hoped its protective spell would work just as well against nightmares caused by pain instead of monsters.

If only such magic worked for myself.

I taught his mother and sister how long to steep each tea, and explained the healing herbs in each salve. I promised to look in on them again.

I hoped it was a promise I would be able to keep. My heart lightened as we left their home. Llewelyn and I were both still alive. He would recover, and I would do what I could to help as long as I could.

As I walked through Shalott, I savored each sensation. The sights, the sounds, the touches, the tastes, the smells. I was taught to identify these things when emerging from an altered state of consciousness. A dream, a sight, a hysteric episode – these all brought risks to mind and body.

I could finally die happy, knowing what the world outside of my tower was like.

I was sniffing a bright red rose when a knight approached me. The sun glinted off his armor, and I found myself blinking, both from the brightness and from the realization that I was experiencing something of which I had dreamed. A knight walking through the sunlight to speak to me, the scent of roses in the air. It seemed too perfect to be real.

"My lady." The knight bowed deeply, then took my hand and kissed it. He was tall, and handsome, and I was entirely unprepared for a chivalrous conversation.

I felt my cheeks flushing. I couldn't help it. No one had ever kissed my hand before, although I had imagined such a moment for years.

Was this what it was like? Were all the village women accustomed to being treated with chivalrous courtesy, or was it because of my power or station that I received such a kind greeting?

I would observe people's behavior on another occasion – if I survived to do so. But for this moment, I would savor the feeling of his lips on my skin until the end of my days. Even if my fate was to come in a few minutes or hours.

"My lord," I finally managed to reply, dipping a curtsey, or at least, what I thought one should look like. "What brings you to Shalott?" I dared ask. Perhaps he would come again, and I could see him again.

A perilous thing, hope was. But I had the sun on my face and wind in my hair for the first time, and I cared not that I would suffer for it later.

"I was hoping to inquire after your Lady," said he, gesturing widely to my tower. "I was gifted an enchanted tunic she wove, and others of my company also wear her crafts. She has saved our lives more than once."

His words stopped my heart. This handsome knight had one of my tunics? My magic had saved lives? I wanted to ask so many questions. I did not want to appear impertinent or irritate him by asking questions. I wanted to continue our conversation. I could have spoken to him forever, about anything and everything. But I couldn't stay trapped in the moment, in my dreams, forever.

Dreams could not compare to the reality before me.

I dared to meet his eyes. "I am the Lady of Shalott."

His eyes widened. "My lady," he began, then shook his head and ran a hand through his hair. "I cannot begin to thank you enough for the gift of your enchanted garments."

"My magic is a gift which must be used," I tried to explain. "No thanks are necessary. I must weave my magic, and I am glad to share it. The more people wear my works, the stronger my magic will become." I did not add that I was cursed to weave alone in my tower for the rest of my life. Nor that I recently failed to protect one of his knights with my magic.

"Would you bring more of your garments to Camelot?" he asked. "There are many who would gladly pay a princely sum for a blanket or a scarf from you, my lady. I would be honored to escort you there."

"That is very kind of you, my lord," I replied. Was what he said really true? Were my works so desired, even after my failure? Perhaps word about that had not spread among the knights yet. It need not, if I survived to make up for the time I had lost at my loom.

My heart raced as I finally answered his request. There was only one way I could answer. "I would be honored to meet you and your knights in Camelot. I will endeavor to weave as much as I can in the meantime."

He smiled, and it was like the sun above. His face was radiant, his eyes crinkling at the corners. "I look forward to it, my lady. May I have your name?"

"Elaine," I almost whispered. I had never spoken my own name aloud before. "My name is Elaine. But I would only be known to your court as the Lady of Shalott. None here call me by my given name."

"Lady Elaine," he said, taking my hand once more. He was still smiling, and my heart was singing. "It is an honor to meet you. I am Lancelot du Lac."

"It is I who am honored to meet you, my lord," I said, lowering my eyes. I couldn't look at his smile, his eyes, any longer, or I would be overwhelmed.

He kissed my hand again before he continued on his way, and I stood still as a statue, trying to believe and process all that had happened.

I was exhausted when I returned home that evening. But I was still alive. My curse hadn't killed me yet.

I suffered the next day with a migraine, but it was worth it. I forced myself to work despite the pain behind my eyes, choosing a simple weave I could do with my eyes closed.

* * *

Lancelot was true to his word, and arrived promptly the following week to escort me and my works to Camelot, an extra horse in tow.

"I've never ridden before, my lord," I admitted, blushing. He did not need to know about my curse.

"She's a gentle horse," he said, helping me into the saddle. I arranged my skirts carefully and tried to sit as straight and tall as I could.

"Hold the reins like this," he said, his hands over mine. It sent an ember through me that lit my entire body on fire. I swallowed, hoping he would not notice I was still blushing, and tried to focus both on my breathing and committing his instructions to memory.

It was not a long ride to Camelot, though it had felt so far away since I was committed to my tower.

If entering the village I called home for the first time overwhelmed my mind and body with sensations, then Camelot surely did. There were people everywhere – selling their wares in the market, hurrying to and fro, stopping to chat with a neighbor in the streets. Skirts and wheels and feet dragged through the mud, dust was kicked up, and the air was full of sounds and smells.

It was overwhelming. It was beautiful. It was alive. I was alive. Leaving my tower hadn't killed me – yet. Perhaps I'd collapse in a puddle of mud or pile of dirt on the side of a street. But until then, I'd enjoy feeling sweaty and dirty and being welcomed.

And welcomed I was, as I rode beside Lancelot. He was clearly popular, receiving many waves and hand clasps and flowers.

And I became popular too. I had saved my earnings to buy new fabrics and yarns, meeting many fine weavers in their own right. As Lancelot requested, I distributed the garments and blankets which I had brought to many grateful knights and their loved ones. He introduced me to many lords and ladies, demonstrating the chivalry for which Camelot was famous.

I felt my energy flagging by the evening hours before dinner. I was not used to socializing, to walking to and fro, to riding horses. But Lancelot seemed indefatigable, his charm never fading.

And the feeling of his hand on my back as he led me around was something I knew I would crave desperately when it was gone. It was something I had always wanted, something I could become accustomed to, if given the opportunity.

I knew it was not a possibility for me. But in the weeks prior, I'd believed that leaving my tower would never be a possibility. That I would never see Camelot for myself.

And here I was, with a purse full of coins, a basket full of new fabrics and yarn, and a handsome knight by my side. A dream come true, really.

I would collapse into bed later and suffer the next day, I knew. I was learning the limits of my abilities after a life of never pushing against them, never considering the shape of the shadows of my curse.

* * *

The knights set out again the following week. I hoped this time, my magic would hold as tight as the weave that bound it.

Llewelyn and the knight he served did not travel with Lancelot and the others, and I was able to visit them again, as I had promised.

Rather than sending baskets to and from my tower with Abigail and Ethel, I began to visit Shalott myself each week. I began to feel that I was earning my title instead of merely having been given it by virtue of my existence.

I was the Lady of Shalott, no longer of it, but in it.

My headaches and nightmares came and went. I weaved and tried new recipes and shared flowers from my garden.

Summer was beginning to turn to fall, and the sun was casting a golden reddish glow over the trees when the company returned.

It was after dinner, the sunset turning to twilight, when I heard horses approaching, then a knock at my door.

I dreaded hearing that my magic had failed again. I swallowed, brushed out my skirts, and quickly twisted my hair into a bun before heading down to the gate, my feet moving as quickly as my mind.

A captain from Camelot was there, along with a few of his companions, who were bearing a wounded, unconscious Lancelot.

"My lady," the captain said, quickly bowing. "His lordship requested we bring him here to you, for your care."

I swallowed, watching the other knights carry him inside my tower. "Why did he ask to be brought to me?"

"You brew remedies and teas, in addition to your magic, do you not?" The captain's tone was matter of fact, as if I should have known what knights like them were thinking. I had never met any of them until those fateful weeks prior.

"I do, my lord," I replied, lowering my eyes respectfully, lest he think I was going to refuse to care for the injured.

He nodded. "Many of us owe you a great debt for your magic. And he will," he gestured with his chin to Lancelot within my tower, "for certain. Care for him well, my lady. I will return in three days' time to check on his progress."

"I shall, my lord. Thank you for entrusting him to my care."

The captain bowed before departing into the night.

I swallowed. Would my teas and salves be enough?

They would have to be. And I could give him an enchanted tunic that was not already designated for someone.

I cared for Lancelot through the night and into the next day before he awoke.

"My lady?" he asked, tentatively. His voice sounded hoarse from disuse, and shouting during the battle, I assumed.

"I am here," I replied. I wasn't sure what else to say. I had been thinking of the conversations we might have, but as before, dreaming and planning were inadequate for reality.

He reached over and took my hand, running his thumb over it. "I thought I was dreaming when I met you. You have such a lovely face."

I smiled and admitted the truth. "I felt the same way, my lord."

His eyes were still closed, and his throat bobbed as he swallowed. "For the first time since I began fighting, my dreams have been pleasant instead of nightmarish. Instead of monsters, you've haunted my dreams. Forgive me for intruding upon your home. But I could not bear to face my pain alone as I recover. And I thought your magic might help."

I did not question why he was sharing this with me. I could understand all too well the desire to empty one's heart due to pain, or before death. If he were speaking his darkest truths, I could not be reticent and not share my own. "I can't use my magic directly on people. I tried, and failed. But I can make remedies in addition to crafting, and I have." I pushed his hair back from his brow. “I have tea and broth prepared, when you’re ready for them.”

“Thank you, Elaine,” he said.

He did not see me shiver.

* * *

Lancelot recovered. I was pleased to know my magic helped, although I thought most of his quick recovery was due to his own inner strength.

I tried to teach him how to weave and knit, but he was terrible at both. I had never before laughed like I did as he struggled to follow my patterns.

It was not as hard to adjust to someone sharing my home as I’d thought it might be. Perhaps it was because I knew not to take such a thing for granted, cradling the precious possibilities in my heart as if I held the most fragile glass in my hands.

We held each other at night, through nightmares and in peaceful sleep.

When we kissed for the first time, I thought my heart might burst. I felt it all so clearly and yet it was overwhelming: our lips, one of his hands on my cheek and the other in my hair. My own hands in similar positions. Our bodies pressed together.

It was perfect despite our own imperfections.

In the quiet of the night, my lover’s soft breathing and heartbeat in my ears, the moon peeked through the window, a light breeze stirring the curtains. My loom cast shadows upon the floor, my knitting needles and his sword and armor glinted in the darkness.

I feared a curse and nightmares no longer. They would always be part of me, trailing me as my shadow. But I no longer had to face them alone. I no longer grieved a life not lived.

* * *

Through glory and woes,
Half made of shadows,
Draw near and fear not, – this is I,
The Lady of Shalott.

Shadows of Silvermorn

AJ Lancaster

Myr, fae King of Silvermorn Court, stared down at the letter on his desk as if it held a darker curse than the one that had ended his predecessor's reign.

Outside his office, batlings were coming in to roost, their eerie cries puncturing the ever-present mist. The legacy of Silvermorn's curse meant the days were always short here, just as the sky was always ash grey and the trees bone white.

Myr stared at the letter some more. Bellicent couldn't come *here*, could she? But that's exactly what the letter proposed, in stilted formal language. Waybloom Court would be pleased to recommend one of its finest warriors, Bellicent Fire-eyes, as his Second. Did he accept?

The carefully neutral offer had Bellicent's fingerprints all over it. He had no doubt this was her idea, giving him the option to refuse with equal neutrality.

Could he refuse?

Between the centuries of rule by his monstrous relatives, a population decimated by a dark curse, and the unnatural horrors that kept spawning, Silvermorn desperately needed experienced warriors. Especially in the palace, where the curse had struck hardest, slaying every member of the royal house down to the last scion. All except Myr, the exile who'd remained safe in an 'enemy' court. Safe in Waybloom, in fact.

He screwed his eyes shut, but that only allowed memories of the last time he'd seen Bellicent to blossom in the darkness behind his eyelids. The day he'd taken up the mantle as king, he and Bellicent had argued as never before. She hadn't understood why he needed to return to Silvermorn alone. He couldn't explain that he was hopelessly in love with her without destroying their long friendship and thus *also* couldn't explain that he needed time away in order to get over her. He'd lashed out at her for her over-protectiveness instead.

Blighted Leaves, he *missed* her. Five years was nothing in the lifespan of fae, but what was the saying? A week of war aged a person as much as ten years of peace? Cleansing Silvermorn had been a long, grim, ongoing battle. He certainly felt like a changed man: harder, stronger. Surely, he could keep his unrequited longing under control now.

He took out his quill and signed, watching the ink disappear into the parchment. Far, far away, in Waybloom Court, the same mark would be welling up on this document's twin, newly wet.

Then he went to work. Foolish to imagine he could fix Silvermorn in the next few days, and yet some part of him clung to the absurd notion of showing Bellicent a court so impressive, so beautiful, so heroically cleansed of all dark curses, that she would…what? Swoon? Bellicent had never swooned in her life.

* * *

Instead, the appointed day of Bellicent's arrival of course dawned its usual dreary grey. Myr waited in the main courtyard with his captain of the guard. Captain Vankia was his usual attentive self, but Myr heard none of his report. Myr's attention was fixed on the flash of green in the sky, drawing closer. His heart beat in time with her wings.

When Bellicent landed, he lost the ability to breathe.

Dark eyes, fierce as a hawk. Burnt umber wings tipped with gold. Lush green hair in a hundred shades of forest. Brown skin glowing with exertion. In the faded land of Silvermorn, she seemed impossibly vivid, luxuriously alive.

Bellicent grinned as if it had been five minutes rather than five years since they'd last seen each other and leaped to embrace him. Her body pressed against his, and every nerve ending lit up.

Vankia gave an outraged squawk at the breach of protocol.

"Myr," she said. Just that single word, thick with warmth, before stepping back as if the world hadn't exploded into dizzying sensation. She grinned. "Miss me?"

Fire-sprites danced over his entire body, as if he were a youth swallowing his first glass of night wine. He hadn't been this touch sensitive before. How was it so much worse after all this time apart?

A trace of a frown appeared between Bellicent's brows. "Myr? Or I should say, Your Majesty, shouldn't I?"

He found his voice. "No – not that. Not you. You are welcome to Silvermorn, Bellicent of Waybloom."

Bellicent cocked her head, the angle so familiar it sent a wave of yearning through him. "Am I truly?"

He refused to have this conversation in front of his court, brief though it might be. "Fly with me?"

"I can accompany you, Sire, if you wish for exercise," Vankia put in, dark wings twitching.

The corner of Bellicent's mouth turned up. "I don't think you're invited, my brave bat."

* * *

She truly hadn't planned to start their reunion by offending Myr's captain in the first two minutes. Dammit. The sight of Myr had thrown her more than she'd anticipated – as had her own fiercely possessive reaction. *Lock it down, girl.* Myr, with his impossibly perfect cut-flower beauty and air of haunted fragility, had been courted and coveted by anyone with eyeballs from the day he'd stepped into Waybloom. He'd hated it, and she'd always sworn not to add to that burden. His friendship was more important than any wistful attraction.

Myr remained silent until they got above the clouds, soaring over Silvermorn's unsettlingly edged architecture. "It would be helpful if you could avoid insulting my staff; they're not so plentiful I can afford for them to quit the court in a huff."

"I know; I'm sorry. I shouldn't have teased him. Boy was just eyeing you like a bee guarding a flower it wants to pollinate, if you know what I mean."

Myr grimaced. "I know."

She gave him a sideways look. "Need me to knock him upside the head?"

He scowled. "I don't need you to defend my honour like a helpless baby bird, Bell." His words held an echo of the last topic they'd argued over.

"I know you don't; I didn't mean to make you think I doubted your strength. It just felt like the sort of thing that might be more politic for your Second to handle. Keep your kingly dignity out of it."

Myr snorted. "I had no idea you harboured such respect for my kingly dignity."

"Just in case you want to start developing some," she told him seriously, earning another laugh. After a moment, she admitted, "It's still strange to think of you as a king. But I really do mean to be a proper Second. Assuming you're not kicking me straight back out again after that fabulous beginning."

Myr shook his head, but he seemed as unnaturally subdued as the landscape they flew over. Eerie forests surrounded the palace, bristling with bony trees that probably drank blood as a hobby.

"I need to tell you something," he said. "Silvermorn didn't Choose me."

Bellicent just managed to avoid dropping out of the sky in shock. "*What!?*"

Myr explained how the curse that had taken out his entire awful family had sent parts of Silvermorn into permanent shadow. His theory was that it had shocked the faeland badly enough to sink it into a state resembling stasis – the frozen cursed sleep of fairytales. He hadn't yet been able to wake it, but as the only remaining member of the bloodline connected to the land, it was *assumed* that he must be its next Chosen ruler.

"We're still dealing with occasional cursed creatures coming from the shadowed parts of Silvermorn. My hope is that if we can eradicate them, get enough *un*-cursed energy into the faeland, it might wake up again."

Neither of them brought up the other possibility; that the faeland might never wake, or that it might not Choose Myr even if it did. She didn't know what would happen in that case. Would the faeland cease to exist entirely?

* * *

Captain Vankia met them the moment they returned to the palace. "Sire! Scholar Skven was just attacked down in the undercroft! It looks like a cursed attack."

Myr stiffened. "Status?"

"Alive, but unconscious. Claw wounds, and he's lost a lot of blood. Sucked out of him rather than spilled. The healers say he's unlikely to wake up any time soon. He's under restraints in the healing wing."

"Why is he under restraints?" she broke in.

"Sometimes bites from cursed creatures are only dangerous to the person bitten, but sometimes it makes them dangerous to others as well. I thought we'd entirely cleared the palace, but one must have gotten back in somehow. The palace wards?" He directed the question at Vankia.

"We haven't found a breach yet."

Bellicent surreptitiously studied Myr as he arranged for hunting parties to begin the search for the cursed creature. It reassured her to see him so competent and assured in his role, and yet…a selfish part of her howled at the proof that he really hadn't needed her here. Had in fact been thriving without her.

Except – Myr was tense as they headed into the bowels of the palace, tense as a dry twig ready to snap under the slightest pressure. Tense in a way that reminded her far too much of his initial Waybloom days – constantly adjusting so as not to accidentally touch anything or anyone. It had taken decades for the ingrained touch aversion to ease, for him to feel safe beyond the horrors of his family's torture.

The tall, narrow door to the lower levels caused Myr to hug his wings in even more tightly. Not the slightest edge of a feather brushed the frame. Bellicent ducked after him, unsure what to think.

The undercroft made her shoulder blades itch with its sheer number of hiding places. Far too many shadowy nooks for her liking.

"Skven was searching the archives for clues on how to cleanse Silvermorn of the curse's remnants," Myr told her.

"Do we know what caused the curse?" Speculation had run rife through Faerie in the wake of Silvermorn's fall, but no official version of events had ever been announced.

"A blood magic ritual gone wrong, we think. There were no survivors at the epicentre, so we may never be sure exactly what my father was hoping to achieve. But we know it involved sacrificing others of royal blood. Personally, I think the ritual was merely the tipping point after centuries of dripping slow evil into the ley lines. It's hardly the first time my family has committed murder. Perhaps Silvermorn had simply had enough of our hubris."

"You're nothing like them," Bellicent said, immediate and fierce.

He subconsciously touched the scar hidden at the nape of his neck, a familiar gesture of unease. It took a lot for fae to scar. "No. But I may not be what Silvermorn wants either."

The archive where the scholar had been working was stuffed with crates, some open and some still closed, a scene caught mid-unpacking. On Skven's desk, an inkstand had tipped over, and a pool of black spread across the floor, merging with a liquid much redder in hue, the surface still wet enough to capture reflections. The coppery smell of blood thickened the air, and spatters of it glistened wetly here and there.

"How big are these cursed creatures?" she asked, inspecting a crate as big as a person and feeling relieved to find it empty.

"Whatever size the original creature was, before it came out of the shadowed areas. We've had everything from horses to wolves to rats. The curse often makes animals larger." He grimaced. "We found a cursed ant once that had swollen to the size of a melon."

She whistled. "Giant cursed ants. Lovely. What about people?"

"Some people, too, at the very beginning. There haven't been more since we mapped the shadowed areas."

Falling into an efficient search pattern without needing to discuss it, they went over the room inch by inch. Their easy synchronisation heartened her, but they found no sign of the cursed creature.

They began to sweep the rest of the undercroft. Beyond the scholar's workroom lay a long gallery crowded so thickly with tall vases and sculptures that she had to edge sideways in places. The sculptures were of belua fae, more bestial than humanoid, beautiful but tormented – and casting shadows far too much like figures crouching in ambush.

"Creepy," she commented, examining the snarling face of a particularly gruesome figure carved in black stone.

Myr sighed deeply. "They used to sit in the main courtyard. At least here I don't have to look at them."

"Is there a reason you didn't cast them straight into a volcano?"

"Apparently they're extremely rare and valuable, made by a demigod sculptor a thousand years ago who might still be around to take offense at the destruction of their creations."

"Unfortunate." Bellicent's attention flicked to a shadow where there shouldn't have been one. She took a step closer—

"Bell! Move!"

She was already moving to meet the second shadow attacking from the side. She whirled away from scrabbling claws, summoning her sword, but before she could strike, metal blurred through the air. A high-pitched squeal abruptly cut off.

She stared down at the enormous, misshapen rat at her feet. It was about the size of a terrier, and its fangs dripped black liquid. One of Myr's daggers quivered dead-centre in its head.

"I told you to move!" Myr's voice was sharp.

"I did move," she objected.

But Myr's face whitened, his horrified gaze fixed on the rip in her sleeve. His remaining dagger clattered to the ground as he closed the distance between them. "Take it off!"

She frowned. "What?"

"Take it off so I can check it didn't infect you. Even a scratch can pass on the curse."

Bellicent rolled her eyes but started unbuttoning. "Usually people buy me dinner first," she quipped, moving away from the dead rat. She flung her shirt aside, leaving her in only her practical bandeau.

Thanks to their warrior training together, she and Myr had seen each other in various states of undress many times. This ought to feel perfectly mundane. And yet, the time apart had shifted something essential between them, made it harder to shut down awareness of him as a man. She patted her bared stomach, covering the traitorous flutter with brash humour. "See? I'm clean. The rat didn't touch me. I'm still a wet dream to behold."

Myr's expression had gone odd, his eyes alive with fractured light. If it had been literally anyone else, she would've called it hunger. But Myr didn't look at anyone like that, least of all her.

He turned away, picking up his sword and methodically slicing open the dead rat's stomach. "Not enough blood," he said grimly. "Plus, it doesn't look large enough to have chewed Skven up so badly. This can't be what attacked him."

She'd forgotten all about the rat and the attack, caught in Myr's eyes. Right. Priorities. She replaced her shirt. "I thought I saw a second shadow before."

An additional search of the gallery turned up nothing. Empty-handed, they emerged into the dreary daylight, only to run straight into an alarmed Captain Vankia. "Sire, there's been another attack!"

* * *

The second victim, this time one of the palace guards, lay in the infirmary beside Skven. Both fae were swathed in bandages and unmoving but for the faintest rise and fall of their chests. Myr's own chest tightened.

"They won't wake?" he asked.

The healer shook their head. "The curse has taken hold of them both. It's stronger than anything we've seen in years."

He swallowed. "Let me try." Putting his hands on Skven's barely moving chest, he closed his eyes and attempted to summon Silvermorn, to share the faeland's power with one of his people. Beside him, Bellicent watched with silent concern.

Of course nothing happened. Of course he was no use at all.

He shook his head, shame acrid in the back of his throat. Thanking the healer, he left the infirmary, taking flight as soon as they were outside.

Bellicent followed him up to land on the tallest tower, where he glared down at the palace complex in a futile attempt to force it to reveal the location of the creature. She laid her wing over his, and he recoiled, his whole body humming from the touch.

"I didn't mean to startle you," she said after an awkward pause.

He knew she'd meant the gesture in comfort, could have no idea the effect it would have on him, touch-starved as he was.

"It's fine." He kept himself angled away, afraid she would see his reaction, willing himself to think of ice showers, willing Bellicent to leave it. He nearly groaned as her expression shifted from concern to determination, because of course Bellicent never backed down.

"Myr, I want to apologise," she said.

He frowned. "You really don't need to apologise for startling me."

"Not that. Well, not only that," she said. "I should have apologised properly as soon as I got here. I was over-protective, before. I *did* treat you as fragile. I'm sorry for that. It wasn't because I doubted your abilities – it was because I was so afraid of you being hurt again after what your family did to you. I hated that you didn't want me to accompany you here when you ascended, but not because I thought you couldn't thrive without me hovering at your back."

Blight, if only she knew, but he couldn't let her take the blame for their split. "I *was* fragile. You were there for me when I needed you."

Bellicent shook her head. "You survived something designed to break you. That's strength. I was the one who was fragile, trying to wrap you in cotton wool because the idea of losing you scared me so much."

He didn't deserve this faith. If he was strong, he wouldn't have needed to run away to control his feelings, wouldn't still yearn for something he couldn't have. Wouldn't be unable to wake his kingdom or save his subjects.

"I missed you," she whispered, offering an up-turned palm.

He slid his hand into hers and squeezed, trying to ignore the wave of heat the touch sent through him. "I missed you too."

"Let's go find your cursed monstrosity, then. Do you have a map?"

* * *

"I want to sweep this area again," Bellicent said, putting a finger on an intersection between ley lines in the water gardens on the map that Myr had found for her. "Easy spot to tap into the ley lines; plenty of hiding places. There's a direct roofline route here from where the most recent attack was."

The phrase 'water gardens' had conjured pleasant visions of tranquil waters amid verdant pools, but of course she ought to have known better. There *was* water, but it was dark and brackish, the plants sickly and yellowing.

The raked paths crunched under their boots as they searched between arched bridges and rust-stained walls. At least the smooth, abstract garden sculptures were nothing like the deformed monsters in the vault.

Except that one. Her attention caught on a statue on top of a pile of rocks. She drew her sword.

"Bell?" Myr asked, immediately sensing her mood shift.

She gestured with her blade. "That statue. There was one just like it in the creepy statue gallery on the lower levels."

They exchanged glances, and Myr drew his own sword this time. She wanted to tell Myr to stay back, that she would go first, but held back from voicing it. She'd promised not to treat him as fragile. "Want me to watch your back?" she asked instead.

She couldn't read Myr's expression, but there was something intense in it. "Always," he said.

Myr drew closer to the snarling statue. The creepily lifelike composition of a malformed fae beast in black stone had bat-like wings and a long rat's tail. Its hind legs were those of a gargoyle, with large, fearsome talons.

Myr aimed the point of his blade at the statue, but the statue moved before he could tap it. Springing to life, it swiped at Myr, who blocked the blow as its tail whipped, wrapped around Myr's ankle, and toppled him. Myr's hiss of pain made something go red inside her.

She charged, but the thing launched itself off Myr with a brutal kick of its hind legs and soared across the garden. She raced after it, dodging plants and stupid aesthetic sculptures. Drawing a dagger from thin air, she threw, straight and true.

The dagger bounced off the creature's neck with a sound like a struck hammer. Its stone-like skin took no damage. Blades would be no use.

Good thing she was Waybloom's finest warrior. Disappearing her sword, she called in a mace. Bludgeoning it was, then.

When the statue shot straight up, she followed, hitting hard at its wings and sending stone fragments splashing into the pool below. The creature shrieked as it lost flight capability, the sound like nails scratching down glass. It landed heavily, snarling.

She landed beside it a moment later, and it leapt for her with its claws out. Calmly, she slammed the creature right in the throat. She kept slamming, smashing stone pieces free with every blow, taking grim satisfaction from pounding it to powder.

She turned back. Myr lay propped up against the rocks, deep gashes marring his chest, his blood obscenely bright against the dull grass. The bottom dropped out of her world. She was next to Myr in a heartbeat.

His face had drained of all colour. "Too damn slow," he slurred. A fae of Myr's age and power should already be half-healed. But instead, the wounds were turning a mottled grey at the edges. The curse.

"Myr!" Hardly knowing what she was doing, she slashed a long shallow cut across her palm and pressed it against Myr's chest. She wasn't of this faeland, and he wasn't properly bonded to it in any case, but there were other ways to share power. Through the mingling blood, she poured her strength into him, heedless of risk.

"No, Bell, it'll take you too—" he slurred, feebly trying to stop her, but the curse was pulling him under. "I'm not worth it—"

"You are worth *everything*," she hissed. "And I'll be damned if I lose you."

But she was losing herself. She could feel her magic sputtering out, pain flaring along her nervous system as she kept drawing power through the shadowed ley lines, ignoring her body's warning signals. The world went dark.

* * *

Myr's heart started beating again, except it was a heart far larger than his own. Vast, ancient, powerful: Silvermorn. The magic of the faeland flooded him, pushing out the darkness, and he came to, gasping. The faeland had finally woken, and he didn't know why—

—and then he did, ancient knowledge blossoming in his mind in answer to his silent question. The faeland, so deeply tainted by darkness, had been forced to retreat. A powerful cleansing had been needed.

Cleansing? Myr asked Silvermorn.

Sacrifice. Blood of hate; blood of love.

Understanding came, horror following on its heels. His blood. Bell's blood. She'd been willing to sacrifice herself to save him, the act the diametric opposite of everything his family had done here. He opened his eyes and found her body collapsed against his.

Save her, he told the land grimly, but Silvermorn had needed no such instruction. Silver-tipped power flowed through him, and petals rained down upon Bellicent's prone form. They covered her body in a drift of soft blossom-pink.

His heart stopped and didn't start again until she gasped. Shedding petals, she sat up so quickly they nearly knocked heads.

"Myr?" She was touching him, frantic, finding only fading scars where his wounds had been. And then she was taking his face in her hands and kissing him, fierce and desperate, shocking him down to his bones. She attempted to pull away after a moment, recalling herself, but he stopped her, wrapping a hand possessively around her waist in order to kiss her back.

They broke apart.

"You want me," he said, not quite daring to believe it.

Her eyes shone like stars. "Oh, we are idiots."

The kiss this time went on for some time, until someone politely coughed and then repeated their cough, less politely.

They reluctantly disentangled themselves.

"Yes?" Myr asked, feeling that everything short of another curse could bloody well wait.

Captain Vankia looked supremely uncomfortable. "Ah, Sire, I thought you would want to see this." He gestured.

The faded, ash-grey colours of Silvermorn were no more. Instead, the landscape unfurled green as far as the eye could see, the silver palace towers shining in the bright sunlight. And all around them, flowers bloomed.

Ring of Wax, Armor of Bone

Jessica Lévai

Once upon a time, during one of those wars that ravage a country and leave no good in their wake, a young witch lived in a cottage in the wood. She had been alone since the death of her mother not long ago, and had taken up her role as a local healer. One day, a horse bearing an armored rider stumbled through her wood. The witch peered out the window of her cottage and gasped at the sight of it tromping into her yard. She pulled away from the window, her heart thudding in her chest. Then, grabbing an iron poker from the fireplace, she stepped out into the sun to investigate.

"These woods are protected!" She had meant to shout this at the rider, but it came out a choked whisper. Blushing angrily, she stumbled through the rest of her speech. "Keep the wars and destruction of men away from my home, or I shall..." She stopped cold as the rider fell out of the saddle to lie in a heap at the horse's feet. Lowering the poker, she approached the fallen rider carefully. The figure on the ground lay still, though the dented and rusty armor creaked a little with breath. The witch tapped the helmet a few times and received no response. She angled the poker just so and lifted the helmet off the rider's head. She peered at the brown hair this revealed, and felt with her fingers for signs of life. The heartbeat was strong, yes, though the exposed skin bore an expected host of bruises and cuts. Something about the face was not expected, and the witch turned the chin a little roughly to get a better look.

"Oh," she said, examining the rider's jaw and figure. "Not just men, I see." The witch pursed her lips and looked at the horse, who returned her gaze with an animal's calm. She looked back at the rider, tugging away the breastplate – the wounds were worse than they first appeared. When the part of the witch that hated to see suffering at last bested the part that hated soldiers, she said aloud, "Well, come on then!" and dragged the rider toward her house while the horse followed.

* * *

The knight awoke to the smell of stew: meat, onion, herbs, and something a little harder mixed into the broth. It was a smell of home and safety, of plenty and warmth on a cold winter's night, and it drew her from the bed before she had a chance to realize that she had no idea where she was, or in whose bed. The knowledge arrived with the pain of her bruised ribs, and she fell back into the bed with a whimper, deciding to enjoy the aroma lying down, for now.

"You're awake," said a voice. It sounded familiar, the way a dream is familiar.

The knight did not trust herself to stand, so from the bed she called out, "Where am I?"

"You are in my house," the voice replied, the corresponding face swimming into view. The face belonged to a woman about the knight's own age, with hair the color of the sky at dawn. The knight blinked, rubbed her eyes, and looked hard as the face smiled at her. It was a shy smile, charming. As comforting as the promise of food, but more wonderful.

"Forgive me for intruding on you like this," the knight said, ever mindful of her manners. "There was a mighty battle, a league or two from here. I made a poor showing..." She broke off, feeling the bruised spots with her fingers. Already the pain was ebbing. "My fellow warriors warned me a witch lived in these woods. And by the state of my injuries, I must assume that you are she, and that you have healed me. But why?"

The witch answered, "Let us say you weren't the person I expected to find in the armor. I figured you had a story to tell, and if you died, I wouldn't be able to hear it."

The knight flushed. "My name is Loren, and you have my gratitude. I am at your service."

"Enough of that for now," said the witch. "Come, eat your stew, and tell me your story."

Loren, grateful, ate three bowls of the stew. The witch watched her eat, asking no questions, but eventually Loren's story emerged. She was an only child and wanted nothing more than to fight and win honor. She had bought her armor for a dear price, but it was old and battered from its service to its previous owner. This recent battle had been her first, and since she kept her identity secret from the other soldiers, she had no true friends to help her.

In her turn the witch, who called herself Anise, told how she was the youngest of seven sisters, all scattered now. How she was the last to live in their mother's cottage and tend to the garden, brewing healing potions and telling fortunes for those who sought her services. How her mother had been brave and powerful, and how Anise feared she would never be her match. Over the course of three weeks they shared not only more stories of themselves, but how lonely it was on the paths they had chosen. The days were tiring, the nights cool and empty. As the sun set on the fourth week, Anise lit tapers and Loren ventured, cautiously, into the woods to gather kindling. Together they stoked the fire until the inside of the cabin was as merry as it had ever been. The moon was high in the sky when they ran out of stories to tell, and they debated who would sleep in the bed that night. Anise insisted her patient still needed rest; Loren was certain she had imposed enough. In the end, they shared it, and found they did not need words any more.

* * *

The next morning, Loren awoke with memories of bliss and a few new bruises. The cottage was full of sunlight, but the bed was empty. Gingerly she arranged herself and threw on a shift that had been left for her. She breathed in deep, testing the pain in her ribs. Once again something in the cottage smelled delicious, this time like wildflowers in a meadow. She hoped it was breakfast.

"Good morning," said Anise, emerging from behind a screen, fully dressed and dazzling, despite some dark circles under her eyes. "There is food for you, but first, I wanted you to see. I… I made something for you." She took Loren by the hands and led her behind the screen, where something was hidden under a length of muslin, and said, "Take a look."

Loren carefully lifted the muslin and was rewarded with that sweet smell again, stronger. Under the sheet stood a breastplate, gauntlets, greaves, and a helmet. The pieces glowed a golden ivory color in the sunlight. Loren touched the helmet with a single finger. It felt warm, almost alive.

"I fashioned these while you slept," said Anise.

"Out of what?" asked Loren, unable to take her eyes away from the armor.

"Beeswax," the witch replied. "And quite a bit of magic."

Loren's awe dribbled away, but Anise looked so proud, she didn't want to say anything to her about the practicality of the armor. Instead she said, "It is certainly lovely, and must have taken a great deal of work."

"But you wonder if it will hold up on the battlefield. Well, let's try it on you and see if it fits, first." Together they angled the breastplate over Loren's head and eased it into position, the witch pulling the straps tight. Loren moved her arms slowly at first, then with more vigor. The armor fit like a second skin. She reached for the helmet and lowered it onto her head. The scent of the beeswax refreshed her. She closed her eyes to enjoy it, and thus was surprised when she felt a slight thud against the side of the helmet. She opened her eyes to see the witch holding the iron fireplace poker and grinning.

"I assure you, the magic that holds these pieces together is strong," she said.

Loren gaped. "I can't believe your magic could do this!"

Anise smiled shyly. "Neither could I, before today. But you inspired me, and… I can hit you again, if you like."

Loren smiled. "Give it all your strength!"

After a few more minutes of testing the armor, the two were exhausted, and hungry. As they were about to remove the plates, Loren said, "You have aided me beyond any obligation or expectation. I will wear this armor with pride, and dedicate my victories to you."

"I don't want warlike victories," said Anise in reproach. "I only want you."

Loren was sad. "I must defend my king. But when the war is over, I will return to you, and stay."

Anise kissed her gently on the lips. Then she scraped the bottom of the breastplate with a long fingernail, golden wax curling away from the armor. She took the wax and breathed on it to soften it, then fashioned it into a ring, which she slipped onto her own finger.

"I'll wear this ring as a pledge. When the war is over, return to me."

"I swear it," Loren replied.

* * *

The knight rode to join her fellows the following morning. The armor the witch had made held true, and as the war dragged on, Loren was safe from all harm and went on to win much glory. Back in her cottage in the wood, Anise wore the ring and waited for her love to return.

There were many who noticed the sudden skill and luck the knight possessed on the battlefield. One of them was a cousin of the king, lord of a once-prestigious house which had fallen on hard times. He took note of the knight in the golden armor, who never removed his helmet. Who never drank with his companions. And the more this one succeeded, the more bitter and angry the lord became, and determined to learn his secret.

The knight was friendly and as gracious in his victory as one could hope, and the lord did not lack for cleverness. But no amount of cajoling, joking, or confiding could reveal the origin of the golden armor. The lord was about to give up, when he conceived another avenue of attack.

One evening, after the knight in the golden armor had once again saved his life, the two of them stood warming themselves by a fire. The lord said, "I wonder that a strong fighter like you has no woman waiting for him back home."

The knight was quiet about this for a long time, then replied softly, "I do have someone waiting for me. I fight so I may see her again, and her faithfulness and love give me strength."

"Where did you meet this wonderful creature?" the lord asked. "And when?" But the knight grew sheepish and would say no more for the rest of the night.

The lord asked around. He collected rumors about a disastrous battle, and a witch who lived in a certain wood. He slipped away, retraced the army's path, and spent three days and nights searching until he came to a cottage in the middle of a clearing. Certain that he had found the healer's home, he took a deep breath and cut a long gash in his leg with his dagger. He did not feign his cry of pain, though he was able to discard the dagger before the witch emerged from the cottage.

She was beautiful, with hair like the dawn. He smiled upon seeing her, as warmly as he could manage with his life spilling on the grass. "Please," he asked, "tend my wound, and I shall pay you whatever you like."

The witch saw the blood and the lord's pained expression. She moved quickly, expertly binding his wound and pulling him to his feet. He leaned on her small but strong frame and let her lead him inside her home, where she gave him a tea to drink. As she did so, he spied the ring of pale gold on her finger and the smell of wildflowers.

"Tell me about the ring you wear," he said to her. "Was it given by a sweetheart?"

The witch fingered the ring, and her eyes were distant for a moment. Then she said, "I have a beloved who is away at war, and this is the link between us."

"And you are faithful to him?" the lord asked, a touch too interested in the answer. The witch fixed him with cold eyes, and he retreated quickly. "I am sorry," the lord said. "It has been a long campaign, and in my pain I forgot myself. I shall leave directly after we eat, but…do you have anything that might help me sleep?"

The witch's face softened, and she went to her table, selecting herbs and grinding them. She presented him with a vial and he thanked her. As they ate, the lord tried to engage the witch in conversation, but her mind was clearly elsewhere. He took no offense. It made it much easier to put the sleeping draught in her cup.

Once his host was sleeping soundly, he scraped some chunks of wax from a taper on the table and worked it until he had formed a ring. The smell of wildflowers filled the lord's nose and he carefully, gently, removed the wax ring from her finger and replaced it with the one he had made. He let himself out of the cottage and was gone, true to his word.

Upon catching up with the army, the lord immediately sought out his companions to tell them of his adventure. Certain the knight with the golden armor was listening, he said, "And then the witch and I passed an evening together.

In gratitude and love, she gave me this ring." He held the wax ring aloft, so the sun made it glow and the smell of honey wafted from it.

The other soldiers laughed coarsely, but the knight in the golden armor was silent. "Who was the lady?" someone asked the lord.

He smiled. "Truly, I never learned her name. She was a healer who lived in a cottage in the woods twenty leagues away." The lord's smile turned sharp. "It's a pretty little thing, like its owner, but neither ultimately seems worth keeping." He turned to the knight, now trembling in the golden armor, and said, "Would you like it? Match that suit of yours." This invited another hoot of laughter from the lord's audience. The knight in the golden armor snatched the ring and drew away to an isolated corner of the camp.

Once she was certain she was alone, Loren tore off her helmet and let herself sob. This was indeed the ring made from her armor's wax, the token she had left with Anise. Perhaps it had all been a feint. Perhaps there were no real feelings between them. Perhaps Loren was as foolish in love as she had been in her desire to be a warrior in the first place.

A horn sounded. Heralds ran through the camp, exclaiming "To your horses, men! Ambush!" Arrows streaked through the air, and Loren slammed her helmet back on her head: angrily, but in time. She ran to her horse and mounted it, the ring still clutched in her sword hand. The wax was beautiful and fragrant and made her heart ache. So she guided her horse swiftly to the nearest cooking fire, and dropped the ring in the flames.

* * *

Anise awoke in her darkened cottage. The fire had gone out, and her guest was nowhere to be seen. She suspected the reason for her sleep, and cursed him. She relit the fire and inspected the cottage by its light. Everything was as it had been. He had not robbed her. He had not…but then she touched the ring on her finger and cried out in surprise. The ring was cold.

No, not cold. For the ring had been cold, those nights when Loren was camped under the stars in unforgiving wind. And the ring had warmed, when she did battle under the sun. It nearly glowed when she and the witch thought of each other. In this way had the witch traveled with Loren, and known her struggles and victories. But now, the ring gave her nothing. It was dead.

She pulled it from her finger and took it to the window to examine it. This ring was wax, but rougher than the one she had made. She remembered how the lord had looked at her ring, asked her questions, and distracted her. Anger surged in her chest and she slammed her fist on the table. There were ways she might punish the thief, but first, she needed to find her love.

This need was complicated by the lack of the proper token. As her mother had taught her, the witch scrabbled up some of the smaller bones from dinner the night before and cast them, but this yielded two answers, one more definite and the other just confusing. She decided to try the first, and packed a bag of provisions for the trip.

Through the forest she traveled and once she emerged, she simply had to follow the path of destruction the king's army had left behind it. For months, scavengers avian and human had been hard at work. There was little left to see. The witch trudged on. She came at last to an encampment where the scars of battle were fresher and the crows more numerous. There were no living human souls as far as she could see, but her stomach cramped with a kind of expectation and she knew she need go no further. She investigated the murder of crows, looking at the remains when they scattered. Not here. Not here.

Here.

The cold mud seeped through her skirt and cooled her skin. The birds cawed impatiently, but she did not stir. Here was her Loren, a puddle of golden wax surrounding her, an arrow protruding from her back.

Anise did not cry, though her eyes burned. She did not scream, though her teeth were on edge, to bite someone. She pulled the bones from her pocket and cast them. Again. Again. Eventually she was satisfied with the answer, and the one remaining path.

* * *

Her mother had taught her about the many entrances to the land of the dead. Some were small and secret, admitting only one at a time. But so close to a battle and its carnage, the door was thrown open so wide that even the living might pass through. So it was that noon when Anise saw a shadow where there should be none, and heard a sound like rushing water when even the blood in the field had dried to dust. She approached. The sound grew louder, the shadow darker, and she was through.

At first the sun lit her path. Before her, stairs shone slick and dangerous. Anise went down and down and down. Behind her the sunlight faded and winked out. She conjured fire and continued her path. Her love was here and she had to find her, but this land was vast and her light feeble. A gust from somewhere blew it out.

"You are neither expected nor welcome here, witch."

Anise heard a familiar strength in this voice, though it had been stripped of its warmth. Slowly a thin light suffused the space, and the witch made out a knight in full armor before her. When the helmet was removed, the witch recognized Loren, and her heart broke. She ran to the knight, who neither approached nor fled, and touched the armor. It glowed pale like the moon and made a rasping sound when she brushed it with her finger, for it was constructed of the cold bones of dead men.

Anise, her hand trembling, brushed Loren's cheek, which was colder. "My love?" she asked.

"Am I?" Loren replied, her voice echoing awfully in the deep dark. "You gave that love away. Look to your finger."

Anise covered the false ring with her hand. "There was a young lord who came to me." At this, Loren turned her face away. "I was deceived," Anise continued, understanding. "We both were. The ring was stolen from me but you…" She choked on the word. "You threw it away. You lost faith, and we have lost everything." Angry, desperate tears fell on her cheeks.

Loren's eyes were dry, for the dead do not weep. But she hung her head and said, "It doesn't matter. We both wear the tokens of others, and I am Death's knight now."

"But Death has gotten you unfairly."

"Have I?" responded Death. For Death is always close, whether we are in that realm or ours, and now her soft voice hummed in Anise's ear. "Perhaps. But what is that to me? That lord came to the borders of my lands on several occasions, but this one saved him. Or you healed him. There is nothing more for you but to say goodbye."

"I will not leave her!" the witch cried.

Death's voice turned adamant. "I am not particular about my guests, but the living may not stay. You tax my patience as it is."

"Then I shall join her in the usual way," said Anise, but her voice held a touch of uncertainty.

"You will not," said Loren, and she took Anise's hand in her gauntlet. "You are alive, and free, and I want you to remain that way for as long as you can. Death must have a champion, and I am rightfully hers. Let it be, and we will see each other soon."

"Yes," said Anise, a thought and a plan taking shape in her mind, "but not soon enough."

* * *

A commotion at his castle door disturbed the lord from his rest. He hadn't yet recovered from injuries he had sustained during the ambush, not to mention his disappointment that, in the fighting, he had not been able to locate his rival or the golden armor. He pulled his robe tightly around himself and went to see what the fuss was about.

"There is a woman to see you," his chamberlain said, matching his step as he stormed down the hall. "She will not be put off until morning, and she claims..."

"Yes?"

"She claims she is your betrothed."

The lord pushed through the crowd of his men surrounding the woman in question. The witch from the wood, her clothes dripping from the rain outside and her boots caked with mud, sank to her knees at his feet.

"What are you doing here?" he asked.

"Where else would I be?" she asked, through tears. She showed him the ring on her hand. "Did you forget that you gave me your ring?"

The lord paled, just perceptibly. He pulled the witch to her feet and led her down the hall, where he might speak to her alone. She went without resisting.

"You should not be here," he said. "I realize that I owe you for treating my injury. I can spare you some clean clothes, perhaps a room for the night, but..."

"I treated your injury because helping travelers is what I do," said the witch, sadly. "You don't owe me for that. You owe me for my heart, which you stole when you left."

"You don't mean..." But she looked at him with such hope, he began to believe it. And he saw that she was more beautiful than he remembered, and something stirred in him. He was at times a man easily distracted by women, yet here he was wary. "You have a love already, do you not?"

She shuddered. "My love is dead."

"I am sorry," the lord said, surprised to find the emotion true. He reached for the witch's hand, only to catch her as she fainted.

* * *

The witch was a week in the lord's castle. He saw her infrequently the first days; he was a busy man. But as they passed in the hallways, or sat across a massive table for dinner, she did not take her eyes off him. This flattered him. He ordered flowers and jewels be brought to her. She wove them into her hair, becoming more lovely. He created excuses to cross her path more often, and she smiled when he did. He wrote letters full of feeling, which he then hid or burned.

On the seventh night, after ordering his servants to leave that she and he might dine alone, the lord heard the witch say, "You have been generous to me. I want to give you something in return."

"What did you have in mind?"

"I would like to build you a suit of armor."

This was unexpected, and the lord hesitated. "I have armor."

"Not as I can build it. The armor I have in mind will not fail you, and will enable you to escape such injuries as you have been prone to." And her gaze flicked to where he had cut himself on his thigh.

"Wait," he said. "Was it you who built the golden armor for my rival, using your magic? Magic that failed him when he needed it the most."

A cloud passed over the witch's face, and was gone. "Perhaps, after receiving you in my home, it failed by my design."

The lord considered. He was a long way from regaining his family's honor. His mishaps in battle had become a joke he could no longer ignore. "What will you require?" he asked.

"Time and privacy."

The lord assented, and the witch shut herself up in the room she had chosen for herself. Through the night there were strange sounds through the walls, and a smell like brimstone and old leather. The lord posted guards, and berated them when they abandoned their assignment. But when he himself stood at the door he felt an unearthly chill, like all the life was being drawn from the air. After that, he no longer insisted on guards.

After three nights, the witch emerged. She sent for the lord who, with some trepidation, entered the chamber. The smell had dissipated, and the air was no colder than the rest of the castle. He gasped at the spells sketched on the floor and walls in ink and chalk, and soon settled his gaze on the armor displayed in the middle of the room.

It was not as she had made for his rival. This armor glowed silver, like the moon. It was cool to the touch. He tapped it, and thought he heard an echo through eternity.

"You mustn't be afraid of it," said the witch, a little playfully, "though you might cover your eyes." She took his sword from him and dealt the armor a mighty blow. The lord's hands flew to protect his face as the weapon shattered. "There is nothing stronger than this armor," she said, dropping the hilt to the floor with a clang. She looked at him. "Do you want it?"

The lord was awed by what he had seen. "How do I know it will not fail me, by your design?"

The witch smiled. "A wise question. The knight of the golden armor forswore a pledge to me, and so the armor failed. But you don't strike me as someone to break an oath. Come. Let's try it on."

The lord accepted the witch's help and together they assembled the armor around him. The fit was perfect, as if the armor had been waiting for him. The witch finished tightening the straps and handed him the helmet. Cool like the rest of the armor, it nevertheless sat comfortably on his head.

"Now you must make your pledge," said the witch, moving from his blind spot to stand before him. "The armor cannot be yours without it. Do you swear your service to its maker, now and forever?"

"I do," said the lord. The armor grew a little more snug around him, and he tested the straps. "Forever. But how do you take it off?"

The witch stepped back and folded her arms across her chest. "You don't."

The lord pulled harder and harder at the armor, tried to prise the helmet from his head. It wouldn't budge. Sweat trickled down his back as he struggled. The armor only pressed more. There was a force drawing him, dragging his feet against the floor. In the midst of his desperation he could see the writing on the floor glow and shift. He screamed, and then could see nothing at all.

* * *

"It does seem a waste of excellent armor," said Loren, as she and the witch sorted through the pile of clothing on the floor for something to cover the now alive but quite armorless knight.

“He’ll have plenty of use for it where he’s going,” said Anise, tossing her beloved a tunic and some shoes. “And anyway, I could make you something even stronger.”

“Stronger than the armor of Death?” said Loren, checking her reflection in the mirror.

“Of course,” said the witch, coming to stand behind her. “The armor of Love.”

Loren winced and began to weep. “I’m so sorry…” she began, but Anise stopped the words with a kiss.

“Enough of that,” she said, pulling on a cloak. And taking her love by the hand, they fled the castle together.

The Hedge Knight Drinks

M. McNamara

Anais was hunting a demon named Zed. And she'd finally found it in the catacombs beneath the village of Blackshear.

There was just one problem: a group of bunglers was in her way.

The competition was a stupid idea; she didn't know what the mayor of Blackshear had been thinking when he made the announcement. *A gold purse to any who can slay the demon of the dark*… Half the knights in the kingdom had already tried to dispatch the beast, as had *all* the criminals; she'd seen more scallywags and lowlifes enter the Blackshear gates over the past few weeks than she had in all the slums of Steephand. Most of them had been killed; a lucky few had only been maimed.

"Don't go down there," one man had shrieked as he staggered up through the trapdoor, his arm ripped off, the socket spouting blood; he'd died shortly thereafter.

So now the only ones left were the young folk, the hopefuls, the desperate, the stupid – and her. She'd been waiting in the town for two months, watching the other challengers and collecting information from those who managed to emerge from the underground tunnels. She always asked them the same three questions:

What did the demon look like?

Where was it hiding?

And most important: *Was it holding anything?*

She received various answers. Some said it resembled a shadow; others, a creature of fire. Some swore it floated in a passage; others, that it lurked in a chamber. But they all agreed on one thing: it carried a metal flagon in its claws.

That was how Anais knew.

She swallowed at the memory of her childhood, the humble village in which she'd grown up, the cruel master who'd taken her as an apprentice...

She banished the thoughts. She wasn't that child anymore. She was a warrior, a woman who had studied demon lore in the great library of Steephand. She focused on her knowledge. Demons belonged to several classes of being. Some were mortals that had made a bad deal; others were wizards' spells that had backfired.

But the most dangerous of all were emanations, dark hungers that issued from the cracks of the world. Scholars claimed they were phantom desires of the gods themselves;

certainly their appetites were vast. Each one was associated with a physical object that reflected its nature – one carried a silver tray and deprived mortals of food; another bore a horn and deafened its victims. Such was the demon of Blackshear – or so Anais thought. It was only a stray thought at first, an unsettling suspicion, but after two months had passed, she had gathered enough evidence to convince her of this fact. Now she waited in the town square, ready to join a fresh group of challengers – ready to battle Zed.

The others were not ready. She felt a momentary stab of pity for them. It wasn't their fault they were doomed; very few people knew how to defeat a Class Three demon.

Very few people had a sword like hers.

* * *

Of course, the question remained: who *were* the other challengers?

Anais stood on the edge of the town square. It was almost noon; the others would arrive shortly. As she waited, she ran a hand along the pommel of the weapon strapped to her back. To the untrained eye, this seemed no more than a large sword. But to those few with specialized knowledge, it was something else: a weapon imbued with spellwork.

She looked up. A group of people had entered the square. For a moment they were obscured by the crowd that rushed forward, by the excited whispers. *The challengers come!* She waited patiently until the group reached the dais in the centre of the square. There were about twenty all told, men and women in various styles of garb – some in armour, others in the robes of mages, a few in nothing but humble peasant clothes. But what struck her was their age – they all looked as if they'd seen fewer than twenty summers. The mayor, however, did not seem dismayed.

"People of Blackshear, please welcome our challengers!" he called, and the crowd cheered. "It is my great honour to greet the brave warriors who will take up this quest." He went down the line as each person gave their name; then he paused, gazed out at the square. "Is there anyone else who will join them? Anyone else who will test their courage?"

You mean stupidity, Anais thought as she made her way through the crowd. She was about to call out to the mayor when a figure pushed in front of her, called out in a rough baritone.

"I will."

Anais scowled. This oaf had just cut her off!

"And who are you?" the mayor asked, focusing on the newcomer.

"My name is Bardolph."

The figure stepped up – a warrior with a silver breastplate and a head of shaggy blonde hair. He looked older than the others, perhaps closer to her own age, and had the sort of features that some might call agreeable. A few of the women in the line cast him eager smiles.

Anais disliked him immediately.

"What do you do, Bardolph?"

"I am a hedge knight."

"What's a hedge knight?" one of the children near the stage asked. The mayor chuckled. Before he could respond, Anais stepped forward.

"A knight so poor he can't afford lodging, and sleeps under hedges."

The crowd erupted into titters as Anais took one long step up to join the others. The mayor glanced at her.

"Ah, here is one more. And you are?"

"Anais." She crossed her arms, gave Bardolph a defiant glance, but he was looking the other way.

The mayor nodded. "Welcome, Bardolph and Anais! Two worthy contenders, I am sure. Any more? No? Then let us delay no longer – it is time for the next round of demon hunting to begin!"

* * *

The mayor led the crowd through the square and down the street, heading for the trapdoor beside the cemetery. "Now remember," he said to the warriors following behind, "to win the gold purse, you must slay the demon and bring back some proof of its demise before dawn. If more than one person is instrumental in the creature's death, you shall split the purse between you. Any questions?"

"Do we get a bonus if we kill it before midnight?" one brash young fellow asked.

"If you slay it before midnight, I will personally gift you a barrel of ale," the mayor replied. A few of the others boasted of their prowess then, how they could complete the deed in less time than that. Then the party reached the cemetery, and the warriors' boasting died away. The crowd, too, fell quiet as they threaded past gravestones; the reality of the quest was starting to sink in. By the time the group reached the trapdoor, all were hushed. The portal was an old wooden thing, carved with the face of a gargoyle. It did not look friendly. The silence was only broken when the mayor crouched down and threw it open.

"Let the challenge begin," he said softly.

For a moment the warriors hesitated, eyeing each other. Then Anais stepped forward. Before she could pass through the door, however, someone stepped in front of her, stole her words.

"I'll go first."

Anais cursed and followed Bardolph down the stairs.

* * *

"Excuse me," she called out as she hurried after him, "but what is your problem? Do hedge knights lack manners in your kingdom? Or is it just you?"

Bardolph did not answer, and Anais ground her teeth. She was stuck behind him, for the stairway was too narrow to allow overtaking; all she saw was the back of his armour. In the fading daylight she noticed it bore an intricate design:

a vine that curled from one side to the other. She was so distracted by it that she didn't notice when he reached the base of the stairs and stopped.

"Ack!" Anais grimaced as she smacked into his armour. Since when had she been so clumsy?

Bardolph examined her with surprise. "I'm afraid I don't know what you mean. How have I offended you?"

"You've cut me off twice!" She glared, rubbing her face. "First in the crowd, and just now, at the door. Perhaps you don't realise there are other people in this realm besides yourself?"

"There are many people in the world, and many creatures," he said solemnly. "And right now there is one standing behind you."

Anais went still. She felt the hairs on her neck rise, heard a gasp on the stairs above. Then she sensed it: a flow of cold air, a brooding malevolence.

A demon.

Her heart thundered. Was it *a* demon or *the* demon? There was a terrible pause – and then, guided by Bardolph's eyes, she ducked and rolled. When she sprang to her feet, she drew her sword, ready for battle, but the creature had already passed her. The third challenger, a girl named Tryn who was proceeding down the steps, shrieked as the demon leapt upon her and tore out her throat.

"No!" Anais ran forward, her sword drawn, but something rushed ahead of her, some flurry of motion from Bardolph; it almost looked as if he had thrown a rope. Whatever it was, it wrapped around the demon's neck. Anais struck with her sword a moment later, burying it into the creature, but it was a pointless maneuver.

The thing was already slain.

She stood for a moment, her breath coming in gasps. Then she bent down and looked more closely at the object around the demon's throat. "Is that…a plant?"

"Yes. A vine, in fact." Bardolph lifted a hand and the vine retracted, flowing back across the floor towards him; then it disappeared in a puff of green smoke.

Anais stared in surprise. "Are you a mage?"

"No. I am a hedge knight. But not quite in the manner you put it; I can summon plants, instead of sleeping under them."

"Ah." Anais bit her lip. "Well, I've never seen such magic. It worked well."

"Not well enough." Bardolph gestured towards Tryn's body, his expression grim. Then he looked at the stairs, where another figure was coming down. "You there…can you give us a hand?"

"For certes." The fourth challenger hurried down; when he saw Tryn's body, he froze. "Gods…is she dead?"

"Yes." Anais stood up. "But so is the demon. Can you take Tryn back up?"

The boy took in the mangled dark shape, and his mouth fell open. "What the…you killed the demon already? Does that mean the challenge is over?"

"No." Anais shook her head. "The demon we seek is a Class Three. That was just a Class One. There must be more than one here; perhaps they have multiplied over the past few weeks."

Bardolph nudged the demon with his boot. "How do you know this thing isn't the Class Three?"

"Because I'm a scholar, and I've been studying demon lore for years." At Bardolph's skeptical look, Anais sighed. "A Class Three entity has great power. The mere sight of it will probably sear your eyeballs. Then, while you try to regain your senses, it will either crush you like a bug, or fry you like a griddlecake. *That* is how I know." She paused. "The demon we are hunting is a particularly treacherous bastard named Zed. I've been tracking him for some time; I'll know him when I find him." She turned towards the figure who was gathering up Tryn's body. "What is your name, boy?"

"Samuel."

"Well, Samuel, don't come back down here. You don't stand a chance against this foe. And neither do the others." Before Samuel could reply, Anais turned and began to walk down the passage. Bardolph cleared his throat and called after her.

"It seems *you* didn't stand a chance, a moment ago. That thing was about to gut you."

Anais scowled. "That would never happen, normally. You distracted me."

"Oh really?

"Yes. I hunt alone. Now if you'll excuse me, I have a Class Three demon to slay, and a purse to claim." Anais kept walking, but she sensed the hedge knight's eyes upon her, heard his retort.

"Not if I kill it first."

* * *

The next hour or so was uneventful. Anais made her way through the tunnel, which soon branched into a network of tunnels. She'd been expecting this, based on what survivors had told her; but even so, it was easy to become disoriented. One thing was clear: she would have made better progress if she hadn't gotten sidetracked by the sound of screams.

Not demonic screams; human ones.

Anais frowned as she doubled back. *I told the others to go home. Now they've gotten into trouble, and I might lose my neck saving them.*

She picked up her pace as the screams grew louder. Suddenly the tunnel expanded, flared into an open room. There before her was a cluster of figures wrestling with a writhing mass of tentacles. It was dark; Anais could only see because the tentacles threw off a bluish glow. The demon was big, and of unusual appearance; it looked like a giant squid.

She sighed. A Class Two shapeshifter.

Anais ran forward and plunged her sword into the creature. At once the blade lit up, as if it had been dipped in fire; a brilliant glow illuminated the chamber. The faces of the challengers flashed into her vision for a moment, astonished and terrified; then, with a hiss, the light winked out. The shapeshifter collapsed, releasing the others from its grasp.

"That is quite a sword."

Anais spun around; Bardolph was behind her. "Yes. Its name is Demon Drinker, and it feeds off demonic souls." She patted the blade. "Only a weapon such as this can conquer the soul of a Class Three entity." She turned to the others, who were sprawled in various places. "Perhaps you will listen to me this time. Go home."

Bardolph regarded her as she turned back. "Demon Drinker? What spell does that use?"

"The incantation of thirst."

He gave her a look she could not read. "I have a proposition for you. Let us hunt together; when we reach the thing, let me kill it, and I will reward you the purse."

"Why?"

"I am thirsty myself." He raised a hand, conjured a flower. "This magic takes a toll. I need to replenish it. A Class Three demon can restore me. And your sword has already had a drink."

* * *

On they went, and there was much work to do, for the place was a warren of demonic scourges. Anais slew the demons with her blade; the hedge knight employed his botanicals.

The hours passed, and they both grew weary. Then they stumbled upon a room whose walls burned red like a magma chamber.

"Oh, shit." Anais wiped her brow, taking in the shadows crawling across the floor – short and squat and crackling with flames. "A nest of fire-imps. Let's get out of here."

But it was too late; the moment she spoke, they were swarmed. Sweat dripped down their faces as they attacked their molten-eyed foes. It took some time to dispatch them all; when they had finished, Bardolph slumped against the wall.

Anais looked up from cleaning her blade. "Is something wrong?"

The hedge knight grunted. "One of the bastards got me." He lifted a hand; it was stained with blood.

She cursed and moved to his side. "Let's see it."

Bardolph removed his breastplate, then his tunic, exposing a jagged gash along his waist. Anais took a breath. The glowing embers behind them cast flickering light along his skin, which rippled with muscle; suddenly she realised how long it had been since she'd enjoyed the company of a man. He grimaced, and she remembered she was meant to be examining his wound.

She ran her fingers across it. "Can you heal it with your magic?"

"No. It is running low…I need to replenish it."

"How do you do that?"

"With water. Or with something that quenches my thirst."

Anais paused; this remark was oddly specific. She fetched the waterskin from his pack, frowned at its flaccidity. "There is not much left." She brought it to his lips.

He put one hand over hers as he drank.

"Thank you." He sat back. "I need a moment to mend this wound."

"Take your time. I don't think Zed is going anywhere." Anais sat down beside him, trying to ignore the sight of his bare torso, the hard lines glistening with sweat. She focused instead on his arms, which bore twining green tattoos. "How did you learn this plant magic?"

"I didn't learn it. I was cursed with it."

Anais raised an eyebrow. "What do you mean?"

"I tried to drink from a rose."

"I beg your pardon?"

Bardolph let out a breath. "I was a wild youth; my appetite for violence was only exceeded by my appetite for wenching. I tried to hide it at first – by day I worked dutifully with my father, who was a botanist and ran an apothecary shop. But by night I turned into a ruffian, drinking and debauching. Every morning a new person was at my father's door with a complaint. I'd broken the innkeeper's window in a brawl; I'd seduced the miller's daughter. One day my father had had enough. *Go from here and do not return until you learn restraint.* So I left, travelled from town to town, offering my services as a warrior. I also crafted herbal remedies, for that much I had learned from my father. But I partook of something else as well."

Anais crossed her arms. "Women?"

"Yes. You see, I loved the pleasure of a kiss, the caress of soft skin. That is no odd thing for a young man, of course, but…I think it meant more to me than it did to most men. And my hunger was insatiable. I wanted to know not just one woman, but all of them – to admire each one, as my father had studied the variety of plants. So I partook of lovers, and each seemed a flower to me – one was as round and welcoming as a daisy; another, as slender and elegant as a lily.

"One day I came to a strange little village. There was not much there except for a few farmers – and a hermit with his apprentice. She was a lovely thing, the loveliest I'd seen – but forbidden. The villagers told me so at once, perhaps sensing my nature. *Her master is a wizard*, they said, *and you must not speak to her, for she is his apprentice*; but I wanted her badly, for she was a rare beauty. A rose. And so I made my advances. And…she accepted. And that was my downfall."

Anais swallowed. "Because of drinking?"

"Yes."

"I don't understand."

Bardolph gave a rueful smile. "To experience a woman fully, one must taste her. This, in fact, was my greatest pleasure…and I think I gave great pleasure in return…or so my lovers seemed to indicate."

Anais felt her cheeks flush. "And the wizard found you?"

"Yes. He discovered us together and cursed me. *You will never kiss another woman again*, he said, *and your only weapons will be flowers. A hedge knight forever.* And from then on I have wandered from town to town, except now my only pleasure is in destruction. As for women – I try to avoid them." He paused. "I may not even notice if I cut them off."

"I see." Anais sat back. "What do you mean, never kiss another woman? What happens if you try?"

He regarded her. "Would you like to find out?"

Anais nodded, for she was always up for a challenge. She leaned over and tried to press her lips against his, but something stopped her; it was as if she hit an invisible wall. She felt something else then, a prickling of her skin, a tingling she had encountered before. She sat back.

"What was the name of the village?"

"Arrowdam."

Anais sucked in her breath. "The man was not a wizard. He was a demon. And I think I can break his spell."

"What?" Bardolph sat up. "How?"

"I told you, I've studied demon lore. This has the signature of such a working."

"Then what do you propose we do?"

"Continue onwards."

* * *

And so they went on, but they progressed more slowly than before, for Anais was clumsy and unco-ordinated; her mind was stirred by Bardolph's story. She could all too easily imagine his skill in the bedchamber, his muscular body executing acts of pleasure. She had a sudden vision of herself as the object of his desire…

Focus, she commanded herself, but it was no use. As they killed an earth demon, she imagined Bardolph's mouth on her neck; as they wrestled with another shapeshifter, she could almost feel his hands on her skin. Soon she was utterly possessed by hot desire, of surrendering to Bardolph's passion. He seemed under a similar spell, for his plants came out swollen and pink: rigid larkspur and phallic laceleaf and great spears of thistles. At one point, after they had crushed a crawling thing with many legs, Anais needed a break; now it was her turn to slump against the wall.

Bardolph came over. "What is it?"

"I am distracted."

"I can see that." He examined her face. "Are you fearful of Zed?"

"No." She shook her head. "You are the cause of my distraction."

Bardolph gave a surprised look. "Me?"

"Yes, you and your stories of seduction. They are stuck in my head. And I fear it will only get worse."

"Ah." He came closer. "I must apologise." He lowered his voice. "Can I help fix the problem?"

"Yes. No. I…I want to kiss you," she stammered.

He did not reply at first, just stepped closer until his face hovered before hers. He waited there, his body a question. Anais said nothing – or meant to say nothing – but the tiniest whisper escaped her lips.

"Yes."

Bardolph nodded. He leaned forward then, as inexorable as a raindrop sliding down a petal, and slowly pressed himself against her. She felt all of his contours, all of them hard.

Oh, gods above.

He made as if to kiss her then, hovering before her lips for what seemed the age of the world. The tension was unbearable. Then he ducked his head and breathed against her neck. "Perhaps," he whispered into her ear, "if you can indeed break the spell, I might be able to resolve your distraction."

Anais moaned. She felt a fire running along her body, a pulse of heat between her legs. Its ferocity was shocking; she'd never been so aroused. Why did this have to happen now, in such perilous circumstances? She needed all her wits about her.

She gasped for air. "I don't know if I can wait much longer."

He stepped back and grinned. "Then let us hurry."

She nodded and hefted her sword.

* * *

They found Zed in the next chamber. He formed into a cloud as they entered, sent flames running along the floor and static crackling through the air. Normally this would have been terrifying, but Anais was so addled by lust that she felt detached from the whole scene, as if she were seeing it through someone else's eyes.

She strained for focus. "Zed. You've hidden yourself well."

The entity swirled; its voice rumbled from the earth. "How do you know my name?"

Anais smiled. "Do you not remember me? I toiled under you for years, back in Arrowdam. Back when you posed as a hermit."

Two eyes formed. "Anais?"

"So you do remember!" Anais clapped her hands. "Perhaps then you will also recall how you tormented me. You and your precious games. I see you still keep your favourite cup."

Bardolph leaned over, whispered into her ear. "What cup?"

Anais gestured to a silvery gleam within the cloud; a flagon seemed to be floating within it. "The battered old thing. It looks fit for the scrap pile, but it is Zed's favourite toy." She raised her voice. "Isn't it? You would fill it with water, but never let me drink. *You can slake your thirst when you have finished your work*, you said. But my work was never done." She gripped her sword. "But that was your undoing, for I realised that you were not a wizard, but something darker. And I learned your precious spell. The spell of thirst, written upon the metal. The nature of your being. And then I escaped."

The demon flickered like a storm-ridden thunderhead. "You did not escape. I expelled you."

Anais rolled her eyes. "We both know that is a lie. I broke free from your clutches and swore to find a way to destroy you. And you, in the meantime, lost no time in finding a new apprentice to torment – and a knight to curse."

Zed's amorphous form went still; his voice became a dangerous hiss. "What would you know about that?"

Anais gestured to her companion. "Because that knight is here beside me. Perhaps you do not remember him either; but I daresay you remember what he did to your apprentice."

At this remark, a blast of wind ripped through the chamber. Zed solidified, becoming a man whose eyes were filled with fury. His voice boomed in their ears. "He defiled her! He ruined her!"

"Why? Because she let him do what you could not?" Suddenly Anais understood. "The girl. You wanted her, but she refused you. She did not yield to your thirst. She was the cup from which *you* could not drink."

At these words, Zed growled and leapt – not at Anais, but at Bardolph. The demon moved as quickly as a passing shadow, as quickly as a flash of dark hunger, but Anais was quicker. She lunged forward and struck with her sword.

"Yahhhhhh!"

She gave an exultant yell as Demon Drinker pierced her enemy's hide – but the blade did not bite. No light flashed along its shaft, no spirit was extracted. She felt a moment of panic, for her attack had caused no injury; now Zed's arm was raised above her.

A dagger appeared in his claws. He was about to skewer her.

The blow did not fall. Instead a thorny tendril wrapped around Zed's hand – a rose with a mighty stem. As Zed struggled, the plant grew outwards, a verdant proliferation that formed a cage, penning the demon in. Anais, whose sword was still buried in Zed's body, put her foot on the lattice and yanked out her blade. Then she retreated to Bardolph's side.

"It's stronger than I thought," she admitted, panting. "My sword is not up to the task. We must break it down some other way."

The hedge knight grimaced with the effort of his spell; he could not defeat the demon either. "How?"

Anais looked over at Zed, who was struggling against his rose-studded prison. His power was wavering...

She had a sudden wild thought. Without reconsidering, she leaned over and kissed Bardolph. This time, their lips met; at the unexpected touch, Bardolph went still. For a moment, he did not react. Then he surged forward, pressing his mouth against hers. At the sight of their embrace, Zed hissed in dismay.

Anais pulled away from the kiss. "I have an idea."

"What?" Bardolph's breath was heavy, his eyes wide.

She gestured to the demon. "Zed abhors the sight of physical contact, for that is what he was denied. It will weaken him – and the curse he laid upon you."

Bardolph nodded. "Then what are we waiting for?" He leaned forward and kissed her again, his mouth hungry, his tongue exploring hers. Zed growled, but Anais did not hear it. She only knew that the hedge knight tasted as good as she thought he would, that they fit together effortlessly.

She could have stayed in that embrace for some time, but Bardolph could not wait. He pulled back, kissed her again and again – not just on the lips, but along her neck, her collarbone. At the recovery of this lost ability, he seemed to go mad. "It's been so long…and you are so beautiful. Oh gods, I need you."

"Do you?" Anais felt a jolt of desire throb in her quim. She was also dimly aware of the demon's yowl of dismay; Zed sounded like a cat whose tail had been stepped on. *It's working.* And something else was working; Bardolph's rose had grown thicker, its stems swelling; she could feel him swelling elsewhere as well. "Then I guess we'd better keep going."

"Oh, yes." He threw off his breastplate, tore off his tunic; in the next moment her vision was obscured by her own vest, which he'd pulled over her head. Her breasts sprang forth. The demon gave a low shriek as Bardolph caressed her nipples. Anais felt another jolt as he sucked on first one, then the other. She felt as if she could reach a crescendo right then, but she held herself off, staving the crest of pleasure; the timing was critical.

"Bardolph…we must keep going…I can't wait much longer…."

He nodded and undid his breeches. His member sprang forth, proud and erect. Anais grasped it with one eager hand; with her other, she slipped off her trousers. The demon was shrieking like a banshee now as she prepared to guide him into herself; but Bardolph held off. Then he breathed into her ear.

"One thing first."

The hedge knight got down on his knees. At the prospect of this intimate contact, Anais tensed; a moment later she gasped as Bardolph flicked his tongue across her slick aperture. At the first taste of this ultimate pleasure, the one he'd been denied so long, he groaned.

"Oh, *yes*."

Then he set to work – first stroking her folds, then teasing her kernel of pleasure. As he circled it, Anais closed her eyes. Sensations washed over her; she forgot where she was. She could only think, *by the gods above, he is good*. He seemed to know exactly what she wanted, caressing her like a creature of clairvoyant pleasure.

Anais could bear it no longer. "Now," she whispered.

Bardolph stood up. His body was framed by Zed's torments now, for the demon was writhing and throwing off sparks, and the knight's every contour was edged with fire.

It was time.

Bardolph thrust his hips forward. As he buried his shaft within her, Anais gasped with relief. All she wanted was to lose herself in the moment, in the ecstasy of wet hot union, but she had one task remaining. As her knight withdrew his shaft, she reached back and grabbed her own. Demon Drinker flew across the room in a glittering arc, its blade lit by the raging inferno in Zed's eyes; then it pierced the hedge of roses and plunged into the demon's heart. Zed shrieked louder and louder, matching Anais's cries as Bardolph thrust again and again; and then, as the hedge knight exploded within her, the Class Three emanation burst into a puff of smoke.

* * *

Afterwards, when they came back up just before the light of dawn kissed the horizon, the mayor asked them for proof of the demon's demise. In response, Anais held out a metal flagon.

The mayor frowned at the humble object. "What's this?"

"It is all that is left of the demon Zed. His essence was imbued into it – you can see the inscription of the spell around the rim – but we captured it and destroyed him."

The mayor raised an eyebrow. "How did you do that?"

"We used his own spell against him. It was quite a battle… you wouldn't believe what we had to do." Anais smiled. "But he's gone. And I believe we've won this." She reached out and gently took the purse from the mayor's hands. "We'd love to chat more, but I'm afraid we'd need a rest and some refreshments…my friend here is thirsty." She turned to her companion. "Aren't you?"

Anais tossed the cup to Bardolph, who brought it to his lips and grinned.

The Gentle Art of Necromancy

S.C. Mills

Cyrus lowered herself into the well, hand over hand on rough rope, walking her boots down the rock wall. Months of digging up graves on an Imperial labor crew had callused her palms, but the wet hemp shredded her skin regardless, dotting the rope with crimson. She fought the temptation to let go. It was right for this mission to extract a price from her flesh.

Her boots struck bedrock. It had been an unusually hot, dry year. Yet another curse the sun-worshipping Imperials had brought with them from the arid north.

Cyrus ran her fingertips over the walls, where stacked rings of stones held back the earth from caving in. She wiggled rock after rock at waist height, like her lookout waiting above had instructed her to do. One would be loose, he'd said. It had been recently replaced to hide the precious remains she was here to retrieve.

A fist-sized stone wobbled under her hand. She pried it out and dug into the dirt behind it. Mud, tiny rocks, and clay caked the raw gaps in her skin where her calluses used to be. Her fingertips skated over something rounded and smooth. She withdrew a curve of white bone, streaked with black char and Uriash's pervasive yellow clay.

Archon Daciana's jawbone fit perfectly into Cyrus's palm. Her hands remembered its size and heft. She could almost smell Daciana's balsam oil and rosewater perfumes. The prospect of seeing her again soon, if only briefly and in front of others, was too much. Overwhelming. Hot shame filled her chest and grief pressed against the backs of her eyes. She shoved it all down yet again with a hard swallow, but memories forced themselves to the front of her mind:

Swearing in as the Archon's royal guard, standing tall in her pressed uniform. Daciana's stern smile, the jeweled hilt of a new sword in her hands—

Cyrus slumped down against the rock wall, clutching the jawbone to her chest.

Daciana's oiled chin, turned aside by Cyrus's sure fingers. Slipping a straight razor over the last ghost of silver stubble on her Lady's delicate jawline—

Cyrus tilted back her head, blinking away tears. Dark clouds rolled across the cutout circle of sky above. A lonely sob rocked her chest, strangled by a fresh wave of shame. Others were waiting on her. An entire rebel cell, held up by this moment of weakness.

"—can't loiter here. All Uriashi cemeteries are the Emperor's property." A voice from above, far away, with an Imperial accent.

Screaming as the living pyre's flames swallowed her lover. The burned husk of Daciana's head on a spike—

"Someone's down there?" Louder, now. Too close. Clearly speaking to her lookout.

Cyrus leapt to her feet and wiped away her tears with a filthy hand. She tucked the jawbone into a small bag hung around her neck and under her shirt, shoved the stone from the retaining wall back into place, and raced to haul herself back up to help. She didn't know if her lookout, Marin, could handle being questioned by an Imperial, but *she* could. She could help.

While she climbed, Marin answered the Imperial soldier's questions in a surly monotone that bordered alarmingly on outright disrespect. Yes, he said, someone was in the well – they were "inspecting" it. And no, he was not any kind of witch or necromancer, nor was he carrying anyone else's bones.

The soldier eyed Cyrus as she hauled herself over the low stone wall around the well. Marin stared at the ground, snow collecting on the shoulders of his coat. She lowered her gaze, too. The last of her open defiance had left her when she'd watched Daciana burn alive.

"The well ran dry, Citizen," she volunteered, right away. That Imperial honorific hardly stuck in her throat at all anymore. She risked a quick glance at his eyes – his irises were tinged fiery orange-red, meaning he was a truth-seer. Her stomach flipped. And they called Uriashi necromancy a dark art.

"You had to go down there to check?" The soldier snorted. His eyes might as well have been burning holes into her forehead. "The empty bucket didn't tell you?"

"Sometimes a collapse can cause a dry well, Citizen. I shored up some of the retaining wall." She'd replaced the stone she'd removed, anyway. "But I think this one is too shallow to reach groundwater after the dry summer."

Silence. That last comment was a mistake. The sun-worshippers knew locals blamed them for the drought. Some deep part of her hoped he would attack her. Both stealing his sword and dying on it had their appeal.

"Look at me, Laborer," he snapped.

She jerked up her chin. The soldier was shivering in his standard-issue cotton tunic and leather sandals. The early autumn frost had caught all the northern invaders underdressed. Perhaps they would march in boots next time they wanted to conquer a southern city.

His irises glowed like hot copper. "Are you a witch?"

"No, Citizen." No self-respecting Uriashi would *ever* call themselves that.

The soldier's jaw clenched, perhaps from concentrating on his truth-seeing. "Are you carrying any bones?"

"I'm yours." Daciana's breathy whisper, her soft body arching beneath Cyrus. "Always yours—"

Probably just a sweet nothing. Cyrus tried to believe it now anyway.

"Only my own." Blood rushed in her ears, each heartbeat loud as thunder.

The fiery hue in the soldier's eyes faded. Cyrus suppressed a relieved sigh.

He turned to Marin, who began visibly panicking. His eyes tracked back and forth across the dirty snow. Cyrus hoped the Imperial took his fear as flattery. Perhaps that was Marin's intent. The soldier squinted at Marin and stepped back, as if sizing him up.

"You're my size, Laborer," he said. "Give me that coat."

Well. Perhaps she should've seen that coming. Marin disrobed and didn't complain, but he didn't exactly say "Yes, Citizen" either. Cyrus was grateful for her narrow shoulders, and not only because of the cold. The burn scars on her wrists would've invited more questions.

They waited after that, eyes averted, while the sun-worshipper tried to yank on Marin's slightly too-small boots. Once he gave up and left, she made another trip down the well to retrieve said boots, where the soldier had thrown them in anger. He'd backhanded Marin and stomped off by the time Cyrus came back up, leaving Marin and her free to continue their mission in relative peace.

* * *

Marin slapped warmth into the ropy muscles of his arms as they trudged in silence across the barren, desecrated cemetery. Around them, empty graves yawned like open wounds. Fresh snow crunched underfoot and blanketed piles of dirt and spent pyres, where the Imperials had unearthed and burned Uriash's sacred dead. Or rather, where they'd stood over Uriashi like Cyrus and forced them to do it themselves. She'd be digging today, in fact, were the ground not frozen.

"You got it?" Marin's blurted question made Cyrus jump.

"Yeah." She glanced at him, but could read nothing but righteous resentment in his tight expression. "I only found a jawbone."

"Yes." Marin sucked his teeth. "That was all that was left. After—"

"I know." Cyrus cut him off. After her beloved's blackened head had been left skewered on a spike over the city gates, a symbol of Imperial dominance.

"No. You don't know." Marin clenched pale, bloodless fingers. "It was my brother who stole it. We created a distraction, and he *tried* to take back the entire—" He shook his head. "Most of the Archon's remains were lost during the chase. Her jaw is all we've got. Now, we only have this one chance." He stared straight ahead at the gutted mausoleum across the sprawling graveyard. "Our people died that day. Friends of mine. My brother broke his legs falling in that well. He still cannot work."

"I'm sorry." Dull rage hummed, buried deep in Cyrus's soul. Harder to suppress, now, with her lover's jawbone thumping against her chest with every step.

"Don't be. I'm not. He isn't. All worth it, for what she can tell us."

Whatever that was. No one had deigned to tell Cyrus, but as the Archon's personal guard, she was accustomed to powerful people not explaining themselves. She'd do her part regardless.

Marin fell silent again after that, but kept stealing glances at her. Dread tightened the muscles between her shoulders. She could guess what was coming. Eventually, he spit it out. "You're that last royal guard, aren't you?"

Cyrus flinched. Shame ballooned in her chest again, her skin burning hot against the cold bone between her breasts. Having survived her Archon's death was inherently disgraceful. She was practically forsworn.

"I was off duty that night," she snapped, shocking herself. She'd never told anyone that.

"That's not the story I heard." Marin's tone leaked disgust. "Everyone says you were with her when they took her."

Imperials shoving Daciana to her bedroom floor, hands bound behind her back—

"That part's true. I was there." Cyrus fixed her gaze on the mausoleum, trying to swallow down shame and keep her lips sealed. To avoid besmirching Daciana's name worse than she already had. To stay on task.

"Why were you in her *bedroom* if you were off—" Marin stopped speaking mid-word. He stopped walking. Cyrus wheeled around to glare at him. He squinted at her, suspicion flickering over his face.

Better to tell him the truth than let him guess a worse lie.

"I was *off duty*," Cyrus repeated. "We were sleeping. They used smoke to keep us that way. I woke up to—" she raised her arms, shoved her coat sleeves above her scars "—Imperial fire-cuffs searing my wrists. Nothing I could do. *Nothing*." Her chest heaved, squeezing up the bile of helpless, choked-down rage. "I was supposed to be burned and staked up over the gates too, before they decided I was just a bedwarmer, so nobody would care anyway. I was of more use on a labor crew." She bit off a sob and dropped her arms.

Marin was staring. The Archon had been ten years widowed, her heirs grown, but Uriashi law and morality both forbade the powerful from fraternizing with their servants.

"Nobody knew but the other guards, and they're all dead," Cyrus said. "I haven't told anyone else. I don't want our people to remember her…that way."

Daciana in bridal yellow, in private, in the dark, gifting Cyrus the traditional golden chain, vowing her love and devotion—

Then, the secrecy of their liaison had made it feel special. Now, standing on desecrated holy ground, wearing her lover's jawbone under a ratty coat instead of a gold necklace beneath fine livery, she doubted. Maybe she'd only ever been a bedwarmer.

"The scion and the bone-slingers are waiting." Marin turned away. "I won't speak of this. No one should speak ill of the dead."

* * *

As sickening as the defiled graveyard was, the mausoleum was worse. In one corner, labor crews had piled up the splintered, rotting wood that had once been lovingly crafted coffins, designed to be sealed and re-sealed for generations. Even the crisp smell of snow couldn't mask the stench of mold, of needless decay, of the generations of descendants robbed of access to their ancestors' wisdom.

Cyrus stood by the barred door, keeping watch through a gap by the hinges. Three necromancers gathered around a chalk circle on the floor where the mausoleum's altar had once stood, skirting around bits of candles, flipping through old tomes, and fretting.

The scion, Daciana's only still-living relative, turned out to be a scrawny boy of about ten. Unsurprising, in hindsight. Any adult relation would've been declared the new Archon by now, at least within the rebel network. The future Archon sat on the floor, absorbed in a game played on his fingers with a loop of string. He didn't look much like Daciana, if you asked Cyrus, but no one did.

"We're ready." The necromancers' leader was a gangly middle-aged woman, wrapped in rags. "Are we clear? This much material only gets us a few minutes."

Cyrus and Marin exchanged glances. He sat across the room with his eye to a crack in a boarded-up window, watching the other side of the graveyard.

"All clear," he said.

The leader gestured to the scion. "Come here, child."

The boy pocketed his string and scrambled over. Perhaps he missed Daciana, too. He knelt at a marked spot on the chalk circle. An assistant pressed a dagger into his hand and murmured instructions, showing him how to cut without hurting himself too badly. The boy nodded and sat up straighter, his expression serious.

The lead necromancer then read from a book written in ancient Uriashi, which Cyrus barely understood. In her experience, necromancy was flat boring, until it suddenly wasn't. Anticipating seeing Daciana again, even for a few minutes, had her stomach churning. She tried to focus on the frozen landscape outside the door, but no one was out there to watch. She couldn't help but catch a few phrases of the ritual that were oft-repeated in other spiritual ceremonies.

"—by their spilled blood, your willing beloved—"

Willing beloved. Just like in wedding vows. Hearing it speared Cyrus's soul. On her request, she and Daciana had once said vows to each other. Alone, with no officiant or witnesses to make it real, but it had *felt* real. Only Daciana's opinion had mattered, then.

Cyrus refocused on the bleak, empty graveyard. A royal guard should hear only what was necessary to protect her charges. Despite kind words whispered in the dark, that was probably all she'd ever been to Daciana: a guard.

"—family of the departed—"

Family. That was what it felt like Cyrus had lost that night. Her lover – her *wife*, some defiant part of her insisted, damn the law – and the rest of the royal guard. They'd always looked the other way when Cyrus sneaked into Daciana's chambers while off duty, never seeing anything but what was necessary to protect their Archon. They'd never judged.

"It's not working." Panic in the leader's tone. "Why isn't—"

"Someone cheated. Obviously." Marin's voice was hard and bitter.

"Imperial propaganda. They lie and cheat as much as—"

"Adopted family still—"

"People died for this!" Marin shouted. "You should've been *certain*." A thump rattled the building, like a fist on a support beam.

Startled, Cyrus whirled away from the door, reaching for a sword that wasn't there.

The necromancers were pacing by the chalk circle. Marin stood in their midst, away from his post, body quivering from some mixture of cold and rage. The candles' flames rose a foot above the floor. Feathers and bone dust swirled in the air, but no spirit had yet formed from them. In the center of it all, Daciana's jawbone smoldered with a black flame, disappearing by the second.

"I didn't cheat." The boy lifted the dagger and his arm. "Should I do more? She sounded like a great lady, and it really didn't hurt—"

"They never even *met*?" Marin threw up his hands. "How is that family?" He stomped across the room and flung himself down to sit on a pile of broken caskets.

"No more, child," said the leader. "You did all you could." She shot a glare at Marin, then took the dagger gently from the boy's hand. "You're probably just…too distant a relation. I'm sorry."

Cyrus stared at the flaming jawbone. Her limbs tingled and her body felt far away. A question burned in her mind, one she wasn't sure she wanted the answer to, but they had no time. No time to find another scion. No time for wallowing or indecision.

She snatched the dagger from the leader's weak academic grip and dropped to her knees by the chalk circle. She yanked up her sleeve and cut deep into the back of her wrist, along the twisted burn scars. She held her arm over the circle, amidst the floating debris, and let her blood drip down and mingle with the thin, palm-sized pool already under the jawbone.

Dust and feathers whirled faster around the circle. A column formed. Hips, then shoulders, and then above them, where it belonged, a woman's head.

"Ancestors below," whispered Marin.

The necromancers scrambled back into position. One spoke in ancient Uriashi again, too rapidly to follow. The figure took on a more distinct form. Soft curves, strong arms, a delicate jawline. Around Cyrus, her compatriots pressed their palms together before their collarbones and dropped their chins. She joined them in saluting her Archon with her hands, but she couldn't look down. Tears ran freely from her eyes as she gazed up at her beloved.

At her *wife*.

Daciana's hand, translucent and smoldering with black flame, reached down to cup Cyrus's cheek. "You're alive," whispered Daciana. "I was sure—"

"Yes, Archon. Daciana." Cyrus kicked herself for wasting precious moments with fumbling words. "It was— I wasn't important enough to kill."

"And they call themselves truth-seers." Daciana scoffed. Her smile spread; her visage shone like obsidian. She tightened her grip on Cyrus's chin and tugged up gently. Cyrus stood, and Daciana pulled her into her arms, as warm as living flesh.

Daciana spoke quickly over Cyrus's shoulder to Marin and the necromancers, her low voice a steady murmur of orders and information.

"—find tomes buried beneath the Myrs River Cemetery—"

"—turn their own dead against them—"

"—my wife's martial expertise—"

Cyrus hardly heard any of it, save for *my wife*. She buried her head in Daciana's shoulder, breathing in balsam oil and rosewater. Holding her tight for what was truly the last time, for this single stolen minute.

"Goodbye, love," Daciana whispered. Too soon. "I know you'll lead them well."

Before Cyrus could process that, Daciana was gone. Cyrus stumbled forward, off balance, squeezing nothing but air. Every candle and lantern in the room went out.

Loss and grief rolled through Cyrus's body, in convulsing sobs that she at last didn't try to suppress. Her chest heaved, then steadied. Her eyes adjusted to the dark mausoleum, now lit only by shards of sunlight through gaps in the boarded-up windows.

This was…better. Not good, but so much *better* – kinder, easier – to say goodbye after death, rather than during it. Necromancy was a beautiful, gentle art, worthy of giving her life to protect. She couldn't have saved Daciana, but maybe she could still help save her people. Peace blanketed Cyrus's mind like snow on a fresh grave.

The room was quiet, aside from the soft sounds of breathing. No one was speaking. No one had stomped out, slammed the door, slunk back to their labor crew. Her scalp prickled and hair raised on her arms. She'd missed something.

Cyrus turned around to a sight that chilled her to the bone: every head in the room was bowed, their palms pressed together beneath their chins.

"Archon Cyrus." Marin stepped forward. "We have an army to raise. What are your orders?"

The Duelist and Dreamweaver

Charity Ogechi

The clash of steel had become Kelvin's constant companion – sharp, cold, and unyielding as the blade he wielded. Loyalty to the crown was all he had ever known, and his reputation as the kingdom's most feared duelist was carved not from grand speeches or courtly favor, but from the precise, ruthless strikes that ended lives without hesitation.

When the Queen's summons came, he answered with neither surprise nor question. The royal court needed a sword, a shield forged by discipline and battle, to guard against the shadows creeping ever closer. Assassins had already slipped too near the throne; whispers spoke of poison, daggers, and veiled plots.

Kelvin arrived beneath the heavy, arched gates of the palace, his boots silent on the cold stone floor. His dark cloak concealed a lean frame honed by years of grueling combat, his eyes sharp – grey as steel, observing everything and nothing at once. He trusted no one but the edge of his sword and the rigid code etched deep in his bones.

The hall was alive with the hum of the court – silks rustling, whispered intrigues, laughter as sharp as a knife's edge. But to Kelvin, it was a cage of delicate masks and fragile lies. The courtiers turned their gazes upon him, eyes narrowed, lips curled in suspicion or disdain. Outsider. Mercenary. Cold blade.

A slender woman stepped forward, the air around her shimmering faintly as if reality itself bent to her will. Elara, the Dreamweaver, the magician whose presence stirred both reverence and unease among the nobles. Cloaked in robes that rippled like liquid moonlight, she moved with an ethereal grace, her dark eyes gleaming with secrets.

Without a word, Elara raised her hands, and the room dimmed. Silken threads of light spun through the air, weaving visions that danced like ghosts before the assembled court. Castles crumbled, alliances shattered, faces of friends turned foes. The illusions revealed cracks deep within the kingdom's foundation – political fractures threatening to split the realm apart.

Gasps and murmurs filled the chamber. Elara's magic was beautiful and haunting, but to Kelvin, it was little more than smoke and mirrors. He watched with skepticism, arms crossed, muscles taut beneath his cloak. "Tricks to distract and unsettle," he muttered under his breath, a grimace tightening his jaw.

A sharp-eyed noblewoman caught his words. "Our duelist doubts the power of the Dreamweaver," she whispered, voice dripping with thinly veiled scorn.

Elara's gaze flicked to Kelvin, a faint, knowing smile playing on her lips. "Magic is no trick, Sir Kelvin. It reveals truths your sword cannot cut through."

Kelvin's reply was ice. "Truths can be masked as easily as lies. I fight what I can see, not shadows."

The tension between them was a silent blade, sharper than any forged steel. The court watched, intrigued by this collision of pragmatism and mysticism – two forces at odds, yet bound by the same fragile thread of loyalty to the crown.

Before the night could unravel further, a breathless page arrived with urgent news. A new threat had been uncovered, a whisper of danger lurking just beyond the walls, intent on striking at the heart of the kingdom.

Kelvin's eyes narrowed, steel already humming in his veins. Duty demanded vigilance. Magic or no magic, he would be the shield that kept the throne standing.

But even as he prepared to face this unknown enemy, he could not shake the silent challenge in Elara's gaze, a promise that this war would be fought on more than one battlefield, and that the clash of sword and illusion had only just begun.

* * *

Kelvin watched from the shadows of the great hall, his sword sheathed but his body coiled like a spring, eyes never leaving Elara. The court had dismissed her illusions as mere spectacle, but he sensed something else, something beneath the shimmering veils of light and shadow.

Tonight, as the courtiers reveled in silks and whispered promises, Elara's magic was different – less show, more subtle. She traced delicate patterns in the air, threads of light weaving themselves into intricate tapestries that only she seemed to understand. Within those silken illusions were hints no one else dared see: hidden alliances, half-spoken threats, the flicker of danger concealed beneath smiles.

He found himself drawn closer, despite every instinct screaming caution.

Later, when the guests had thinned and silence settled like a cloak over the palace, Elara found him near the arched windows overlooking the moonlit gardens.

"You watch too closely," she said softly, her voice barely above a whisper, yet carrying the weight of secrets.

Kelvin met her gaze, the cold edge in his eyes softened by curiosity. "Your illusions are not mere tricks."

She stepped nearer, the air around her pulsing with quiet power. "They are threads of truth, yes. But more than that – they glimpse possible futures. I see paths the kingdom may take, but the magic to look beyond the now is forbidden, dangerous."

He frowned. "And yet you risk it."

"Because the future is not fixed," she said, her voice fierce. "I cannot fight with a sword, but I fight with visions. They warn me of what may come if we do nothing."

Kelvin's jaw tightened. His life was forged in certainty – steel met steel, honor upheld or shattered in the moment. The unknowable terrors of visions unsettled him, but he could not deny the urgency in her eyes.

That urgency became undeniable days later.

During the preparations for the Spring Festival, a vision seized Elara in the quiet of her chambers. A shadowed figure slipped through the crowd, a dagger glinting beneath the lantern light – aimed at the Queen.

She sought out Kelvin immediately.

Together, they moved through the throng like two halves of a reluctant whole: Kelvin's eyes sharp, sword ready; Elara's hands weaving soft illusions that cloaked their presence, masked their intent.

When the shadowed figure lunged, Kelvin intercepted with fluid precision, steel flashing and meeting steel in a whispered clash. Elara's magic swirled around them – misty tendrils that blurred vision, confounded senses, turning an assassination into a dance of light and shadow.

Breath heaving, Kelvin pinned the would-be assassin beneath his blade. Yet even as his grip tightened, his eyes found Elara's, flashing with equal parts frustration and something unspoken, fragile.

"Your magic saved us," Kelvin admitted grudgingly, voice low.

Elara's lips curved, a hint of a smile. "And your blade kept us alive. We are stronger together, if only you would trust it."

Kelvin's gaze darkened. "Trust is earned, not given."

"And neither is blind skepticism," Elara shot back, eyes sparkling. "You see only the blade's edge; I see the threads it cannot cut."

Their words hung between them, sharp as their weapons. Yet beneath the friction, a subtle shift began, an unspoken respect that wove through their interactions like a fragile thread pulled taut.

As the festival lights flickered and faded into dawn, Kelvin found himself reconsidering the rigidity of his beliefs. Fate was no longer a certainty etched in stone but a tapestry woven from countless choices – choices he might no longer face alone.

And somewhere deep beneath his cold exterior, a spark kindled – an ember of something dangerous, something like hope.

* * *

Whispers spread through the marble halls like wildfire, curling into every corner of the court with venomous delight. Elara had done the unthinkable. One of her illusions, a fleeting glimpse of shadowed figures huddled in a secret council chamber, had unveiled a conspiracy against the throne. The nobles, already wary of magic's unpredictability, seized the moment with cold teeth. Treason. Sedition. Witchcraft.

The Queen, bound by justice and court protocol, could not shield her magician forever. A trial was demanded, and

Elara was brought before the gathered lords and ladies, her fate balanced precariously on a knife's edge.

Kelvin stood near the chamber doors, his posture rigid as steel, the weight of his new responsibility settling heavy on his shoulders. He had been named Elara's guard – an honor, but also a prison of duty. Bound by his oath, yet torn by the complex tangle of his growing feelings for the woman who wielded illusions like whispered truths.

The chamber itself was cavernous, lined with towering pillars that seemed to watch like silent sentinels. Nobles sat in judgment, faces carved with suspicion and fear. Elara's hands were folded calmly before her, eyes steady, but Kelvin glimpsed the flicker of pain beneath her serene mask.

She began, voice clear and unwavering. "I have only ever sought to protect this kingdom. My visions reveal threats that lie hidden, secrets that, if ignored, will bring ruin. I am no traitor."

Murmurs rippled through the assembly. A grey-haired lord scoffed, his voice thick with disdain. "Protection through deceit and dark magic? Your illusions cast doubt where there should be loyalty. You threaten the very order we uphold."

Kelvin's gaze flickered to the Queen, who sat silent but resolute, weighing justice against fear.

In the tense silence, Elara's mind drifted back – memories surfaced like shards of glass. She had been a child when the Edicts against magic users were decreed, her family hunted like vermin. Years of isolation and persecution hardened her resolve; loyalty to the kingdom was not a choice but a necessity. She alone bore the burden of keeping the realm safe from threats unseen.

Her voice softened. “Magic is not a curse but a tool. It has saved lives, revealed treachery, and warned of futures dark and uncertain. I ask only for trust, not fear.”

Kelvin’s heart clenched. He had always believed in simple lines – right and wrong, friend and foe. But here, in the flickering torchlight and whispered lies, those lines blurred.

As the trial wore on, Elara’s illusions flickered behind her, a silent language none but Kelvin could decipher. Scenes unfolded: visions of chaos, bloodshed, the throne overturned. Then, the most harrowing of all, a shadowed glimpse of Kelvin himself, struck down in battle, his death marking the kingdom’s fall.

Kelvin’s breath caught. The vision was clear and cruel. Death was no longer distant, it loomed, tethered to the fate of a fragile woman who had become impossible to ignore.

After the court adjourned, Kelvin approached her quietly in the dim corridor, his voice low, rough with conflict. “I do not understand your magic, nor do I fully trust it. But I cannot deny the danger we face.”

Elara met his gaze, hope flickering in her dark eyes. “Trust is a choice, Kelvin. Not given lightly. But without it, we fall.”

For the first time, Kelvin felt the weight of fate, not as an unyielding chain, but as a thread they might weave together. He would walk this uncertain path with her, guarding not only the kingdom but something more fragile: the promise of what might be.

* * *

The palace after midnight was a labyrinth of shadows and whispered secrets. Flickering torches cast long, twisting shapes along the stone corridors as Kelvin and Elara moved with practiced stealth, two predators in a dangerous game.

They had become an unlikely pair, bound by necessity, mistrust, and a fragile thread of growing respect. The court's gilded masks no longer held meaning here; only survival mattered.

Kelvin's eyes scanned every corner, sword drawn and ready. "You see too much in your visions," he murmured, voice low. "Fear twists truth."

Elara's gaze flashed with quiet fire. "And your blade sees only what it can cut. But some dangers lurk where steel cannot reach."

Their verbal sparring was a rhythm, a dance as old as time – sharp words, sharper minds. Yet beneath it pulsed a deeper connection, unspoken and electric.

The illusions had grown darker in recent nights. Threads of shadow weaving grim possibilities: Kelvin's death igniting chaos, the throne bleeding into ruin. Each vision tightened the noose around their mission.

As they rounded a bend, the faintest whisper of movement caught Kelvin's attention. Figures cloaked in black slipped through the corridors – assassins, silent and deadly.

"Ambush," he warned, tightening his grip.

Elara's hands fluttered, weaving a veil of mist that shrouded their presence. "Follow my lead."

The clash was sudden and brutal. Steel sang as Kelvin met the first attacker, every strike precise, every parry a promise of death. Elara's magic swirled, a phantom dance of light that disoriented their foes, turning the shadows against themselves.

But the enemy was relentless. A blade found Kelvin's side – a searing pain that stole his breath. He staggered but held firm, his determination burning more fiercely than the wound.

Elara knelt beside him, fear threading through her calm exterior. "This magic," she whispered, "is forbidden. But I will not lose you."

Her hands glowed with an otherworldly light, tendrils of healing magic wrapping around Kelvin's injury. The pain ebbed, replaced by warmth and renewal.

The risk was immense. Should the court discover her use of forbidden magic, the price would be exile...or worse.

Kelvin's eyes fluttered open, meeting Elara's gaze, a moment suspended between life and death, truth and longing.

"Why save me?" he rasped, voice raw.

"Because without you," Elara replied, her voice trembling, "this kingdom falls. And because..." She faltered, words caught in the fragile web between them.

Kelvin reached out, his fingers brushing hers, a touch heavy with meaning. The cold barrier around his heart cracked, revealing something fragile and vital beneath.

They stood in silence, the world outside fading until only the quiet between them remained. Neither dared to speak the name of the feeling blooming in the shadows, but both knew it was there, defiant and undeniable.

The dance of blades and shadows was far from over. But in that fragile moment, sword and magic, duty and love, found a tentative harmony.

* * *

The grand hall shimmered beneath crystal chandeliers as nobles gathered for the Queen's banquet, a night meant for celebration now thick with tension. The air was heavy with whispered alliances and veiled threats, eyes flickering like embers, waiting for the spark.

Kelvin stood near the Queen's throne, blade concealed but ready. Elara's fingers brushed the air, weaving illusions only he could perceive: subtle distortions of reality that cloaked their movements and revealed hidden truths.

The traitors moved among the crowd, high-ranking lords whose smiles hid serpents. Their plot was no mere whisper now but a deadly snarl aimed at seizing power by toppling the throne.

Elara's voice was a low murmur in Kelvin's ear. "They believe themselves safe behind masks. But tonight, their dance ends."

The moment shattered when a gilded goblet shattered on the marble floor, a signal. Steel flashed as conspirators drew weapons, chaos erupting in the midst of nobles frozen in shock.

Kelvin surged forward, sword singing through the air, meeting the lead conspirator...Lord Velran...a man as ruthless as he was cunning. Their blades clashed in a brutal duet, sparks flying as steel met steel.

Elara's magic shimmered around the Queen, crafting illusions that hid her from harm, phantoms that twisted the conspirators' senses, turning their confidence into confusion.

The duel between Kelvin and Velran was fierce, every strike a question: Would duty alone be enough to save the kingdom? Or was there more at stake, something he had fought to deny?

In a brief pause, Kelvin glimpsed one of Elara's visions flickering before him: himself fallen, lifeless on cold stone, the kingdom plunging into darkness without him. But alongside it, another future, a fragile light where they survived, ruling not as sword and sorceress apart, but as partners entwined by trust and love.

Breath ragged, Kelvin made his choice.

With renewed strength, he pressed the attack, not just for duty, but for the promise of a future with Elara. His sword found its mark, disarming Velran and ending the threat.

The hall stilled as the conspirators were seized, their plot unraveled by the fusion of blade and magic, love and loyalty.

Kelvin turned to Elara, eyes heavy with unspoken words. "The future is uncertain," he said softly, "but whatever comes, I choose to face it with you."

Elara's smile was a whispered vow. "Then we weave that future together."

As dawn broke beyond the palace windows, light spilled over a kingdom battered but unbroken. Kelvin's wound from the confrontation throbbed, a reminder of the cost of choice.

Yet within that pain was hope: the delicate beginning of something neither blade nor illusion alone could forge.

Together, they would walk the uncertain path ahead, bound by a love that had been born in shadows but now shone like a beacon.

* * *

Months had passed since the night the kingdom had teetered on the edge of ruin. Now, peace settled like a soft cloak over stone walls and bustling streets. The court moved with cautious confidence, guarded not by fear, but by the steadfast union of blade and magic.

Kelvin stood beside Elara on the balcony overlooking the palace gardens, the rising sun gilding their silhouettes. His hand found hers – steady, warm – a silent vow spoken without words.

Elara's fingers danced lightly through the air, weaving strands of light into a final illusion, a tapestry shimmering with possibility. Before them unfolded a vision of a kingdom reborn: fields rich and golden, laughter spilling from village squares, and a throne guarded by two who chose love and duty in equal measure.

"This future," Elara whispered, "is ours to shape. Not bound by prophecy or fate, but forged by the choices we make."

Kelvin's gaze met hers, the cold edge long softened into quiet strength. "Sword and magic," he said, "love and loyalty. We are more than what we were – something new, something stronger."

Together, they watched the dawn crest the horizon, a day bright with promise.

The past, with its shadows and fears, lingered only as a memory, a reminder that even in the darkest moments, the heart's courage could weave a new tomorrow.

And so they stood, partners in every sense, ready to face whatever the future held, not as isolated guardians, but as a single, unbreakable thread woven through the tapestry of their kingdom's fate.

Always for Her Favor

Jennifer R. Povey

Sometimes, I have fallen in love with a curve, or the flow of hair unleashed from braid or helmet. I keep no secrets about my proclivities…unlike in some kingdoms, women who wish to wed women are as accepted here as women knights.

So, yes, sometimes…but this time that was not the first thing I noticed. The first thing I noticed was her poise in the saddle.

I did not even know as yet that Alastria was a woman. Full armor conceals gender unless you are wearing foolish ceremonial armor designed to reveal it. Such armor might be suited to a queen in a parade, but not to a knight on the field. It looks bad and protects worse.

So, no, I did not know, she could have been a slender young man, too masculine for my personal tastes, although I do, I will note, have a sister. If she ever settles down, she will be the one to easily grant my parents grandchildren of the blood. They have accepted that any children I bring into the family will be wards. Hard to accept, but I did convince them.

It would be some time before I saw her without the helmet. In fact, the first time I saw her, my duty was to try and slay her or, at least, to drive her back.

They called it the War of the Azaleas, which is pretty, isn't it? There is nothing pretty about war. Oh, *tournaments* are pretty. We wear armor designed to ensure that nobody actually gets hurt and show off our horsemanship and swordsmanship for the favors of ladies and gentlemen. Afterwards, we drink together and enjoy fair foods made by those who have traveled to show off their wares, and compare horses.

War is nothing like that. True, there is drinking afterwards, but it is not drinking to have fun or to celebrate a victory or commiserate a loss.

It is drinking to chase off the ghosts that haunt the battlefield...ghosts of knights and soldiers and horses.

Putting a pretty name onto it does not make it anything other than a war. What was it over? In many ways that is not important to our story, but it was about what almost all wars are about: money. You want to say they are about land, but land is valued by what it produces and what it produces is valued in money. The war was between Queen Iosepha and King Ramon over a fertile valley, and it was resolved with a deal everyone was happy with except the dead. They attend each other's birthday parties now and laugh like none of it ever happened.

I serve a Queen. That does not mean I like her. Truth is, for my skills, there is no other way, and until I retire to a farm and breed jousting horses, I will serve Queen Iosepha.

Just as Alastria serves King Ramon.

But I get ahead of myself, for I must take this story back to the last days of the war.

* * *

The end of a war has a peculiar tension to it. There comes a point when you know peace will be agreed. There is the point when it has been agreed, but you don't know yet, so you keep fighting.

I had been unhorsed at some point and could only hope my mount had run out of there and not been injured, killed, or captured.

Every kingdom trains their horses slightly differently to reduce their value when captured. A good knight learns how to adapt quickly.

If I could grab a horse, any horse, I would be back in the fight, but an unhorsed knight is a fancy infantryman...and less effective than one. I had my sword out and was hacking away at...at what I realized was the same knight whose horsemanship I had admired days before, the way they sat, the way they held the reins, light and consistent, not yanking on the horse.

And I won. I had my sword blade touching their gorget when the trumpet sounded to stand down.

I kept the blade up a moment longer, then lowered it. Stand down?

The banners were being struck. The rumors were true; peace had been agreed. Trades would happen. Possibly some poor noble kids would find themselves child-betrothed to somebody on the other side. I was glad my family was not of such rank.

We looked at each other then, almost simultaneously, lowered our swords and took off our helmets, looking at each other.

She was auburn haired and fair skinned. I knew I was southern-dark, descended as I was from spice traders. "I'm Paria."

"Alastria. I would have surrendered."

"So would I. But I don't need to take your surrender now. Although I wouldn't mind." It came out without thought.

She had every right to hit me with her gauntlet for the implication. Instead, she smiled speculatively. "Perhaps one day."

Then we both turned to find our horses. Mine was slightly injured; nothing the farrier could not fix, and I led the limping beast back to camp.

If I saw her ride again, it would be in tourney. And I wondered who would win.

* * *

She won.

The next time I saw Alastria sans helm, she was offering me a sportswomanlike hand up after having neatly unhorsed me with one shot.

To make it worse, she was smiling about it. Which meant I had to smile too, even though the padded armor had only *reduced* the bruises she inflicted. "Good riding."

"Good riding."

I wore the favor of Lady Jana of Marlow, who preferred to play the game with female knights. Rumor had it that she had gone beyond playing the game a couple of times and her husband held no objection, as such liaisons could not lead to questions of paternity.

Part of me was tempted; Jana had lovely blonde curls and, shall we say, substantial assets to bring to the bedroom along with those she had once brought to the marriage contract.

However, not as much with Alastria there in front of me, even with the armor concealing her form.

"As victor, I claim your company at the feast tonight."

She could have claimed my horse, my armor, a kiss…I had half hoped for the last. Of course, claimed horses were always ransomed, typically *not* for their full value. We trained our horses not just to be good at their jobs but to work with us specifically.

I did, however, know one knight who rode a stallion and it had become traditional to claim breeding rights. To the stallion, not the knight, although he was a handsome enough man and there were rumors…

Men who could not father children with their wives would often…well, that is enough of that. And women married to another woman who *did* decide to have offspring of blood had the same options.

But the stallion was a fine beast and my sister *did* have a mare that would…but never mind that, again.

Company at the feast was not a claim I had expected and I felt the blood flush to my cheeks. Was she implying?

A kiss would imply she desired me.

Company at the feast implied she wished to know me better. We were of age and rank to court, too.

Could she…

Could this be…

…a date?

* * *

As vanquished, I had little choice. Alastria, it turned out, was not one of those lady knights who preferred doublet and hose when out of armor.

Neither was I, and I have no doubt but that we looked striking together…I in a red gown and she in a rich blue that perfectly set off her hair.

I did not dare ask her intentions regarding me, but as she led me to the table reserved for those who had competed that day (and piled accordingly with food; the cooks and servers knew how hungry knights were after a tournament), I followed appropriately, taking on a slightly subservient role.

She grinned as she sat me down. "This might be the only chance I get…"

"…to have me…shall I feed you, my lady?"

She laughed. "No, I feel no need to take this that far, and besides, your blow was almost as good as mine. If your horse had not mis-stepped, our roles would be reversed. Tell me, what would you have claimed of me?"

I looked down, but only for a moment before, once more, my voice betrayed me. "A kiss."

"Is that all you wish?"

I shook my head. "No, but it is…less complicated."

There might have been peace for a few years, but the one obstacle to our courting was the border that lay between us.

"You do not wish to court a Velonian."

I shook my head. "I do, but my family might…present some complications. They have long accepted I will not court a man, but…"

"But a foreigner…then we will simply have to convince them. Assuming you *are* interested in courting me?"

I flushed again. "I am interested in finding out if you are the right one to court."

She laughed. "A good answer, fair Paria."

I had received compliments, but few, thanks to my ancestry, called me "fair". "We both ride again tomorrow," I said, in part by way of excuse as I piled my trencher high.

"And whose favor will you carry? The Lady Jana again?"

"All part of the game. I note, though…"

"The one whose favor I asked refused me. No doubt they are now regretting it."

But we would ride again. She in the higher division, I in the lower after she had knocked me out of the running for the championship. This time.

"What are you asking?"

"I will decide in the morning."

And it was not just the feast we spent together that night.

* * *

It was the worst tournament of my life. Tournaments are dangerous, though we take steps to keep them from being so, including armor so carefully put together our squires put some of it on us *after* we mount.

Unlike battle armor, which is designed to fight and remount, tournament armor is designed solely to prevent serious injury.

Alastria lay on the ground, a heap of armor, and she was not moving. Her opponent, the same knight I had mentioned before, Erus, whose stallion was so in demand, had already dismounted and cast aside pieces of armor to rush to her side.

I left my horse with my squire and rushed into the lists. It was not entirely proper, but everyone had seen us leave the feast together.

She could be dead.

She could wake and never again be herself.

I knew all of those risks, for I took them myself. "Alastria." In that moment I knew.

A wise woman once told me that you do not marry the person you want to live with, but the person you do not want to live without. I am not saying that I could not imagine life without her, because I could…it would simply be grey and dull and anyone I wed instead would run the risk of knowing they were the second choice.

Erus was gently removing her helmet. "I think she just took a knock."

I hoped so. The surgeon was also rushing over, and I let her past, let her examine the fallen knight.

Stood there not even knowing what to think, let alone what to say, what to do. I am not a praying woman but I went through the names of every relevant god, demigod, and saint I could think of in that moment.

Every *remotely* relevant one.

Please let her be alright. Please let her be okay.

We carried her from the lists and I knew this was not going…she could not be okay. She had to be okay.

I did not wish to leave her side, but the surgeons threw me out, and I went instead to the shrine of Jivia, the goddess of healing.

I did not leave that shrine for two days. My squire brought me food and I forced myself to eat enough to stay alive, barely.

I just wanted her to be alright.

* * *

The surgeons said she would live…but not ride or fight again.

I was at her bedside, and it seemed likely, for she could not walk. She could crawl like a child, as if everything had been taken from her.

I brought roses, the symbol of love.

"How can you court me now?"

"You are still you." It had been her riding I had first been drawn to, but it was her laugh I wanted to hear again. "And I do not want to live without you."

"I am nothing." She turned her face away from me. "Go away."

I knew I had a battle indeed, a harder one than I had ever thought. My uncle had broken his back in a fall and he too had thought himself to be nothing. He was now an advisor on warhorse bloodlines to the entire kingdom. True, he would never ride again and required a wheeled chair.

And that was when I knew what I had to do. I rode to his estate on a borrowed palfrey, my own being, in this time of peace, otherwise occupied…producing another palfrey.

"Uncle Calwin!"

He wheeled his chair out, and I dismounted to greet him. "I need your help."

"Is it the foal?"

"The foal will be here in about six weeks, if all goes well. But it is not a horse I need your help with."

"It is not?"

"A knight who took a bad fall. She may not ride again. She is…"

"As bound to despair as I was. Say no more. I will arrange my carriage."

He might not be able to ride, but he could still drive. I knew he would come. And when he did, he entered her room, and he did not leave for many hours.

I stayed away, for I feared I would only get in the way of what healing he could offer.

But heal she did. She did walk again, unsteadily, although it was true she would never again have the co-ordination to fight.

And at first I could not get her to tourneys, but we did court. I may have helped save her. Certainly Calwin did, if only by showing that he was still useful.

Six months passed. Another tourney came and went, but now there was one coming up that was for the ages… knights from seven kingdoms.

Part of me thought of not riding, but she told me I must.

* * *

I had trained, even though part of me had wanted to retire. Again, she would have none of it.

And this time she watched, sitting in the lists next to Calwin. I had a new horse, or rather a horse that was finally ready, a red mare who stomped and snorted, but was never out of control in the lists. I thought her possibly the best I had ridden, certainly one of the best.

She watched as I unhorsed opponent after opponent, as I rode better than I had ever ridden.

There is something to be said for favors. And as I stood over my last opponent, I offered him a hand up.

"Whose favor do you ride for?"

I smiled, helping him back to his feet.

"I ride for the favor of Alastria."

"Not *Lady* Alastria?"

I shook my head. "She is *my* lady, for she is my betrothed."

"And what do you claim from me?"

"A young horse from your mother's bloodlines."

"From our *palfrey* bloodlines?"

"One with a quiet temperament and smooth gaits."

For while she would never fight again, I knew that with the right horse, Alastria would ride.

And that at least we could have a knights' wedding, meeting on horseback under the arch of roses, in the presence of all those we cared about.

"Make it a white one if you can."

And perhaps something in his eyes understood, as he looked over at the redhead in the stands and the man next to her in his wheeled chair.

Not nothing. Never nothing. My future wife is never *nothing* and I will defend her honor for the rest of my days, until I too have to hang up my spurs.

And may I never fight again for anything *but* her honor.

It Befits Her

Ziggy Schutz

The whisper of armour over fabric is reverent, amplified by the hallowed hall that they've made their home since the end of the world. The Knight breathes deep, standing scarecrow-still as clever hands slide each piece of armor home. Repetition turns to tradition turns to ritual, giving each movement an elegance in its purpose.

The most important thing to remember when surviving the end of the world is to find the beauty in things, and the girl in front of the Knight has beauty in every inch of her, every stitch and muscle.

One greave tightens, then the other. They used to talk their way through this. Her Squire naming each piece and how it protects her, her repeating the words back, not sure whether the point was to memorize the words or the way the Squire looked saying them. Her favourite times were when the Squire would get distracted, a lace half-done up as she rattled through a history half a world away from the Knight's own, how the Squire would light up with every question or bit of laughter. Then came a day where a loose strap almost prevented her from making it back at all. The Squire had removed each piece of her with fingers that shook, whispering prayers into every new mark in the metal. The helm was last, split almost in two, stained with red.

"You look like a martyr," she had breathed, and the sentence fell into the hollows left exposed by the rain that had eaten away half her breastplate.

"I won't become one," she remembers promising. She would look up the word later. "I won't leave you."

Like makeshift armour forged by a classics major and worn by a badly translated fairytale, their relationship is unconventional but stronger for it. Somewhere between the stained-glass windows of this church, framed by each other's bodies, they have gone from surviving to living.

Now, they dress in silence. What started as a fear of repeating mistakes has grown into something powerful, something neither of them name. As if to name it would make it dissipate, like trying to hold smoke up to the light.

The Squire rises, as calm as any weapon from some fated lake, and the Knight fills her lungs with air as the breastplate slides over her head. In the echoes caught in her own fabricated exoskeleton, she hears the crowds again.

Silence frightens her. She remembers waking in silence, ears ringing with the weight of it. Before she found her Squire, that's what her journey was made of. As if her brain couldn't handle things falling apart around her, and she'd reached over and muted the world. But the Squire has the power to turn silence into a weapon, into something like strength that she folds into each knot and buckle. The Knight's fingers are not that clever, hands built for wielding weapons but not forging them. And outside their doors, silence finds the chinks in her armour, makes her jump at things no one else can see.

So, as her Squire pieces her together, she builds the scene. A skills exhibition, vivid enough that she can almost see each individual crest, held aloft by proud standards. A crowd stamps their feet, and across the tiltyard another Knight mirrors her. It's only a game in this fantasy, one pieced together from fragments of the stories her Squire weaves for her.

Sometimes she closes her eyes and the crowd expands and multiplies, and she swears she can feel the heat on her skin. There are more people and less armour, her arm raised in victory, a crown that means life but not freedom. She doesn't like this story, doesn't like how strongly the sand reeks of blood.

When she thinks like this, her tongue feels heavy, and English comes to it even more slowly. Once she spoke in a language she didn't even know the name of, and her Squire asked her where she'd learnt Latin. She asks for more stories about chivalry, pretends not to understand the questions in the Squire's eyes.

With each piece of hammered metal, she lets herself grow larger. Who she was before, the dreamer and whoever came before that, they cannot survive what waits outside. She doesn't even let them try. She is a storybook hero, in this armour, without face or fear. The Squire fills her head with the history of women warriors, and with each name and deed she stands taller.

She is a Knight made of salvage and salvation. In the new world that is forming, phoenix flame forged, she is the impossible.

Eyes from the windows stare down at them, and she imagines this is what it feels like to be them. Stained-glass sainthood, where details are pushed aside in favour of one's true shape, delicate and tempered and held together by a metal that hasn't yet learned to kill.

Vambrace to gauntlet to gatlings, and when she moves her fingers, they sound like wind chimes. The Squire smiles, as beautiful as any church window, and the Knight thinks about their lessons on idioms, thinks about hearts like lead, about how worry will only slow her down. She reaches into her own ribcage, redefining the words, because it's their world now and language must grow to live, just like people. She slots coloured glass in each crack, so if she falls in battle even the vultures who break her open for her marrow will see the Squire's image in the art of her corpse.

The Knight thinks of her own death and feels stronger, and here is another reason to be grateful for the quiet. She knows her Squire would frown to hear it, use big words like *fatalistic*. The Knight has another theory, because she remembers how her blood steamed, the day she almost died. Because when the Squire talked of phoenixes, she inhaled the ashes of their world and her breath came out as smoke. She thinks of the crowds screaming in her head, about other big words like *reincarnation* and *immortality*. Those words she learned all on her own. She hasn't figured out what part they play in the story the two of them are writing, but that's okay. Words like that have more power when left unspoken, and her tongue is bound to trip on them anyway.

Death is so often where stories end.

"I'm not sure I like your legends."

It was a softer moment, the two of them curled up together, listening to a storm.

"Why not?"

The statement rang false, because every word the Squire spins is filled with passion and care, and it is all beautiful. But they wear on The Knight sometimes. In the dark, as thunder crashed, it was a physical weight on her chest. She felt buried.

"So often, they end sad," she tried to explain. "I love how your voice sounds when you tell them, but I think I like my legends better."

"And how do your legends end?" She was teasing, and the Knight loved her, loves her, will love her.

"I don't know. We haven't gotten there yet."

Death can be a beginning, too.

Her armour bears no heraldry, but she thinks when she returns she'll ask her Squire to help her paint it. It doesn't have to be beautiful or even lasting. She just wants it to be bright. She wants it to be seen through the mist. She wants to be known.

The weight of her hammer feels right on her hip, and she is almost complete. This is where the Squire's nerves show, checking over each piece three or four times before she brings over her helm and sword.

The helm is the newest part of her armour, made to replace the one that had failed. When the Squire is anxious, she polishes it until it shines. It does not touch the floor. If it does not know what the ground feels like, it will not know how to fall. The Squire believes it, so it must be so. Standing on her tiptoes to place it on her Knight's head, she whispers, as if the sound doesn't escape the helmet it doesn't count.

"I love you," she says. "Find victory and then find home again."

The Knight nods, pretending it's tradition and not emotions that keep her from replying. The Squire slides the visor down, and her vision fragments. Her eyes will adjust, but for now she just stares at her Squire's fractured smile. If she turns her head, the room around her will start to flash, the crowds visible even with her eyes open. Inside of her helm, everything feels like an echo, and so everything seems real. But if she looks only at her Squire until her eyes remember where she is, then she knows she is in the right moment. She will stay here, where she is needed and needs in return.

The Squire stares back, until something in the Knight's eyes betray she is ready, and then she leans in, presses her lips to the visor, and disappears.

The Knight does not turn to watch her walk away. She knows she will return.

Hands slide around her waist, and she is grounded. Scabbard to sword belt, and she stands whole. The Squire steps into view again, fists clenched. The Knight knows her Squire is working on a second suit, how she hates being unable to follow her out. The Knight wishes that she could see the importance in what she does, because the Knight knows that she is a warrior but also a distraction, drawing trouble to her so that her Squire can collect all the little things they need to keep living.

The doors open, the creaking of them magnified by the silence they're interrupting. The Knight moves towards them, then turns back to her Squire.

When she draws her sword, it sings. She practised this, over and over until she could do it in one motion, and the ringing of the metal fills her with pride. She lowers the blade until it rests level with her chest. In this moment, it is not a weapon but a promise, and it is pointing right at her Squire.

She does not reply to her Squire's whispered confession. Not out loud. But every movement makes her armour speak, and it says *I love you* again and again. Everything she does is for the woman in front of her, and she can see in her eyes that she knows it.

She is only a Knight because her Squire made it so, after all. Her Squire beat the metal into protection, hammered her heart into beating again, forged them into something like stories, bright glass with bones defined by lead. The shined surface of the sword reflects all of this, catches every light in their lives here and helps it grow. The Knight wields this sword, but it was the Squire who bled for it, who willed it to sharpness, who pulled it from the fire and gave it a name.

"It's a silly name," she had said, when she'd given her the sword. "I was just scared."

But hope is what her Squire gave her, and the Knight does not think there is anything silly about that.

Spero shines between them, and the Squire bows. The Knight bows back. Then she turns, steps out of the doors and into the colosseum, into legend, into sharp relief.

The Thornblade's Promise

Laura Shenton

The roses in the royal garden bloomed dark crimson, their thorns gleaming like tiny daggers in the moonlight. Each petal seemed to pulse with its own malevolent life, fed by centuries of royal secrets buried beneath the ancient soil. Princess Calindra pressed herself against the marble pillar, her heart hammering against her ribs as she watched the shadow-cloaked figure move between the flower beds, graceful yet predatory. The silk of her midnight-blue gown whispered against the stone, and she cursed the court seamstresses who had insisted on such impractical beauty even for a woman marked for death.

She shouldn't be here. The Shadow Court's assassin had come for her, just as the prophecy had foretold – the one written in blood three centuries ago, when her ancestor had first claimed this throne through conquest and dark bargains. She was supposed to be safely locked in her tower, protected by her father's guards and his desperate hope that mortal steel could defeat destiny itself. The old king had aged a decade in the past month, ever since the seers had confirmed that tonight would bring the fulfilment of ancient words: "When red roses bloom beneath the hunter's moon, the last heir shall taste the Thornblade's kiss, and the old kingdom shall know peace through ending."

But Calindra had never been one to cower, not even as a child when the nightmares came crawling through her dreams like smoke given form. She had faced down court conspirators, rebellious lords, and even the dragon that had terrorised the eastern provinces last spring. She would not spend her final hours weeping in a tower like some tragic helpless maiden.

The assassin stopped before the ancient rose bush at the garden's heart – the one that had grown there since the kingdom's founding, its roots intertwined with the very stones of the castle. The bush stood taller than a man, its trunk thick as a warrior's torso, covered in thorns that could pierce chainmail. Legend claimed it would bloom black when the royal bloodline ended, that it had been planted by the first king as both monument and warning. Its roses were the size of saucers, their petals soft as silk but their stems armed with cruelty. Tonight, those petals remained red as fresh wine, red as the dress she had worn to her eighteenth birthday celebration, red as the blood that would soon fulfil the prophecy.

"You came," the figure said, his voice like silk drawn over steel. Each word carried the weight of years and the promise of violence. He turned, and moonlight caught the angles of a face she knew too well – sharp cheekbones that could cut glass, eyes like winter storm clouds heavy with unshed snow, lips that had once whispered promises against her skin in stolen moments between duty and desire. A scar she didn't remember ran from his left temple to his jaw, silver against his olive skin. "I wondered if you would."

The years had changed him. Gone was the lanky boy who had helped her escape etiquette lessons to climb trees and race horses through forbidden meadows. This man before her moved with lethal precision, his shoulders broader, his hands marked with calluses that hinted at weapons training and harder purposes. But his eyes – those storm-grey eyes that had haunted her dreams – remained achingly familiar.

"Sarion." His name escaped her lips, carrying years of sleepless nights and unanswered questions. The boy who had been her dearest friend, her first love, her greatest betrayal. The one who had vanished on the night she was to announce their engagement to a court full of scheming nobles who had never thought a stable boy's son worthy of their princess. He had left only a letter that shattered her heart into a thousand pieces, each shard of pain cutting deeper than the last: "I am not the man you need me to be. Forget me, and find someone worthy of your love."

She had burnt the letter, but the words remained carved into her memory like scars on her soul.

Now he stood before her in the garb of her enemies, leather and shadow-silk that whispered of dangerous allegiances. The Thornblade of legend gleamed at his hip – a sword forged from meteoric steel that had fallen from the heavens themselves, bound with magic darker than midnight and hungrier than winter. The weapon that could cut through any defence, pierce any heart, end any life. Including hers. Its crossguard was wrought to resemble thorny vines, and rubies like drops of blood adorned its pommel. In the moonlight, it seemed to pulse with its own malicious heartbeat.

"You're the Shadow Court's champion," she whispered, pieces of the puzzle clicking together with devastating clarity. Stories uttered in the castle's dark corners suddenly made sense – tales of an assassin who could walk through walls, who could kill with a touch, who served the ancient enemies of her bloodline with absolute devotion. "The Thornblade Bearer. The one they sent to fulfil the prophecy."

His smile was almost menacing, but she caught the tremor at its edges, the crack in his assassin's mask. "Did you think I abandoned you for coin? For power? For the embrace of some foreign courtesan?" He stepped closer, and she caught the familiar scent of cedar that had always clung to his skin, now mixed with steel and something darker. "Everything I've done, every life I've taken, every piece of my soul I've bartered away – it has all been for you."

"By joining those who would see me dead?" The accusation came out stronger than she intended, her voice steady despite the tears threatening to spill. "By becoming their weapon?"

"By becoming strong enough to protect you." The words cracked like a whip, raw with years of suppressed pain. "Do you know what it's like, loving someone you can never have? Watching from the shadows as they parade suitors before you – princes and dukes and heroes with bloodlines pure as mountain snow? Knowing that your love is nothing but a childhood folly to be discarded when duty calls?" The Thornblade sang as he drew it from its sheath. But instead of pointing it at her heart as she expected, he reversed his grip and offered her the hilt, his knuckles white with the effort of restraint. "The prophecy speaks of the last royal heir dying by this blade on the night the red roses bloom beneath the hunter's moon. But prophecies, my love, can be…creatively interpreted."

The blade was beautiful in its deadliness, etched with runes that seemed to shift and writhe in the moonlight. She could feel the power radiating from it, cold as winter's heart yet somehow alive. The metal hummed with ancient magic, and she could see why legends claimed it could cut through the very fabric of reality itself.

She stared at the weapon, overwhelmed by sudden understanding. "You want me to fake my death."

"I want you to choose your fate instead of letting it choose you." His eyes burned with desperate intensity, and she saw in them the frightened boy he had once been – the one who had held her during thunderstorms, who had sworn to protect her from all the monsters in the world. "Take the blade. Cut yourself – just enough to draw blood, to make the magic believe. Let them think the prophecy is fulfilled while we disappear into the shadows together. I know paths through the Whispering Woods that lead to kingdoms beyond the reach of courts and prophecies."

"And abandon my people? My kingdom?" The words tasted bitter, but she had to voice them. She thought of the farmers struggling with failed harvests, of the villages on the border constantly under threat from shadow-beasts, of the growing darkness that crept closer to the capital with each passing month. "They need their princess. Their hope."

"Your people will survive. They always do." But she heard the hollow ring in his voice, the lie they both recognised. "But you…" His composure cracked entirely, revealing the terrified young man beneath the assassin's cold exterior. "You're all I have left, Cali. All I've ever had. When I close my eyes, I still see that little girl who found me crying in the stables because the other boys said I didn't belong. You were seven years old and you looked at me like I was worth saving."

The memory hit her hard. She had been so young, so certain that kindness could heal any wound. She remembered taking his bloody knuckles in her small hands, remembered declaring with all the fierce authority of a child princess that anyone who hurt her friend would answer to her.

"I remember," she whispered, her voice thick with emotion.

She remembered the day they'd first met, two lonely children in a castle full of courtly intrigue and adult games they didn't understand. He'd been a stable boy's son with clever hands and eyes that saw too much, beaten for the crime of daring to dream beyond his station. She'd been a princess trapped in silk and expectations, suffocating under the weight of a crown she would someday wear. They'd found freedom in each other, had sworn oaths of eternal devotion with rings made of braided grass and promises sealed with innocent kisses stolen in hidden alcoves.

They had built a world of their own in stolen moments – chasing fireflies through moonlit fields, sharing books in dusty library corners, planning impossible adventures to distant lands where birth meant nothing and love meant everything. He had taught her to pick locks and climb walls, to see the castle's secret passages and hidden ways. She had shared with him her dreams of being more than just a pretty face to be married off for political advantage.

But innocence was a luxury neither of them could afford anymore. The world had intruded with all its cruel realities, and childhood dreams had withered like flowers in brutal frost.

"Tell me why you left," she whispered, reaching out with trembling fingers to trace the scar that ran along his jaw, a reminder of the violence that had shaped him in their years apart. "Tell me the truth. All of it."

His eyes closed at her touch, and for a moment he was just Sarion again – her Sarion. "Because I found out what you were. What you could become."

She didn't understand. "What I…?"

"You're Flamehearted, Cali. The last of the old bloodline, the one the prophecies really speak of. Not just any royal heir – you're the one who could burn down the Shadow Court with a thought, who could reshape the very foundations of magic itself." His hand covered hers where it rested against his face. "They would have used you, controlled you, turned you into a weapon. So I made myself into one first."

The revelation stole her breath. She'd always known she was different – the way flowers bloomed brighter in her presence, the way injured animals sought her out, the strange dreams that felt more like memories. But this…

"The Shadow Court offered me power, position, anything I wanted in exchange for your death," Sarion continued, his voice raw. "What they didn't know was that I'd already chosen what I wanted most. You. Alive and free, even if it meant you could never be mine."

Tears pricked her eyes like thorns. "You fool. Did you never think to simply ask me to run away with you?"

"A princess and a stable boy's son? They would have hunted us to the ends of the earth."

"But an assassin and his victim might simply disappear." She understood now, saw the twisted brilliance of his plan. Let the world think Princess Calindra was dead, murdered by the Shadow Court's blade. Let Cali the Flamehearted be born from her ashes, free to choose her own destiny.

The Thornblade hummed as she wrapped her fingers around its hilt. The metal was warm, almost alive, and she could feel the magic thrumming through it like a second heartbeat. This was the weapon that had ended dynasties, that had drunk the blood of kings and queens.

"If I do this," she said slowly, "there's no going back. Calindra dies tonight."

"I know." His hand covered hers on the blade's grip. "Are you ready to become who you were always meant to be?"

She thought of her father, grey-haired and weary, ruling a kingdom that grew smaller and weaker with each passing year. She thought of the people in the villages, struggling to survive as magic drained from the land. She thought of the Shadow Court, growing stronger in their hidden realm, preparing to sweep across the mortal world like a plague.

And she thought of the power sleeping in her blood, the fire that could burn away the old world and forge something new.

"Together?" she asked.

"Always."

She pressed the tip of the blade to her fingertip, just hard enough to pierce the skin. A single drop of blood bloomed. A bead of ruby, born of sharp pain but not unwelcome.

"By blood and blade," she whispered, the old ritual words coming to her lips unbidden. "By love and sacrifice. Let the old world die so a new one may be born."

Magic erupted around them like wildfire, turning the air itself to flame and starlight. The ancient prophecy shattered, its power redirected by will and love and the bright courage of a girl who refused to be anyone's pawn.

Sarion's arms came around her as the transformation took hold, as Princess Calindra dissolved into light and shadow, leaving only Cali in her place – Cali the Flamehearted, whose story was just beginning.

"Where do we go now?" she asked against his shoulder, feeling the new power singing in her soul.

His smile was beautiful and full of promise. "Wherever we choose. The Shadow Court thinks they've won, but they've created their own destruction. We'll teach them what it means to underestimate love."

Hand in hand, they walked into the darkness beyond the garden, leaving behind the echo of a prophecy fulfilled in ways its makers never could have imagined. Behind them, the castle slept on, unaware that their princess had died and been reborn, that destiny itself had been reforged in the space between one heartbeat and the next.

The Thornblade rested at Sarion's side, no longer a weapon of assassination but a guardian's promise, while magic flared beneath Cali's skin. They had work to do, a world to save, enemies to face.

But they would face them together, as they always should have, bound by a love stronger than any prophecy and sharper than any blade.

Libeunfeyer

S.S.N. Smith

The air was sour with the scent of sweat. The sound of thousands of boots crunching under the sand filled the air, like thunder in the heavens. Ashia gripped the hilt of her sword so tightly it felt like it was molding into her palm. Her soldiers surrounded her in perfect formation. All watched as she waited for the oncoming procession to stop short.

"We can still fight," Pasha's strong voice said from behind her.

Ashia shook her head.

The opposing army halted, and she finally laid eyes on the man sitting atop the throne, carried by servants. She saw the ornate gold ornamentation and no longer wondered why they were here. For five years, the rumor of starvation had snaked its way through Ashia's land. She'd heard stories of children punished for stealing loaves of bread, mothers clutching their children in their arms as they cried themselves to death, and people dying in the streets from starvation. Ashia couldn't think of how a kingdom as big as

Harata could have starving people, when her small kingdom with far less land and half the population was bountiful.

As the king was carried toward her, dressed in silk robes with woven gold and matching slippers, Ashia had the full picture. The jewels on his fingers, the gold armor plate on his chest, the only piece of armor he wore, said it all.

"Queen Ashia," the king said.

She thought maybe his lips were painted a deep red, but upon further inspection, she knew they were stained from hibiscus and cherry mead, a rich drink that required costly imported fruit and honey. Ashia cringed at the thought of him sipping on wine as his people starved.

"King Kumarian," she bowed her head slightly, "we meet."

"We do," he chuckled. "Who would have thought it would come to this?"

They both knew it would come to this. Even as Ashia watched her advisers draw up peace treaties that would allow for Harata to receive subsidized goods from her land, she knew it would come to this. Kumarian wasn't there for the good of his people; they both knew this.

Ashia stood poised. "I want to spare our soldiers. I see no reason to shed the blood of thousands."

He leaned closer. "And what do you have in mind? A surrender, perhaps?"

"No," Ashia said, "your best fighter against mine."

Kumarian leaned back in his chair and clapped his hands together, his dark curly hair flopping in his face. "A one-on-one for the kingdom of Sambia."

Ashia wanted to jump across the neutral zone and split him in half. "One fight, one death."

"I agree," he said in a high voice. "Where is your fighter?"

Nurian had been her loyal guard and friend since they were children. She remembered him when he was baby-faced and as thin as a twig. Now Nurian stood two heads taller than the tallest soldiers, his shoulders so wide he turned to the side to fit through doorways. His legs were like tree trunks, and his arms were so big that Ashia could hang off them when he flexed.

The mountain of a man left craters in the sand as he marched to her side. He stood, fearless, with his hand on the hilt of his broadsword.

"Nurian will be the champion of Sambia," she announced.

Waves of sound crashed against the silence of the moment as the army cheered, stomping their feet and shaking the earth to clear any doubt in the minds of others that they would come out victorious.

Kumarian smiled as he motioned behind him.

A small figure in black steel armor walked forward as if they didn't want to be there. Their steps were light, as if they walked on petals floating in the water. They stood paces away from the king. They undid the leather helmet straps and bowed as they pulled the black steel from their head. A puff of curly black hair came from the top, and as they stood straight, brushing the locks from their face, Ashia took a sharp breath in.

Her body felt heavy as images flashed before her, and her mind was transported to a new time and place.

She stood on the edge of a garden, the flowers behind her waving in the wind, as she placed her hand above her eyes to shade them from the sun. She saw the figure coming towards her, and her body ached for them.

The figure morphed into the fighter from the field. Instead of the steady scowl on her face, deepening the frown lines on her light brown cheeks, and the darkness that burned behind her deep brown eyes, Ashia saw a smile and light.

She grinned, big and hopeful, as if all the cares of the world were behind her, and she was simply happy.

Her off-white tunic blew in the wind, the braided belt keeping it tied around her waist as she came closer, and Ashia knew she was coming home. Her dark hair was longer, tied in the back, and Ashia remembered oiling her hair that morning before she took off.

When she came to her, an overwhelming sense of comfort and happiness overtook her, and she opened her arms to be scooped up and pulled into the air. As she was set down from the hug, Ashia stared into her eyes, safety and comfort surrounding her. Her eyes flicked down to plump pink lips as she waited for a kiss that she had been desperate for.

"My queen," Pasha said.

Ashia was pulled from her thoughts. She looked ahead of her at the fighter, knowing she had the same vision. Ashia tore her stare away from her and turned to her adviser.

"I need counsel."

* * *

"Something happened," Kumarian said.

He jumped off his gold throne and rushed over.

Xiron shrugged. "Nothing happened."

"Don't play me for a fool, sister," the king snapped. "I saw the look you shared."

He crept closer, and the smell of incense wafted in the air. Xiron hated the way he smelled: exotic incense. She hated the way his eyes were lined with black soot from rare minerals, hated that his hair was shiny from oils extracted from imported plants.

The thing she hated the most about her half-brother was knowing that he knew everything. He knew when she was upset, when she was trying to refuse a command. No matter how hard she worked to mask herself from him, Kumarian always knew exactly what she was thinking and feeling. She knew he knew, and he was already crafting a plan to use her feelings to his advantage as he always did.

"Libeunfeyer," she said.

Kumarian's laughed boomed. "I knew it."

Xiron sat in a chair, her armor digging into her side. She couldn't get the image out of her mind. The vision of Ashia smiling at her, as if she, Xiron the soldier, hung the moon and painted the stars. It pushed into her mind, etching itself into the recesses of her brain, the way it felt to wrap her arms around Ashia's waist, to pull her in so close that even light couldn't pass between them. She could smell the flowers in the garden, the scent of lavender on Ashia's skin. She could feel the warmth of her body. She knew what it was like to run fingers through her spice-colored curls, to kiss her cheeks, to stare into hazel eyes and be lost for hours.

Her mother warned her about Libeunfeyer and the magic that coursed through her. Xiron grew up listening to her mother tell stories of how Xiron was descended from witches and thus had a deeper connection to the magical world. She remembered sitting on the edge of her seat as her mother explained the idea of love that burned instant and hot. She was in awe of the idea that she could meet her soulmate and see their love, knowing there was no turning back.

Xiron was young when she swore her blood oath to her half-brother. She had used her magic to make a dark deal. She'd transformed herself into The World Ender in the name of his greed. After six years of slashing down all that stood against her half-brother, turning her blade on innocents, setting fire to land and standing above as it burned, she assumed the gods had taken away the good magic as punishment. She assumed she would never have love, that she didn't deserve peace.

"You will fight it," Kumarian said.

She was pulled from her thoughts and looked up at him. "Kumar, I don't—"

"You will fight it," he repeated with authority in his voice. "I don't care how strong the magic is; a blood oath is stronger."

Xiron looked at the scar on her palm. "How long must I continue?"

Kumarian smirked. "You give me this and I will give you the quietness you desire."

Xiron's head jolted up to try and glean any sign of lying.

"Libeunfeyer; soulmates, yes?" He gave an evil grin. "Instead of chopping her head off, as I should do, I will give her to you." He moved around the room to pour himself a glass of wine. "You can go live on a goat farm or whatever silly life you think you want."

Xiron stood. "And you'll release me from my oath."

Kumarian turned, spilling some of the dark wine on his gold cloak. He motioned for a servant to come over and clean him up.

"You're asking a lot," he said.

"I'm giving you a lot," she told him. "Sambia is the only kingdom on Dryland you don't rule over."

"And what of those beyond the ocean?" He pushed the servant away.

"Use your legionnaires." She stepped closer to him. "Brother, I am asking, humbly, for my king to grant me a wish."

"That you be set free of your oath?"

She took a deep breath. "That I give him all of Dryland, and he allows me to live in peace with the woman I love."

* * *

"You're insane," Pasha shouted.

Ashia stood straight and watched her best friend as she unbuttoned the top of her tunic to allow herself to cool down.

"Libeunfeyer," Ashia repeated for the third time.

"I know what it is," Pasha said, as she sat down.

"Then you know it can't be fought." The queen moved closer to her crumbling friend. "Pasha, I saw it. I saw our love. I felt her hands on my waist, her breath on my skin. By the gods, that fighter is my love."

Pasha brushed her flyaway hairs from her tanned face. "Her name is Xiron, and she is the bastard half-sister of the king. Daughter of the Witch of Harata. She is dangerous. They call her The World Ender."

The knowledge sank into her heart. Xiron was the fear in the darkness, the idea that kept warriors awake at night, the form that crept into the dreams of the bravest.

Yet she didn't feel that way when they locked eyes. The soldier didn't feel like the ghost of nightmares in the image of her holding her so close that they felt like one person. To her, Xiron felt like a meadow filled with flowers that bloomed with hope.

"You saw you two together." Hypten came from the corner. "Does that mean we lose?"

"No," Pasha scoffed. She stood up and walked over to the man in the chair, ruffling his hair as she always did. "Libeunfeyer is just a possibility. It doesn't mean the vision will come true, only that it might."

Ashia nodded. "Father always said he had it with mother."

Her mother denied the magic with her father, claiming she married him for his money to make him chuckle. A queen marrying a farm-boy, nothing but the magic of the gods could make that happen, her father would say later.

"Either we lose and this Xiron character stays alive long enough to make your vision come true," Hypten told her. "Or we win, and Nurian kills her, and you'll never love again."

"I need a second," Ashia said, excusing herself.

She didn't have long. Her army was lined up and waiting for her command. They would fight if she ordered. Or she could keep her word to save their lives and ask Nurian to cut down the person who made her heart ache. She barely knew Xiron's name, and yet the idea of losing her felt worse than the idea of losing her brother.

She stood outside her tent and watched her soldiers talk amongst themselves; fathers, mothers, sisters, brothers, and children of Sambia. She knew the answer.

* * *

Hours had passed since the royals had met in the neutral zone. Xiron marched next to her half-brother's throne. She halted at the edge of the sandy patch that separated the armies and separated her from Ashia. She looked over to see the queen standing tall and brave; they locked eyes, and the image struck Xiron like a bolt of lightning.

She felt the sun against her skin as she walked out into a dirt path. Her hand went out to touch the soft petals of the flowers that bloomed, and she remembered Ashia planting each seed into the dirt just months before. She could feel the soil against her bare feet as she reached the point in the path that led to an open field of grass and white clover.

Ashia sat on a white blanket facing the open field, watching as a child ran around, chasing butterflies that escaped her. Xiron wanted to stand and watch the scene for as long as she could, but her chuckle gave her away.

Ashia turned, her hair longer, flowing in waves down her back. She grinned at the sight and turned more to show a baby at her breast. Xiron grinned as she approached to sit behind her wife and wrap an arm around her to touch her son's cheek.

"You let me sleep in," Xiron said as she kissed Ashia's bare shoulder.

"You deserved it," she said, leaning back into her.

They both looked up as laughter filled the air—

* * *

"Ready!" Kumarian shouted.

Xiron tore her eyes from Ashia to look behind her at her half-brother. She gave him the signal that she was ready to carry out his commands, as her oath demanded.

Ashia looked over to Nurian as he donned his helmet. She told him to defend the country and not her. Nurian, the kind friend, told her he would end Xiron quickly and with mercy.

The two warriors met in the middle. Xiron was two heads shorter and looked as if she could ride on Nurian's back without him breaking a sweat, yet her sword was drawn, and she showed no sign of fear.

The first clank of the swords proved to the audience that Xiron would hold her own. Ashia watched as the fighter moved smoothly around Nurian. She was quick, easily dodging swings of the broadsword and pushes with the shield.

Her moves were deliberate, knowing where to be and what to cut. With a swift slash of her sword, she cut the back of the man's legs where his armor didn't cover.

Nurian bellowed with pain and anger, but righted himself, watching the smaller warrior dance on the sand. He swung his sword wide, then grabbed Xiron as she tried to duck under his swing. His bear claw grasped tightly around her arm and pulled so hard that you could hear the snap at her shoulder.

Xiron cried out.

Ashia could feel it in her gut.

As Xiron knelt on the ground, her left hand going to grab her right shoulder, Nurian kicked out his foot, smashing into her chest plate and launching her ten feet across the sand.

Kumarian stood up as Nurian approached the unmoving Xiron.

"Get up!" the king shouted.

Ashia wanted to repeat his sentiments. She watched her fighter stand over Xiron. Ashia had to grip her sword tightly to ground herself and keep from shouting out for Xiron to get up, to keep fighting, to stay alive.

Nurian clasped his sword with two hands, aiming it down at Xiron. With all his might, he thrust it downward, but he hit dirt.

Xiron had rolled out of the way, forcing the broadsword to stick into the thick sand. She stood up, and with her left hand she pulled the dagger from her waist, and screamed as she thrust it towards Nurian.

Ashia felt her heart sink as she watched Nurian's hand go to his neck. Xiron fell backward, kicking away from the tree-sized man as he pulled the small dagger from his neck. The blood spurted out in short bursts, and Nurian knelt, staying on his knees for a few moments before the ground shook as he fell and took his last breath.

Xiron scrambled to her feet and removed her helmet to look at Ashia, frozen in awe.

Kumarian chortled as he jumped off his throne. "The beast is cut down. I won Sambia!"

The king motioned for his advisers and laughed as they moved over to Ashia.

"Oh, don't look so shocked, queen," he sighed, then laughed. "She is the World Ender, after all."

The king's men quickly set up a small table, bringing over a quill and ink, and laying out a long contract on rolled parchment.

Ashia was still staring down at her childhood friend, dead in the sand. She could see her army in her peripheral vision, and she wondered if they were going to panic. She wanted to scream that it was unfair. She wanted to face her army and tell them that everything was going to be okay. She wanted to curl into a ball and cry. She wanted to drown in a barrel of mead with her brother and best friend. She wanted to leap from a cliff and break her body on a pile of rocks below. She wanted anything but to face the idea that Nurian was dead, and Sambia was lost.

"Come," Kumarian chuckled. "Papers must be signed."

She took a single step forward, knowing she was walking to her death.

"At least you won't go the way of the other rulers," Kumarian told her. "I won't have your head on a pike." He looked her in the eye and sighed. "You will be Xiron's prize."

Ashia turned to the warrior, who was still standing in the same place where she had watched Nurian die. Again, they locked eyes, and Ashia was overwhelmed by the image of her future.

Ashia leaned comfortably against Xiron, knowing that she would never let her and their son fall back. They watched as their daughter jumped in the air, trying her best to catch the butterflies, laughing as they came close, but they were always too fast for her tiny hands to get a hold of one.

"Nia," Ashia called out. "Come say good morning to your mama."

The little girl giggled as she ran over to her family and sat on the blanket. "Did you see, Mama, I almost caught one?"

Xiron reached out and touched her little cheek. "I saw, princess."

She looked down at the sleeping baby in her mother's arms. "Can we wake Nurian?"

"Babies need their sleep," Ashia told her in a soft voice.

She scrunched up her nose. "Then I'm going to catch a butterfly."

They watched as she shot up from the blanket and raced back out into the field.

Xiron chuckled. "She's going to make a good queen, just like her mother."

"Sign the contract," Kumarian said as he rushed over and grabbed Ashia's hand, forcing her to take the quill.

Ashia could still feel Xiron's kiss on her shoulder. She could feel her son in her arms and hear her daughter's laughter. She looked over to Xiron. Her dark eyes, previously filled with fear and anger, grew softer, and a smile pulled at the corner of her mouth as she nodded for Ashia to sign.

The fear that she once had subsided, and Ashia put quill to paper and signed away her country.

Kumarian screamed with joy, "Dryland is mine!"

He was about to say something else, but Xiron was standing behind him, having crossed the neutral zone as the king celebrated.

"My oath," Xiron said, holding out her hand.

Ashia saw the scar on her palm.

"Can't even let me celebrate," Kumarian said.

Xiron gritted her teeth. "Release me. You gave your word."

He scoffed and waved his hand at the servants. "Fine."

Xiron stood in rapt anticipation as her half-brother ran the dagger over the scar on his palm. The memory of them as teenagers, days after their father's death, when Xiron promised away her life to keep her mother from being killed by her half-brother. She took the dagger and cut open her palm, and before her half-brother could pull away, she grabbed his hand and squeezed as hard as she could.

Kumarian winced at the pain, then schooled his face.

"Release me," Xiron demanded.

He smirked. "Xiron, daughter of Gillia, Witch of Harata, I release you from your blood oath sworn to me."

The chain once around her neck was finally lifted, and Xiron took her first breath as a free person.

Kumarian turned away from his sister to look at Ashia. "You're both free. Go live on a goat farm, or whatever it is you two want to do."

Xiron rushed over to Ashia and reached out for her hand. As they touched, she felt her body catch fire. For the first time in her life, she felt whole.

Ashia took a tentative step closer. She looked up to peer into the eyes of her love, allowing the warm feeling to spread throughout her body.

"I want you to know that after this…" Xiron squeezed her hand, "I want to live in peace."

She couldn't help but smile. "I promise."

Kumarian stood, leaned over the contract on the table, his hand spread out as he basked in the glory of becoming king of everything and everyone to the water's edge. Xiron watched him as she had done her whole life. She watched as he took pleasure in her horrible actions. She watched as he relished the idea that she had slain another warrior, a son, a friend. Kumarian never cared; he never watched the light leave the eyes of another person. He never washed blood from his hands or watched as the dead were buried. He never cared that Xiron was now and would remain forever haunted.

Without thought, Xiron walked behind her half-brother and stuck a dagger into his throat. He turned around to see her and reached out to grab her as she stepped back from his reach. Emotionless, she watched him fall to the ground as no soul made a move to help him. Xiron watched as the last person she would ever kill died at her feet.

Ashia moved to her side, looking down at the king as he took his last breath.

"It's over," Xiron said.

Ashia nodded. "It's over. No more death."

Xiron turned to her queen, and breathed a final sigh of relief before going in for their first kiss.

Oberon's Rose

Gemma Sterling

Cressida humped her milkmaid's yoke up a long hill. The sun blazed down on her. Her bosom sweated. She chafed. She stared ahead at the manor house a league away.

"Nuts to this," she muttered, shrugging off her yoke. She used it as a makeshift seat, putting her chin in her hand and blowing a raspberry. Beyond the manor house, she saw a band of minstrels and jugglers tumbling and playing on their way to the fairgrounds. She yearned to leave the drudgery of being a maid behind. She wished to be a fine maiden at the tournament. The prize was Oberon's Rose, a black rose said to grow on the Fae King's grave. She hung her head. Such a prize was not meant for one such as her.

Her eyes drifted to the woods behind her. She spotted a fine gown caught in the branches of a bush. Her breath caught in her throat. She hopped to her feet, looking about her. She saw no one – no horse, no carriage, no one. How did the dress come to be here? Had it fallen from a lady's trunk atop a carriage?

Cressida edged toward the dress, unsure if this was a Fae spell meant to lure her into a fairy trap. It was a fine dress: red satin with green sleeves and fine embroidery. She rubbed the fabric between her fingers. The collar was miniver.

A shiver of appreciation ran down Cressida's spine. Not only was this a dress, but it was also the finest dress she had ever laid eyes upon.

She bit her lip and looked up and down the road. She saw no one coming from the farm or the manor house. If she stepped behind the bush and switched her milkmaid's dress for this fine one, no one would be the wiser. However, should the bailiff see her, she might find herself on the chopping block. Nobody in the kingdom could dress above their station, on pain of death. The thought of the executioner's large axe filled Cressida's stomach with icy dread. She dropped the sleeve in her hand and backed away as though the gown were a coiled cobra.

She turned back to her milkmaid's yoke. The sun beat down harder, reaching its zenith. Flies buzzed around her milk buckets. It was another league to the manor, and the buckets were heavy.

"Come, Cressida," she said aloud to herself. "You only live but once."

She rushed back, plucked the gown from the brambles and hurried behind the bush. She blushed as her milkmaid's gown dropped around her feet and she stood in her shift in the open air. Once she shimmied on the fine gown, she smoothed its wrinkles out with her hands. Her heart beat wildly. She spun around, letting the dress swirl about her. Never in her wildest imaginings did she think she would dress in so fine a gown. She bowed and curtsied like a lady at court. She danced about, spinning into the wood, wanting to shield herself from the eyes of passersby so she could thoroughly enjoy herself.

So enthralled by the dress was she that she flounced deeper into the wood, nearing the lake the wood encircled, unaware of the thick oaks and boughs about her.

The sound of clanging armor made her freeze. She stopped mid-spin. Her eyes shot to the shore of the lake, where a Knight's armor gleamed in the sunlight. Not far from the armor, the Knight it belonged to stood on a large rock, dipping his toe in the lake, naked as Adam, preparing to bathe. It was like a bolt of lightning hit Cressida. She found herself unable to move, unable to breathe, unable to look away. The Knight looked like a Greek statue, his muscles like carved marble; although his member was longer than that of the statues in her Lord's home. His large, piercing blue eyes focused on the water circling out from his toes. Cressida felt an unfamiliar heat rise through her body, bringing a blush to her cheeks.

She gasped.

The sound drew the Knight's gaze. His eyes widened. His skin flushed. His hands jumped to cover his member (although Cressida wished they hadn't). He averted his gaze and bowed.

"Milady, milady, please forgive me. I do stain your honor by allowing myself to be skyclad before you."

He backed towards his armor, where his leggings and tunic lay. Cressida had never known such embarrassment. She felt her face turning as crimson as a tomato. She wanted to look away but found her eyes following the Knight's prostrating form.

He kept his eyes averted but glanced up as he reached for his tunic. He froze. His mouth fell open.

"Are…are you some glamor? Some fairy enchantment meant to place a spell upon me? I…I have never seen such a beautiful lady in all my life."

Cressida's heart fluttered. Her hand jumped to her throat. Her? He thought that about her? As red as she was with embarrassment, her hair unbonneted and a mess, he still found her beauteous?

The Knight quickly grabbed his leggings and pulled them on, talking all the while.

"I travel the land, looking for a lady that has a quest for me. One that I can commit valorous deeds for. I shall bring you back to your castle, see that no harm comes to you from thief or beast…"

As he spoke, his words faded in Cressida's ear. Now that the Knight was clothed, her senses began to return to her. The fine dress she wore began to feel hot and scratchy. She dug her finger in her collar. Should the Knight discover that she was but a milk maid dressing above her station, he would forget his profession of love and turn her over to the bailiff. She had to flee before he discovered the truth. She grabbed up the fine satin dress in her hands, turned and darted into the woods like a bluejay.

"Milady! Milady..." she heard the Knight call after her as she crashed through the woods.

When she burst back upon the commons, she lifted the gown over her head, flung it back upon the bush and hopped into her milkmaid's dress. She slumped her yoke over her shoulders and hurried down the lane.

She dared not look back, but kept marching forward, her heart hammering in her chest the whole while. Her thoughts turned to the nude form of the Knight by the lake. She ached to see him again, yet such a thing might mean her death. As she rounded the bend and the imposing façade of the manor house appeared before her, she tried to convince herself that it was all but a dream, a glamor created by Fae people to confuse her.

The steward of the manor noticed that it took her much longer to reach the house from the farm than was normal. He docked a florin from her pay for indolence and sent her on her way. As she strode home over the dusty lane with her pocket lighter than normal, her heart sank. The excitement of wearing the dress, seeing the Knight and escaping, had faded. Now, she felt a yearning to look into the blazing blue eyes of the Knight once more. Wearing the dress had been a fool's errand.

She hung her head. Her feet felt heavy, so she dragged them. She wanted to return to the wood, search out her

Knight, and hear the sweet poetry that fell from his lips. Yet she knew that he would not even recognize her dressed in her common garb. The beauty of the gown was what had filled his heart with love. Should he see her as she was, he would think her nothing more than a farm strumpet, unworthy to be the object of his desire.

Lost in thought, she did not hear the clump of a horse approaching behind her on the lane, until its rider's voice broke out, "I beg your pardon, good maid. I seek the lady to whom this garment belongs."

Cressida froze in place. Shock stole her breath away. She dared not turn to see who addressed her, for she recognized the voice. It was the voice of her love, sweet and lilting in her ear. She was filled with dread at the thought that he would realize that she had dressed above her station. She kept her gaze straight ahead, refusing to look back.

"I know of no dress," she said.

"My good woman," the Knight responded, a note of amusement in his voice, "should you not look upon the dress first before you make such a proclamation?"

Cressida looked at the ground and shook her head furiously.

"My good woman, I do but ask that you look upon the garment," he said, trotting his horse around Cressida so he could face her. "The lady to whom it belongs may be in distress and..."

Cressida's chest fluttered when she heard the Knight gasp. Her eyes shot up to the man mounted on the steed before her. He sat on the saddle, shining in his armor. He gaped at her.

"'Tis you. You are my maiden fair."

The dress was laid upon the horse. Her Knight in his armor shimmered like a diamond in the light of the sun. He slid from his saddle, kneeled before her, took her hand and kissed it.

The touch of his lips on her flesh sent bolts of passion shooting through her.

"I do pledge myself to you. I am your Knight protector."

Breathlessness overwhelmed Cressida. She felt faint as blood rushed to her head. She brought the back of her wrist to her forehead.

"But…but I am but a milkmaid."

"Were the Empress of the world standing before me, she would not have a tenth of your beauty or your worth."

It was like a dream, a dream that Cressida did not wish to wake from. She found herself falling into his arms. He placed her in his lap upon his saddle, letting the dress fall back to the road without a care. They kissed, long and passionately, the touch of his lips bringing sensations like exploding fireworks to her body. They trotted to a secluded glen, where a glade rounded by trees could be their boudoir.

She trembled when he removed her dress and then her shift, and laid down his cloak as a bed on the soft forest floor. He was not like the fumbling farm boys Cressida had known. He treated her like a flower, teased her breasts delicately with his fingers until she took his strong hand and drew it down. When their love began, all thoughts fell away. Cressida climaxed with a shuddering release that felt like the ground shifted beneath her. She lay back as though in a pleasurable death, utterly contented. He snuggled against her and together they fell asleep in the quiet glade.

After a time, a soft glow, like the luminescence of a firefly, warmed Cressida's eyelids. They fluttered open. Her breath caught in her throat. Above her, droning as their wings flapped with the speed of a hummingbird, a swarm of fairies buzzed. A cold snake of terror wove its way down her back. Her eyes jumped to her feet. She saw that without knowing it, her Knight had laid her down in the middle of a fairy ring. Her feet had crushed the clovers. Breaking the ring would draw the wrath of the fairies.

She shook her Knight awake.

He looked around as though in a daze, but the instant he saw the Fae people darting about, he jumped to his feet, bringing Cressida with him and placing his body between her and the fairies.

She flushed at the sight of her protector standing tall against the threat. The largest among the Fae people, a crowned woman the size of a small doll, clad in shimmering samite, darted from the rest, and hovered in the air before Cressida's Knight.

"I am Titania, Queen of the Fairies. You have disturbed our sacred grounds. You have looked upon the Fae people, and for this we must rob you of your sight."

Cressida felt her Knight's powerful muscles tighten as he readied to defend her. She tried to hold him back, for might is no use against magic, but alas he sprang for his sword, which rested just beyond the Fae circle.

Titania waved her imperial scepter.

With a spray of sparkling dust, Cressida's Knight turned into a stark nude statue, frozen as he reached for the sword.

It felt like her heart ripped in half. She flung herself at the feet of the statue.

"Oh Queen," Cressida cried through a veil of tears, "how can you so cruelly rob love from its cradle? It was said you loved Oberon more than the blood that pumps in your veins."

Cressida let the wracking sobs out. She brought her head to the stone feet and gave a silent prayer to Venus that she would see her love again in the world after this one. She waited for Titania's wrath to befall her. It did not come. Curious, she wiped her eyes and turned to the Fae Queen. Titania gazed down her nose at the prostrate maid, looking imperious, but with a softness in her eyes that had not been there a moment before.

"Do you know of Oberon's rose?" the Queen asked.

Cressida sniffled, nodding, looking at the frozen leg of her love and stroking it longingly.

"'Oberon did lay his head in a field…'" she began to recite the song.

"Silence!" Titania cried, her voice becoming like a clap of thunder.

Cressida bowed her head and prostrated herself on the ground.

"Sycorax, jealous of Oberon's love for me, grew an ill rose in our fields. When my love did innocently pluck the rose, he laid down upon the ground and died. There in his place grew a black rose that did contain his magic within it. The Queen of these lands had her King pluck the rose on the hunt, not knowing what it was. She holds a tournament today. The prize is the rose. Win it for me, and I shall free your love."

Cressida's head swirled in disbelief. She looked down at her rough milkmaid's hands. How could such a small person win a tournament?

"Milady, I..." she began.

Titania silenced her with a wave of her scepter. Cressida felt a pull in her stomach, like someone held her hand and spun her about. A wind carrying the perfumed scent of roses breathed through the glen and rifled her hair. Her heart drumming, Cressida looked down at her hands again. She had the hands of a man. She could feel the strength twinging within them.

"I have placed a glamor upon you to give you the appearance of a young Knight. You have the strength and skill of one as well, but it is you who must decide the outcome of the contest."

Cressida rose to her feet, seeing the silver armor plate covering her flattened chest gleaming in the sunlight. A black mare appeared from the air and trotted along the glen until it nuzzled Cressida's arm. She stroked the beautiful creature's mane. She turned to thank the Fae Queen for this chance at redemption, but Titania and her host had vanished, leaving the naked stone form of her love standing in the glen. Cressida kissed his cold, marble lips before she mounted her mare.

"I shall place Oberon's rose at your feet," she promised him.

As she trotted to the game field, the heaviness in her chest began to lighten. She lifted her chin high as the tents and banners came into view over the horizon. She felt somewhat guilty for feeling excited at the prospect of the tournament. She had always been a milkmaid. She rose, milked the cows, then returned home. She rose, milked the cows, then returned home. Each day, for her whole life. For the first time, she understood what it was to be a man. Washerwomen and farmers bowed their heads to her as she passed. They scuttled to the side of the road to clear her way. It was the first time she could recall, besides the good love her of Knight, that anyone had given her any deference.

By the time her horse trotted onto the fairgrounds, she felt ready to best all of the King's Knights singlehandedly.

A squire greeted her by the tents.

"Begging your pardon, Lord," the young squire said, bowing his head and removing his cap, "but do you carry your Lord's seal, the one that permits you to enter the games?"

Cressida's breath caught in her throat. She looked about her gleaming armor for a scroll. Titania had not anticipated such a request. Her stomach dropped as she realized that her quest had died before it began.

"Ah," the squire said suddenly, "here it is."

Cressida's stomach fluttered to see a parchment in the young squire's hands. Titania had summoned it from some Fae spell. Her mistress must be watching her from the Fae realm.

"Why, good Knight," the squire proclaimed enthusiastically, "you are being called for the final joust! The rose is within your grasp!"

Before she could object, the squire grabbed her mare's reigns and tugged her along to the jousting grounds. Cressida quivered from fright as she looked upon the gleaming Knight waiting across the field, mounted on a powerful black steed. Behind him, Cressida saw the Queen and King in the stands, and the rose resting on a pillow on a seat beside the Queen. Cressida gritted her teeth and prepared to meet her adversary. The squire handed her a great lance. To her amazement, the heavy lance felt light in her grip. The peasants about the field clapped wildly as the Queen rose, bearing her handkerchief in her hand.

"When I drop this token, the joust has begun," she cried to uproarious applause. "Whosoever wins shall be gifted Oberon's rose!"

Her rival's squire handed him a mighty lance, and he trotted his horse to the beginning of the tilt rail.

Now, Cressida shook from head to foot. She pulled her lance tighter to her side. She imagined the fine point of the Knight's lance piercing her heart. She was about to cry out to Titania that she did not wish to die on the field this day, but the Queen dropped her token.

The Knight dug his spurs into his steed.

He charged.

The booming of his clanking metal armor sounded like thunder. Cressida saw the point of his lance aiming for her heart. It being too late to flee, she dug her spurs into her mare's sides. The horse shot forward with blinding speed. It was all Cressida could do to hold on.

She felt the tip of her rival's lance smash her chest plate. The blow rattled her teeth, and the world spun around her as she smashed upon the ground.

The crowd let out a mighty roar.

Cressida lay on her back, her eyes locked on the sky, her head spinning as though she had crossed a ship's deck in the middle of a storm. She closed her eyes to stop the spinning and gave a silent prayer for her love to forgive her failure. When she opened her eyes, the Knight stood above her, brandishing a morning star. He lifted the spiky iron ball over his head, ready to bring it down on her helm unless she yielded.

Cressida's eyes dropped to the hilt of her sword. Her heart hammered in her chest. She was not bested yet. She rolled out of the way as the Knight drove his weapon into the ground with a mighty wallop. Cressida used her lithe muscles to roll further from his reach, drawing her sword at the same time. She crouched, sword in hand, ready to meet her rival. He charged, wielding the morning star over his head. Her breath caught in her throat. She prepared to meet his blow. Then, a sudden inspiration hit her. She watched his iron shoes clamping on the ground. She waited for him to stand on his front foot with all his weight, then smashed her sword into his ankle.

The Knight wailed, collapsing in a heap on the ground, clutching at his ankle. Cressida rose to her feet and lifted her sword overhead.

"I yield! I yield," the Knight shouted, lifting his arms to shield himself from the blow.

The crowd erupted in cheers.

"Come, my good Knight," the Queen said, beckoning Cressida forward.

She mounted her mare and galloped to the stands where the Queen presided.

"Remove your helmet, good knight," said the Queen, beckoning. Cressida's throat thickened, for she feared the Queen would know her to be a woman, but when she pulled her helmet off, the crowd roared, for Titania's glamor gave her the form of a young man. The Queen placed the softest kiss Cressida had ever known upon the milkmaid's lips, then gracefully handed the rose to her champion.

Cressida held the rose aloft, her heart singing with joy. The crowd roared. She put her spurs in her mare and galloped off. Her heart raced as she flew across the fields back to the glen, where her love stood still frozen in stone. Cressida dropped from her mare and looked about the clearing, searching for her benefactor. Her stomach knotted when Titania did not appear. Had it all been a Fae game?

"My love," the imperious voice of the Fae Queen said behind her. Cressida turned and saw the Queen hovering near the stone form of Cressida's lover. She waved her scepter, and shock filled Cressida as the black rose in her hand transformed into a bearded Fae-man with a crown upon his head – Oberon!

The Fae King buzzed to his love, and the royal couple kissed each other with the tenderness of lovers reunited after a long parting.

"I knew this girl had the spirit to be our champion when I saw her upon the road. I did lure her to my service with a beautiful dress, which she deserves as her reward."

Cressida felt a quickly melting anger over Titania using her in such a way. However, once the Fae Queen transformed her armor back into the lovely dress she'd found on the road, gratitude quickly replaced her heat.

"Come, my love, let us away," Oberon said. The pair vanished in a puff of sparkling Fae dust.

Cressida's heart jumped into her throat. Had the Queen forgotten her lover?

"My Queen! Wait!" Cressida cried.

"My maid," a voice said from behind her. "Why do you shout so?"

Shock froze Cressida in place. She turned slowly towards the sound. Her lover stood nude before her. He rubbed his head as though waking from some fugue. Cressida's singing heart drove her into his arms. She kissed him fiercely about the face and neck as though he may vanish should she stop.

"My love," her Knight said, smiling at the warmth of her affection, "you act as though I have returned from a quest. Did you fear I would leave you?"

"No," Cressida said through joyful tears, "the Gods forged our love. I will never part from your side."

And with that, she kissed him passionately and deeply, the kiss of eternal love.

Sometimes a Sword is Like a Lover

Celia Winter

The squire is afraid of dying more than he is afraid of death. Death is final, finite; dying freshly bloodied on a battlefield means he will not know rest. Resurrection and putrefaction will await him.

Each day, he trains with his peers as the trials of knighthood loom like the pregnant autumn moon over the end of the month. He tries not to think about how most of the young men he'd known as boys, who'd passed their trials with thunderous applause, stand ranks with the enemy now. Whenever he does, his hand tightens around his practice sword. It is heavy and dull to make him stronger without threatening his sparring partners. Partners and peers, because it would break his heart to think that these friends might one day become his enemies.

Sometimes the sword in his palm feels like his only friend.

* * *

"I have need of a worthy sword for my squire."

The apprentice looks up. Swords are his specialty. The master blacksmith prefers armor since there is more money in armor, especially decorated armor, especially decorated armor for rich lords who are never found in a practice yard, even if decorated armor protects the same as plain.

But the apprentice likes swords. When the dead are at the door and fear is a weapon as sharp as a knife, a good sword is the difference between survival and destruction. He's good at swords too, which he thinks is as vital as wielding one. Even if he's just an apprentice, he, too, can keep people alive. Fold the steel, beat it, then fold and beat it again, over and over and over until the edge is so sharp, so fine, it could kill with a sigh.

The squire stands behind his lord, his hands clasped behind his back, his gaze lowered. Well trained – well honed. The apprentice suspects he, too, could kill with a sigh.

* * *

On a rainy afternoon, three days before the trials, the apprentice arrives with the sword in a fine leather sheath.

The squire tries not to be disappointed. It is a simple sword, but he shouldn't have expected something glorious from his ascetic lord. *You want a sword that will keep you alive, don't you? Staying alive will set you apart from half the green boys who die on their first battlefield.*

He wants a sword that will keep him alive, but he also thought the sword would be a little finer than this. There is no gold filigree in the hilt, no gemstones in the pommel.

But when the blade is in his hand – oh. He didn't know it could feel like this. Practice swords were made for different grips, their weight good for training. This one is light, its steel beaten so thin he could thread its edge through a needle. When he swings it, the air around him sings.

"You like it?" the apprentice asks, a trickle of delight weaving through the words.

"Very much," the squire replies breathlessly, turning to face the apprentice again. With the sword in his hand, the world seems brighter now. Less frightening.

The apprentice has broad shoulders, bright eyes, and the beginning of an unkempt dark beard. The squire stares at him as though seeing him for the first time, though he has seen him both at the forge and before he'd taken the sword in hand.

This is a young man who will not die in battle and become his enemy.

The thought pierces him as the apprentice's eyebrows knit together, curious at the extended silence.

"You do fine work." He keeps his words simple, but wonders if the apprentice can hear the sudden thickness in his throat.

The apprentice inclines his head, but the squire sees heat climbing his neck, bursting into a sunrise blush along the horizon of his cheekbones. "I had a good master."

"But you're the one who made and brought me a sword that might save my life," the squire says. He doesn't know why it is important to him that this apprentice recognize his work, but it is. "Becoming a knight means your master can't teach you anymore. Only your duty can. I suspect it is the same with blacksmiths."

* * *

The trials will give him nightmares for the rest of his life, but the squire becomes a knight. Every time he blinks, a shadow fills his mind, corpses with his peers' faces encircling him, smothering all life from this earth. His breath is shallow, and the air tastes like death and decaying flesh, though he is far from the battlefront.

He is glad of a sword made by a knowing hand that sighs when he swings it while he presses his face to his pillow and screams until his throat is raw, dry, hot, as if he'd been forged in flame like the sword resting by the door.

* * *

The newly-minted knight brings his friends to the smithy. "You'll never know a finer sword," he announces as he walks through the door, but they care that there is no filigree in the hilt, that the leather sheath is simple if supple. "You can always buy a new sheath," he points out, but the crossguards – don't you see the crossguards? – they should have a little more art to them.

"It is kind of you to bring me custom," the apprentice murmurs while the knight's friends examine the blacksmith's armor. ("See this? This is worth the gold!") After years of honing his craft, knowing he makes finer swords than any other blacksmith, it hurts to see them ignored like a healthy clever mutt in favor of a beautiful purebred.

"Their loss," the knight replies, resting his hand on his hilt. He swallows, licking chapped lips. "I'm trying to keep them alive."

The apprentice has heard that the trials of knighthood are more trials of the mind and spirit than trials of the body. He's always wondered what it must be like to have priests try to crush your soul for you to prove your valiance. He wonders what it must be like to have your very being beaten the way he beats steel against an anvil.

When the knight had been here as a squire, his gaze had been low out of training; now the apprentice wonders if it might be fear that keeps his eyes on the ground.

His stomach sinks. *This is a knight who will protect us all? At least he has a good sword.*

As if he heard the apprentice's thoughts, the knight's eyes are suddenly locked onto his, brown flecked with gold that flashes in the reflected firelight of the forge.

There's definitely fear in his eyes. Fear can break a man as it can break a dog or a horse, but the knight before him doesn't look broken. He looks defiant.

The apprentice stands straighter and the knight does too. He's only an inch or two taller than the apprentice, narrow as a knife, where the apprentice was always built like the hammer he wields.

"Your sword can protect them if theirs can't." *It will protect us all.*

The knight bends slightly from the hip and the apprentice's breath falters. Knights don't bow to him, but this one is. Suddenly it doesn't matter that his friends thought his swords were drab.

This knight knows his worth.

* * *

A month after he becomes a knight, he rides out into a dawn that reminds him of an apprentice's cheekbones with a line of fresh knights. They will ride for three days to reach the front and then he will test his knighthood.

His sword sits in its scabbard on his hip, its gentle weight a reminder of purpose. It is a good sword, the best his lord could have given him. Even though he rides in a line of knights, it is the sword that makes him feel like he isn't riding alone to his doom.

* * *

The master blacksmith brings a new boy into the forge who has the overgrown tree look of becoming a man. As he sets the new boy to work at the bellows to get used to making the fire too hot to survive, unease grows in the apprentice's stomach.

"Is this because you have nothing left to teach me?" the apprentice asks, his heart in his throat. In his mind's eye, he sees a squire swinging a singing sword, an elated smile on his face.

The master blacksmith sighs. "I could teach you more about armor, but you want to make swords. They shouldn't be left in my shadow."

There are no trials for blacksmiths, no formal way to rise. On his last day as an apprentice, he finds an empty forge down by the river so long disused that its beams might need replacing in the next year, whose hearth needs new mortar, and which has definitely become home to a colony of feral cats. But it is his now.

His master promised to send him anyone looking for a sword, and he will always send someone looking for fine armor to his master. And the knight – he will be proud to become the new blacksmith's patron.

If he lives.

If the sword keeps him alive.

* * *

His peers' frivolous blades shatter and they fall to the hordes. But if the trials didn't break him three moons before, he can't break now, so his grip tightens on his sword.

He does not run, he does not hide, he fights, and fights, and fights. The leather-wrapped hilt warms in his palm as he roars like a lion and hacks the dead to the ground. In the months he's had it, it's come to feel like a part of him. Not an extension of his arm, not an item in his hand, but steel in unity with his soul. It flashes its rage with every strike he makes, straight and true. A good sword, sturdy and strong.

But before the day ends, the sword chips, and though he lives, though his commander credits him with the victory, he feels like he failed.

* * *

A parade of knights and heroes weaves through the city streets and the blacksmith puts down his hammer, wipes sweat from his brow, and goes to the front of the smithy. It's small, and not well stocked, but it's his. His and the cats', who seem very pleased about the addition of the fire. They keep rodents away, so he isn't ready to evict them yet.

Flower petals are thrown through the air, songs praising the moon and sun echo even in the darkest alley. There was a victory. Death has been thrown back another day.

The blacksmith watches the horses mount the hill towards the castle. Their armor is freshly polished, their faces too forced to be truly relieved. *War does that to a man*, his master told him when he was still a sapling boy watching his first parade, wondering why the knights didn't seem gladder.

Knight after knight rides past, but he doesn't recognize faces. He recognizes armor – some of them are fitted in his master's armor and he feels a shiver of pride every time he sees the work. But he wants to see a sword. Wants to see a familiar hilt, and the knife-like knight who wields it.

Maybe his defiance wasn't enough in the end, the blacksmith thinks sadly as the parade fades. He wonders if the sword is lying on the battlefield while the knight shambles on, unable to blame the blacksmith whose sword wasn't enough in the end. What does it matter if the sword endures when the knight does not?

* * *

The knight doesn't return on horseback, doesn't return armored and celebrated. His commanders think he is mad, but he leaves his horse and his gear with his squire and returns to the city on foot, sword strapped to his back as if he is a mercenary or a road warrior, not a knight of the realm.

"As long as you are back tonight so that you can be properly honored," his commander tells him when it is clear the knight will not cede ground.

"I will be," he swears.

Once he is through the knot of people watching the parade, the streets are empty. He moves quickly, his breath shallow in his chest, his heart beating as though he is in battle. He needs his sword repaired. This sword that saved his life, this sword that endured where the faintest shadows of friendship could not. He needs the apprentice to be alive, because he needs someone to be alive after all the death and dying and undying again.

But when he reaches the forge the apprentice isn't there. "Is he ill?" he asks the master blacksmith.

"What?" Then the master chuckles, and the knight's stomach swoops in a way that, for the first time since the battlefield, has nothing to do with fear. "Never knew him to get sick. No, it was just time for him to blossom. He's started his own forge, down by the river." The master blacksmith points back in the direction the knight had come from.

"Thank you," the knight says before retreating.

Before he knows what they're doing, his feet are running, flying down the road, towards life and bright eyes that will never go empty, dull.

* * *

"Can you fix it?" the knight pants. A scar slashes his cheek and cuts across his brow-bone; his face is unshaven and there are dark, sleepless circles under his gold-flecked eyes. "I didn't trust the castle blacksmiths with it."

The blacksmith stares at the sword. The hilt's wrapped leather is well oiled and apart from this chip, the blade is properly honed and sharpened. Cared for deeply where so many misuse their steel, especially young knights so unused to having to care for a fine blade.

"I'm sure they could fix the steel," he says, unwilling to speak poorly of them when his shop is so new and he might need to beg their help one day. But still – he is glad the knight came to him. He doesn't like the idea of their hands running along his blade, even if it's not his, not anymore. He doesn't trust them to know his steel the way he does, and if they overworked it, they might ignore the care he'd put into crafting it. He doesn't want anyone but him bringing the sword back to life.

"They couldn't make this sword in the first place, and it kept me alive where no other blade would have." The knight swallows. "I wouldn't want repair unequal to its creation." He stares at the blacksmith and the blacksmith stares back. There's no defiance now, just the flicker of something akin to an ember that can be stoked to a roaring fire.

The blacksmith lifts the sword, his fingers brushing the knight's. The lightest touch jolts through him as though he'd been struck with his own hammer.

"I will," he vows. He feels like a blossoming cherry tree in spring.

The knight's relieved sigh reverberates through him. It stops his heart; it starts his soul.

Light Tangled in Shadow

Aubrey Wroth

Twice a year, when sun and moon share equally in the sky, we pause our endless war for a tourney between our two courts. Each day, from twilight to twilight, for one week, we partake in the games: jousting, melee, archery, and others. Each night, the Unseelie Court, our rivals, provide a great feast, dancing, and performances from their best bards to commemorate the games. The following seasons of autumn and winter belong to them, and every part of the spectacle is designed to impress.

Now, on the final day of the tourney, I, Prince Fionnlagh, face my greatest rival: Dùbhghlas, the Unseelie prince. Only the crowning events remain: the final joust and the melee. First up? The joust. As my squire Kevoca helps me into my rose chafer shell armor, I take the opportunity to measure up my competition.

Dùbhghlas's armor is made from the skin of a spider, and though he ordinarily cuts an imposing figure on the battlefield with his short but broad figure, the woody brown of his armor gives his night-dark eyes a fiery determination. His armor is polished and new, and a cloak of green and brown moth wings hangs from his shoulders. I can't see his face through his helmet, decorated with the pincers of the spider he'd hunted for his armor, but I know he must be smirking at me.

We have met many times on the battlefield. Always, always, he wears that taunting expression, and he always has equally snide words ready for me. At least there's the scar I put on his face, his very skin proof that I can get the better of him. I remember the day I put it there: the blood on his face, the wound deep red and shiny with muscle with a hint of white bone showing. How it had bled. How he had screamed as I had left my mark on his skin. That sound sank into my very soul, leaving his brand in the fiber of my being. I'd defeated him that day, but he has defeated me on the battlefield too. And at the tourney, well, we are each other's fiercest competition, determined to win more events than the other. Right now, we're tied.

At least the structure of a joust means he must forgo words in favor of actions, though it means I must save any clever replies of my own for the melee later. Or perhaps during the banquet. I ready myself on the back of my warbird, Uarraig, planting my feet firmly in the yellow-black feathers of his back. He may be only half the size of my opponent Prince Dùbhghlas's nightjar, but Uarraig is more ferocious than any steed. I would know, I had raised him from an egg myself. My balance secure, I lower the visor of my helmet.

Across the way, Prince Dùbhghlas does the same.

I'm prepared. I am as sure-footed as any fairy must be – proven as I have yet to be knocked from my trusty bird. If I lose now, I can only imagine the words Dùbhghlas might have for me during the melee later. I've already begun to plan my own insults for him.

The herald signals for us to go with a sharp note from his horn, and our birds take off. The strong wingbeat of Uarraig matches my racing heart, and I ready my lance to knock Dùbhghlas from his bird. I ready the tip, aiming it just so, as we race ever closer to one another. Our birds swoop toward each other, flying closer together. A confident grin curls my lips.

3…2…1… My lance connects with armor.

And then…I am falling.

I curse.

I shouldn't—

What have I done wrong?

Was I not steady?

But no, I see Uarraig flapping above me, and the receding tailfeathers of Dùbhghlas's nightjar.

And I am *still* falling.

I've failed my people. I'll have to redeem myself in the melee.

I grasp the ragwort stem from my belt and mutter the charm to make it fly. I pull myself atop it to stand and fly gracefully the rest of the way to the ground and preserve whatever dignity I have left. As my feet hit the grass, I take a bow. But the crowd doesn't pay me any mind as they are far more focused on Prince Dùbhghlas's victory lap around the arena.

Comforted by the fact I know no one will hear me, I growl in frustration. I was supposed to win. The way I do on the battlefield. Like I did when I gave him that damn scar on his cheek that he thinks makes him look so rugged.

And look at him take off his wretched helmet. Look at him free his shimmering brown hair from the braid that secured it. I scowl. And everyone is cheering for him, even those from my court. I hate it. I hate him.

Sure, it's no mean feat to come in second in the whole joust, having achieved victory over the rest of the contenders. But losing to *him* just makes me furious. I remove my own helmet. It glimmers beautifully in the sunlight, the usual green shifting into purples and golds, but no one notices. All the attention is on my rival. I always win when we fight for real – why have I lost now?

Uarraig lands next to me, and I pet his chin. He leans into it, and despite my frustration, I can't help smiling at him. At least my loyal companion hasn't forsaken me for my Unseelie counterpart. I climb on Uarraig's back, and we take off into the air. Just when we're leaving the arena, Dùbhghlas catches my eye and frowns. I scowl back at him.

I return Uarriag to his nest. I change from my armor to allow my squire to polish it and ready it for the melee later. I have perhaps an hour or two for lunch and entertainment, and then I must compete in the melee. I'll need my strength, both physical and mental, to wield my sword and magic with my usual accuracy and win. I'd rather head down to the market to sample food there and see my people, let their love bolster me, than request something from the Unseelie Court's kitchens. It's as likely to be laced with traces of iron as it is to be a restorative.

As I walk down to the market, I take my time to breathe in the autumn air. It smells slightly wet, as though it might rain later, though no clouds dot the vivid blue sky. I have almost reached the market when I run into the one person I should have liked to avoid: Dùbhghlas himself.

He, too, has changed out of his armor. At least I won't have to stare at those damn pincers any longer. I shudder. Of course, that leaves me staring at his actual face instead. The sunlight dappling through the trees is flattering for his face, highlighting the planes of his cheeks. He alone stands between me and leading the Seelie Court to victory, and I hate him for it. So I meet him on battlefields and in tourneys. My perpetual enemy.

"Your Highness," Dùbhghlas says, his tone derisive.

My lips thin. "Prince Dùbhghlas. Not still parading yourself around like a jester?"

He laughs, the expression lighting up his face. I had not meant to be funny. "Is it wrong to enjoy those admiring my skill? Especially when they come from *your* court. Why, it's like they've never seen anyone so adept with a blade before."

That stings. "Or perhaps they're simply shocked that you understand which end of the lance to use, after what happened in the spring."

His face colors, a rosy blush spreading from the tips of his ears down his neck. "Your people make the best mead, what can I say?"

I keep my scowl firmly on my face. My stomach rumbles, much to my embarrassment. But it has been a long morning, watching others joust under the heat of the sun. Despite the refreshments the Unseelie Queen has provided, nothing is as filling as good Seelie fare.

"I'm heading to the market. Walk with me?"

That's almost enough to make me turn and request food from the Unseelie kitchens just on principle, but the market is closer. And I am hungry. "Fine," I grumble.

* * *

Melee is exhausting, and I could have done without my earlier encounter with Dùbhghlas stealing some of my energy. Fortunately, I had been able to slip away when we had reached the market. Still, I would have preferred to avoid the encounter altogether, as any encounter with Dùbhghlas takes energy that I need to reserve for the competitions. The sun beating down is tiring on its own, even before factoring in the hours of physical exertion. The melee started with all the fairy knights taking part, but now that it's twilight, we're down to the last few. The fatigue wearing on me makes me miss the archery contest or the earlier rounds of the joust – pure fun and victory, instead of this wearing exhaustion. The fight had begun on our warbirds, but as it progressed, we each dismounted for close combat on the ground.

As the fairy princes, the leaders of our troops, it is expected that either I or Prince Dùbhghlas should win. After my defeat earlier today, I am behind. I won the archery competition, but Prince Dùbhghlas had won both the joust and the quintain. The pas d'armes had come to a draw. The melee will determine whether the whole tournament is a draw, or if the Unseelie will return to our usual combat victorious.

It's hard on morale to lose a tournament, and to lose it when your opponent's season is coming? Disastrous. While in our world, we fight a never-ending war. On the other side of the fairy mounds in the human realm, our combat determines sickness and health for whole regions. Who will come home to find their sheep ailing and who will come home to find their wagon suddenly repaired.

My magic swirls around me like golden sparkles. It rushes from me to meet the dark shadows emanating from Dùbhghlas. Light ties around tendrils of night. Shadow slashes against my armor. My armor resists tearing, but I still feel the pressure of it against my ribs. My magic lashes back out against him with similar results.

A stray arrow embeds itself in my armor, hitting hard enough to bruise me. I turn and fend off an Unseelie knight with my sword while blocking Dùbhghlas's magic with my own. The knight falls to the ground. He's out. There's only five of us still competing. I can't wait. I just have to defeat Dùbhghlas. That would be such a satisfying end to this week. To see the look in his eyes when he removes his helmet. To have him, for just a second, at the mercy of my sword. To force him to yield. I can almost taste it.

Dùbhghlas turns and clashes with the one of the final two Seelie knights, defeating him quickly. That leaves us each with a single ally, each preoccupied fighting the other. I can't afford to lose track of their fight, should my knight lose. It wouldn't do for some random knight to vanquish a prince. My sword clashes with Dùbhghlas's, the metal denting slightly where the edges meet, causing them to stick. The opening gives me a moment to step behind Dùbhghlas and put him in a hold.

"Think you've won?" he asks, as he struggles in my grasp. "After you've lost multiple events?"

I growl, furious at the reminder. He takes the opportunity to headbutt me. I stagger backward, making sure to keep a good grip on my sword. *Oh, he's in for it now.* "Oh, not yet. Don't let your success go to your head. It might throw you off balance." I ready my sword to slash at him, and he prepares to block.

We circle each other, throwing taunts back and forth.

"Does that mean you've been admiring my success? Wishing you could be as good as I?" I can hear him laugh, and I hate it. I lunge toward him, but he dodges with ease. He slashes down from the right, and I block with my sword again.

The blades lock again, and I am able to use that to press forward, stepping closer to him. I twist my blade until his fingers are forced to open. He drops his sword, which falls into the trampled grass. He's down to just his magic, while I still have both my magic and my sword.

To the side, the other knights incapacitate one another.

It's just the two of us left. *As it should be.*

I slash at him with my sword, and his shadows stretch to block. They take the form of a blade. Unlike a physical blade, impervious to magic, his dark to my light. Whoever's will is stronger cuts through the other's magic.

In my free hand, I create a dagger out of pure light to give myself the advantage. My copper sword collides with the shadow-sword, but shadows aren't like metal. Dùbhghlas's magic shifts form, morphing into a hand to grab my sword.

I push toward him, getting close enough to sever the shadows' connection to his body. As my light hits his shadow, our eyes meet through the small slits in our visors. Something changes as he stares at me.

My light cuts off his shadow, and I slip my sword forward until the point is against his neck, beneath his helm and above the cuirass. "Yield," I demand. I savor the moment. It feels like victory, like power, sweeter than the sweetest honey wine. My eyes bore into his. I swallow. My chest heaves as I catch my breath. We stay still, each daring the other to back down first.

"I yield," Dùbhghlas says.

It feels like the world has exhaled. I feel dizzy as the moment ends.

"The Seelie Court wins!" the herald exclaims. I hear my mother, Queen Órfhlaith, cheering. We've tied on the tournament overall – the same number of events have gone to each court. But as some of my less-wounded comrades lift me up on their shoulders, I find myself unable to enjoy the victory. I'm almost positive that *Dùbhghlas let me win.*

And how dare he? I want to win on my own merit or not at all.

* * *

My squire helps me out of my armor and padding, and I leave him in our tent to return to my guest chambers in the Unseelie Palace. There, my valet helps me change into my clothes for dinner: breeches made from white poplar leaves sewn together with a blueweed-petal tunic, carefully embroidered with images of flowers and household spirits. Over the top, a mantle of pale green butterfly wings completes the outfit. It is a different kind of armor to what I wore in the tourney, but it is armor all the same.

My valet braids my hair into a knot on top of my head and places a crown of blueweed and polished agate atop it. From my ears hang gems carved in the shape of foxgloves, large enough to brush my shoulders. As I walk toward the great hall, I find Dùbhghlas there, his arms crossed. His mother, the Unseelie Queen Neachneohain, is scolding him, but I am too far away to hear what she says.

Dùbhghlas's head hangs down, his dark braids obscuring his expression and his response. Finally, his mother breezes past him into the great hall. I can't help but taunt him for it, as I know he would do the same to me.

"Your mother must be disappointed in your performance in the melee," I comment.

He glares back at me, his heavy brows drawn together in a scowl. "Your mother cheered for me in the joust. How disappointing that must have been for you."

I curl my upper lip at him, anger rising in me like a flame. "How dare you! At least my mother can be proud that my effort to win was earnest!"

Eyes widening, he takes a step back. He stares at me, his eyes locking with mine. I can see the surprise in them. *He hadn't expected me to call him on that, had he?* "How does it feel to win only because I let you?"

"And what in *elfhame* would cause you to do that, hmm?" I say, leaning closer in my ire.

Only, in a second, hands grip the back of my head as Dùbhghlas pulls me into a kiss. My hands flail in an unseemly fashion as I try to comprehend what's happening. *Dùbhghlas is kissing me?* Dùbhghlas, whose face I've permanently marred, is kissing me? But he *hates* me. I hate him. But his lips are on mine, and it feels so good.

His tongue licks into my mouth, and it feels as though, somehow, he's winning, which just won't do. I bite down, catching his tongue between my sharp teeth and drawing a little blood. But he moans into my mouth and pushes me back toward the wall. *Absolutely not.* I trip him so that he's the one pressed against the wall.

Finally, we break for air. "What," I ask, staring into his eyes, "was that?"

"A kiss," Dùbhghlas says, breathlessly. "What else?"

I snort. He's the worst. I hate him. "It was that. But why?"

"Have you seen yourself?" he asks. "I've seen how you try to do your people and your mother proud, how much you value them. How you help your wounded on the battlefield. How you look in that damn armor. It'd be so much easier if you weren't – I hate you, but then, there you are, and ah!"

"And that's worth betraying your people for?!" I exclaim.

He looks me up and down. "You kissed me back."

He's right. That's the worst part. This man who always gets in my way, who meets me on the battlefield blow for blow, who torments my every waking moment, whose face I envision on every archery target. I'm so wrapped up in him, in trying to surpass him in skill, that I hardly know what I'd do if he were gone. I don't know who I am without him, like a tree strangled by a vine. I can't argue with him, so instead I kiss him again, pouring all my anger and resentment into it.

He meets me in that kiss like it's just another battlefield. I grab at his mantle to pull him closer to me, and he clutches the back of my neck with his long fingers. I want to make myself a part of him, mark him with my essence, something—

—something like that scar I'd already given him.

A mark that shows that I'm irretrievably a part of him.

Something feral inside me shouts that this prince is mine.

Do I love him? I ask myself. *Could I love him?*

I don't know. But I keep kissing him anyway until we have to go into the great hall, with our clothes rumpled and strands of hair loose. People will look at us, and they'll *know*. That's a mortifying feeling, that my people could see right through me. If we're lucky, perhaps, they will assume we got in an argument or a fight in the corridor outside as the last ones in.

I take another look at Dùbhghlas, and I feel a tickle of pride in my chest and a rush of fondness in my gut. It's not love, not yet, but it could be. Dùbhghlas smiles at me, a more genuine expression than I have ever seen on him. "Tonight, come to my room?" he asks.

I bite my lip. "And what about tomorrow? We're back at war."

"It can be war between our peoples without it being a war between the two of us." He leans in closer so that his words caress the shell of my ear. "Secret rendezvous under the cover of night? Sneaking away during battle to have my wicked way with you? Think of the possibilities."

I am. And that's a problem when we're about to be in front of both our peoples. I feel flushed right down to my core, the blood rushing in my veins. I nod, swallowing thickly.

"Tonight," I tell him. "And tomorrow, we'll see."

Biographies

Erica Barnes – *The Pixie's Ploy*
(First Publication)
Erica Barnes likes pretending to live in a variety of worlds, whether by writing, reading, watching movies and television, or playing lots of video games. She has had short stories featured in *It Came From the Trailer Park: Vol 5, Santa Rage*, and in Flame Tree Publishing's *Pirates & Ghosts Short Stories*. Erica can usually be found with her boyfriend, David, and her stepsons, Hunter and Bradley. She currently lives in West Virginia with her family.

Keyan Bowes – *The Queen's Eye*
(First Publication)
A peripatetic writer of short fiction, Keyan Bowes grew up in India and currently calls the West Coast of the US home. She's had around forty-five stories published, some more than once. Her stories have been translated into Italian, Spanish and Polish. Keyan's work can be found online in magazines such as *Escape Pod* and *Fireside*, and on paper in twenty print anthologies. She's a Clarion graduate and an SFWA member.

Kim Chance – *Red Like Blood*
(First Publication)
Kim Chance is a fantasy and romance author who survives almost exclusively on coffee and daydreams. When she's not crafting magical kissing scenes or obsessing over her own characters, she teaches high school English Language Arts. You can also find her re-reading her favorite comfort novels for the millionth

time, falling down True Crime rabbit holes with her husband, or living her best soccer-mom life with her three incredible kiddos. For more information about Kim or her books, be sure to check out kimchance.com.

Kristen Cipriano – *Foreword*
Kristen Cipriano is a romantic fantasy author whose novels are inspired by her own journeys of overcoming psychological trauma, healing from emotional abuse, learning to love herself, and finding her inner truth. She loves to showcase how even the most broken characters can heal and triumph and expertly combines darker themes with lightness and humor, resulting in novels that take readers on wildly entertaining adventures that stick with them long after the story ends. *The Queen Rises* is her debut series with the second book arriving in late 2026.

Deborah L. Davitt – *A Silken Bridge to Bind the Stars*
(Originally Published in *Cossmass Infinities*, July 2023)
Deborah L. Davitt was raised in Nevada, but currently lives in Houston, Texas with her husband and son. Her award-winning poetry and prose have appeared in over seventy journals, including *F&SF, Asimov's, Analog*, and *Lightspeed*. For more about her work, including her poetry collections, *The Gates of Never, Bounded by Eternity, From Voyages Unreturning, Xenoforming*, and *To Love Unquietly*, please see deborahldavitt.com.

Sarina Dorie – *Monster Masquerade*
(First Publication)
Sarina Dorie has sold over 250 short stories to markets like *Analog, Daily Science Fiction, Fantasy Magazine*, and *F&SF*. She has over one hundred books up on Amazon, including her bestselling series, *Womby's School for Wayward Witches*. You can find info about her short stories and novels on her website sarinadorie.com. The best way to stay in contact with Sarina, hear about what she is writing, and know when she has a new release or books offered for free on Amazon, is by signing up for her newsletter: sarinadorie.com/newsletter-sign-up. She can be found on Facebook @sarina.dorie1.

Umenyi Chisomaga Evelyn – *When Frost Loved Flame*
(First Publication)
Umenyi Chisomaga Evelyn is a Nigerian writer whose stories travel from the streets of Nsukka to the upcoming issues of *Ake Review, Uncanny Magazine* and *Stripe Magazine*, among others. Her writing explores the edges of magic, identity, and human emotion and daily life. When not writing, Chisomaga is a Pharmacy student mixing chemicals and wondering what the hell she's doing.

Jonathan Ficke – *By Any Other Name*
(First Publication)
Jonathan Ficke lives outside of Milwaukee in sunny Wisconsin with his wife and children. His fiction has been translated into several languages including Bulgarian, Romanian, Estonian, Galician, Spanish, Farsi, and Greek. Find more of his work at jonficke.com.

Jess L. Freed – *Stolen Shadows*
(First Publication)
Jess L. Freed is a mom and brain tumor survivor living in Massachusetts. She has multiple short stories published in a variety of literary magazines and anthologies. Her manuscript *Dare to Believe* was selected for the 2024 Smoochpit Mentorship Program and she is represented by Grace Demyan. See more at jessfreedwrites.my.canva.site or Instagram: @JessFreedWrites.

M.A. Gardner – *The Rose and the Blade*
(First Publication)
M.A. Gardner is a US Navy veteran who lives in northern Arizona with his wife, three children, and a few spoiled dogs. With multiple degrees under his belt, he works in post-secondary education, where he is passionate about fostering learning and growth. Mark's diverse experiences inform his writing, infusing his stories with authenticity and depth.

Georgina Kamsika – *Fragments of Us*
(First Publication)
Georgina Kamsika writes about monsters and ghosts and swords and magic. Sometimes the people rebel, other times they'll kiss. Georgina

is currently writing an interactive fiction game for Choice of Games, but when the coding gets too much, she finds she must write a short story or two. This is one of them. For more information, find her at kamsika.com and @GKamsika on most socials.

A.L. Keane – *What Honor Dictates*
(First Publication)
A.L. Keane is a queer artist and speculative fiction writer from the Pacific Northwest. Her work often delves into themes of connection, melancholy, and individuality, with a preference for queer and morally ambiguous characters. When not writing or sketching in her notebook, she can be found reading literary classics with an iced coffee in hand and obsessing over stories that refuse neat endings.

Sasha Kielman – *Half Made of Shadows*
(First Publication)
Sasha Kielman is an attorney in Washington, DC, USA. In addition to her story in this anthology, she has short stories published in the anthologies *Living With Demons, Crimson Bones, Unleashed: Set Your Monster Free, Wickedness and Wonder, Of Love and Dragons*, and the forthcoming *Wichelen Vol. 2*. You can find her on BlueSky and Tumblr @SashaKielman.

AJ Lancaster – *Shadows of Silvermorn*
(First Publication)
Growing up on a farm in rural Aotearoa New Zealand, AJ Lancaster's first job was finding lost people in a corn maze. AJ's post-farm life has included a geography degree, environmental planning, and editing maths exams. Now AJ Lancaster lives in the Manawatū and writes romantic, whimsical fantasy books. AJ is best known for the *Stariel* novels, a series about a country estate that chooses its own ruler, beginning with *The Lord of Stariel*.

Jessica Lévai – *Ring of Wax, Armor of Bone*
(First Publication)
Jessica Lévai (she/her) has loved stories and storytellers her whole life. You can find her work in *Strange Horizons, Translunar*

Travelers Lounge, and *Reactor*. Her first novella, *The Night Library of Sternendach: A Vampire Opera in Verse*, won the Lord Ruthven Award for Fiction. Her second, *The Glass Garden*, combines family drama and cosmic horror. She lives near Boston and dreams of collaborating on a graphic novel. See more at JessicaLevai.com.

M. McNamara – *The Hedge Knight Drinks*
(First Publication)
M. McNamara is a Brisbane-based author who dabbles in fantasy, science fiction, and a smidge of horror. She has written three books and many short stories; her work has appeared in *Of Metal and Magic, The Pink Hydra*, and the *Of Love & Dragons* anthology by Flame Tree, among other publications. Her short story 'Welcome to the Fantasy Fair' is also a podcast on Connor Reads Books. If you like her work, please visit her website at mmcnamarabooks.com, or on Instagram @m_mcnamara_books.

S.C. Mills – *The Gentle Art of Necromancy*
(First Publication)
S.C. Mills writes speculative stories set in worlds that might be dark and fearsome, but where love is still alive and bright. They're a Viable Paradise graduate and NYC Midnight winner. They live in Seattle, where they like to hike in the dry season and train martial arts while it rains. Find them at scmillsbooks.com and everywhere online @ scmillsbooks.

Charity Ogechi – *The Duelist and Dreamweaver*
(First Publication)
Charity Ogechi is a Nigerian speculative fiction writer whose work explores the boundaries between myth, memory, and the uncanny. Her stories often weave African folklore with contemporary emotional landscapes, creating vivid worlds shaped by longing and resilience. She has contributed to various storytelling communities and continues to expand her craft through dedicated reading and mentorship. When not writing, she enjoys studying mythic structures and observing the quiet magic in everyday life.

Jennifer R. Povey – *Always For Her Favor*
(First Publication)
Born in Nottingham, England, Jennifer R. Povey (she/her) now lives in Northern Virginia, where she writes everything from heroic fantasy to stories for *Analog*. She has written a number of novels across multiple subgenres. She is a full member of SFWA. Her interests include horseback riding, *Doctor Who* and attempting to out-weird her various friends and professional colleagues.

Ziggy Schutz – *It Befits Her*
(Originally Published in *Forged*, 2017)
Ziggy Schutz (she/him/he/her) is a queer, disabled, proud previvor mess who is at all times looking for ways to make his favorite fairytales and horror stories reflect people who look a little more like her. In addition to his few dozen published shorts, Schutz's first novella, a space mermaid tale called *twice-spent comet* (Meerkat Press) was released in 2024. You can find more about his writing at linktr.ee/ziggyschutz.

Laura Shenton – *The Thornblade's Promise*
(First Publication)
Laura Shenton is probably best known for her music non-fiction, particularly *Dance With The Devil: The Cozy Powell Story* (Wymer Publishing) and *Tommy Bolin: In and Out of Deep Purple* (Sonicbond Publishing). Her fiction books are character-driven with a short, punchy narrative that gets straight to the point – typically novellas and novelettes. Genres include gothic, fantasy, and adventure (mostly, with the occasional diversion). Laura's children's books are simple, accessible, and fun – an excellent choice for youngsters with fertile imaginations who are just beginning their reading journey.

S.S.N. Smith – *Libeunfeyer*
(First Publication)
S.S.N. Smith is a cross-genre writer living in Kalamazoo, MI, with her wife and three dogs. She is a graduate student in Liberal Studies and serves in the US Air Force. When she is not working hard or writing, you can find a guitar in her hands. Her recent publications include *The Writer in Black Cat Tales: An Anthology of Black Cats* and 'Molly, From Data Analytics' in *Fearmoji: A Queer Horror Anthology*.

Gemma Sterling – *Oberon's Rose*
(First Publication)
Gemma Sterling is a writer of SFF and Romantasy. As the grandchild of Norwegian immigrants, Gemma grew up hearing tales of Norse gods and myths from her grandfather. Her fantasy writings draw on this tradition, informing her characters and worldbuilding. Her writing aims to transport readers to long-forgotten eras where magic was a part of everyday life. Gemma currently resides in Nova Scotia, Canada, with her husband, daughter and two cats.

Celia Winter – *Sometimes a Sword is Like a Lover*
(First Publication)
Celia Winter is a Chicago-based award-winning knitter whose bachelor's degree in history only tangentially helps her in her career in Data & Analytics. Her speculative and romantic fiction has been published in *Plott Hound, Heartlines Spec, The Dark*, and several anthologies. When not knitting, she can be found writing; when not writing, she can be found bothering her two fluffy cats.

Aubrey Wroth – *Light Tangled in Shadow*
(First Publication)
Aubrey Wroth is a queer, disabled author who writes the representation they always wanted to see. Primarily a fantasy writer, they have been known to dip their toes into other genres. They deeply appreciate classic literature, folklore, and philosophy, which inspires their work. When not writing, they can be found experimenting in the kitchen, snuggling their cat, or exploring indie cafes.

Illustrations

Key cover art: Xinyue Chen
Xinyue Chen is an illustrator and book artist based in New York, mostly working in traditional media. Since receiving their BFA from the Central Academy of Fine Arts in Beijing and their MFA from the School of Visual Arts in New York, they have provided editorial illustrations, book illustrations and designs for many renowned clients, including

the *New York Times*, *Scientific American*, NBC News, NPR, Bloomberg and many more.

Illustration page 7: Ayush Pradhan

Ayush Pradhan is a young artist who frequently finds inspiration in genres like adventure, fantasy, science fiction and emotions. His work demonstrates an interest in how ideas influence people and vice versa.

Illustration page 13: Betta Crotti

Betta is an Italian illustrator and merch-designer who loves sword-bearing women, tabling at cons and gifting cute trinkets to her loved ones. She pretends to be a cinephile but her movie-related tastes are those of an 8 year-old kid.

Illustration page 405: Rita Földessy

Rita is a passionate hobbyist artist of Hungarian origin based in Austria. In her youth, she was inspired by anime/manga which has had an influence on her style and linework. She then spent time at the Visionary Art Academy in Vienna, where she learned from artists such as Rebecca Yanovskaya and Olga Klimova. In her personal work, she uses traditional and digital ways of creating art.

Illustration page 414: Faziela Harris

Faziela is a Cape Town based anime artist and self-published author of two urban fantasy novels, writing stories driven by action, heart, and transformation. A creative builder at heart, moving easily between coordinating on the ground teams, crafting fantasy stories, and designing original characters. She brings a grounded, real-world perspective to every project, always with a touch of magic.

Romantic Fantasy

Flame Tree Romantic Fantasy is a captivating blend of our signature Gothic Fantasy collections with the passion and magic of Romantasy. This new series featuring stories selected from open submissions is an exciting addition to Flame Tree's Beyond & Within, Myths, Gods & Immortals, Gothic Fantasy, Classic Stories and Epic Tales Collections, all beautifully presented, perfect as a gift and offering a lifetime of reading pleasure.

FLAME TREE MYTH, FOLKLORE & FICTION